MW01193341

THE RETREAT

B. E. BAKER

Purple
Puppy
Publishing

Copyright © 2022 by B. E. Baker

All rights reserved.

No part of this book may be reproduced in any form or by any electronic or mechanical means, including information storage and retrieval systems, without written permission from the author, except for the use of brief quotations in a book review.

❄ Created with Vellum

For my mother

If books didn't require conflict, all the mothers I wrote about would be as great as you are.

The terrible mothers in my story are no reflection of you. <3

Thank you for being unfailingly supportive—basically, nothing like any of them.

The Battle of Bunker Hill
By Izzy Brooks

The Battle of Bunker Hill is a rather famous victory for the British military in the American Revolutionary War. After all, the colonists ran away.

Just before the conflict, Boston was under siege by a newly formed revolution. Determined to put down the revolution before it could take hold, the British sent a large and well-armed contingent of troops to destroy the militiamen who were gathering. Wave after wave of British troops landed, and the colonial leaders had a decision to make.

As the British climbed Breed Hill (toward Bunker), they fired down on them, killing more than a thousand Redcoats.

Should they hold their line and fight to the end, like Leonidas and his 300 at Thermopylae? Or should they flee, hopefully making them able to fight again another day? In the end, with no ammunition, they didn't opt to make a charge with bayonets.

They fled.

At the time, the British judged them harshly for that decision. Even other colonists were nervous, wondering if they would have the grit it would take to win. But had they held their ground, the men would all surely have died, even if only because they were ground out one by one like grains of wheat in a mill.

And sure, a well-respected colonial officer named Joseph Warren died, inspiring more colonials to join the fight. But many others lived because they retreated. John Stark (who actually was quite a hero, like John Snow from *Game of Thrones*!) went on to be the hero of the Battle of Bennington. Also, George Claghorn was shot in the knee, but didn't die, and he went on to build the USS Constitution. And finally, Thomas Knowlton survived that battle to become the leader of Knowlton's Rangers—America's first spy organization.

In summary, some people think that retreating means you're a coward. But sometimes you have to be brave enough to face life after a defeat, or you can't accomplish the things you're supposed to do here on Earth. I think we can all learn a little bit more about the importance of knowing when we can't win, and taking a measured loss so we can keep on going to win greater battles in the future.

Sometimes it's the losses that prepare us for the wins.

1

ABIGAIL

When I met Nate's parents, I was already pregnant with Ethan. We were determined not to tell them, and they were equally determined that I taste a few different vintages from a winery they had invested in. . .

It was a bumpy start to a difficult relationship. But this time around, I vowed that things would go much more smoothly.

"I wish I'd started on the remodel of the kitchen right away," I say. "Because this kitchen looks awfully run down, especially by comparison to the new addition."

"Abigail." Steve grabs my forearms and stares into my eyes. "None of that matters."

"They'll be here any minute, and I didn't even think to ask what kinds of foods your dad likes."

His half-grin annoys me. "If you had, I wouldn't have told you. Who cares what he likes? Make something you like."

"What?"

"You're almost forty," he says. "So am I." He shrugs.

3

"We can do what we want, and if our parents want to be involved in our amazing lives, they can get on board."

"But what if he doesn't like me?"

Steve laughs. *He laughs.*

"I'm not kidding right now."

"Everyone likes you. I mean, the women are jealous of you, and the men are jealous of me, but everyone likes you."

I don't have the bandwidth right now to argue with him about that. "But what if he doesn't?"

"Then we're even," he says. "Because most days it doesn't feel like he likes me all that much."

"You're kidding."

He shrugs. "I hear from him a few times a year, Abby. He's coming out because his new wife is curious, and that's it."

"He's your dad."

"And when Mom died, he checked out of my life. It is what it is, and I don't get upset about it anymore."

I have trouble believing that's really true, but I believe that he *thinks* it is. "Alright, well, I hope he likes lasagna and garlic knots, because—"

Steve releases one of my arms and spins me with the other until I'm pressed up against the wall. "He's going to love your lasagna, and he's going to love your garlic rolls, and he's going to love you." He's still holding my left hand, but he runs his other hand down the side of my face, his fingers stopping by my mouth. His eyes drop to my lips, and then his head dips slowly.

When his mouth covers mine, the rest of the world drops away and I *melt*.

The oven buzzer goes off.

"My garlic knots!" I wiggle away from Steve—who

looks a little dazed—and pull them out of the oven. They're just barely golden, which is perfect.

Unless his dad and stepmom arrive late. The longer they're out on the counter and the cooler they get, the less delicious they'll taste.

The front door bangs open—Izzy and Whitney dash inside, both puffing from their run to the house from the barn. They're both smiling and rosy-cheeked, though, and I can't tell whether it's from the exercise or from the chilly weather.

"Shut the door," I remind them. Why can't kids ever remember to close the door? Summer, winter, it doesn't seem to matter. They push on through and let it swing open, cool air billowing one direction or another.

"They're here!" Izzy wheezes. "A big blue car just pulled up."

"It's a Cadillac," Ethan says as he breezes through the door, thankfully closing it behind him. "A brand new one."

"That would be Violet's doing. If it's not shiny and new, it's not worth having." Steve reaches into the cabinet and pulls out a stack of plates. His next words are muttered so softly that I can barely hear them. "Why she wanted my dad, I'll never understand."

"Come now," I say. "I'm sure your dad's shiny enough."

Steve snorts.

A moment later, when his father's escorted through the door by Gabe, I understand why. His father's much shorter than Steve, and his hair is entirely white. His nose is slightly bulbous with age, and his back is a little bit bowed, too.

He's definitely not shiny, but he looks affable and open.

"Welcome," I say. "I'm so pleased you could make it. I know it's quite a drive."

Steve's father hisses like a leaky gasket. "Pshaw. Seven hours? I used to do that down and back in a day when I was younger."

My ever-patient, ever-understanding fiancé rolls his eyes toward the ceiling in an uncharacteristic move and shakes his head. "Here we go."

"I'm Abigail." I extend my hand.

Steve's dad takes it and pumps it up and down vigorously. "Meacham Archer," he says. "Glad to meet you, finally."

I can't quite help furrowing my brow. "Finally?"

Meacham's laugh sounds like a chuckle and a guffaw had a baby. "Steve ain't no spring chicken, that's for sure. You can't possibly be worse than his last wife, so at least there's that."

Oh, good. Steve's rolling his eyes and his dad's insulting Steve right back. We're off to a spectacular start. "Stephanie's a very beautiful woman," I say, proud of my diplomacy.

"Speaking of beautiful women," the lady next to Meacham says. Then she, honest-to-goodness, bats her eyes, like a debutante in an old Southern movie. "I'm Violet. It's such a pleasure to meet you." Her hair's been permed, I think, and the sheer volume of her makeup makes it very hard to guess how old she might be. But the upper limit of that span stops at least ten years younger than Meacham.

"Abigail." I hold out my hand again.

Instead of shaking it, Violet frowns, slightly, and pats my shoulder. "Yes, dear, you already said."

Maybe in-laws just aren't destined to be easy to get along with, no matter your age or maturity level.

"I hope you like lasagna," Gabe says. "Mom was really worried you wouldn't like her food."

Meacham laughs. "I love lasagna, young man, and the fact that she cares what we think already makes her head and shoulders above that other woman."

"Miss Stephanie's not very nice," Izzy says, "but Steve's daughter Olivia isn't so bad."

Meacham freezes.

Violet's jaw drops open.

I elbow Steve. "Was that a secret?"

Steve laughs. "I just don't talk to Dad much. Sorry— meant to tell you myself. Turns out the baby Stephanie had right before we divorced actually *was* my daughter after all. Didn't know until a few months back."

"How can that be?" Violet looks terribly displeased.

Meacham practically jogs across the room to pat Steve on the back. "That's the best news I've heard all year."

"It *is* only January," Whitney says. "Not much has happened yet."

"Although, Mom's marrying his son." Ethan coughs. "Might also be good news."

Meacham turns toward Whitney as though he didn't even hear my teen. Let's hope he didn't. "How old are you?"

Whitney raises one eyebrow, like the jury's still out on this guy. "How old do you think I am?"

"Well, I'm old enough not to guess a woman's age." The corner of Meacham's mouth lifts.

7

"I'm old enough to make macaroni and cheese and do my own laundry." Whitney folds her arm. "I like Olivia, but I don't love that *you* seem to like her better than us without even meeting her." She huffs. "I don't mean to be rude, but I don't think you'll make a very good grandpa."

Steve's jaw dangles open.

Violet chokes.

Meacham lets out a belly laugh. "Good on you, young lady. Way to put me in my place. I'm delighted to hear that Steve's got a daughter."

Whitney places one hand on her hip. "But?"

"But I should have been just as excited to meet the four of you."

Whitney shrugs. "That's a little better."

"Well, Steve, you're just full of surprises lately," Violet says. "Anything else you need to tell us? Maybe we should get it all out right now."

"Mom and Steve are pregnant," Ethan says. "With twins."

Violet's eyes widen so dramatically that I worry they'll pop right out of her head.

"That's a joke," I say. "I'm not even close to pregnant, not with any number of children."

"Not yet." Steve wraps an arm around my shoulders.

"Okay," I say. "Maybe it's time we all have something to eat."

"Yes," Gabe says. "I'm so hungry I could eat an elephant."

"And do you like lasagna, young man?" Meacham asks.

"I'm really into it," Gabe says. "And the knot rolls are even yummier."

"I'm really into it?" Ethan mouths at me.

I shrug and smile. Gabe's a funny little guy, with his teenage expressions he picks up from Ethan. Keeps us all on our toes.

Once everyone has gotten a plate and filled it with food, and once we're all seated and we've said a prayer, everyone starts to eat.

"See?" Gabe has somehow already gotten tomato sauce on his cheek. "It's really good, right?" He lifts a fluffy garlic knot into the air.

"It sure is," Meacham says. "Your mom's a great cook."

"She's an even better lawyer," Izzy says. "So don't do anything mean, or we'll sue."

"Is she really?" Violet asks.

"She is," Steve says. "She recently left a huge firm in Houston to open her own practice out here."

"You're okay with living here?" Violet asks. "In the middle of—"

"Don't say nowhere," Whitney says. "It's rude."

"Everywhere is somewhere," Gabe says. "We're learning about Utah in school right now, and I just found out that these mountains, the Uinta Mountains, are the only mountain range that runs east to west." He beams. "Plus, there used to be a fort here called Fort Davy Crockett. You've heard of him, right?"

Violet blinks.

"He was really famous, so if you don't know who he is, you probably didn't go to school for long." Gabe smiles. "Or maybe you just didn't listen very good."

Steve's not doing a great job suppressing his laughter.

We may call Manila 'the middle of nowhere' with some regularity, but by golly, no one else better make fun

9

of it, or even seven-year-old Gabe will pull out a pitch-fork, apparently.

"They're turning you into a downright Utah zealot at that school," Ethan says. "I'm not sure whether I'm horrified or impressed."

"Well, I'm impressed with these rolls," Meacham says. "That little man was correct—these are tasty."

"Thanks," I say.

"Steve," Meacham says.

"Yeah?"

"I'm proud of you. This is a mighty fine lady, and her kids seem to be quite bright as well."

"Yes," Violet says. "They've even done enough school to know a lot about Utah." If her voice is a little flat, well, I can't entirely blame her. We're kind of a fearsome pack.

"Thanks," I say.

"It was well worth the long drive," Violet continues.

And if I hadn't been a lawyer, or if I hadn't been a good cook, would it *not* have been worth it for them to drive out to see Meacham's son? I don't like qualifications when it comes to parental approval. I was raised with enough of them to last a lifetime. "I'm happy you came. We'll have to come out soon to see your place in Idaho as well."

"We'd just love that, wouldn't we babe?" Meacham asks.

For some reason, hearing a sixty-something year old man say 'babe' makes me want to giggle. I restrain myself, but it's hard.

"Why don't you tell us about the wedding plans," Violet says.

It's not lost on me that she changed the subject without saying she'd love to have us come visit.

"My plan's to pay for anything and everything this woman wants, and provide whatever input she asks for," Steve says. "I'm all about the marriage—the wedding doesn't mean as much to me, but I want to make her happy with it."

"That's why we're thinking we'll have a small wedding," I say. "Something local and probably in the near future."

"May," Steve says. "That's the plan. May twenty-fifth."

"It shouldn't be *too* cold then," Meacham says. "And things are starting to sprout. Nice idea."

"It's well before the cows go up to the forestry land," Steve says, "but should be after all the calving is done."

"I don't miss that at all," Meacham says. "Planning all my life events around cattle and animal seasons was a real drag."

"It's not that bad," Ethan says. "Plus, Steve seems to like planning his life around horses."

"Only because he didn't have anything more important to do until now," Violet says. "Surely now that he's got a wife and a child, he'll let all that go and focus on being a doctor, a father, and a husband." She lifts her eyebrows.

"I'll definitely prioritize those things," Steve says.

"So a simple wedding, somewhere close, and relatively soon," Violet says. "I think that sounds very sensible, for a second marriage for you both."

Something about the way she says it irritates me, but I don't want to argue with them, so I let it go.

The rest of the evening goes about the same as the

beginning—but compared to my first 'meet the parents,' it's a walk in the park. Once they leave to drive over to Steve's, I breathe a hearty sigh of relief.

"That wasn't so bad," Steve says.

"It could have gone worse," I say.

He drops a hand on either side of my hips. "You're a delight, you know. They got that right. A brilliant lawyer, an inspiring mother, and a stellar fiancée." He drops a kiss on my forehead. "And if I didn't have to leave right now to let my dad into my house, I'd be elaborating."

"That's alright," I say. "We have plenty of years of *elaboration* ahead of us."

Steve beams. "That's the best news I've heard all year." This time, when he kisses me, it seems that he's forgotten that he has guests waiting. And that's alright with me.

2

ABIGAIL

I was twelve years old the first time I ever received a grade that wasn't an A.

My older sister Helen never did.

We hadn't built blanket forts in years. We were far too old for that sort of nonsense. But when Helen got home from school that day, and a misplaced comment on her part left me in tears, she pressed until I confessed.

"I got an eighty-four on Monday's test," I said. "Chemistry's confusing, and I hate it."

I brace myself for her disapproval, or even her disappointment, but instead, she ducked into her bedroom and emerged with her arms full of blankets.

"It's not cold," I said.

It was pretty much never cold in Palo Alto in September.

"Thank you, Captain Obvious," Helen said. "No wonder you got a B." But her smile's not mean—it's kind. Kinder than I was used to seeing from my sister.

She set to work right away, building the biggest

blanket fort I'd ever seen. Thanks to the addition of a few kitchen stools in the center, it maintained its height across the entire structure. With Helen to direct the construction details, it was no surprise it went up perfectly. Once we were out of blankets, Helen laid a few pillows on the ground in the middle, lay down on one, and patted the one next to her.

I dropped down flat on my back beside her.

"We're inside the Helen Bubble," she said.

"Huh?"

"Your grades don't matter here. Your report card can't come inside. You never have to show it to Mom and Dad, and you don't have to do homework, either."

"I love the Helen Bubble," I said.

"Of course you do. Everything to do with me is awesome," Helen said.

It was pretty much true.

She pulled two snack bags of crackers out of her purse—I wasn't yet old enough to pull off a purse, but after I discovered you could store food in them, I really wanted to be—and handed one to me. "When you're in here, you can talk about the future. You can talk about your grades. You can talk about people you like and don't like, and none of it can make you sad or hurt or angry."

We talked under that magical canopy for almost an hour.

I didn't get any more Bs that year, but I did ask for the Helen Bubble a few times for other reasons, and every time, Helen set up a blanket fort with me. Every time, we would talk about what we wanted without worrying about what our parents would say, what our teachers would say, or whether it was even feasible.

Some days, I still think about those blanket forts,

and I smile. Helen told me about all her dreams while lying on the floor under those blankets, and now, every single one of them has come true.

Mine, not so much.

Maybe I should have envisioned things that were a little more reasonable. I'll never be a rock star, although I might know one, and I doubt I'll ever be tapped for the Supreme Court. But in other ways, my real life is far better than anything I dreamt of as a child.

Just not right now.

Cows, as it turns out, need their hooves trimmed twice a year. And one of those trims happens in January, and it *is* January, unfortunately. As if the miserably cold mud and manure and constant feeding isn't already bad enough, now we need to immobilize and cut their dirty feet.

"Once it's in the chute and restrained, this band of rubber here will lift it with that hydraulic hoist," Kevin says. "Jeff's been doing this for years, and he's really good, but you only really learn by doing it, so he's going to teach you."

They don't remind us that they won't be working here forever, but now that the ranch is ours, it's one of the only things I think about. Eventually, we'll need to know how to do everything without their help.

"It gets pretty messy, too." Jeff glances at my boots. "You should at least put on gloves."

"Mom's just going to hand us stuff," Ethan says. "I'm sure she'll be fine."

If my cowboy boots, my jeans, or my coat get a little dirty, it won't be the first time. "I still don't totally understand why the cattle even go down the chute to begin with," I say. "Can't they tell that bad things are waiting on this end?"

"All of them naturally want to escape—break out from wherever they are," Kevin says. "It's a cow thing. They're always looking for a way. Luckily, they're kinda dumb, so if there's a light at the end of a little tunnel, they can't seem to help themselves. They scramble right in."

I've seen horses' hooves trimmed, and I've seen shoes put on, dozens of times now. But trimming a cow's hooves is apparently totally different. Most well-trained horses stand still and calm while their hoof is trimmed and the frog is shaped. They've done it a million times, and they know what's happening.

Cows?

Kevin's right. They're not smart. It's a total fiasco of chaos and thrashing.

Even though I'm essentially acting as a gofer, my fingers are still stiff from the cold weather, and it makes me fumbly. I accidentally drop the bolt-cutter-looking tool that Jeff uses the most and have to brush the mud-manure slurry off of it and onto my pants before handing it over.

Hoping we might be close to done, I ask, "How many are we doing today?"

"Whatever we don't trim today, we get to do tomorrow," Kevin says.

"Or the day after that," Jeff says.

"Hopefully a hundred and change a day," Ethan says.

We've done thirty, and I thought maybe we were almost done. No such luck. Most of the cows are fairly calm, but some of them, and sometimes surprising ones, really struggle. By the time we finish our hundred and twelfth cow, my back aches and I can barely feel my fingers.

Jeff glances at the next pen, his eyes resting on the huge bull in it. "Let's call it a day."

"Agreed," I say.

"That was a pretty good first day," Jeff says. "You'll be great at this after another few hundred trimmings."

"Goodie," Ethan says. "Can't wait to claim expert status on this."

"Your mom's a champ, too," Kevin says. "Thanks for the help."

My whole body's one enormous shiver. A very disgusting, very muck-spattered shiver. "But we're done now, right?" As if the weather could hear me, it starts to snow.

"Done, yeah," Kevin says. "You head back and get a really hot shower, hear?"

"Thanks." In my glee, I spin just a little too fast. . .and slip. I land face first in a pile of manud—the word Whitney made up for the cow manure and mud combination that took over our pens and nearby pastures around January first.

Ethan helpfully pulls me to my feet by grabbing the back of my coat. Even he looks disgusted by the front of me. The walk back to the house doesn't usually feel too long, but this time, it stretches. Knowing I'll need to be rinsed off before I can even go inside is almost too depressing for words. But the alternative—going inside my house coated in manud? Flooding my pipes with it?

Impossible. Some aspects of ranch life are really miserable.

I'm nearly to the side of the closest barn, where there should be a hose in a wash rack with a drain I can use that won't be frozen, when a shiny black car pulls up the driveway. I'm not expecting anyone, so I pause and squint. It's a country thing—the pause and squint we do when we're trying to piece together who has come to visit.

It's not a car I know, and I'm actually baffled about who might be inside, until the door opens, and my older sister Helen stands up. When her eyes find mine, they widen at the exact same time as her jaw dangles open.

I can tell the precise moment that my smell reaches her nose. She scrunches up first, as if that will help, and then covers her face with her gloved hand.

She's wearing a sleek black dress coat trimmed in grey fur—certainly real—and shiny black boots. Her grey handbag's too far away for me to make out the brand, but I already know it's one of the most expensive designers money can buy.

Because that's all Helen would purchase. Always.

And I'm covered in drying manud. Fantastic.

"Helen?" I raise my voice. "You weren't supposed to be here for three more days."

"*Abigail?* Is that really you?" I didn't think her look of shock could become more pronounced, but miraculously, it does. She takes a single step closer and even from here, she's sniffing the air with extreme distaste. "What in the world happened to you?"

"It's no big deal. I was a little clumsy when I turned to—"

"I don't mean *literally* what happened today. I mean, what the heck are you doing out here?" She gestures around her. "It took me *forever* to even find you. You're not close to anything."

I sigh. "Let me get rinsed off and shower. We have a lot of catching up to do."

She doesn't argue with me about that, at least. After a miserable hose down, I try not to pay attention to Helen's expression as I peel off my outerwear and head inside to shower.

But eventually I'm done, and I have to face her. At least this time, I don't smell like manure or look like I'm wearing a full body mud mask.

Helen's staring at her phone in frustration when I emerge from the bathroom. I'm guessing Ethan didn't give her the wifi password yet—actually, he's notably absent. That coward is probably hiding across the yard with Kevin and Jeff.

Lucky little jerk. "You surprised me," I say. "I thought I had a few more days."

Helen looks up, her grey eyes focusing on me with the same intensity with which they had previously been focused on her phone. "You sound like you're upset that I'm early. My deal closed quickly, and I have less than two weeks before I acquire a new company. I thought a little extra time would be a good surprise."

"It is," I say.

"And I think the person *most* surprised today was definitely me," she continues. "I had no idea my sister, the Harvard lawyer, who just called me for the first time in months to say she was engaged to a doctor no less, would be caked in mud like a creature from the Black Lagoon."

I roll my eyes. "Please. It wasn't that bad."

"You were in *boots*, and your hair around your face was *dripping mud*, and you smelled like an airplane restroom. No, worse than that. I just can't think of

anything that really corresponds with the actual odor."
She scrunches her nose. "Have you noticed that *every-thing* around here stinks?"

I've gotten used to it. "Cows don't pay attention to where they poop, and today we spent eight hours trimming their hooves."

Her lip curl tells me everything I need to know. Though, to be fair, if this had been my introduction to ranching, I might have felt the same.

"There are a lot of good things to offset the distasteful ones," I say. "Fun things. Cute things. Rewarding things." I think about that. "But there is a lot of poop."

"You're reinforcing my decision never to have any animals."

"You can't even keep plants alive," I say. "I'd never have tried to talk you into a pet."

She shrugs. "Nurturing was never my thing."

It certainly wasn't.

"When do your other kids get home?"

I glance at the clock. "In about twenty minutes."

She whistles. "How do you find the time to do any work, if it's cows all day and kids all afternoon?"

I wasn't looking forward to explaining my lifestyle here to her. "Ethan usually runs most ranch things himself, but I do have a lot fewer commitments than I did."

She frowns. "What does that mean?"

"I quit my job," I say. "I'm going to start a practice here—and I already have my first client." Not that I really think of Donna as a client. I've never even charged her before. "I'll have the flexible hours I need to parent my kids, and I'll be able to—"

"Oh, Abby." Helen's shoulders slump. "You got engaged and then quit your job? Really?"

"It wasn't done in a fit of pique," I say. "And I certainly didn't do it because I plan to be the perfect little homemaker for Steve. I thought about it a lot before—"

"We've all been waiting, you know," she says, "for exactly this to happen."

"For what to happen?"

"You handled things inhumanly well after Nate passed. I mean, you've always been reasonably competent, but even so, we knew that eventually you'd implode. I just didn't expect it to be quite this bad."

Thirty minutes, most of which I spent in the bathroom. That's how long it took from the time my sister arrived until I want to slap her. "Implode?"

"What would you call it, if you were me?"

My hands fly to my hips. "I'm sure if I were you, I'd say *implode* as well. You always were horribly rude, improbably uninsightful, and miserably officious."

Her laughter sounds more like the barking of a seal. "Officious? Well, at least all that legal training isn't going entirely to waste while I'm here. But once I leave and you only have country bumpkins to talk to again, will any of them even understand you?"

"You came early, which means you can leave early, too. Tell Mom and Dad you saw me, and that I'm falling apart." I step closer. "But mention to them that anyone who comes into my house and tells me how to live my life will be shown right back out."

"Are you actually going to kick me out for telling you the truth?" Helen drops her purse on the table and crosses her arms. "Well, if that's your plan, you'll be disappointed. I'm your sister, and I'm staying here until I have to go back to start securing investors for my new acquisition." She mutters so loudly that it's clear she wants me to hear her when she says, "Looks like that's going to be a walk in the park compared to dealing with this."

"I don't need you here, Helen. I thought you might be happy for me, in light of the miserable last few years that I and the kids have endured, but if you're not, there's the door." I point.

She unfolds her arms as she strides across the room to move away from said door. "You're a lawyer. I shouldn't have to tell you this, but isn't it funny how the people who need help the most think they're totally fine?" She arches one very carefully manicured eyebrow. "You'll thank me, eventually."

"For what?" I glare. "For being condescending? For channeling your best impression of our mother? For disapproving of me now, just like you did when I first met Nate?"

Helen braces her hands against the smooth granite of the kitchen counter and leans toward me. "At least Nate didn't drag you all the way out—"

"Did you forget what you said about Houston when we decided to move there?"

She straightens. "Abigail, I really am here to *help* you. I love you, and if you would calm down enough to—"

"Get out," I say, pointing again. "Before the kids get here and have to see us fight again. Before my fiancé shows up and shoves you out the door himself with his own brand of cowboy indignation, just leave."

"Fine. Answer a few questions honestly for me, and I'll do it," Helen says.

What do you know? She can still surprise me. "Really? You'll go?"

She nods. "I swear. But first, tell me how many people you've told about the wedding."

"You, Amanda, Mom and Dad, and the kids."

"Eight people?"

"I could name the other friends I've got here, but you don't know them. Suffice it to say, it's not a secret."

"So your best friend Robert Marwell knows?" She arches that same eyebrow again.

"No," I say. "Nor do I plan to invite him."

"Why not?" her lips are compressed, but she'd be smiling if she didn't have her face on such a tight leash.

"He hit on me, if you must know. Apparently he's been in love with me for years." Let her chew on that.

"Of course he has." Her smile is almost catlike. "Everyone in the world knew that, other than you. But notwithstanding that fact, he's also your and Nate's oldest friend."

Everyone in the world knew? I splutter. "Was that enough questions for you?"

"It's a big wedding that you're planning?" she asks.

"No, small."

"And you're planning to have it, when? Next year, to give the kids time to acclimate? To make sure that this huge move is the right one?"

"In May," I say. "As soon as the weather's nice enough and the calves are all born."

"I think I've heard enough." She throws up her index finger in the universal symbol for the number one. "You've essentially told no one that you knew before you moved here six months ago."

This time, I fold my arms. "My life is here now. I also haven't told my friends back home that I quit my job."

She holds up a second finger. "You're doing a small wedding, and you're having it as quickly as possible."

"I don't have the energy to plan a big one."

She holds up one more finger. "Third, you quit your job. You're carefully isolating yourself out here in the middle of *nowhere* with no other options."

Arguing with her is pointless. She thinks what she thinks no matter what I say. "How many questions do I have to answer before you actually leave?"

"Doesn't any of this sound like a downward spiral to you? If you're really excited to marry this guy, if you're really not embarrassed at all, if you're positive that this is the right call not only for you, but for your *many* darling children, then why the rush? Why the tiny wedding? Why aren't you shouting it from the rooftops and really celebrating?" That stupid eyebrow arches yet again. I hate that eyebrow.

"I already told you," I say. "I don't have the energy to plan something huge precisely because I prioritize my children." Something my sister knows nothing about.

"What do you think people will say about you getting married again this fast?"

"I don't care."

"Really?"

I shrug.

"You're starting your own legal practice, your kids have only you to turn to for help with school and life, and you're running a cattle ranch." She sits down at the kitchen table. "I know you want me to leave, but you need me." She smiles. "I can raise two hundred million dollars in a week, you know. That's what I'll be doing

24

when I return to New York. But for now, I'm not going anywhere. I'm going to either help you with this huge transition, or I'm going to convince you that it's a mistake and help you get back on track."

"Helen, I—"

"Let's just get some of the big details worked out for this wedding, and *then* I'll fly home with a clear conscience."

The bus pulls up outside.

"And for now, I can't wait to see my nieces and nephews. I can barely even imagine how much they've changed in the past year."

As the kids rush up the drive, ogling her black BMW, I have a split second to decide how to handle Helen. In the end, I opt for classic Abby. When the door swings open, I force a smile. "Look, kids! Your Aunt Helen arrived early!"

❧ 3 ❧

AMANDA

Border collies never get tired.

I wish that was a joke or an exaggeration. I throw an orange rubber ball for Roscoe for at least half an hour, sometimes closer to an hour, every morning, and it's never enough. When I stop, he's always still staring at me with longing eyes.

"My shoulder hurts," I say. "And there's snow on the ground. That can't be fun on your feet." It doesn't seem to bother him much, if I'm being honest.

His eyes plead with me. *Just one more throw.*

"Oh, for heaven's sake." I chuck it as far as I can, but it's never far enough.

When he drops the ball on my left foot a moment later, I groan, massage my shoulder a little bit, and pick it up with my gloved hand.

"If my tendonitis comes back thanks to you. . ." I shake my head at him, but he doesn't seem to be the slightest bit worried. The second I toss it, Roscoe's off—he usually leaves just a hair early, his faith is so absolute that I'll throw it for him.

He comes bounding back immediately, begging me yet again.

The cycle will never break. Once, a few weeks ago, I decided I'd just throw it until he got tired. I finally quit around lunchtime, because I was hungry. He was still bringing me the ball.

That's when my tendonitis flared for the first time. Luckily, Steve's suggestion of Voltaren worked, but he said not to push it.

"Where, Roscoe?" I crouch down, and he slathers my face with dog kisses before I can stop him. "Where does this energy come from?"

If I knew the answer to that, I could bottle it, sell it, and make a fortune.

Eventually, I have no choice but to smash all Roscoe's hopes and dreams. I do have work to do, after all. These new homes and offices aren't going to remodel themselves.

Things have been awkward with Amanda Saddler ever since Christmas. I wasn't sure what to say about it, so I haven't said much at all. When Abby and her kids moved out, I helped them pack. When my girls begged to go with them, I said no. After all, we don't own it. They do.

But the upset feelings her generous gift caused in me haven't faded like I thought they might. I used to love to be around the funny old lady, but now I always feel like a loser around her. I met her first. I made friends with her before anyone else, and even *she* likes Abigail better.

I get it.

I like Abigail better than I like myself. My kids like her better. Everyone likes her better. She's a better person. She's less whiny and more impressive. Certainly she's less selfish than I am. I think it hurts *more* because I understand it.

I guess I just wanted one person to like me more, to understand me, and to support me.

"I need to shower and get ready," I say to no one but Roscoe. I have four different contractors to meet for bids today. "You ready?"

Roscoe wags his tail.

"I'll take that as a yes."

By the time I get out of the shower, Amanda's waiting on me. "You still angry?"

That I was not expecting. "Angry? You think I'm angry?"

"That I bought Abigail the ranch."

I swallow.

"Guess so."

"Angry's not the right word," I say. "Hurt."

"I have something for you, too," she says.

"What?"

"I said I've got something for you, too. I've been thinking about it, and even though it's something I've had my whole life, even though it's something I love, you've got more people you answer to. I feel like it's fair."

"What's fair?" What is she talking about? Is she giving me. . .her ranch?

"I'm gonna give you the name Amanda. Everyone can start calling me Mandy."

It's a joke. It must be a joke.

"Before you argue with me, it's too confusing, all this Amanda Brooks, Amanda Saddler business. And I know you don't like when the kids call you Aunt Mandy. I've seen you cringe. And if Abby says 'Amanda Saddler' where I can hear her one more time, I swear. My blood pressure shoots up every time. The only person who ever called me that was my ma, and only when she was mad."

"Amanda—"

She holds up her hand. "May as well get used to it. Say Mandy."

I grit my teeth. "Mandy."

"Don't say anything about it. I promise not to be sore over it, and I promise I'll get used to it." She beams at me. "I shoulda just said that at Christmas. That would've been a good gift, but it took me some time to wrap my head around the idea."

That's her idea of a comparable gift? Abby gets a ranch, and I get. . .to keep my name? "We're moving out," I say.

Mandy blinks. "What?"

"I've been thinking about that since Christmas, too. Abby told us we were welcome, and the girls really miss being with their cousins."

"But you all have way more space here," she says.

"When you really love the people you're with, you don't want space from them."

She flinches.

That's when I realize that I wanted to hurt her, like she hurt me. But I also didn't want to hurt her, because I love her. "I'm sorry," I say. "It's been a hard decision to make, where to live. We feel like we're imposing here."

"You're not."

"And I'm hurt," I say again. "You don't have kids, so you probably don't know this, but you have to be really careful when you give your children gifts."

"Why don't you explain it to me, then?"

"At Christmas one year, I gave Maren a phone. Emery was younger, and clearly not ready for one, so I gave her a new dollhouse instead. The dollhouse actually cost more, but the phone was much more exciting."

"Okay." Amanda crosses her arms. "And?"

"Emery was really upset. She felt that Maren had the better gift, and it meant that I loved her more."

"You're saying that Abigail and you are like my daughters, and that I gave her a phone?" She arches one eyebrow.

I shrug. "I'm not saying that exactly, but I am disappointed that you clearly care a lot more about—"

"Child, do you think I care more about the charities I donate money to than I do about you?"

"Charities?"

"I donated three million dollars to a charity that feeds children in Africa the year before last."

Okay, that kind of hurts, too. Clearly she has money to throw around, and what do I get? *I can call her Mandy.* Awesome. "I know that you don't owe me anything."

"And yet I helped you with your cookie business. I offered to let you live here—"

"If Abigail came along."

Amanda scowls. "At some point, you're going to have to get your head out of your butt, Amanda. Do it sooner, rather than later. Take it from someone who has tried waiting too long. It's a mistake."

"Excuse me?"

"I made you bring Abby along for *your benefit.* You were the one hurting over the fight you two had. You were the one suffering, and you were the one who was wrong, and if I hadn't given you a mighty good reason, you'd never have overcome your pride to fix that mess

30

you made." She folds her arms. "Stop obsessing over what you don't have and worry about what you do." She pivots on her heel and stomps off. "I'll see you on site in half an hour." She pauses and looks back over her shoulder. "Unless you're quitting our partnership?"

I shake my head.

"Great. See you then."

I knew she'd be upset, and that's why I told her we were moving out. Abby didn't actually invite us, because I haven't even asked. The girls have been clamoring to go back 'home' as they call it, but I like having a little more room and a few less judgmental eyes on what time I wake up and how I parent.

My pride really is a problem. It's always getting me into trouble. Amanda—*Mandy*—got that much right, at least.

I try to step back and listen to what she said. She did help me when no one else had. She gave me not one, but two big business opportunities, and moreover, she told me I could succeed at them. She believed in me enough to offer me free rent and a place to stay, and she was right about another thing, too.

It was my fault—the fight with Abby.

She did me a favor by making me fix things with her, and having my stay at her place be contingent on the repair.

The thing is, I know I shouldn't be upset that Abby and her kids got a two or three million dollar ranch, and I got nothing. I know Mandy has been more than generous every step of the way.

I know.

But I can't help my feelings.

It *feels* deeply unfair. And it makes me feel like she thinks Abby's worthy and I'm not.

That Christmas, I didn't give Emery a phone because she didn't need one—is Mandy trying to say that she didn't give me a ranch because it's not what I needed? What about a pile of money? A nice house? *Anything at all* that was sort of, kind of, a little bit on par with that ranch? Or with a huge donation to starving children.

Even I want to slap myself.

I wish I was a bigger person, the kind of person who could let this sort of thing go.

But I'm just not.

I think about how happy the kids will be when I tell them we're moving back in with Abby. That means I should probably call Abby and confirm that we *can* move back. I'm not totally sure which room each of her kids took, and she may need to check with them before telling me whether it's alright. Also, the timing may be tricky. I know she's going back to Houston soon to pick up all their stuff—their house sold, which is great news.

I'm sure another enormous check will really help her.

Gah, stop it already, Amanda. I need to stop measuring my happiness by what other people have and what I don't, but it's easier to say that than to do.

Right as I'm pulling out of the driveway, Eddy calls.

"Hey," I say. "I'm about to meet some contractors, but I'd love to get lunch today, if you have time between patients."

"I'm in the middle of teeth-floating purgatory," he says. "But I can always make time for lunch with my favorite person. Message me when you're finished, and I'll take a break."

"Perfect."

Talking to Eddy always sets everything else right.

He still hasn't given the studio an answer about the new album, and I think he has to tell them by tomorrow. We still haven't talked about it, not really, and I'm not sure what to say. I don't want him to do it—he'd have to leave to record the album, and he'd have to be gone on tour to promote it—but I'm not willing to tell him that. What kind of relationship can survive when one person squashes the other person's dreams?

I've been the one being squashed, and I want no part in doing it to Eddy.

But hoping that he'll make the right decision for *us* himself is a little nerve-wracking. I mean, he's a forty-year-old man. Surely he'll realize that the time for chasing his dreams of being a rock star is past, right? He can't really want to travel all over the country promoting a new album that also happens to be his first solo album, and his first album in twenty years?

He's only getting all this attention because of my posts, anyway. Wrecking my entire career boosted his—life isn't always fair.

Although if *I'm* being completely fair, my career would be resurging right now if I had any real interest in reviving it. Technically, it was Abby who boosted Eddy and saved me, by revealing the truth about his past.

I reach the first home we're thinking of remodeling with two minutes to spare. Of course, Mandy's truck is already there. I've noticed that for her, ten minutes early is barely on time. I can't decide whether it's her age, or her generation, or just a personal thing that she's always so early.

At least I'm not late.

"Good morning," I say.

The man Amanda Saddler's talking to has the largest pores I have ever seen. It looks like his face is made of lava rock.

"Amanda," Mandy says. "This is Todd Hesslup. He's the best tile guy in Utah, and the fastest too."

"But not the cheapest," he says.

"You can get two of three," Mandy says. "Quality work, speedy work, or inexpensive work, but you can't get them all."

"Who's quality and cheap?" I ask.

Todd chuckles. "That would be Frank Johnson, but good luck ever finishing anything when you're working with him."

"Frank's always biting off more than he can ever hope to chew," Mandy says.

"Let's walk the property," I say. "Then if you have any questions—"

"We walked it before you got here," Mandy says. "Todd's got another appointment he's off to, so he needed to get this done quickly."

"Oh," I say. "I'm so sorry. I could have come earlier if I'd known."

"Just got a call this morning," Todd says. "I told you I'd work on this, but this other project is supposedly huge, and it's a rush job. So let me know if you want me to do the work ASAP."

"As soon as we get your quote," Mandy says. "Plan on us first."

"This job is supposedly going to take up to a year," he says.

"A year?" Mandy frowns. "What kind of job is it?"

Todd shrugs. "Not a lot of details yet—some big thing over in Dutch John—near the Flaming Gorge."

"Who told you to go bid?"

"Referral from Frank Johnson, actually. He knew this was too big for him. He said some guy called him out of the blue—said he heard he was good work for cheap."

"It's a house? That will take a year?" Mandy asks.

"Not a house—bigger than that. I heard it's a resort or a hotel or something."

Over the next two hours, more than two-thirds of our contractors admit that they've been called over to bid on the same thing: a new resort in Dutch John.

Mandy's lips are pursed and her eyes flashing by the time we're done. "I try to keep my guys focused on one thing at a time," she says. "That's why we have them bidding on this one house first—but we have a long list of properties to make ready. I can't have some stupid, ill-advised project over on the Gorge driving prices up." She pins me with a look. "Go poke around over there—no one knows you. Act confused and bat your eyes and find out who's the driving force behind this."

"Bat my eyes?" I can't believe she's actually suggesting that I flirt my way around to the information.

"Use what God gave ya." She smiles. "Or are you morally opposed? The same woman who was very recently dating on social media for the promotion of a clothing line?"

I straighten my shoulders. "I'm not morally opposed, no."

"Good. Then remind me why I hired you, and go figure out who our opponent is, and what their weak spot is. It would be great if you found out they didn't really have funding, or that the whole thing was just speculation. Then we could lock our people down much easier—but we should probably hammer out a chain of importance on these remodels to make the jobs with us more attractive, don't you think?"

"I'd do it now, but I told Eddy I'd meet him for lunch."

Mandy waves. "It's getting late—go and meet him. We can go over it tonight." She quirks her eyebrow. "Unless you'll already be moving out?"

I roll my eyes. "No move date set."

"Good." Mandy nods. "That's good."

When I call, Eddy has one question. "Brownings? Or The Hub?"

"You know, I still haven't eaten at The Hub."

"Don't let the gas station-bar-grill-convenience store combination confuse you. If you like things that are smothered in gravy and/or cheese, you will *love* it." I can almost hear his smirk. "Plus, I can get gas while we're there."

"You had me at smothered in cheese," I say.

"I knew that would sell you."

Less than five minutes later, I'm looking over the menu. That's the best thing about Manila. Nothing is very far from anything else. "The menu is more robust than I expected for a gas station," I say. "Chicken fried steak and burgers, but also pizza, quesadillas, cod, a burrito, and even prime rib."

"You pick anything you want, hot stuff," Eddy says. "We're here to celebrate."

At the words, my heart skips a beat. I can barely force out my next words. "Celebrate what?"

"I've finally made a decision," he says. "You're looking at a soon-to-be Comeback Kid." His eyes study my face.

I slam on the mask I wore for more than a decade

around Paul—my impenetrable smile. "I am? You decided to do it?" Beam, beam, beam. I'm just *so excited.* Or at least, it has to look like I am. "I'm so proud of you."

"Are you really?" His head bobs a little. "I haven't told them yet—I wanted to make sure that you were really okay with it first."

I push that smile a little harder. "Of course I am. If that's what you want, then I think it's fantastic news. I can't wait to hear what new songs you'll—"

"That's the thing that decided me," he says. "I stopped performing, but I never stopped singing or writing songs. I gathered up the ones I've written over the years, and I sent them to the studio, and they love them. They've already got band members for me to choose from—I can assemble whatever team I want. And they've approved fourteen songs already. Two will be released as singles to precede the album, and then twelve would be released as the album itself."

"Wow," I say. "I had no idea you'd been talking to them about all this."

"Nothing is signed," he says. "I haven't made anything official or formal, but I wanted to make sure that they'd really let me do what I wanted—that they'd honor their word things with them will be different than my first label."

"Of course it will—you're an adult for one. A compe-tent, intelligent, savvy businessman, who knows what he wants." Unfortunately, what he wants is to leave me and the life we have here and chase fame and fortune by traveling all over the world.

I mean, it's hot.

But it's going to be really lonely.

During a large part of our marriage, Paul travelled for work three weeks out of four. With him, I didn't really mind it. It's not like I wanted him around. But lately, Eddy has felt like air to me. I'm already suffocating, thinking that he's going to be gone for. . .how long will he be gone?

"Do you have details yet? When will you be recording and touring?"

"Not yet," he says. "But it's all negotiable, and I promise I'll go over it all with you. Anything you need, we'll block that off and I'll be here."

I want him here all the time. Not at prearranged times. What if there's a cougar attack? What if I've had a bad day?

But Eddy needs a girlfriend—actually, most everyone needs someone—who isn't so pathetic, so needy, or so desperate that she can't handle things on her own. I need to *be* the kind of girlfriend who isn't wrecked by her boyfriend's success and whatever else that means.

So I paste a smile on my face and I gush and I congratulate and I die a little bit inside with every word. And when my girls come home from school, I do the same thing in front of them.

"Of course it's a good thing," I reassure Emery. "Eddy's pursuing his dreams, and I couldn't be more delighted about it."

❧ 4 ❧

DONNA

No matter how bad things got at home, no matter how much Dad yelled or how many times he hit me with his belt, when I got to school, I was safe. It's funny that, even now, school is my safe place. After all, who would come to my place of work and accost me?

Patrick.

That's who.

I can barely believe my eyes when he strolls through the front door. I cast around the small foyer of the school, checking to see whether anyone else might be close to keep his behavior in check.

No luck.

"Why do you look so panicked?" he asks. "I'm your brother—or did you forget?"

"I'm at work," I hiss. "Can you please hold whatever you plan to say until after I'm no longer at work?"

"You're threatening my entire life right now—laying claim to what's mine—and you think I should be more accommodating of your piddly little secretary job?"

"How am I threatening your entire life?" I know I shouldn't get drawn into this discussion. He's clearly baiting me. But I can't seem to help myself. "Mom and Dad executed a new will, and it doesn't write me out because they helped me with school. *They* did that. You were the one lying to me."

"Dad wasn't in his right mind when he signed that." Patrick crosses the space between us and drops a stack of paper on the desk in front of me with a flourish. "You may not want to hear this, but that will isn't valid. Mom marching Dad into the law office to make that will was a game of make-believe. Dad never would have done it if he'd been in his right mind—which you know—and that's why it changes nothing."

Without even touching me, he's managed to strike a pretty painful blow. That was where Patrick surpassed my dad. He doesn't need to use his fists. His words are plenty awful all on their own.

"I hear that idiot blonde quit her fancy job and that you're her first client. I thought you might like to know, before you go off spending money you don't have, that your efforts will be a total waste."

"You came to warn me?" I ask. "Out of the kindness of your heart?"

Patrick sighs. "You're my sister. Of course I want what's best for you. I even talked it over with Amelia, and we're willing to give you a hundred thousand dollars from the life insurance proceeds." His voice shifts up almost an octave. "Not that we think we should or even that Mom and Dad really wanted us to, but we're willing to give you that, if it will make you happy. But you have to drop this nonsense about the new will."

"Your lawyer executed this will you say isn't any

good." My voice is flatter than I mean for it to be. "You're saying that he shouldn't have done it?"

"It was always just a farce—he did it to placate Mom so she wouldn't get herself into trouble by arguing with him. You know how angry Dad could get. Mom wanted to change her will, and Dad wanted to keep his the same. In the end, we knew that it wasn't binding for Dad when he redid it. He barely knew up from down most days."

I should have known that even with a valid, witnessed, executed will in my hands, one that he had been hiding from me no less, Patrick would somehow manage to make me doubt everything. "Go away, Patrick. We can talk about this later."

"This isn't an offer you can just hold in your back pocket," Patrick says. "I'll forward you the settlement agreement my lawyer drew up, but you should know that it's got an expiration date on it. Think of it like a gallon of milk. Make up your mind in a few days, and it's fine. Wait too long, and you'll get nothing, which is exactly what you deserve."

Something has been bothering me for a while. "If you really want me to consider the offer, then give me some information to show me you're here in good faith."

Patrick's hand is already on the door. He turns and looks at me over his shoulder. "What?"

"You wanted the Birch Creek Ranch really badly. You lied and cheated and even risked committing fraud to get it. I just can't figure out *why*. Any way I look at it, you don't need more land for your cattle, and having it be practically contiguous with your land isn't enough of a reason. You could be pressuring the Langleys on the other side, if that's all you want. Why did you want that place so badly?"

Patrick's smile is forced. "Donna, your biggest problem has always been that you think you're so much smarter than everyone else around you." He pushes the door open. "But you're not."

And then he's gone.

I'm still shaking.

By the time school's out, I'm not shaking nearly as badly, but I'm still shaken up. I called Abby, but she hasn't called me back yet. I need to find out how big of a deal this is, Patrick's argument that Dad wasn't in his right mind and that this was just some kind of make-believe will.

"Mom?" Aiden, oblivious to everything else that's going on in our lives, gives me his biggest grin every single day when he sees me. It does remind me of what matters the most, and it's not money, no matter how obsessed Patrick seems to have become with it.

"Hey, sweetheart."

"Are we going to check out the new house now?"

My seven-year-old is reminding me of things on our to-do list. How pathetic. "Of course we are."

Amanda Saddler offered to rent us a little house on the edge of town. It's on the Birch Creek side of Manila, which is nice. It won't be a long drive to school for Aiden, and it won't be annoying to go see my new friends.

"We better hurry," I say. "I'd hate to leave Amanda waiting."

"Will Gabe be there?" Aiden's eyes light up.

I shake my head. "Not this time, sweetheart. We're just meeting Ms. Saddler."

"Oh." His tiny shoulders slump, and I try not to feel as deflated about it as he looks.

Once I hear back from Abby about the will, I'll see if we can set up a playdate as well. I know she's busy, but once we have a place of our own, I could even bring Gabe home from school with us and take him over to Abby's after dinner—no extra imposition on her.

Aiden's pelting me with questions about a house I've never seen the entire time we walk to the car. "Sweetheart, I don't know anything about the yard, the bathrooms, or the size of the family room yet. But we're on our way over, so I'm sure we'll both find out soon enough."

He sighs. "Do you think Mr. Will really has Legos?"

I wish adults wouldn't offer things unless they were one hundred percent positive they would be able to follow through. After offering to let Aiden play with his Legos before Christmas, Will seems to be struggling to find them. His mom probably threw them out years ago. It would be totally fine, except first graders are like dogs who have been given one little taste of bacon. They cannot let it go.

"I'm sure that if he can find them, he'll honor his promise," I say. "But sometimes when it's something you haven't used for a really long time, like Legos for Mr. Will, what we want to do isn't really the same as what we can do." I grit my teeth and hope that Aiden doesn't press the issue.

"Do you think—"

After a loud popping sound from my front right tire, my car starts pulling heavily to the right. I finally pull over onto the dirt curb of the small road heading out of town.

"What was that?" Aiden asks.

I've needed new tires for a while. I should have gotten them replaced a while ago, but driving all the way into Green River just hasn't been in the cards for me. Not to mention the expense of a whole new set of tires. They're probably going to cost more than my car is worth. But now that I'm stuck on the side of the road, without a tire shop within an hour's drive, I'm wishing I'd made time and found money.

"Mom?"

"Everything's fine, sweetheart," I lie.

Tears well up in my eyes. You can only tell yourself that everything is fine for so long before it stops having any meaning.

"How are we going to see the house?" Aiden asks. "Is someone going to fix the tire?"

I'm not the kind of girl who doesn't know how to change a tire. I don't like doing it, but Dad made sure I knew how. Only, it's hard to change a tire when you haven't got a spare. I should have one, I know. But we're already using the spare, thanks to the last time we had a tire go flat. At least that time it had the decency to happen in the driveway of our house.

I call Amanda Saddler and tell her we're going to be way late—my phone says it's a mile and a quarter hike. Not bad for an adult, but between the seven-year-old and the snow, we won't be getting there any time soon.

"Why?" she asks. "What's going on?"

"Oh, nothing horrible," I say. "I just managed to hit a nail in the road, and now—"

"Flat tire?" She sighs. "Maybe if I call—"

A truck passes us and then slows and parks not far down the way.

"Someone's here," I say. "I'll call you back."

Not any truck, I realize as I hang up the phone. Will Earl's big black truck. The door opens and he hops out and circles around to where I'm still parked. I scramble out of the car as quickly as I can.

"Hey, it's Mr. Will," Aiden says.

"Shh," I say.

"Looks like you lost a tire," Will says. "Not a big shock. They look a little worn."

I sigh. "It just hadn't quite made it to the top of my list."

"What with the funeral, the holidays, your son, work, and living in a hotel?" Will smiles. "It doesn't help that the closest tire shop's nearly fifty miles away."

I kick at a snowdrift just to have something to look at other than his face, but I regret it immediately. My sneakers are now wet and cold and I feel even more idiotic. "It's fine though," I say. "You didn't need to stop."

"Triple A's already on their way?" He raises one eyebrow. "Really?"

"Well, not exactly," I say. "But—"

"How about this. You tell me where you were headed —since it clearly wasn't to the hotel—and I'll give you a lift."

I open my mouth to argue, but before I can say a word, Aiden starts hooting in the back. I should've closed the car door. "Yay! We're going to see a new house. And now you get to come."

"A new house?" Will asks.

"It's a rental that Amanda Saddler's showing us," I say. "Nothing special."

"Want a ride?" he asks. "I'm happy to take you back to the hotel when you're done."

"I'm sure Amanda can take us," I'm quick to say. "No need to stick around the whole time."

"Alright." Will wipes the side of his nose with his finger, and it leaves a big black smear.

"Uh, you've got a—" I point. "A smudge."

"Oh." He wipes at it and the black spot grows.

I laugh. "That didn't exactly make it better."

"It didn't?"

Aiden says, "You look like a Dalmatian. They're dogs with big black spots."

"They do have spots, but I'm not sure how big they are," I say.

"One day, I want a Dalmatian," Aiden says.

"That's very specific," I say.

"It's good to know exactly what you want," Will says. "A man should be able to make up his mind."

Something stupid shivers inside of me when he says that, but I squish it down hard. It's not like he really meant for any of that to apply to anything other than Aiden wanting a white dog with black spots.

"Let's go." Aiden's unbuckling.

I text Amanda Saddler to tell her we're on our way to her again, and then I hold Aiden's hand as we walk over to Will's truck. I'm a little surprised to see that Will actually thought to grab Aiden's booster seat. He's buckling it in before I can even try to do it myself.

"When am I going to get to play with your Legos?" Aiden asks.

"That's a good question," Will says. "I was actually on my way to Mom's hotel to tell you that I found something."

Aiden's eyes widen. "What did you find?"

"What do you think?" Will asks.

"Your Legos?"

"Not only *my* Legos," Will says, "but my sister's Legos too. I asked her whether she cared what I did with them, and she said no." He smiles. "I figured maybe you'd want to keep them at your place for a little while."

Aiden's mouth drops open. "Really?"

"Your mom may not want them underfoot while you're staying at a hotel, but if you're going to check out a house right now, who knows? Maybe they'll have a new home soon."

"Mom won't care," Aiden says. "Right, Mom?"

I open my mouth, but I'm not sure what to say. "Let's go look at the house, and we can make a decision after that."

When Will finally heads down the road toward the address and makes the tiny turn onto Oriole Lane, I brace myself. For the rent Amanda Saddler quoted me, four hundred a month, and given the excellent location, I'm pretty sure this place is going to be far worse even than the old farmhouse Dad grew up in where we were living for months before the hotel.

I'm not sure how much worse I can handle.

I think about the gummy linoleum floors, the scratched and discolored mirrors in the bathroom, the water-stained windows, and the faded and ratty carpet, and I shudder.

When I left Charlie, I knew things would be rough for a while. I guess I didn't consider exactly how uncomfortable they might get, or for how long. Maybe I can work with Amanda on getting a few things upgraded here and there for a slight reduction in rent. It would be a win-win. I'd be more comfortable as things are fixed up, and she'd have a nicer place to rent or sell when we finally leave.

But how much lower on rent could she really go? Clearly she's already giving me a deal.

"I think this is it." Will points.

Time seems to slow down as I turn toward his outstretched finger.

And stare at the cutest little white and yellow farmhouse I've ever seen in my life. Amanda's standing outside on the front porch, which someone has cleared of all the snow and ice that must have accumulated there in the most recent storm. The porch is white. The main house is yellow. And the windows have dark blue shutters that look absolutely precious.

No part of it looks run down.

Nothing about it screams neglect or channels a depressing vibe. Amanda told me it's a three bedroom with two full baths. It even has a little picket fence around the back yard that still somehow doesn't disappear entirely in the snowy landscape.

That's when it hits me: there's no way this house should be renting for four hundred bucks a month.

I want to cry.

With my paltry salary and the cost of utilities and food and a car payment, which I will very likely soon have when this junker dies, I can't afford much more than six hundred a month. And this place would be a steal, even at that. If I paid what it's worth, I'd have to invade the principal of the money I got in the divorce, and I promised myself that I'd save that for my retirement. Honestly, even with all of that saved, it's not likely that I'll have enough for Aiden's college *and* a comfortable retirement, but if I start spending it now?

Forget it.

I can't even go inside. If I do, I'll never walk away from it. And if I take it at a dramatically reduced rate, it's charity. Letting Abby help me for free has been enough.

"That's really cute," Will says. "I approve."

"I can't go in," I say.

"What? Why not?" Will sounds as confused as I feel.

"Mom! Come on." I hear Aiden unbuckling.

Amanda Saddler's walking toward the truck, her bright and intelligent eyes scanning the glass to figure out who gave us a ride. What am I going to say to her?

But I can't hide in here forever. I screw up my resolve and open the door.

"Well you look terrified," Amanda says. "And you should." Her lips purse.

"I should look scared?" What does that mean?

"I started remodeling this place a few months ago, and we knew winter was coming so we started with the exterior. New siding, new paint, replacement porch boards, repaired electrical."

"Oh."

"The inside won't be ready for a while yet, and it's a mess." She crosses her arms. "If you're worried about that, I can show you some other places."

So it's a fixer upper? So what? Wasn't that what I was hoping for anyway? That could bring the rent down some, right? And maybe I can do some of it myself. That could justify the lower rate for a while. . .or is that still wishful thinking?

"To be honest, I'm worried that I can't really afford

this place," I say. "I know that my budget isn't exactly grand, and—"

"You get a friend discount," Amanda said.

"I've never heard of you offering anyone a discount," Will says.

"Maybe I'm getting soft in my old age." Amanda shrugs. "So sue me."

"I'm already using a lawyer more than I want to," I say. "No more lawsuits from me."

"That's a relief," Amanda says. "I think we have the same lawyer, and I'm not sure she'd pick me over you."

"I'm pretty sure lawyers pick whoever has the most money," Will says. "I think you're safe."

"This one's different," Amanda says. "She's got principles."

"Wow, imagine that," Will says. "A lawyer with principles."

"I have principles too, and a friend discount is one thing," I say. "But I've been searching online in neighboring towns, and a place like this should be at least a thousand a month."

Amanda cringes. "You haven't seen the inside yet."

How bad could it really be? I guess it's time to find out. I jog up the steps and open the door, bracing myself for the absolute worst.

And I did not prepare well enough. Not even close.

I stifle a scream when something darts across the very dirty, very outdated olive green linoleum floor.

"I didn't know cockroaches were out and about in the middle of winter," Will says. "You've got to give it to them. They're resourceful."

"Ooh." Aiden pokes his head around my waist. "Look!"

I'm afraid to.

"There's a lizard in the window."

And he's right. Sort of. I shuffle a bit closer, knocking over a can that's thankfully empty. "That *used* to be a lizard," I say. "Now it's a skeleton."

"You weren't kidding," Will says. "This place is. . .rough doesn't feel like the right word."

"It has a lot of potential," Amanda says. "Once we get it cleaned up, put in some new floors, and use a little elbow grease."

"I think it's going to need more than new floors," I say.

"It will," Amanda says. "So here's the thing. I can either come out here every single day and meet contractors for all the things that need to be done, and then come hover over them. Or you can live here once we get it livable, and you can be here to open the house and answer questions and pick colors yourself."

"So the four hundred a month would be because I'd need to supervise?" I ask. "And make design decisions?"

"Amanda Brooks will make most of the design decisions," she says. "She'll decide on tile and whatnot, but you can give input on colors and style, as the renter."

"What exactly would you do before I move in?" Because there's no way I can live in this.

She sighs. "I've got an appointment with a contractor tomorrow to go over a comprehensive list, and I thought we'd try and prioritize. You'll need at least one bathroom that's done, and a working kitchen. But paint and finishing touches could probably wait."

"I agree," I say. "But I need a house that heats and can securely close. And I need it to be safe and toxin free." I scrunch my nose.

"Absolutely," Amanda Saddler says.

"Let me know when you hear back what kind of timeline we're looking at," I say. "But I think this could work. I'd love to see the list and kind of go over what things I could live with and what might be too much."

I walk through the disgusting place, making note of the things that should stay. Two of the rooms have stained glass windows that are just gorgeous. Or they will be, once we get them cleaned up. The back bedroom has wood floors that look pretty bad, but I think they might be salvageable if we can refinish them. I rented an old house in California for a while that had the most beautiful old wood floors, and if they're as old as they look, they could probably be buffed down. I'd love real wood floors...

Will's pointing out something about the closet to Aiden, and Amanda sidles over next to me. "What do you think? Be honest."

"I really like the layout," I say. "But it needs a lot."

"How much longer can you stand that hotel?"

"It's hard to live in a hotel with a kid," I say.

"I'll prioritize this, I swear," she says.

I check on Will and Aiden again—and Aiden's shouting about something, so they aren't paying us any attention. "I don't want to be a charity case," I say. "I don't need the Taj Mahal, but I think when this is done, it'll be a little too nice for us. I'm worried we'll move here and endure the remodel, only to have to leave again."

"Donna Ellingson." Amanda's normally genial voice is whip sharp. "You listen to me, and you listen good. I'm an *old* lady."

"You're not—"

"Eighty-six years next month. I think by anyone's standards, that's old. And do you know what I've learned in my almost nine decades of life?"

I swallow.

"Never argue with a genuinely kind gesture. Not as a recipient, not as a giver. Kind gestures are the best thing about humanity. I think you can agree that I don't stand to gain anything from charging you lower than market rent." She wiggles her eyebrows. "I'm not some horny young man hoping to get you into bed, so this is just genuine kindness." She releases my wrist and folds her arms under her chest. "My joints ache. My head hurts most days. My eyesight's not what it once was. Even drinking wine isn't as fun as it used to be. My brain fogs up too quick, and I get hungover like a lightweight. But one thing still makes me happy, and that's helping the deserving members of the family I've chosen."

"But—"

"I didn't actually pick you, but I picked those two little gals who moved out here, and Abby picked you, and that's good enough for me."

"I would feel—"

"You'll feel *grateful* that because you were willing to take a chance on a ramshackle pile of moldy bricks, I'll keep your rent low while you're staying here, and you'll promise to come to dinner at my house with your sweet little boy whenever I ask."

I open my mouth, but she's not quite done.

"And with the money you save, you can pay a sitter and come to some girls' nights. Have you ever seen the show *Bridgerton*?" Her eyes sparkle.

"Um, well—"

"I'll take that as a no."

"Mom!" Aiden races across the room, literally kicking up dust with every step. "You are never going to believe this."

Oh, no. What did he find now? More dead critters?

"This house—" His eyes widen and his lips clamp closed.

"Will?" I quirk one eyebrow. "Did you tell him it's haunted? Because it may seem funny now, but it will *not* be funny at ten p.m. when he can't sleep."

He frowns. "I didn't tell him anything."

"It's *so* cool, but the more people that know about it. . ." Aiden trails off again, glancing pointedly at Amanda Saddler.

"She owns it," I say. "Anything you've discovered probably ought to be brought to her attention."

Aiden whispers, his eyes as round and shiny as boiled eggs. "There's a secret passageway from the closet in one of the bedrooms to the other one."

I stifle my laugh. "Wow."

"Mom, it's *so* cool. Can one of those rooms be *my* room? And then the other one can be for my little brother or sister?"

"Aiden, I'm not—"

"I know I don't have one now, but like, later. When I do?"

My heart breaks just a little bit. I have no idea if he'll ever have a brother or sister, and it'll just be one more disappointment in a line of disappointments he'll have to deal with.

"Or maybe you could have a friend come stay and do sleepovers in there." Will nods. "That would be awesome too."

Aiden's mouth forms an 'O.' "Gabe would love that!"

54

"I'm sure he would," I say.

"Note to self. Do not eliminate secret passageways," Amanda says.

"No!" Aiden grabs her hand. "Please don't!"

"So if we get this fixed up, you're interested?" she asks.

"Please, Mom!" Aiden would move into a latrine if it had a secret passageway, clearly.

"I suppose so," I say.

It occurs to me, then, that I have not a single stick of furniture. Not only will I need to come up with a deposit, and whatever oddball things you need once you own a home, but I'll also need to buy furniture. Maybe it's good that I have a little time. Hopefully air mattresses aren't too pricey right now. The list of things we'll need starts to crowd into my brain, but I refuse to dwell on it, not right now. I have other, more pressing issues to fret about.

"Thank you so much, Amanda. I'll text you my email address and I look forward to working together on this. But for now, I really need to see whether I can figure out how to get my flat tire fixed."

"I can tow your car to my place, Dee," Will says. "I've got the stuff to fix it."

"I couldn't possibly—"

"Oh, let the boy show off."

"Show off?" Aiden asks.

"You haven't seen his shop," Amanda says. "But once you have, you'll understand."

"Your shop?"

"A guy needs a hobby." Will ducks his head a little so I can't stare right at his bashful smile head on.

"I doubt you can fix my tire," I say. "I'm pretty sure it

was a combination of being way too old and worn, and a rendezvous with a nail."

"I just pulled a set of tires off a car I bought and replaced them with much wider ones. You're welcome to have the old ones, if you want them. They should have at least another year or two in them."

"I'd have to pay you something for them—and for putting them on."

"Sure you would." He rolls his eyes.

"Why don't you buy him dinner to repay him?" Amanda cackles. "And *dessert*."

I am going to slap her if she's not careful. "How will we get it there?"

Will looks at his truck and then looks back at me. "I can tow it, no problem."

"Oh, great."

He's not wrong. He's got all the things he needs in the back of his truck, and he carefully hitches my janky little car up to the back of his huge truck and loads Aiden back in. "It really won't take me that long."

Amanda wasn't kidding about his shop, either. I'd never even seen Will's house, which we drive past too quickly for me to form much of an opinion. It's a boring grey brick.

But his shop? You can tell this is the place he loves to be. It looks like a modern art deco garage you'd see on the cover of *Car and Driver*. The majority of the exterior is a slate grey metal that's ribbed. The trim and some of the siding is made from a knotty pine. It sounds crazy, but it really works. It's all sharp lines and angles, with custom rectangular windows over each garage bay and a sloped roof. There are six garage spaces, one door to which he opens with the click of a button. Even pulling my car behind him, he turns easily and backs my car into an empty bay.

"I can't believe how simple you just made that look."

"It's basic geometry," he says. "I never quite got it in school, but angles and pivots just make sense to my brain when I'm behind the wheel."

I always thought he was kind of an idiot when we were growing up, although we never had classes together. Or maybe it's because we never had classes together that I thought that. I was always in the advanced classes, while he was in with the boneheads. Maybe I was paying attention to the wrong things.

Aiden's desperate to get out and look around. He's wriggling like a worm on a hook. "Is it okay if I let Aiden out? I can keep him out of the garage."

"He can come inside," Will says. "How'd you like to be my helper, buddy? I mean, otherwise I might need to charge your mom."

"Yeah." Aiden's eyes widen. "I'm really good at tools."

He's good *at* tools? Oh my word. How on earth would he think he's good at 'tools'? What does that even mean? Ridiculous. "Actually—"

But he's already scrambled down and Will's walking him through the names of a few things. "Once I unhook this car so I can lift it, I'll need you to hand me the right thing. Think you can do that?"

Aiden's nodding vigorously, and my heart constricts. Why couldn't Aiden's dad have been like this? Why couldn't he have care and interest in his son instead of using him as a prop whenever needed and shelving him the rest of the time?

"See those tires over there?" Will points. "They've been gathering dust. I won't get much for them if I sell them used, not around here, but shipping is so high that it doesn't make sense to try and sell them elsewhere. Really you guys are helping me out by taking them off my hands."

He's such a bad liar. I can tell that Aiden doesn't even really buy it.

I turn to look at the cars he's working on and bump into a rolling chair. It hits the table with a keyboard and computer on it, and the movement wakes up the computer. I'm not snooping, but I can't help noticing the huge sad face in the middle of the screen. "Uh, oh," I say. "Looks like you lost your bid."

Will groans. "I always lose. I've tried for ten of those, at least, over the years, but they're always either fully restored and so expensive it's insane, or the decent ones always get snaked at the last minute."

I lean closer, since he doesn't seem distressed that I looked at it. "A Ford Mustang? I feel like I see those pretty often, even the old ones."

"It's not just an old Mustang." He shakes his head. "It's a 1967 Mustang Shelby GT350 Fastback. They're rare, trust me. There's one more for sale that ends in a few weeks, and I just bought this software that's supposed to help me win the bid. I just have to decide how much I'm willing to pay."

I can't help it. My eyes dart to the winning bid amount. It's more than I would make in *years*. How could Will even consider it?

"Alright," he says. "Let's get started."

It's hard not to get distracted by Will's muscles rippling while he changes my tires, but I really do need to pay attention to Aiden's safety in a garage like this.

"Why do you have so many cars?" Aiden asks.

"I guess I started working on them when I was young and I just fell in love with it."

"Do you think I'll like Legos my entire life, then?"

"I don't know, buddy." Will chuckles. "For me, it's more than just liking it as a kid. My dad and I don't have much in common, but we can always talk about car stuff."

I think about that for a bit—the value of using things to connect with people. I'm surprised that he has that kind of insight.

"My dad only likes money," Aiden says. "Maybe if I make a lot of it, he'll want to talk to me more."

Will's hands tighten on the wrench he's holding until his knuckles are white. "Some people aren't worth the —" He grits his teeth. "That's a good idea, buddy. I'm sure you can do it. Keep studying."

ABIGAIL

Between the two of them, my parents knew everything about everything when I was growing up. Dad's a professor of mathematics, and Mom's a professor of English. I suppose you could say that one of us took after Dad, and one of us took after Mom, but I think that since neither Helen nor I went into academia, they'd argue with you about that statement. And once Mom and Dad start arguing, you're doomed to lose.

As a child, I was the one person in the entire house who was willing to admit when I was wrong. I was the peacemaker right up until the day I left for college. It nearly gave me an ulcer, but I managed to keep the peace between everyone in that house for eighteen years.

Once I escaped that environment, I never went back for more than a few days at a time. But now that Helen's here with me, I'm remembering exactly how tense and horrible it was. It's amazing that, alone, she can still channel all that anxiety, stress, and shame, but here we are.

Which is why I'm hiding in the icy manud at six in the morning with my son Ethan.

"Mom, I told you I didn't really need help feeding the cows. You could've stayed inside where it's warm."

Warm's a relative term. Nothing about Helen makes me feel warm inside. Although, out here, I'm sitting next to Ethan as he drives the tractor with a spiky front-loader thing on it, and we're bumping and whirring and lurching our way toward the hay barn, wind gusting against our backs and around our heads.

When he lowers the lever and the spiky thing stabs the dead center of a round hay bale, I gasp. "That was great."

"Yeah." Ethan bobs his head with round eyes that clearly say I'm acting strange. "It's about my eight hundredth time doing it, so I'm glad you're proud of me. I'm pretty sure my skills can be credited to all the hand-eye coordination I gained from playing video games."

I frown. "We didn't have any video games in our house."

"Why do you think I spent so much time over at Chad's?"

My head spins to glare at him, but he's not too worried. He's too busy laughing.

"I'm kidding, Mom. Calm down."

A very large part of me doubts that he's actually kidding, but seeing as he's now an adult, it's not like I can really do or say much about it. The brisk wind continues to blow around us, like a skeletal hand, clutching at us from the grave. I shiver involuntarily and pull my heavy farm coat tighter.

"What are you really doing out here?" Ethan's voice still bristles with irritation, but there's also a very clear note of concern.

"I'm hiding," I finally confess.

"From Aunt Helen?" His hearty laugh rubs me the wrong way.

"You don't know her very well. She was always too busy conquering the corporate world to come see us, but she's not an easy person to deal with, and I think she's determined to stop my wedding."

"I never thought I'd see the day that *my mother*, the wrecking ball of Houston, would *hide* from someone else —another tiny little woman, no less!"

I jab him in the side.

It's significantly less satisfying given the sheer volume of coat between us. He squirms anyway—out of habit, probably.

"Look, she may be tiny, but she's awful. She's telling me that if I don't want a huge wedding, and if I'm not keen on inviting everyone I know, it means I'm ashamed of marrying Steve."

"Are you?" Ethan stops the tractor and turns toward me, leaving the enormous bale of hay bobbing up and down in midair, thanks to the jerky stop. Meanwhile, the cows in the pasture we're driving alongside are huddled up next to the fence, lowing and jostling one another, desperate for their breakfast.

"Of course not."

"Why don't you want a big wedding, then?"

I shrug.

"Your problem is that you don't *know* why you don't want a big one, and you're afraid she's right." He puts the tractor back in gear and when it starts lurching along again, mud spatter from the enormous tires flies up and covers my pants.

"Ugh."

"Are you saying that about the mud?" Ethan asks. "Or my insightful truth bombs?"

I roll my eyes, not that he sees it.

"Once we feed the cows, can I suggest that you go inside, clean up, and then actually have a talk with your sister? Tell her why you want a small wedding, and then stick to your guns."

His suggestion's not bad, but I don't take it. Instead, I run inside, shower as quickly as I can, and then escape out the front door before she sees me. It may not be a good long-term strategy, but she only has ten days before she's due back to start raising gobs of money for her next venture. If I hide successfully for long enough, she might get bored and leave. It was a classic move for me in my family growing up, and no matter how old we get, those kinds of baked-in habits die hard.

Plus, I'm running late to meet Amanda Saddler at the office she said might work for my law practice.

Okay, fine. Maybe I'm not actually late, but I *could* be late.

By the time I reach the address she sent me, which just happens to be next door to Amanda's failed cookie shop, I'm almost forty minutes early. Even so, I probably needed to walk the perimeter four or five times to make sure it looks like I want it to look before going inside to check out the office's interior. Right? Right.

"Should I be contacting the police?" a deep voice asks from behind me.

I spin around.

It's Eddy, and he's smirking. "What on earth are you

doing out here so early, circling the old post office like a bank robber scouting a job?"

"Everyone's a comedian today," I say. "I'm meeting Amanda in a few minutes to check it out. I might use it for my law practice."

"Oh." Eddy bobs his head. "Amanda Saddler, not my Amanda."

My Amanda. Even though I know they're dating, it still sounds strange. "Right, Amanda Saddler."

"I guess Amanda hasn't told you yet. They struck some kind of deal, and now you can refer to her as Mandy."

"But I thought she hated when the kids called her Aunt Mandy."

He shakes his head. "Not my Amanda. Amanda Saddler agreed to go by Mandy."

"She did?" My brow furrows. "I thought she hated it even more than *your Amanda* did. Plus, she said she's too old to start using a new nickname."

Eddy shrugs. "No idea how they worked it out, but that's what Amanda said. No more confusion. That's the good part."

"I guess so," I say.

"Is Mandy late?" Eddy asks.

I glance at my watch. I still have fifteen minutes until she's due to meet me here. "Not exactly."

"You're ridiculously punctual," Eddy says. "But I do hope you take this place. You can keep an eye out for the vet who's moving in to take over for me."

"I'm sorry, what now?"

"Didn't Amanda tell you that either?" His eyebrows rise. "I'm leaving tomorrow to go to California. I'll be recording a new album and then touring to promote it."

"That feels. . .sudden." And I'm starting to feel like I have no idea what's going on with Amanda now that she doesn't live with me.

"That's why I'm surprised you didn't know," he says. "I told her my final decision a few days ago, but we've been mulling it over as an option since Christmas."

We've been. Clearly Amanda's okay with it—sounds like she was part of the team who made the decision. "Well, that's exciting. Congratulations."

"I just hope it ends up going better than the last time I went on tour."

No kidding. "I'm sure it will," I say. "You're so much wiser, now."

"I certainly hope so," he says.

Amanda Saddler's—Mandy's—truck pulls up out front, the tires crunching on the gravel area in front of the office space. "I'd better head out front," I say.

"Right," he says. "But hey, if you have any energy or time for it, can you make sure Amanda's doing okay without me around? I doubt she'll tell me if anything goes wrong."

"Of course," I say. "And I'll keep an eye out to make sure your replacement isn't edging in on her."

Eddy laughs. "Well, I can't say Buff might not be interested—Amanda is a gorgeous spitfire—but I doubt she'll pose much of a threat. She's been happily married for more than thirty years, or together that long. Not sure when they got married."

"She?" I shouldn't be surprised, I guess, but I just assumed that the new vet for cows and horses in the area would be a man. "Wait—"

"Buff was one of my favorite instructors back in vet school, and she just retired and sold her practice at home so she could spend more time at the cabin she bought in Colorado."

"Oh."

"She about ripped my head off when I first suggested she come here, but even though she's got a huge bark, she never actually bites. She's one of the kindest-hearted people I know. Her partner Deb might roast me on a spit, but hopefully she won't see me." Eddy's shoulders straighten and he smiles. "Until she sold her practice, they actually lived somewhere outside of Houston. You'll probably get along with her great." He leans a little closer and drops his voice. "But be warned. She could talk the hair off a mule."

Now I kind of can't wait to meet her.

"Abby?" Amanda—er, Mandy—is calling for me around the front. This new name thing might make it easier to avoid confusion, but it's going to be a rough adjustment.

"Coming!"

When I reach the front of the shop, Mandy's already unlocking it. Like always, she gets right down to business. "I warned you that this hasn't been remodeled in a while, and I'm willing to offer you a rent concession for the first month or two so you can change the things you want." Her hair, which is usually down around her face, is pulled under a fluffy white knit cap, and when she turns around, she looks like a Q-tip.

I can't help my smile.

She quirks an eyebrow. "What's so funny?"

"Nothing." I shake my head. "You're offering me concessions off the bat, huh?"

"I expect that I'll get a discount on all the legal work

I need," she says. "I know if you take this place, I'll have a lawyer as a lessee, so I'm ready to bargain."

"You *gave* us the ranch," I say. "I'll pay whatever rent you name."

She straightens, the door hanging open. "Now, Abigail, I didn't expect to need to tell you this. I gave you the ranch as a family member, but I'm renting you this office as a landlord. Make sure you behave accordingly."

I blink.

"Got you." She slaps her knee and laughs.

I swear, she is a real hoot. "Do you really think you'll need legal work?"

"Amanda and I are remodeling places to sell or rent. That all requires a lot of paperwork. I was planning on transferring my legal work to you, unless you don't want to do real estate law stuff."

"I haven't done a lot in the past, but I'd love to do it, of course."

"Great! Then I'll be your first client."

Frankly, that's a relief. I was genuinely worried that other than Donna, I'd never get another client. It's not like there are a lot of people living out here, and I only know a handful of them as it is.

I take a good look around after walking inside—and Mandy wasn't kidding. It's a real mess. It was clearly used for a post office, but it also looks like it might have been set up as a shop of some kind for a while.

"Did you say this was a Post Office?"

"It had one in that corner." Mandy points at the far corner where there's a large counter with an open space behind it. "But it was actually a secondhand shop for a while. I don't think they did great business, seeing as there aren't many people to buy things around here, but they hung in there for almost ten years."

"Interesting."

Mandy walks past the big open area and toward a closed-off room near the back. "I figure you'll want to make this back room your office, and you could make that big front area a sitting room and a secretary station."

We'll need to knock out some of the counters and redo the floors, but it's not a structural overhaul.

Then I open the door to the bathroom.

"Whoa," I say.

"I think that may need some work." Mandy scrunches her nose. "Maybe someone came in who didn't realize the water was turned off."

It smells like someone pooped. . .and then died in the toilet. I take a few steps back and shake my head. "I'm seeing a little more why you were willing to offer concessions right off the bat."

"The other place I could offer you that's clean and in working condition is Double or Nothing, but it's now been set up as a bakery, and I doubt you need the ovens in that kitchen or the front display counter."

I think about the setup there. It's smaller, but it's already been cleaned and refurbished. "What would the rent there be?"

"How's six hundred a month?" She tilts her head. "No rent concessions there—it's in fine shape. It's just not set up for a law firm."

But I could probably arrange legal books and whatnot in that front window until I have the money or inclination to remodel the area, and I don't really need my own dedicated office. It's not like having ovens and a fridge would really wreck anything.

"Let me think about it?" I ask.

She shrugs. "Of course."

The bathroom there's clean and in good working order. The outside's attractive and recently power washed. "I would hate it if taking that one made people gossip about Amanda."

"She's an influencer who was recently doing a Bachelorette series to generate buzz. She was also secretly dating our resident rock star. Nothing you do will keep people from gossiping about Amanda."

Fair point. "I'm leaning toward Double or Nothing. Can we go take a look?"

The more I walk around the formerly-bakery-occupied space, the more I think of ways I could transform it down the line, if this crazy scheme even works and I don't have to crawl back to Robert and beg for my job.

"I'd love to run it by Steve," I say. "And make sure Amanda's okay with me taking her space, but this might work."

"That's too bad," Mandy says. "I was hoping you'd clean up that mess next door."

I laugh. "That's your and Amanda's job."

We're walking out of Double or Nothing when a tall woman with broad shoulders and short, tightly bobbed hair nearly runs into me.

"Oh, excuse me." Her tone's brusque, almost stressed.

I look around to see where she came from—the streets, er, *street* of Manila isn't exactly hopping. There's a small white Camry parked right in front of Double or Nothing.

"I'm sorry," I say, "but the cookie shop's closed. Indefinitely."

"Actually," the woman says, "Venetia told me you might be over here—she said next door, though. She says you're a lawyer?"

I was not expecting that. "Um, yes. She's right. My name's Abigail Brooks—"

"Jed's nephew's widow, right?" She's looking me up and down like someone might evaluate a horse they're looking to buy.

"Right."

"Small towns," Mandy says. "They're the best." She looks utterly unfazed, standing there, listening in on every word of our conversation.

The tall woman's head snaps sideways. "I was hoping to talk to her alone, if you don't mind, Amanda."

"Oh, alone, is it?" Mandy's eyebrows creep upward. "Something embarrassing, then?"

"I will likely have an office soon, but for right now—"

The woman thrusts a piece of paper I hadn't even realized she was holding at me. "I'm almost out of time. I got this letter a while ago, but didn't realize I'd gotten it."

"Oh."

I take the paper and scan the message. It's from the IRS. They believe she owes quite a lot of money in back taxes. She has two days to file a protest. "It does look rather urgent."

"Can you help me?" she asks.

"Er, well—"

"Don't mind me," Mandy says. "I'll just be on my way. Gillian, you won't find anyone better to help you than Abby. Trust me on that."

"I heard she lost in court on the case for keeping her own ranch, though." As if the words slipped out, she clamps her hand over her mouth.

"I did," I say. "But that was less of a legal issue and more of a mistake. We didn't think we wanted it and left, violating the terms of the bequest in the will."

Gillian nods.

"It was Jed's fault. He always was an idiot," Mandy says.

Gillian laughs. "True."

I end up following Gillian to her house, which isn't too far away. It takes me nearly two hours to evaluate the basics of her tax situation, and the good news is that, with a little elbow grease, I think we can reduce her liability by more than half.

The bad news is that she has less than no money, which means that she'll struggle to pay the IRS any of it. And if she does manage to pay them, there's no way she can possibly pay me.

"I knew I needed to pay them something," she says, "but by the time I realized how much it was, I was already pretty far behind. I hadn't filed in years, so I kind of plowed ahead with my life, not paying, not filing, and trying not to think about it. That makes me sound pretty bad, doesn't it?"

I will never understand that kind of non-action, but she's not alone. Plenty of people I've met ostrich their way into big trouble.

"And then when I hurt my back. . ."

She hasn't worked in a while. I get it, but she's not exactly the kind of client I was hoping to attract.

But sometimes we're in the right place at the right time to help someone. Last month, I'd have had to wish her luck and send her on her way. I had no time. Now I have loads of time. "Well," I say. "My other client with cash flow issues recently came into some money and is going to be able to pay me, I think." Donna's going to have a fight on her hands with her brother—she's actually called me twice in the last hour, and I owe her a call back as soon as I leave here. "But that means that I've got an opening."

"You can help me?"

"I can, and for the time being, I'll keep track of my hours, but I won't demand payment. Sound alright?" Telling people up front that I'm not going to make them pay usually puts me in a bind. In my experience, knowing my services are free leads people to impose more and more, not less. Thinking she may have to eventually pay should keep her motivated to mitigate the amount of time I put into this by doing her part.

"What do you need?" she asks.

I walk her through the documents I'll need to see. "Bring them to me tomorrow, to the Birch Creek Ranch. Can you do that?"

She nods.

When I stop at Steve's on the way home, he's out in the middle of his covered arena. The little grey he's on is bucking up a storm. Once he finally calms him down, he notices I'm standing near the fence and walks him over.

"That was exciting," I say.

"I'm getting too old for breaking horses," he says.

"You look pretty good to me." He does—he didn't even lose his hat. Even with a coat on, you can tell he's in good shape, and even though the horse is green, he moves him effortlessly.

"How'd the office look?"

I sigh.

"That bad?"

"The bathroom was. . ." I pull a face.

"We can get it cleaned up," he says. "I'm sure Eddy will—"

"You didn't hear either?"

He frowns. "Hear what?"

"He's leaving," I say. "He's going to California to record a new album and then he's going on tour. They're setting up dates now."

"You're kidding." Steve tips his hat back an inch or so. "Does he think he's a teenager again?"

I think about Ethan and how he's pursuing his dreams right now. "Maybe since his life got shut down back then, he never really got to be a teenager. I hadn't thought about it, but that could be the reason he's so excited to go."

The grey's stomping and pawing at the ground, and I don't blame him. It's cold, and I interrupted their session. "Worry about the horse," I say. "But I wanted to talk to you about this. We also took a look at the Double or Nothing building, and it's in way better shape. I was thinking about taking that one instead."

"With the full kitchen and the display counter?" Steve scratches his chin and frowns.

"It's odd, but this was never going to be a really traditional law office no matter what we did."

"It's better than working on your bed with your laptop in your lap, I guess." He smirks. "I'm just not sure you should rush into anything. People out here won't be critical no matter where you work, and I want you to get a place you'll stay in for years."

"That's true," I say. "Actually, I got two new clients today."

"You did? Who?"

"Amanda Saddler and another lady named Gillian, although I doubt she can pay me."

He scowls. "Abby, I know you like to help people, but trust me when I say that no one around here will have money, and even if they do, they'll pretend they don't. No other lawyer is going to do the work for free, so if they need it, you'll need to hold the line."

"I know." I sigh. "I'll try and keep that in mind in the future."

"Well, whatever you decide, I'll support you and I'll put my back into it."

And that's why I love him. "Be safe. I need that back."

He shifts the grey horse toward me slowly, and tries to lean toward me for a kiss. But when I go up on my tiptoes, the grey decides he's done and shoots forward.

"This guy," Steve says, "is in for it, now."

"I'll see you for dinner?"

"Night shift tonight," he says. "Remember?"

I still struggle to keep his shift schedule straight. "I feel like I need a dedicated calendar just for your work shifts."

"I'll be sure to order you one on Amazon," he says. "Maybe a horse calendar." He winks.

"Good idea."

I wave on my way back to the car, but when he tries to wave, the grey dives forward again. I call Donna on my way back home and do my best to calm her down. I didn't realize that Patrick would be claiming *non compis mentis,* but it'll be hard for him to prove given that the will was both witnessed and notarized.

By the time I get home, I'm exhausted.

I haven't been seeing Amanda nearly enough lately, but I'm a little disappointed when she's waiting in her car in my driveway. I was hoping for a late lunch and a little break before the kids got home from school. When I pull in next to her and open the door, she opens hers, too.

"I know you're probably busy," she says. "So I'll get right to the point."

Usually she's the kind of person who schmoozes and chats for twenty minutes before asking for a favor, so I kind of appreciate her changing up her normal behavior for me. "What's up?"

"How upset would you be if we moved back in with you?"

That wasn't what I expected to hear. "I thought you liked living at Mandy's?" I'm proud of myself for remembering to use the new name.

She grimaces. "How'd you hear about 'Mandy'?" She leans against her car. "Right. You met her to look at the office this morning."

Sometimes I forget how up in each other's business Amanda and Mandy are right now. "The partnership's been a bit rough?"

"It's not that—working with her has been great. But I guess I'm still—" She cuts off and her mouth clicks shut.

"You're still what?"

"We just miss you guys," she says. "Emery and Maren are lonely, and so am I."

I don't mention that Amanda Saddler—er, Mandy—

75

would be lonely if they leave. She must know that, and her reasons for moving back must be more compelling. "Of course you can move back," I say. "But I have one caveat." I drop my voice. "My sister's here right now. She's leaving in the next ten days, or if I get my way, sooner. But while she's here, your room's temporarily occupied." I don't think I can handle another family moving in *and* Helen breathing down my neck at the same time.

"Oh, right. Of course. I wondered who that car belonged to." She glances at my sister's black M4. "But once she heads home?"

"Sure," I say. "If you're positive that's what you want, you're always welcome with us." Even if I was a little bit relieved to have just my family in our own four walls with no one poking their nose into every part of my life for a change. The kids do miss their cousins, and it was nice to have another adult around. Plus, you don't turn family down, and Amanda is family to me now, more than she ever was when Paul was alive. More than Helen is now.

"Thanks."

I wonder whether it was hard for her to ask. I hope not. We may have had our ups and downs, but surely she feels comfortable asking me for favors when she needs them, right?

❧ 6 ❧

AMANDA

I t's hard to rummage through a box while wearing gloves.

Our stay with Amanda Saddler was meant to be temporary. I just assumed that Abby and I would be looking for a new place, or that Abby would head back to Houston and I'd either find a place here, or. . .I don't know. At no point did I think that we'd be staying at Amanda Saddler's house for *months*, and now Abby's sister Helen seems to be camped out permanently at Jed's old farmhouse, and I'm going crazy.

I can't even find my favorite pair of sunglasses, the kind that looks great and doesn't constantly slide down my nose or cause a headache by being too tight.

Perfect sunglasses are hard to find, and I *need* mine.

It's possible they're lost. Or that one of the kids sat on them and threw them away. But it's also possible they were tossed in one of the STORE IN GARAGE boxes by accident, which is why I'm out here, rummaging. Even with thick gloves on, my fingers are stiff from the cold. If I could just shift this blanket to the side. . . But my hands push a little too hard and the entire box falls on its side.

The contents spill out all over the dirty floor of the never-used garage.

I groan.

After righting the box, I start to stuff things back in, but when my fingers close around the shiny cover of a *Luxe Interiors & Design* magazine, I freeze. I still remember the day they contacted me, asking if they could photograph my apartment. *My apartment.* My friend Chloe had told someone with their team that my apartment was a dreamy oasis on the Upper East Side, and that they'd be lucky to get photos. I squealed at the thought of everyone drooling over *my* life.

After that article came out, I'd had quite a few friends reach out and ask if I'd be willing to decorate their apartments. Delighted, I started with Chloe's—she had been the one to get me the attention. It seemed fair.

But meeting with vendors made me late to pick up the girls from dance. Waiting for the carpet install guy had me scrambling to beg favors from friends so that the girls would have someone to meet them after school. And a traffic jam after a long morning spent looking at light fixtures meant I missed my normal time slot as an aide at Maren's school.

"You can't keep playing around," Paul had said. "It's great that people liked our apartment—they should. God knows you spent enough money on it. But I can't deal with work and home while you flit around like a socialite. You have to do something of value around here, too."

His words stung. I wasn't getting paid for Chloe's—I needed to build a portfolio first. But plenty of interior designers *did* make good money. And I was developing contacts with vendors and boutiques. It was work for me, and an unparalleled opportunity, but his message was loud and clear: his job paid the bills, and his job mattered.

Mine didn't.

That was the first time I realized, deep down in my bones, my place in our marriage and in the world. My life was meant to complement his, to make it easier, and smoother, and more gratifying. But I should never, ever interfere with the smooth operation of his life.

I was an accessory, nothing more.

I've never felt that way around Eddy. He sees me as someone talented, someone feisty, someone worthwhile. He works hard to make sure I feel valued, cared for, and cherished.

Or at least, he did.

Until his name was cleared and this opportunity arose for him to record an album and go on tour. A chance he'd never have had if Abby hadn't cleared his name, and my IG account hadn't made him famous by resurrecting his past. I mean, sure, his good looks and talent factor into it as well, but without the megaphone of my platform, no one would have noticed him in a veritable sea of gorgeous faces.

Now I feel a bit like I did with Paul, like I don't really matter. Like his life is more important to him than our shared future. I mean, technically I told him that he should make the decision irrespective of our relationship, but I didn't think he'd *really* do that. I thought he'd dig deep and find out what I wanted. I thought he'd ponder on the strain that leaving might put on us and decide to stay.

He didn't, though.

But I'm not the same person now that I was then. I won't accept a position as an accessory, not ever again. I'm afraid that Eddy's imminent departure will break us. For the first time in my life, the thought of a relationship with a man ending makes me quake with fear. With sorrow. With longing. My life is better with him in it, but maybe he doesn't care about that as much as I do and that's a terrifying thought in and of itself.

My phone buzzes in my pocket, and I drop the magazine into the box. My fumbly, thick fingers manage to swipe and answer the call, thanks to special tips on the end of the glove on each finger that somehow register on the touch screen. "Hello?"

"Hey—you still coming for breakfast?" Eddy sounds nervous, like I might stand him up.

"I have half an hour still, right?"

"Yeah, you do," he says. "I just know how busy you've been, so I wanted to make sure you remembered."

"You leave the state in three hours. You think I'd miss my last chance to see you for the foreseeable future?"

"Planes," Eddy says. "Trains. Automobiles."

"That is a funny movie," I say.

He chuckles. "There are many ways that we'll be able to see each other. Don't get all melodramatic on me now."

If he thinks a little whining about his departure is melodramatic, he's in for a rude awakening. "I'd better go change clothes," I say. "Unless you'd like everyone to mistake your girlfriend for Big Foot."

"I doubt that Hunter's winter line of boots and a fluffy hooded parka will actually make anyone think you're Sasquatch, but I appreciate your ongoing efforts to look amazing at all times. It's nice to see everyone I grew up with looking pea-green with envy every time we meet and I have you on my arm."

He can't know that I've been worried that he saw me as an accessory, so I push that thought out of my head. "See you soon."

As I drive to Brownings, I think about the advantages to living in a small town. I know the owners, I'm used to the menu, and there's always a table available. Of course, there's not a lot of variety, and if I had a fight with the owner, things would get awkward in a hurry.

My phone rings before I'm halfway there.

"Mom!" Maren never sounds panicked.

"Is everything alright?"

"No!" she wails.

"What's wrong?" I pull over on the shoulder. I don't trust myself to be safe while driving if her news really is bad.

"I started my period today three days early and—" Her voice drops to a distressed whisper. "I bled through my pants, Mom."

I don't laugh—at least, not loud enough that she can hear me. It's practically a rite of passage for a high school kid. "I'm on my way to meet Eddy for lunch, but as soon as we're done, I'll head home and get you some new pants."

"Not as soon as," she says. "*Right now, Mom!*"

I doubt anyone has even noticed anything, but I don't bother arguing. She'll only get more hysterical. I'm sure in the moment this really is horrifying. "Does the nurse have other jeans you could borrow?"

My sympathy evaporates when she says, "They're

generic." Like wearing non-brand-name clothing would *ruin* her.

"Eddy has to leave—"

"*Mom*, if I come out with these on, everyone will know something happened, and I'll never—"

"Spilled a soda, ripped the butt, pooped your pants. And that's just off the top of my head."

"*Pooped my pants?*"

Some days being a parent is really annoying. "Fine. I'll go get you jeans now and bring them over before I meet Eddy."

He's so understanding when I call to tell him I'll be late that I'm even more annoyed about my daughter only caring for herself.

When I finally reach the restaurant, I'm definitely late. "Sorry," I say as I breeze in and sit down next to Eddy.

He looks up with a smile. "You're not the one leaving. I should be saying sorry. Never apologize to me for your life or for taking care of the people you care about."

"Speaking of, how's Buff getting along with Snuggles?"

"So far, so good," he says. "If something changes, you'll be the first to hear."

Of course, that's when my phone rings. Since it's a local call I don't recognize the number for, I'm kind of stuck answering. "Work," I whisper to Eddy. "Sorry." Then I pick it up.

"Hey, Amanda."

"Hello, um, I'm sorry. Who is this?"

"It's Adam," he says. "Tile guy?"

"Oh," I say. "Right. We're meeting later so you can walk me through what the process will be—"

"Actually, about that." He clears his throat. "The thing is, something has come up. I'm not going to be able to do the job we talked about."

"We were going to sign a contract today," I say. "We agreed on terms."

"I know," he says. "I'm sorry about changing things, but I just won't have time."

"Can I ask what came up?" I shouldn't press. It's not super professional, but I have a hunch.

He sighs.

"You don't have to say, but if I guess, can you confirm at least? Are you working for a project in Dutch John?"

"It's a big project," he says. "And the director's paying huge bonuses."

This is the third contractor to pull his bid *this week*. It was hard enough just competing with Derek's stupid factory for the cattle processing. At this rate, the only way we'll be able to remodel the homes on our short list is if Mandy and I shackle the kids and start laying tile ourselves.

I don't swear. I don't scream. I remain polite and professional, but it's hard. Really hard. "Thanks for letting me know."

We manage to order, and even to eat, before another contractor calls, cancelling for the same reason. I'm about ready to smash my phone against the counter when Eddy takes my hand.

"Oh no," I say. "Is it time to go?"

"My dad wants to take me to the airport," he says. "If I leave now, we'll just make it."

I leap from my chair and hug him tightly. His hands —smelling slightly of french fries—brush my hair back from my face. "You, Amanda Brooks, are one-of-a-kind. I love you."

"I know."

"It feels long," he says. "But these five months are going to fly by, I know it."

"It's not like I won't see you for that whole time," I say. "I'll come visit."

"And so will I, whenever I can."

Even so, it feels. . .transformative that he's leaving. He's about to live somewhere else. I'll be left behind. Before I can start to spin out, his mouth captures mine. His lips press against me, demanding I stop thinking.

I capitulate.

After all. Eddy is many things, but more than all the others, he's compelling—no, he's downright hot. I have no idea how he stayed single all this time. His hands hold my face in place, refusing to release my mouth.

I sink into him and try not to think about the fact that this feeling will be gone very soon for a very long time. When he finally leaves, I can't help crying, at least a little. Something huge is changing, and I hope we can survive it.

His dad must be driving, because a few moments later, the text messages start rolling in.

REMEMBER TO TEXT OR CALL IF YOU NEED ANYTHING. I'LL BE WORKING, BUT NOTHING MATTERS MORE THAN YOU.

ALSO, IF THE GIRLS NEED SOMETHING, MY PARENTS ARE CLOSE. THEY CAN HELP. MY DAD SAYS HE AND MOM ARE HAPPY TO DO WHATEVER, BUT MAYBE DON'T ASK THEM TO DO IT TOGETHER. THEY FIGHT A LOT.

AND ANOTHER THING. I MISS YOU.

MAYBE CHECK IN ON SNUGGLES FROM TIME TO TIME. BUFF'S NOT THE KIND OF PERSON WHO ASKS FOR HELP.

He keeps texting me the entire way to the airport, it feels like. I stop reading them quite as religiously when I start calling all over the place, basically haranguing people for referrals. And then the girls get home and they're unusually needy today, for some reason, as if they know I need a distraction.

"Mom!" Emery's beaming from ear to ear. "Did you hear that Steve's giving Izzy a foal? We have lots of room here. Could we get a baby horse?"

"A baby horse?" I ask. "You must be kidding."

"I would do everything," she says. "I swear, you wouldn't have to do a thing. Plus, Ms. Saddler has that barn she never uses."

"We store stuff in there," I say. "Lots of stuff."

"The goats are kind of funny too," Maren says as if she didn't even hear me. "And they'll eat almost anything you don't want."

"Like my boxes of stuff?" I ask. "Is anyone even listening to me?"

"Yes! I would love a goat." Emery's bouncing on her toes and it's probably my fault for not shutting this down right away.

"We have a dog now," I say, rubbing Roscoe's head. "And Jed the Pig! Let's wait and see how hard it is for Abby's family to deal with a baby horse, and we can go from there."

"Remember how much you hated my candles at first?" Maren asks.

Her candles litter half the surfaces in poor Mandy's house, now. She became obsessed with them a few years ago when she learned how to make them at a friend's sleepover. Now she puts them all over, and I'm always worried she'll burn the house down.

"At first?" I shake my head. "Maren—"

"You said you liked that magnolia one the other day," Emery says.

"Liking something doesn't mean that I love it," I say. "And besides, candles and goats?" I snort. "Not even close."

I've almost stopped the begging when Mandy gets back home.

"You can change back into your sweats." Her voice is flat.

"What?" I frown. "I don't wear sweats." What on earth is she talking about?

She harrumphs. "Whatever."

"We have that meeting in twenty minutes," I remind her.

She shakes her head. "No, we don't. Peter called to cancel just now."

"What?" My heart sinks. "Did he really?"

"At this rate, we may as well just quit trying." Mandy sinks onto the sofa, as dejected as I've ever seen her.

"We're in a rush because of all the people who will be moving in to staff the new meat processing plant and leather treatment plants," I say. "That hasn't changed. It has made things harder, but—"

"But we can't find a single decent contractor." Mandy chucks her purse down on the kitchen counter so hard that a package of Kleenexes rockets out of it and flies into the sink.

"It's that stupid retreat in Dutch John again, isn't it?" A rage builds up inside of me. We were here first. What are they doing, stealing all our contractors? Bidding double? Have they gone insane? "I'm going over there right now, and I'm going to give them a piece of my mind."

Mandy's eyebrows rise. "You're what?"

"That director who keeps offering everyone incentive bonuses and luring them away from working for a woman they've known for decades?" I cross my arms and fume. "He's going to get a piece of my mind."

I expected her to stop me, but she doesn't. She merely grins like an idiot. "You do that."

I grab my jacket and my purse. I'm on my way out the door when I turn back. "By the way. The girls want a baby horse *and* goats." Let's see how much smug smiling she does while she tries to figure that one out. I'm actually sad to miss it.

The entire drive over to Dutch John, I review the numerous instances of injury this stupid man has inflicted on us. I review the name of each contractor he's *stolen*, and I mentally tabulate the costs and delays he's created on our end. By the time I arrive at the little temporary building with the sign, "The Flame and the Heart" in front of it, I'm ready to spit fire myself.

I march up the steps, and I yank the door open, and I come face to face with David Park, the artist with whom I shared an amazing first date in Chicago.

"I wondered when you'd get here." He smiles. "Actually, if I'm being honest, I've been hoping that you'd show up pretty much every day."

7

AMANDA

David Park was my nearly-perfect first date in Chicago as part of the Bachelorette thing Lololime set up. And now he's standing in front of me in teensy little Dutch John.

"What are you doing here?"

He smiles. "I thought that's why you were here." He tilts his head. "You have no idea how much distress the thought of upsetting you has caused the contractors I've been hiring."

"*You're* the jerk who's been stealing my people?" I can't seem to process what's happening. "But you're an artist."

He shrugs. "My parents decided it was time for me to stop messing around with that and focus on the family business instead."

"The family business?"

"You knew I was Korean, right?" His smile really is killer. Like, I can't stop staring at it, and it's hard to hang on to my righteous indignation when he's being so utterly charming. "We own a lot of hotels in Asia, and we've been expanding into the American market for a decade or so, now. When Mom told me she wanted to open a few retreats—places that tired, worn-out business people could go to escape from everything?" This time he *beams*. "I immediately thought of the tranquility of your new home that you kept talking about on our date."

"You're saying it's *my fault* that you're here?"

He shrugs. "I suppose I am. If you hadn't fallen in love with this area, as a dyed-in-the-wool city girl from New York, I'd never have considered it for a retreat. But I have to say, you were right. The area's stunning visually, and the land prices?" He whistles. "Can't be beat."

"David." I need to think this through. I'm too flustered to really rip into him like I planned. "Find somewhere else." I realize that sounds a bit like a command, so I soften it. "Please."

"Somewhere else?" His eyebrows rise and his forehead furrows. "But I've already bought the land. The wheels have been set well into motion."

I clench my hands at my side. "It's too remote out here. How will people even *reach* it? It's a three-hour drive from the closest airport. You did look into that part, right?"

"And did you hear that there's both a premium beef and a leather company putting in processing plants here?" He's surprisingly well informed. "Between that and this, I think we'll have a regional airport sooner than you might expect."

A regional airport? Ohmygosh. "There must be plenty of places that are a simple forty-minute drive away from a major city that would make more sense."

"We're selling this as literally being away from everything—too remote for the people who come to be dragged back easily. Plenty of people want something that's truly remote, and we're going to cater to them."

"But—"

"Think about it." He's so excited that he's selling me on the idea. "If you live in New York City and you go to the Hamptons, and then your job has some emergency, what happens?"

I can't help scrunching my nose. "You hop on the jitney—"

"And you head back into town." He wiggles his eyebrows. "But if you've taken two flights and then made a four-hour drive to get where you are, they'll badger someone else. You'll get to stay put."

"There are plenty of places that are more remote that would work even better for that. Bora Bora, for instance, or, like, Australia."

"They're *too* far," he says. "You need a vacation from your vacation after a trip like that, not to mention the jet lag and the time zones and the unfamiliar languages and the currency exchange. We'll offer the best of all worlds, but here, supporting the good old United States economy."

Ugh. "Can't you just bring in your own contractors, then?" I ask. "I mean, the reason you feel bad about stealing my—" Suddenly it hits me. "How did you know you were stealing them from *me*?"

He starts to walk toward the window, dragging me with him against my will. "I had no idea you were doing remodeling or building or whatever. I swear, I didn't. When we went out on that one amazing date, you had a cookie shop and you were an influencer. I had no reason to believe that wasn't still the case."

Exactly. "But you said—"

"I won't lie and say that I wasn't hoping I might bump into you. You clearly had something going on with someone else—we had a connection that night, but you walked away without a backward glance."

My relationship with Eddy is all over the internet at this point. If he really cared to know about me, he'd be following all that, right?

"But that's not why I came here—and then when I did, and I started looking for people, they kept telling me that they were going to be working with an Amanda. I asked. . .'Amanda who?' They told me it was someone named Amanda Saddler. Obviously that's not you, nor did I have any reason to believe it was you."

"So then—"

"But last week." He leans against a large window—the only nice part of this little command center trailer—and smiles. Then he bites his lower lip. "Last week, when I selected *this* site, I had a new batch of contractors come out and presented them with the timeline."

I arch one eyebrow.

"And for the first time, one of the contractors said he wanted to do a small job for someone named Amanda *Brooks* before he started work for me." He swallows, his Adam's apple bobbing faintly. "I thought I'd misheard at first, and if I'm being honest, my heart skipped a beat." He grins again. "Or three."

His grin shouldn't be so charming, not when he knows I've got a boyfriend. Actually, his entire face is the problem. He has a deep dimple on the right side, and he tilts his head when he smiles, and his longish hair falls forward across his eyes, just a little bit. His jaw is so square he almost looks like a cartoon, and his skin is so beautiful, it actually makes me feel bad about mine.

He may be one of the only men I've met who's *almost* as good looking as Eddy. What is with all these gorgeous men in one place? And why is he showing up in my life right as Eddy leaves?

"David, the thing is, whether you knew it or not, my cookie shop folded, and this is what I'm doing now. I've partnered with a local friend, Amanda Saddler, and we're remodeling and renovating various properties in the area—"

"So that they'll be ready to sell or rent when the plants are complete." He lifts his eyebrows. "Gorgeous, funny, *and* business savvy." He whistles. "A triple threat. I knew I was in trouble."

"I do have a boyfriend," I say. "If you hop on my social media, which takes half a second, you'll see that it's been quite a salacious story."

That dimple comes out to play again. "The infamous rock star with a killer bod? The one who's also a vet?"

My jaw drops.

"I'm fairly internet savvy for a forty-something, I think you'll find."

"But—"

"I also saw that he's leaving you here, alone in this remote area, while he goes to California to record a new album and then go on tour." He shrugs. "And I just happen to be here." He shakes his head. "I swear, it didn't actually occur to me that I'd run into you—I did pick Dutch John after all, knowing that you're in Manila. There's a forty-minute drive between us. And yet, here we are. Fate's funny, isn't it?"

"David, if you think that manipulating me into—"

"Manipulating?" He frowns. "I assure you, I neither had nor do I have any plans to do anything of the sort."

My past with Derek might be coloring my view, and that's not really fair. He certainly hasn't tried to pressure me in any way. In fact, I'm the one who came here, to yell at him.

"If you give me a list—two, no, three—contractors whom you want back, I'll tell them they're fired. You can have them."

But he's paying more than I am, and all the people I've met really need the extra money. My gain would literally be their loss. Ugh. "No, no, don't do that. Business is business and my budget isn't the same as yours, clearly."

"I'm sure if you cast a wider net, you'll be able to find some people who can help you," he says. "Especially since you're connected among the locals."

"Ha," I say. "You don't even care."

He drops his arm from the windowsill and steps closer, moving right inside my personal space. "Actually, you're wrong about that. I never would have come to do this if I thought it might hurt you. I liked you from the first moment. Do you know how long it has been since I went on a date with a girl and she told me the truth?"

"What are you talking about?"

"Most girls will hop on a bike even when they don't want to. They'll do the activities I plan, even if they don't like them. It was refreshing to have someone tell me that I was wrong—that I hadn't given enough thought to what you might want to do. You were right."

He's too close for me to be able to think properly.

As if he knows he's getting to me, his lip quirks and he presses on. "We had a great date, in spite of all my plans falling apart. You know someone's a good fit when you have fun doing *anything at all* with them."

That reminds me of the night I spent mopping the cookie shop with Eddy and cleaning toilets. He's right. I know that Eddy's right for me because I have a great time when we're together, even if we're troubleshooting issues with an animal or cleaning an office. "David, I love my boyfriend."

He steps back and holds his arms out to his sides. "Understood. I'm coming on too strong, and I'll stop. My apologies."

"I came here today to tell you that you're wrecking my plans," I say. "I don't want you to back out of anything on any of the contractors you've hired. But can you promise me that, in the future, you won't throw insane amounts of money around, offering to triple what they've quoted me?"

David nods slowly. "Of course I will."

"Thank you."

"Can I double it?" His dimple is just barely poking out, and a hint of a smile is playing at the corners of his mouth.

"Are you messing with me?"

He shrugs. "Just trying to find out what I'm *allowed* to do."

I huff, but before I can speak, my phone rings, loud and clear. The caller ID says UNKNOWN, which sometimes happens when my reception is quite poor. Since I left Mandy to watch my kids, I can't ignore it. "Hello?"

"Amanda?"

"Hey, Donna," I say.

"When I went by to sign the lease, your girls said you went to Dutch John, and I actually had to drive out here anyway for the school. I thought you might want to meet for dinner or something. You know, like a girls' night."

"A girls' night sounds really good," I say. "And the thought of eating somewhere other than just Brownings or the Grill sounds amazing."

"Girls' night?" David asks, butting his way into my phone conversation. "I'd just like to mention that I have a company card, and I'm not afraid to use it. You could yell at me some more."

"Who's that?" Donna asks.

"Just a guy I'm *not* working with and hope never to see again."

"But did he really offer to pay for our dinner?"

"He most certainly did," David says.

Clearly the volume on my phone is set too high. "You must have been a nerd," I say.

"What?" Donna asks.

"Huh?" David asks.

"Not you, Donna," I say. "But my *dear friend* Mr. Park must have been a serious nerd. He clearly didn't listen to music that was nearly loud enough in his teenage years, if he can eavesdrop on a *private phone conversation.*"

"Is he hot?" Donna asks. "He sounds hot."

"He is hot," David says. "In fact, the *Chicago Tribune* called me one of Chicago's hottest men under fifty last year."

"Under fifty?" Donna sounds skeptical. "That means he's forty-something."

"Hey," I say. "I'm over forty."

"Sometimes I forget that," Donna says. "Your skin is amazing."

"I'm hanging up now," I say. "I'll text you about dinner."

"I'm driving—"

I hang up anyway. I'm about done having David standing over me, listening to every word. My fingers fly over the keyboard as I text, GREEN RIVER GRILL. Then I stuff my phone into my purse and turn to brush off David. "If I'd known you were here, I'd never have come."

"Ouch," he says.

"I'm not trying to hurt your feelings," I say. "But I have a boyfriend, and I've already done the whole 'I'll push until you love me' routine and it was horrible. I have no plans to go back down that road, thank you very much."

"I would never push anyone, and I know that won't make anyone love me." David frowns. "Although I do want to push until I know what loser treated you that way. It makes me angry—males in general are being wronged by one lousy idiot."

"It's fine," I say. "I'm capable of dealing with that kind of thing myself." As I say the words, I realize that while I'm defending my own capability, I didn't really do anything to Derek, even though I'm reasonably certain he's the one who leaked Eddy's history to the press. In the end, that worked out just fine, and my righteous indignation kind of fizzled.

Actually, maybe I should send him a thank you card. That would really frost his cookies.

"You're more than capable. That's what I like about you, but you shouldn't have to. That's my point."

I wave off his words, but as I'm getting in my car and heading over to the Green River Grill, I wonder why *Eddy* didn't do something to Derek. Maybe it's something to do with AA. Maybe he can't really take revenge, or get into that headspace. Or maybe it's just not who he is.

It didn't bother me until David pointed it out, which is just one more reason for David Park to get out of my life and out of my head. The fact that he's making me annoyed with my boyfriend's lack of grudge-holding is very unwelcome.

When I reach the Green River Grill, Donna's already there, waving at me from a corner booth. "I've never been here before," she says. "Is it good?"

I wait until the hostess has walked away. "Not really," I say. "But it's not horrible. Usually." It's not like I've been here a lot either, but with so few places to go, Eddy and I have driven over once or twice. It has happy memories to go along with the mediocre food.

Like Eddy blowing bubbles into his too-weak chocolate milk shake.

Or Eddy making plane noises and trying to get me to eat overcooked chicken fried steak, as if I was a little kid.

The time Eddy charmed the waitress into bringing us free dessert because the fries were burned.

"So you don't think the food's great, but you suggested we come here anyway?"

"The food is fine," I say. "It's just that sometimes the cook or the waitress doesn't pay the *most* attention to detail."

"That's one of the things we'll be focusing on," David Park says as he sits down at the table next to us.

"Details, I mean. Every single one matters at my new retreat."

My eyes widen, and my jaw drops. "What are you doing here?"

"It's a free country," David says. "If I happen to be eating at the same place as the two of you, well." He shrugs.

I stand up. "You have got to be kidding me right now."

"I'm deadly serious." But the corner of his mouth is twitching. "Aren't you going to introduce me to your friend?"

Donna grabs my arm. "Who is that?" she hisses.

"I am not going to introduce you to my friend," I say. "Because you're not my friend. You're a malingerer."

"That's a pretty fancy word," he says. "Word of the day?"

"I have a brilliant sister-in-law who—you know what? I don't have to explain."

"I think you might have used it wrong," he says. "It's not someone who's evil. It's someone who kind of lays around or is lazy."

"That's what I meant," I lie. "So you just shut up." I fold my arms.

"Wow, I thought you were forty. I didn't realize you were secretly also twelve." His stupidly adorable grin tells me that he thinks we're flirting.

I sit down and turn away from him, pointedly. "So Donna, tell me what brings you to Dutch John."

"I had to pick up some forms for a school thing," she says. "I told you that."

"Right. How fascinating."

Donna leans toward me and whispers, her eyes

darting behind me to where David Park is surely smiling like an evil mastermind. "Who is that guy?"

"He's the nuisance who has been *stealing* all my contractors and ruining my life. He's building a misplaced, ill-conceived resort here in Dutch John."

"There already *is* a resort here," she says.

"Currently," David Park says, "there's an overinflated hotel that calls itself a resort. But it has none of the hallmarks of an actual resort, and anyway, I'm not building a resort. I'm building a *retreat*. A getaway from the modern and demanding world. A place where someone else takes care of the stressful parts of everything and you can simply relax in whatever way you'd like. Spa treatments? Yes. Fishing? Of course. We'll take care of the supplies, the cleaning, and even the cooking of your fish to perfection so you can photograph what you made and post it anywhere you like. Hiking? Plentiful. Kayaking or canoeing? Of course. When weather permits, snowshoeing, wildlife watching, or bird watching? Absolutely."

"What about river sports or helicopter rides? Horse trails?"

"I like the way you think," David says. "What's your name?"

"I'm Donna—"

"Stay away from my friends," I shout.

"That's a really long and kind of odd name, but I think I can remember it," David says. "It almost sounds Native American. Donna Stay-away-from-my-friends. Does that mean that you're a very protective person?"

I roll my eyes so hard I'm worried they might stick in the back of my skull.

"I think your retreat sounds amazing," Donna says.

"But it would be awesome if you could make it that way *without* upsetting my friend Amanda."

"I agree," David says. "But business is business, so I'm struggling to figure out how to accomplish both. See, we're fundamentally at odds. Small town, small region, and very few skilled workers."

"Maybe, since you have big city contacts, you could bring some people in?" Donna asks.

I can't help sneaking a peek at his face to see how he responds.

He nods, running one hand over his jawline. "I've been offering city rates to locals. But if I can find some local housing, I could offer city rates to city people and only be out the extra costs of lodging and travel."

"As an added bonus," Donna says, "you could ask those city dwellers for their thoughts on the area. Maybe you'd get some extra marketing or attraction information out of them."

"Brilliant." David beams. "You know, I'd be delighted to take you to lunch any time to pick your brain. Your friend Amanda's right that I simply don't know enough locals."

Donna grins. "I'd love that."

"She would not." I slam my hand down on the table. "She wants nothing to do with you, today or any other day."

"She doesn't like to share me," David says. "And as much as I love that little flash of jealousy, I have no interest in Miss Donna Stay-away-from-my-friends. My desire to talk to her is purely professional."

I wave at the waitress. "This man right here is bothering us. He'd like to—"

Donna cuts me off. "He's too far away. He'd like to join us at our booth."

I'm going to strangle her.

In fact, *not strangling her* is a move I regret for the rest of lunch, while he charms Donna and goads me until I can barely eat a bite. When he picks up the check, it's too much.

I stand up. "We have to go."

"What?" he asks. "No 'thank you' for the intelligent conversation and picking up our meal?"

My hand tightens on the handle of my purse. "Should I thank a lion for bringing me the hind quarter of a gazelle when he's already eaten all the antelope in the savannah?"

"Amanda," Donna says. "David's not eating anyone. The business world can be a little rough sometimes, but he's been perfectly pleasant. Surely you can handle a little healthy competition."

David's eyebrows lift. "Healthy competition. I think that should be my new nickname."

I grab Donna's arm. "We can talk about it later."

"Speaking of competition, I could use a smart, business savvy local to help me make the connections I need for this project to succeed." Out of nowhere, he's flourishing a card in front of Donna.

And she takes it with a stupidly girly giggle. "Thanks."

"If you have any interest in being that local, give me a call."

"There is *no chance* that Donna is going to work for you. None at all." I pull on Donna's arm until she finally stumbles out the door with me.

David's laughter follows us out.

And if my day hasn't already gone poorly enough, on my way home, I get a call from Abby's sister. . .the one who's currently keeping us from being able to move back in. And she wants a favor.

8

DONNA

I've watched Abigail in a lot of legal situations in the past few months, and she always seems utterly unflappable. A nurse yelling at her? No problem. My brother scowling and fuming and shouting? Who cares? My ex-husband's super fancy lawyer breathing down her neck? She practically grinned at him.

But today she seems off her game.

And I need her in top form.

"Are you alright?"

Abby starts. "Me?"

"Don't take this the wrong way, but you seem a little. . .distracted."

"It's my sister," she says. "She keeps texting me about my trip to Houston. I sent her the itinerary, and she knows that even though she's here, I have to go. It's not like our house full of stuff is going to move itself, and my house is under contract. I didn't pick when she would come out, so it's not my fault that she chose a bad time."

"Right. That sounds fascinating," I say. "But in about

five minutes we'll be starting the deposition with Patrick and—"

Abby puts her hand over mine. "Donna."

I meet her eyes, and they're not distracted anymore. They're confident, like before, like the eyes of the Abigail Brooks who eats fancy suits like my ex-husband's lawyer for dinner. "We've got this."

I've doubted her in the past, repeatedly. I was there when she handled the case that was, sort of, against my brother and lost the ranch. But that time, she was nervous, she was not at all sure, and she was not shocked when it happened. I have to remind myself that I trust Abby *because she's trustworthy*.

"Your parents loved you," she says. "They didn't want to rip you off, and they realized their mistake, or at least, your mother knew it and eventually prevailed upon your father."

"Yes. Right." I nod. "And today is only a deposition." Which she told me ten minutes ago. "It's not the trial."

"We're gathering information, and probably important information, since your brother plans to argue that your father was *non compis mentis* when he executed that will."

"Non what-is?"

"It's Latin for 'not of sound mind,'" she says. "And what he may not know, but his attorney will, is that he only had to be of sound mind during the period of time when he executed that will, assuming he knew the importance of the change."

The deposition goes about as I expect it to go, with Patrick testifying on multiple occasions that Dad was fumbling and bumbling and confused even as he walked into the law office the morning of the will execution.

"Your testimony, then," Abigail says, "is that you were with your parents when they went to your lawyer's office to execute that will?"

"How else would I know how he was acting?" Patrick rolls his eyes. "Of course I was there."

The stenographer's fingers work furiously as she records everything.

"You physically walked inside the law office with your parents and watched them execute what you previously described as a. . ." She glances at her notes. "A 'farce of a will.'"

"Yes," Patrick says. "I walked right next to them into the office, like I already said."

"And did you meet them there? Or did you all go together?"

"It's a long drive," Patrick says. "Why would we drive separately?"

Abigail shrugs. "So you didn't, by chance, go the night before and spend the night inside the office or anything like that?"

"Have you lost your mind? Why on earth would I do that? Of course I went with them in the very same car. In fact, I drove."

Abigail nods. "Alright, and you are basing your opinion that your dad wasn't in his right mind that day on your physical presence before, during, and after that execution?"

"Is this the only kind of lawyer you can afford?" Patrick asks, ignoring her and facing me. "Someone this stupid? Someone who asks the same questions over and over?"

"Would you care to address your client's accusatory tone?" Abigail asks, clearly addressing Patrick's lawyer, the same man who drew up the will that we're now contesting.

"Why would I stop him?" The lawyer's grin is cocky and self-assured.

I'm beginning to wonder whether Abigail might be in over her head.

"Was your lawyer present as well?" Abigail asks. "When the will was executed?"

Patrick sighs. "Of course he was."

Abby's eyebrows shoot up. "Really?"

"I think you may be recalling that incorrectly," his lawyer interjects. "Think carefully." Under his breath, I can barely hear him mutter, "I never attend executions. Remember?"

"Did you get that?" Abigail asks clearly. "Patrick Ellingson's counsel indicated to his client that he never attends executions of wills."

"Right," Patrick says. "I mean, I forgot for just a moment. There was another lawyer who greeted me—I can't remember his name, but of course you weren't there just for us to get it notarized."

"It's interesting to hear you reversing your position," Abigail says. "Are you sure you wouldn't like to do that about your presence at that signing?"

"I'm absolutely positive." Patrick crosses his arms. "A momentary bit of confusion over whether my lawyer— whom I saw all the time—was present isn't relevant."

Abigail nods and presses a button. A television in the corner of the room turns on. "I'd like you to all direct your attention to the screen here. This is footage from the cctv camera across the street. It happened to record footage of your parents arriving, and as you can see on the date and time stamp, this is the very day they came to execute the will, is it not?"

Patrick's face drains of blood.

"The curious thing, as you watch this video, is that you are, most notably, not with them. And as you were quite clear about earlier, you didn't, say, spend the night in the law office."

Patrick swallows.

"I'm just trying to reconcile what I'm seeing with my own two eyeballs, and what the judge will most certainly see as well, with your very clear, very adamant statements about the day of the will execution."

Oh, shabam. She nailed him, and it feels really, really good. The best part is that she's acting utterly calm and nonchalant, just as she did when Patrick and his stupid lawyer were acting like she was an incompetent idiot. She played into that, so that there would be enough rope for him to hang himself.

"I suppose my question, Mr. Ellingson, is how could your previous statement possibly be anything other than a lie to serve your own greedy purposes? Do you possess superhuman powers that allow you to become invisible?"

"You're a real bi—"

His lawyer grabs his arm. "Patrick."

"If you had that video, you should have shown us right away."

"You had as much access to it as I did," she says, "and you didn't ask for it in any of the document requests you provided, nor did you ask for it in interrogatories."

"But you knew—"

"Are you meaning to imply that I knew that you would *perjure yourself* after swearing an oath?" Abigail asks. "I suppose I had an idea, after all the lies you told and the fraud you attempted to commit when trying to buy the Birch Creek Ranch, but I didn't *know* you would lie this time as well."

"Objection," his lawyer says.

"I would also like to point out, for the record, that I did ask for any video footage or records of the actual signing of the will, and when I went to your office last week to hand deliver my discovery requests, I noticed that you had a camera, both in the front lobby and in the conference room. When I asked your secretary how long it had been there, she bragged to me about how high tech your firm is and that you've had it for more than five years." Abigail smiles. "Seeing as you never provided that footage, should I assume you deleted it in anticipation of this trial, fraudulently, or that you're withholding it in bad faith?" She taps her lip. "I can't decide which is worse, honestly. I doubt the judge will like either one."

Patrick stands up. "This deposition is over."

Abigail's lips twitch in bemusement. "You don't get to decide that, unfortunately." She turns her face toward him slowly. "There are some things in life, Mr. Ellingson, that are outside of your control, and I aim to show you just what a few of those are."

His lawyer stands up, too. "If you want more time, you'll have to file a motion with the court."

"Oh, it would be my pleasure to do that," she says. "And you can look forward to my notice of your deposition as well, Mr. Scholes. Frankly, I'm shocked you're handling this case, seeing as you're likely to become a defendant in a related civil suit yourself."

I've rarely seen two men like a woman less than these men like Abigail Brooks. If I were her, I'd be nervous.

But she just looks triumphant.

"Did you have something else to say?" she asks. "Some additional threats to make, perhaps?" She stands up and braces her hands against the top of the table. "I'd rather you make them right now, while we're on the record." Her smile is borderline wicked. "Then I might even get a restraining order from the judge. I imagine if he could see your scowls and glares right now, I might get one without you saying a word." She gestures behind herself. "And even after today's lesson in not lying or doing other evil things, you don't think to look for cameras." She tsks. "Criminal *and* stupid. If law school didn't teach you that's a dangerous combination, I doubt anything I say will help."

They both storm out the door, and once they're gone, I don't know whether to laugh or cry.

"That was pretty awful." Abigail looks like a marionette with cut strings when she sinks into her chair.

The stenographer is all packed up. "I'll be in touch about my bill." She glances from Abby to me and back again. "Are you two alright?"

Abby sighs and nods. "Thank you." Once she's gone, Abby almost whispers, "I'm so sorry you grew up with a brother like that."

As if her words summoned them, tears start streaming down my face. I've made excuses for Patrick my entire life. He wasn't as bad as my dad. He wasn't really vicious. He cared about me, in his own way. But every single thing I told myself had a qualifier. It was never just that he cared about me. It was never that he wasn't bad—just not as bad as Dad.

Abigail puts one hand on my shoulder. "You're not by yourself," she says. "And the louder you bark and the more viciously you snarl, the less likely they are to move against you."

But Abby has Steve backing her up.

I have no one.

"Sometimes I wonder whether it's worth it. He offered me a hundred grand from the life insurance, and that's way more than I ever expected to get. Maybe I should just take it and be done with the fighting."

"This is where you think I'll give you a pep talk and tell you that you deserve all of what the will says you should have and more. It's where I'm supposed to tell you that, since your brother acted in bad faith, you could actually request and possibly be granted the entire estate, including his ranch. I bet it would feel good to kick your brother and his horrible wife off their property."

I think about it.

"But that's not what I'm going to tell you." Abby's eyes are sad. "Knowing what I know about you, I doubt it will feel very good. Family and home are complicated, and you'd probably regret doing something like that your entire life. Only you can decide what the emotional toll this is taking will be worth. But I will just add one thing. If you believe that your brother will be fine with you taking a portion of the life insurance because he's offered it, if you think that will repair your relationship, I think you'd be wrong. I don't think your relationship with that man can *be* repaired, because I think the only part that wasn't rotten was on your side."

After Abby drops me off at what's apparently becoming my long-term hotel room, I think about how lucky I am that I met Abigail Brooks. I might not have custody of my son if she hadn't moved here. I might have lost my dad sooner and missed out on the few positive memories I have of him. I certainly would never have found out that Dad redid his will.

Would Patrick and I have been fine, relatively speaking, if I hadn't found it? If I'd lost my son, and my dad died leaving me nothing, but my brother got to keep everything? Would he, at least, have taken care of me? Would he have had my back?

The worst part is, I'm not sure that he would have. Even if he had gotten away with stealing everything from me, and stealing the Birch Creek Ranch like he planned, I'm still not sure he'd have been happy. After I pick up Aiden and make it safely back to the hotel we're still staying in, I notice I have several text messages, two missed calls, and a voicemail. I plonk Aiden down in front of the television and walk into the bathroom to check them in peace.

The first text is from Abby. YOU AREN'T ALONE. YOU'RE A GOOD PERSON. YOUR PARENTS KNEW IT.

Another text is from an obnoxious car wash in San Francisco. I should never have signed up to get their messages just to save ten percent.

The last message is from Patrick. THERE ARE MORE WAYS TO WIN.

More ways to win? What the heck does that mean? If he loses in contesting my probate of Dad's will. . . he'll do what? I'm still thinking about what that might mean when I press talk on the voicemail.

"Donna," a tinny voice blares from the speakers of my older model iPhone. "This is Linda Ferguson, the chairman of the board of education for Daggett County. I hate to do this over the phone, but I did try calling you several times. The board has decided that, in light of your numerous absences from work, we're going to have to let you go from your position at the school. We will, of course, pay you through the end of this pay period, but we have already replaced you."

The bottom drops out of my stomach. I need this job.

And they've already replaced me? They didn't even tell me they were unhappy. This is the first I've heard about any of it. I don't understand. My time off has all been taken with accrued vacation and the approval of the principal.

There are more ways to win.

Patrick's ominous text message was sent less than thirty minutes before the voicemail from Mrs. Ferguson. Patrick's best friend is on the school board. I have no proof, but it's the only thing that makes sense.

He cost me my job.

My fingers itch to call Abigail. I know she's planning a wedding. I know I'm not paying her much and she's done most of the work she's done for me for free, but she did just say that I'm not alone. Maybe she can work her magic and undo whatever just happened.

I know what she's going to ask for, though. She'll want to see my employment agreement. I think it's in one of the boxes stacked in the entryway. My hands shake as I rummage through it, jostling things around as I do. A dead cricket freaks me out and my hand flies backward, sending a stack of papers careening into the bedroom.

"What are you doing, Mom?" Aiden's eyes are wide, his mouth open just a little bit.

"It's fine, honey. I'm fine."

He frowns. "I said what are you doing. I didn't ask if you're okay."

I clear my throat. "I'm just looking at some papers. Don't worry about that."

My phone buzzes in my pocket. I whip it out. Maybe it's the school board calling me back. Or my principal.

But it's not a call. It's a text.

From Charles. Nothing my ex-husband would send me could possibly make me feel any better, but I force myself to read it anyway.

YOUR BROTHER TELLS ME YOU'VE LOST YOUR JOB. THAT'S A SIGNIFICANT CHANGE OF CIRCUMSTANCE, AND IT GIVES ME A RIGHT TO PETITION THE COURT FOR A REVISION OF THE PARENTING ORDER.

I'm an inch away from a full-on meltdown, but I can't collapse in front of Aiden. I can't. None of this is his fault, and he's too young to know what's going on. Above all else, he has to feel safe. He has to know that I can take care of him. I bend over to grab the papers and start gathering them to put them back in the box, and something under the edge of the bed catches my eye.

A tiny square of paper, er, technically, it's a rectangle. I crawl across the floor and retrieve it, my eyes scanning over the words obsessively.

Park Hyun Capital.

David Park, Vice President of New Projects.

Before I can second guess myself, stiff fingers fumble with my phone, pinging the numbers listed after his name. My mouth has never been drier than it is in that moment, as the phone starts to ring. I try to lick my lips, and my tongue practically sticks to them.

"Hello?"

I try to say hello back, but no sound comes out.

"This is David Park. Who is calling?"

What should I even say? He was probably kidding when he said he wanted someone who knew the locals. And with Patrick mad at me, I might do him more harm than good. If he knew the whole story, there's no *way* he'd consider hiring me.

But I'm not in a position to fully disclose. Arguing with whomever Patrick coerced to get me fired will take too long, and I'll be right back in court, my life being judged and displayed in order to justify keeping Aiden with me.

He can't be raised by Charles. He just can't.

"Okay, I'm going to hang up, now. If we have a bad connection, which seems to happen pretty often around here, call me back."

"Wait," I manage to croak. "Don't hang up."

"Hello? Who is this?"

"I'm sorry," I say. "I'm not sure what's going on with the phone tower around here." Yes, David. Thanks for giving me the idea to blame my silence on the crappy reception.

"Tell me about it," David says.

"This is Donna Ellingson," I say. "We met at lunch a few days ago with Amanda Brooks."

"Donna!" He sounds as if he's delighted to hear from me. That's promising, at least.

"My circumstances have changed a bit, and I remembered something you said. That you'd like to find someone local who knew people to help you—"

"Please tell me you're calling because you want a job."

I swallow a lump and blink back tears. "Actually—"

"Whatever you're currently making at that school, I'll offer benefits *and* I'll give you a twenty percent raise. I know you have a kid, so I'm okay with you leaving early and working from home when you need to do that."

"I mean, we'll have to discuss what exactly you want, to be sure I'm a good fit."

"I need someone to manage things for me, to organize files, to take calls, and to help me find people." He sighs. "But most of all, I need someone who knows the people around here and can give me an accurate and honest assessment of what's really going on."

Now that? That I can do. "When do you want me to start?"

"Is tomorrow too early?"

I breathe in a sigh of relief. "Not in the slightest."

✾ 9 ✾

ABIGAIL

There are many things I love about my new life out here. The wide open spaces. The trail rides. The horses and goats and cows and chickens and dogs my kids play with daily. The fresh air. The family that's close, and the found family like Amanda Saddler and Donna Ellingson.

But one bad thing is the limited array of options. In everything.

"You only lined up three places for us to consider as wedding venues?" Helen's nose scrunches. "Three?"

"Frankly, we're lucky to have three decent options," I say. "Most of the people in the area go to the same church, and their congregation's willing to let us use their building even though we don't attend." I don't mention that it's an orange brick structure that was built back in the fifties. At least it has a nice little mountain behind it, and a cute white spire at the top. With a vintage filter on the photos, it could work.

"And?"

"There's also the Daggett County Rodeo Grounds, if

we wanted to chance holding it outdoors, and the view from the far side showcases the mountains and the Flaming Gorge. It's hard to beat."

"The *rodeo* grounds?" Helen blinks. "Please tell me you're kidding."

"I know it's not your thing, but I'm marrying a horse trainer. We could do the ceremony on horseback." I know full well even mentioning that will make her go crazy. I never understood why anyone would poke a bear, so that phrase didn't make much sense, but for the first time in my life, I get it. She's already spinning out. May as well enjoy her overreaction.

"Abigail."

I don't wait for her to rant. "Last but not least, there's the Flaming Gorge Resort, which features a scenic bridge nearby with soaring lines that look great in photos. It has the added advantage of offering rooms onsite for anyone who travels in from out of town to come to the ceremony."

"Which would be *everyone*." Helen whips out her phone and taps the screen a few times. She flips it around and shoves it toward my face. "Is this the Flaming Gorge Resort?"

I stare at a tiny rectangle that's far too close to my face until my eyes focus, and then I evaluate the photo. It appears to be two full size, or perhaps twin size, beds, covered with a yellow striped bedspread from the eighties. I scrunch my nose and look at Helen. "That's just the inside of a hotel room. How am I supposed to know if it's the right resort?"

Helen's nostrils flare. She swivels the phone back around and taps a few more things. When she flips it back, it shows the iconic Flaming Gorge bridge with that steel arch structure I'll never forget.

"Yes, that's it."

Maybe she likes it. That would be a nice change. Helen closes her eyes. "Let's save that option for last. It sounds like our best one, which is really depressing."

"Why would we save it?" I ask. "We should go there first. If we love it, we'll have saved lots of time." And I won't have to deal with her mocking and criticizing everything about the church or the rodeo grounds.

"Abby, the fact that you're encouraging me to express my satisfaction with a three star hotel out loud should be embarrassing enough. The fact that you're being sincere. . ."

I roll my eyes. "Really, Helen, you're being so obnoxious that I may send you home." I don't think I can take another week of this.

"*I'm* being obnoxious?" Her mouth dangles open.

"Yes." My phone rings, saving her from the earful I've been trying really hard not to give her. "Hello?"

"Hey, sweetheart," Steve says. "I have bad news."

My heart flies into my throat. "What's wrong? Did you get bucked off? Did you break something? Do you need me to come get you?"

He laughs. "I'm completely fine, but I've got a horse who's colicking, and I need to take him over to Rock Springs for fluids and to be monitored."

"Oh no," I say. "Don't worry. I'll reschedule the trip to check out wedding venues."

"Your sister's with you, isn't she?" Steve asks.

"Yeah."

"Why don't the two of you go? I'd hate to delay wedding things, and there's not a place on this earth I wouldn't be willing to marry you. Anything you pick is more than fine. I was going along so that you didn't have to make the decision without any input at all, but I'm sure Helen's opinions are more helpful than mine."

I'm not at all sure of that, but I don't argue with him in front of her. No reason to add an accelerant to a bonfire. "Alright, well, be safe."

"It's a boring drive," he says. "If this idiot hadn't gone off his grain this morning, I wouldn't need to make it, but with colic, catching it early matters."

"It's fine," I say. "Go."

"Alright. I'll call you when I'm on my way back."

"Great," I say. "Dinner?"

"I'd love that. Should I bring something from Green River?"

"How long will this take?" I was secretly hoping he'd be able to make it back by the time we reached the resort at Flaming Gorge.

"Since I have to go that direction anyway, the hospital asked me to come in and sign some charts I missed. I'll be home before dinner, but not by much."

I sigh. "Don't bother picking anything up." It would be soggy and cold by the time it got out to the ranch anyway. "I'll see you then."

"Is this common?" Helen asks.

"What?" I slide my phone into my pocket.

"You didn't seem surprised that he's going to skip our plans today."

She's so irritating. "You never know what may come up when you have horses," I say. "But colic isn't something you ignore."

"What is it, exactly? Is this horse *dying*?"

I grit my teeth. "Horses can't puke. So if they get

dehydrated or have other stomach problems from eating something they shouldn't, for example, because they can't poop the problem out, colic can kill them, yes. He didn't say the horse is rolling, which means that with some extra fluids, hopefully he'll be fine and he won't need surgery."

Helen grabs her purse off the counter. "That was way more than I wanted to know." She strides toward the door. "I take it we're going to soldier on without him?"

"Soldier on?"

"I'm sorry." Helen's smile is catty. "What I meant to say was that I can't wait to go and check out the delightful local venues where you'll be marrying your handsome and rugged rancher." She drops her voice. "Was that better?"

I consider all the times over the past thirty-nine years that I've really let Helen have it—none of them have gone well for me. She always seems to make me look and feel like a moron. I think it's because, while I regularly pull punches to keep from harming the people I love, Helen never relents. It gives her an edge I've never been able to overcome. "Sure. Let's go."

As we walk out the door, Ethan's climbing into his beat-up old truck.

"Where are you going?" I ask.

"Steve said he's going to stop in Green River on his way back from Rock Springs," Ethan says. "I figured I'd ride down with him."

"Your fiancé ditches you but takes your *son* along with him?"

"I need some supplies for fixing fences," Ethan says. "And Steve said they'd fit in his horse trailer better than they would in my truck bed."

I'm glad that Steve and Ethan talk, and I'm delighted that Steve's helping Ethan with things. I don't find it incongruous at all that he'd be taking Ethan—or that he knows what Ethan needs already. I do, however, wish I wasn't stuck spending the day with Helen while the two of them are talking and laughing it up comfortably.

Before I can climb into my SUV, Helen gestures toward her car. "I'll drive."

"Let's go past the church and the rodeo grounds on our way to the resort," I say. "We may be able to rule them out without even going inside."

Helen arches one carefully manicured eyebrow. "*May* be able to? I bet I can rule them all out before we even leave the property."

I don't grit my teeth. I don't even sigh. "I don't want to rule them all out, Helen. I want to pick the best option, even if it's not one that you would want for yourself."

As if she can sense she's pushed me as far as I'll bend without snapping, she backs off. "I'm kidding. Geez."

When I slide into the seat of her posh sports car, I can't help comparing it to what I drive. Other people might be unhappy with their full size SUV by comparison to her BMW M4. Helen's car is sleek, shiny, and the inside is luxurious. If I didn't have four children, I might drive something similar. That's the one thing that keeps me from ever regretting my choice. It's also something Helen will never understand. She may tolerate my children, and now that they're older and more interactive, she might even like them. But she'll never quite comprehend why I had so many when they cost me my enjoyment of the finer things in life.

Kids are a nuisance to her, whereas to me, they're the

source of most of my joy and fulfillment. Even with our differing outlooks on life, I strive to find common ground. "These seats are nice. I'm surprised you could find a rental this fancy."

"Oh, it's not a rental," she says.

"It's not?" I buckle so that I have something to do other than gape at her. Since she's buckling too, it's not like she has even noticed my shock.

Her head turns toward me slowly, her eyes narrowing. "The worst part about sleeping somewhere away from home is the sorry state of the mattresses in most of the world. Once you grow accustomed to a ten thousand dollar mattress, your body just cannot rest properly on anything less."

A ten thousand dollar mattress? I can barely process that. She must be hating sleeping in our house on that old ancient ranch house bed. "But surely you didn't drive here?" I ask. "All the way from New York? How long did that even take?"

She snorts, and it's one of the least ladylike sounds my sister has ever made. "Drive here?" She rolls her eyes. "I flew, obviously, and my assistant had this waiting for me when I landed."

"Your assistant?"

She keys the address of the resort in Dutch John into her navigation system. "Yeah, his name is Roger. I don't know how I lived without him."

"And yet somehow, I've never even heard of him before."

Helen's mouth turns up into a half smile as she floors it and we shoot forward. "A good assistant is one you'd never need to hear about. They make my life easy and much, much more comfortable without ever taking up any of my time."

I know she works hard in New York. I know she's taken a few companies public, but I'm beginning to think I don't know Helen as well as I thought. "Didn't you say you just finished a project?"

She keeps her eyes on the road, but with the satisfied grin on her face, I can tell she's been wanting to tell me about it. "I did. It went *very* well. Even better than the last three."

I'm not entirely sure what my sister does. As I understand it, she has ideas, and then she finds people she can pay to make the things she thinks up. She handles the business end, but she never actually does or invents or creates anything herself.

I still remember her condescending tone when I asked her what she dreamt of doing after her college graduation. Her dream was to make a lot of money, and she had to analyze the market to really do that effectively. It had nothing to do with what she 'wanted' to do, and everything to do with what would sell the best.

Finding something the world is eager for but doesn't have is much more lucrative than making something and trying to find people you can convince to buy it.

"I still don't understand why you sent this car all the way out here," I say.

"I didn't have it sent out." She says that as though I'm the idiot for not understanding.

"You couldn't have driven a Corolla for a week?" I had no idea she was so high maintenance, but I guess I should've known.

"A Corolla?" She presses her lips together in distaste. She shakes her head. "No thank you. This wasn't a hassle at all. Roger arranged the sale and had the dealership bring it to the airport."

Holy cats. I had no idea divas like her really existed. "But you'll take a bath when you sell it back. Don't cars depreciate the second you drive it off the lot?"

"Not in this instance. I have something I like to drive to make my stay more palatable, and then when I leave, Izzy can keep it as an early graduation present."

This time I actually do choke. "Izzy? As in, *my* Izzy? She's years away from graduating—years away from driving for that matter."

"Years? Please. I bet they let them drive at fourteen in this backwoods province."

"You want to give her *this* car? It's brand new. And it's a sports car." Ethan's head would explode. "What about Ethan? He can drive right now." Or me, for that matter. Oh my word, she's totally thrown me off with this oddball tangent. "Why on earth would you leave *a car* at all? You could have your trusty assistant resell it for you."

She waves her hand through the air. "Whatever. If you don't want it, that's fine."

"Helen, what's going on?"

Her hands tighten on the steering wheel. "What do you mean?"

"You flew in for Nate's funeral for less than twenty-four hours. Other than that, I haven't seen you in three years. My kids barely knew your name before you showed up early a few days ago. For the last twenty years, you've called me once a month as though I'm a scheduled tooth cleaning, and now you show up here for an extended stay and spend all your time criticizing my decisions, belittling our town, and talking about giving my way-too-young daughter a hundred thousand dollar sports car." Something grotesque occurs to me then. Nate, my level-headed, solid, dependable Nate, began making wild suggestions near the end. Very out-of-character, very strange suggestions. "Helen, are you sick? Are you—" I force myself to choke out the words. "Do you have cancer?"

"You think I'm dying?" She sighs heavily. "Don't be absurd. I'm healthy as a horse."

"Actually, that's kind of a stupid cliché. Horses are constantly falling lame due to something or other."

"Fine." Helen's fingers tighten until her knuckles turn white. "I'm not sick, but I've been busy. So busy that most nights over the past few years, I barely slept. It's not like I planned it that way, but business opportunities don't sit around and wait for a convenient time. When both of my last two deals finished, I had another deal lined up that I had to hit the ground running on immediately."

"And this time you don't?" My eyebrows rise. "You're here because you're bored? Really?"

"I'm not bored. I have another deal in the works. In fact, it was just coming together when you called and told me that you were engaged." She slams on the brakes and pulls off on the side of the road. She turns her entire body toward me, her eyes flashing. "This next project looks like it could be far better than the last three. I could double my very substantial net worth inside of two more years."

"I'm delighted to hear that you'll be able to make even more money," I say. "Heaven knows that's all you care about."

Helen's hand moves so quickly that I don't even see it coming before my cheek starts burning like a bonfire.

She slapped me.

"How dare you?" This time, I'm the one who's incensed. "You storm in here with your sports cars and your expensive clothes and you make fun of me, and you criticize me, and you mock the place we've moved to, and now you slap me? Unlike you, I manage the future of four other people. I don't have the bandwidth or the desire to spend my entire life focused on myself, and I refuse to feel guilty about not living up to your arbitrary standards."

For once, she doesn't have a quick reply. She merely looks at me, her shoulders drooping, her chin lifting slightly.

And I look right back at her. I don't glance and run, I don't steal a look sideways. I really *look*. Her light blue eyes are utterly familiar, and so full of sorrow that I don't know how I didn't see it before. There are faint lines around her eyes I didn't notice either. Her hands twist in her lap.

"I'm sorry if I was mean," I say, and I'm surprised to find that I actually am. "But you haven't been acting like someone who came to help. For the first time since my husband died, we're happy here, and I don't need you to wreck it. I've been counting down the days until you leave, since we're being almost unbearably honest."

"You have, huh?" Helen's eyes flash. "Well, you shouldn't be. I'm the only person in your life who's brave enough to tell you the truth. Steve's a rebound you're stupidly marrying, and if you go through with it, it'll be the dumbest thing you've ever done, and that's impressive since you didn't go to Stanford, you got knocked up in grad school, and you had at least twice as many kids as you should, sacrificing your career in the process."

And there's her real opinion, finally. No digs, no sideways jabs. Her unadulterated opinion of how absurd I am.

"In spite of all that, you loved Nate," she continues. "You built a life with him, a real life. Your many, many kids adore you. They trust you, even Ethan. I can't believe you're letting him throw his life away, and if that's not bad enough, you're dumping the other kids' lives down the drain at the same time."

She means that bringing them here will drag them down as well. I thought that way once, so I understand why she feels that way, to a certain extent.

"Not everything in the world revolves around Ivy League schools and money," I say. "I did build a life with Nate, but I'm not bound to him, not anymore. And as you said, I'm responsible for making sure my kids are happy." I've found that when you really want people to listen, you should talk quietly, so I drop my voice to a whisper. "We are happy here, Helen. Or we were, before you came." And we will be again, when you leave in six days.

"For now."

And now I'm itching to slap *her*. "Just drive."

I don't see how even Helen could criticize the beauty of the Gorge. But she does. Oh, she does. It's not nearly as tall or majestic as she thought it would be. It's flatter than in the photos. And the air is smoky. (It's not). The birds are too loud. (They aren't.)

"The rooms are an utter disgrace," she says. "Plus, the staff doesn't seem very well trained." She scrunches her nose. "Did you see the woman wiping down tables? She just went from one to the next, never even rinsing her rag."

127

"Helen, stop pushing your version of perfection on everyone else and try to imagine what I want—a spacious place where any of my family and friends who want to celebrate this new step for us will feel welcome." I push past the doors of the resort and step out into the clean, crisp air. The mountains have snow on top of them, and the vivid crimson of the stone that graduates to a sandy color halfway up is still breathtaking to me, even now.

"Fine, fine. If this is what you want, I can negotiate you a rock bottom price." She folds her arms. "I'll stop complaining."

It would be a miracle if that was true.

"I'll even admit that it has a sort of Wild West charm."

The heavens have cracked open and the world is turning inside out. I'm not sure quite what she means by Wild West, but the word charm certainly implies that it's a sort of compliment. "Let's go see if they're available to talk to us."

I do have to give it to Helen. She wasn't just bragging about her skills. Somehow she knew about the new resort opening up, and she used both that, and the presence of a famous influencer at the ceremony, to negotiate a lower price for the event.

"I hope you'll be the one to tell Amanda that she has to post about the wedding." I hide my smile with a cough. "Three times." Amanda's going to be majorly annoyed.

"Tell her that can be her wedding gift. Judging by what I've heard so far, it's better than anything else she would have gotten for you."

"Actually, she's getting me a great deal on the invitations. She has a connection with a printer who helped her—"

"Oh, please," Helen says. "If she's counting the use of her connections as a wedding gift, she's not a very good sister."

"She's not a sister," I say, playing a hunch. "She's a sister-*in-law*."

Helen beams.

I was right. She's heard me talk about Amanda and the kids talk about her, and she's *jealous*. My sister who has, of her own volition, been a footnote in our lives for the past twenty years, is jealous that someone else matters more to us than she does. I don't understand the reason for the change, but it's definitely there.

"Come on." She slings an arm around me, as if we're actually quite close.

I want to dart out and away to freedom, but acting like she cares about me must be a good thing, so I suppress that urge. "I'd better get home soon and start making dinner."

"Actually," she says, "You don't need to make dinner tonight."

This time, I do pull away. "What are you talking about?"

"Don't worry. I called *Amanda*." She says that the same way she'd say she called the septic company to report a backup in the tank. Talking to Amanda was clearly a distasteful necessity. "She's stepping in to make dinner and do whatever other mundane things you would have otherwise had to do over the next few days."

"Mundane?" I glare. "The reason my kids trust me is that I am there for all those boring things that need to be done. You can't—"

"Oh, just come with me, will you? If we don't go now, we'll be late."

"Late for what?" I splutter.

"I guess it doesn't really matter if we're late." Helen laughs. "It's not like my pilot will take off without me."

"What are you talking about?"

"You were planning to fly home to Houston this weekend," she says. "But as you know, I can only stay a few more days, and I'd rather not have you leave and miss the last few of them."

"I can't just take off—"

"Why not? It's not like you'll be missing out on work. You have two clients, and one of them is *pro bono*."

I really hate having her around. "What did you mean, your pilot?"

"My pilot's name is Chris, and he's been sitting on the airway in Vernal for two hours waiting for us."

"I can't just leave," I say.

"Izzy helped me pack your bag," she says. "I even cleared it with your little boyfriend."

"Steve knows we're getting on a plane?" My voice has become so shrill that I'm worried I may crack the glass on her car.

"He did a good job ad libbing with his offer of bringing you dinner and all." Helen's smile doesn't show any stress at all. She must be telling the truth. "Actually, Steve was supposed to be coming along, but thanks to his stupid horse, it'll just be you and me."

I have clearly dramatically underestimated how much money Helen has. "When you said 'your pilot,' I was envisioning we'd be flying in a crop duster," I admit.

I've already counted at least three different flight attendants, and this jet seats at least twenty people.

Helen rolls her eyes. "I bought this so that I'd be *more* comfortable than if I was flying commercial, not less."

"You own this plane?" I ask. "Outright? Just you? How is that possible?"

"I asked if you needed help after Nate died," Helen says. "On more than one occasion, I asked if you needed money, I'm quite sure."

"I thought you meant, like, to pay the mortgage on our house," I say. "Or, like, to help pay Ethan's tuition. I didn't know you meant you'd dedicate a wing to Nate at Harvard to get Ethan in."

Helen rolls her eyes. "You're the Harvard fan. I went to God's school."

Of course she did. Mom and Dad almost died when I picked Harvard over Stanford. "Do Mom and Dad know?"

"Do they know that I went to Stanford?" She lifts one eyebrow. "Uh, yeah. I think they do."

"No, idiot. Do they know you're as filthy rich as a maharaja?"

"Oh, that." Helen shrugs. "Doubt it. How often do you talk to them?"

"Not much," I say. "And that's how I like it."

She chuckles. "Same."

"So they don't know either?" I shouldn't care, but for some reason the idea of knowing something they don't makes me happy.

"If you tell them I have this," Helen says, "Mom would be calling me all the time to try and fly places—I bought this to make my life easier, not to help Mom see the world more conveniently."

"She can already afford to fly wherever she wants to go," I say.

"Exactly."

The rest of the flight—direct from Vernal to Houston—passes quickly, once we start complaining about Mom and Dad. It's always been the most solid of the common ground between us. Before I know it, we're landing.

"I've lined up a hotel that's—"

"Oh, we don't need a hotel." I pause. "Or maybe you do, if they have ten thousand dollar mattresses underneath their beds. But I'll just call an Uber and head for the house. I can get a lot of packing done between now and bedtime, and my bed's still set up."

"Oh, fine. Have it your way." Helen sighs, but when

we deplane, there's another black sports car waiting for us.

"Did you buy this one too?" I squint. "Is that—what kind of car is that?"

Helen shakes her head. "It's an Alpha Romeo, and no. I didn't buy it. The rental car companies here have a lot more options, and they promised Roger this had *never* been smoked in."

Once she's behind the wheel, my sister looks impressed. "Seeing as it only has eighty-seven miles, I think their promise to Roger was correct."

"If I'm ever as high-strung as you, feel free to slap me again," I say. "You and I both know you're comfortable with the slapping part."

"Why yes, Abby, I do accept your gratitude for setting up this trip, flying you out to Houston so you can get your house packed, and even coming with you to help."

I roll my eyes.

"And of course, it was my pleasure to line up a suitable rental car."

This time I laugh. "It was a pretty cool way to travel."

"And since we're at a regional airport, we're only twenty minutes from your house."

"I'm shocked you know where my house is," I say. "I don't recall you ever coming to visit."

"Roger knows everything—I had your address saved."

She isn't great with birthdays, as those happen all over the calendar, but she has always been a pretty reliable sender of lavish Christmas gifts. I should've known she had my address in order to do that.

Since we ate a pretty great pasta dish that had both cherry tomatoes and black olives, as well as some kind of sweet and crispy kale salad on the plane, we don't even need to stop for food on the way to my house. When we arrive, I notice for the first time—since there's no one to unload the car for us here—that her bag is actually quite small. Mine is much larger.

"You packed light," I say. "I hope you have some warmer-weather clothing in there. January in Texas isn't very cold."

Helen's smile is wry. "I have this little app on my phone." She waves it at me. "It's like magic—it tells me what the weather is like in places I haven't recently been. . ."

"Yeah, yeah." I slide my key into the lock, which is harder than usual thanks to the dumb black lock box that's scratching up my beautiful wooden front door. "Well, don't come whining to me if you're all hot while you're helping me pack the kitchen."

"Oh, I don't whine, but I hate packing. My assistant sends me clothes by courier when I reach a new location."

It's like she's gone entirely insane. "How do you know they'll fit?"

"I have a personal shopper." She's looking at *me* like *I'm* the crazy one. "Two, actually. Jessica is terrible at formal wear, so I hired Trish to handle that."

Because that makes sense.

"But back to the packing."

I turn to find out what she's saying, but she waves me inside.

"Go, go. Geez. You planning to keep me out here on the porch all night?"

I'm grumbling as I walk through the doorway, my much larger bag packed by Izzy hefted over my shoulder. "Maybe I should."

Once we're through the door, Helen drops her bag and leans over it, rummaging around in the smallish front pocket. "Aha!" She straightens and brandishes something small, square, and bright yellow.

"Aha?" I ask. "What is that? Why are you aha-ing me?"

She steps closer, her arm still outstretched, thrusting the small yellow square item at me. "It's a pad of Post-Its. Duh."

I blink at her, but I don't take them. "Yeah. Those are really neat, but if that's a prototype for your next idea?" I lean a little closer and drop my voice. "I'd be careful about raising funding for it, cuz someone else beat you to it."

She presses them against my hand and rolls her eyes. "Absolutely hilarious, I tell you."

"What are these for?" I ask.

"My wedding gift," she says. "To show you that I support you."

"You're being supportive. . .by giving me Post-Its?" I can't quite keep my lip from curling. "The woman who has a private jet, a pilot who works for her full time, and sports cars in every time zone is being supportive by giving me Post-Its?"

"With those, we'll mark your belongings," she says. "Storage, trash, donate, or pack and move."

"Why would we do that?"

"I've hired packers and movers. They'll show up here tomorrow, so we don't have to pack a thing." She grins. "You're welcome."

I put one hand on my hip. "Confess. Did you do this for me?" I arch one eyebrow. "Or for *you* so you wouldn't have to help me pack?"

She sighs. "Fine. It's not a wedding present. It's self-interested. But it's also supportive. I want the credit."

I want to complain and tell her I don't need her to pay for movers, and that I need to go through all the stuff and sort through things more deeply than I can while slapping Post-Its on things, but I can't say any of that convincingly. From the time the plane landed, the idea of sorting through our belongings, my mementos of memories with Nate, and the accumulation of a lifetime in this house has weighed on me.

I hate procrastination, but this one time, maybe she's actually done me a huge favor. I can send things I can't deal with to storage, things I want up in Utah to be shipped, and I can eliminate stuff I know I don't want. "Thank you."

Helen's smile this time is genuine. "You're welcome."

She doesn't even complain when I show her to our guest room, which boasts a bed with an eight hundred dollar mattress. She just asks me what time we should wake up in the morning. She's obnoxious as all get out sometimes, and she's one of the most self-centered people I know, but she is my sister, and I think she does love me, deep down.

The next morning, she's up right at six a.m., and she does her very best to pre-sort the office, the bathrooms, and the kids' rooms for me. With her help, and a huge crew of movers following behind me, we actually finish the entire house by four in the afternoon.

A single day.

That's how long it took to complete a task I thought

would take a week even with Helen's help. She's effective, I'll give her that.

The moving company and their crew of twenty are just going over some paperwork with me, confirming the address in Utah, the address of my preferred storage unit, and the location where I'd like everything we aren't keeping to be donated, when my phone rings.

It's Robert.

Does he know I'm in town? I can't help cringing a little. He doesn't even know I'm engaged yet, and now I'm physically in Houston without telling him. "Hey, Robert."

"Abby?"

"Yeah."

"Are you in Houston?" How could he know that? He's like a bloodhound chasing a fox.

"Who—"

"I called the ranch when you didn't pick up last night, thinking maybe your internet was down, and Izzy answered. She said you came out here early to pack things up."

"Yeah, it wasn't the plan, but Helen surprised me—"

"Is she there?" he asks. "I've missed her." That's a big fat lie, but I don't call him on it, since Helen's watching me interact with him with a little too much interest.

"She is," I say. "She helped me get things taken care of way faster today than I thought possible."

"Really?" Robert asks. "Because I'm almost to your place. When I realized you were in town, I took off early to come help."

Panic pulses through me—I have no idea why, but I don't have time to question it. "Oh, no." My voice is way too high and squeaky. I clear my throat. "We just left."

"You did?" Robert sounds deflated. "Could you turn around?"

I snatch my purse off the counter and gesture wildly at the door. "Go, now," I mouth to Helen. "Oh man," I say. "I wish we could, but we have to—er—Helen set up an appointment to—"

"Abby's trying on wedding dresses," Helen shouts. "Not much time between now and the wedding, so we're hoping to get something that won't need many modifications."

Maybe he didn't hear. Maybe Helen seems way louder to me because she's essentially shouting in my ear.

"Wedding—" A choking sound comes through the line. "Did she say something about wedding dresses?"

"I've been meaning to call and tell you," I say lamely. "Steve proposed."

Robert hangs up.

"Let's go." I practically rip her arm off dragging her to the car.

"Why did you tell him we were already gone?" Helen's expression is so smug that I want to kick her.

In all the world, no one makes me more violent than my sister. I wonder whether that's a common sentiment. "I told you already," I mutter. "He likes me, and it's awkward." I rush to the car and yank on the handle like a preschool kid until she unlocks it.

"Wow, you're a mess."

I expect her to go on some tirade about what my reaction means. I expect her to scold me or berate me or argue with me, but she's miraculously silent. We've been driving for nearly ten minutes when my heart rate finally calms enough to realize that I have no idea where we're actually going.

That's when my irritation flares again. "Why did you have to yell that we're going to look at wedding dresses? You knew that—"

"Because it's true," she says.

That catches me off guard. "Huh?"

"I made an appointment a few days ago."

"At a wedding boutique?" I can hardly believe it. "*You*, the person most opposed to this wedding in all the world, other than maybe Robert—who just hung up on me—made me an appointment to look at wedding dresses?"

She shrugs, her hands remaining at ten and two. "If my mule-stubborn sister is insisting on making a big mistake, I'd at least like her to look nice while doing it."

That makes me smile. Even if she's being annoying, at the root, she's being supportive. "Thank you."

She stares straight ahead, but I can tell she's pleased.

"How did you know we'd be able to go today?" I ask. "I have a huge house."

"I set up five appointments over the next twenty-four hours," she says.

"Whoa," I say. "Weren't you worried we might piss off the boutiques?"

"I made them at five different places," she says. "And even if we annoy all the Houston shops, there's always New York."

It must be nice for her, that money is no object. "I can't fly to New York—"

"I'd take you, obviously," she says, her voice soft. "The movers may have been set up to keep me from having to perform backache-inducing manual labor, but this is actually just something nice I want to do for you."

"Thank you," I say. And I mean it.

The shop owner is an older lady with a heavy accent, but she's nothing but smiles, and not the fake kind—the wide-mouthed, eye-crinkling smiles that mean she genuinely loves her job. It must be fun, finding the perfect dress to celebrate the perfect day.

The first dress she brings me is vintage—ivory bodice, cream skirt, and thick, hand-crocheted lace on the long sleeves and trim. It looks like a gown that would have been worn in the eighteen hundreds.

"Oh, no." Helen waves. "I get what you're going for, but no one who's as close as you are to forty wants to have a vintage theme." She shakes her head. "Hits a little too close to home."

I laugh.

The woman laughs along with us. The next dress she brings is bright and white and hugely puffy.

"Now *that* you're trying on just so I can laugh at you," she says.

I hate it on sight, but I comply. I mean, isn't that half the fun? Trying on the duds so that when you find the right dress, it really stands out? Over the next hour, I try on a form fitted dress with fur trim. I slide into embroidered and bejeweled gowns that look like they were made for Queen Victoria herself. I shimmy into several more cupcake inspired fluffs. And I even wait patiently as the proprietor laces up the slinkiest, the *naughtiest* looking wedding gown I've ever seen.

But after so many losers that I've mentally lost track of them all, the woman brings out a gown that's in a protective rubber case. I can tell by the careful way she's holding it that it's hugely pricey. She looks like the jeweler who has brought in an unmounted diamond that was resting in a huge black box kept in the safe in the back.

"I doubt that one's really in my budget," I say. "Judging by that bag."

"Oh stop," Helen says. "Just try it on."

The smiley woman carefully begins to extricate the gown from the bag, and I catch my first glimpse of the bottom. The skirt is full but not floofy. It's clearly made up of several layers, but the overlay is made of a delicate lace shaped like flowers—it reminds me of the yarrow flowers that overran the meadow the first time Steve took me on a trail ride.

Layers and layers of tulle and organza lie beneath it, helping it look full without resembling a cupcake.

But the bodice is the most perfect part. It's simple, clean, and elegant. It's a clean-cut sleeveless bodice that's tightly overlaid with the same yarrow-covered lace, and around the waist is a bright but thinly embroidered ring of turquoise-colored flowers.

They're just the pop of color that it needs to say, "I'm elegant and mature, but I'm still fun."

It practically screams for a pair of turquoise and gold cowboy boots to be worn with it.

My hands tremble as I undo the laces in the back. Will my back and my arms look too old? Will this gorgeous dress look ridiculous on me? Will people laugh at me for trying to look much younger than I am?

Strong hands tighten the laces behind me. "Careful," I say. "You haven't told me what it costs yet, but I bet it's not cheap."

"It doesn't matter." Helen's voice surprises me. I

assumed the older shop owner was still helping me while Helen lounged. "This is the dress."

"But do my arms look—"

"It's *the* dress." Helen steps aside and points at the wall-length mirror.

Even without the boots, without yarrow flowers woven into my hair, I can tell. She's right. I look thinner than I am. I look younger than I am. I look more country than I am.

And somehow this dress makes it all look just *perfect,* like I'm the Abigail I was born to become. "Imagine how it'll look with a pair of turquoise cowboy boots and a bouquet of Indian paintbrushes and yarrow flowers."

Helen sighs. "Tell me you don't have any doubts at all, and I'll stop haranguing you and be the perfect Maid of Honor."

Maid of Honor? She's lucky I even asked her to be a bridesmaid at all. "I don't have any doubts."

"Really?"

Normally I'd brush her off. You don't feed a bear, after all. That's how you end up mauled. But something about her tone makes me turn to meet her eye. And for once, my armored sister almost looks. . .vulnerable. She looks worried about me.

She looks genuine.

So for the first time since she showed up, I think about her question. "Do I have any doubts?"

I almost laugh. I've been nothing but doubts since Nate died. I've doubted myself. I've doubted our future. I've doubted the children. I've doubted God.

"Steve and I are so different. I wonder almost every day whether we're a mistake. He lives and breathes for horses, and he literally spends all his free time with them. He'd live in a barn if he could."

"So you have thought about it," Helen says. "And you do see that it's not a simple, uncomplicated pairing."

I stare at the image in the mirror. "From the outside, to everyone in Birch Creek, yeah, we look perfect. We're both well educated. We both have money. We're close to the same age. He seems to never have wavered, but I'm not Steve. My life is complicated. I'm the one giving everything up while he just kind of coasts along. He has a daughter he barely knows. I have no idea whether he'll be a good father to my kids in the long run. He wants at least one more child, and I don't think I do. He's country, and I'm a city girl. He's a doctor who fixes things with his hands, and I'm a city girl who uses my brain. Yeah, I have a lot of days where I wake up in a panic, thinking maybe this entire thing is a terrible mistake."

Helen grabs my hand.

"Look, I know that you're just going to double down now, but you shouldn't. I'm trying to be honest with you, and—"

Helen yanks.

I finally turn to look at her and realize that her eyes are wide and her mouth is dangling open. She glances pointedly to the side and tosses her chin at the door.

Where Steve is standing, his eyes as hurt as I've ever seen them. "I guess now I know why it's bad luck to see the bride in her wedding dress before the big day." He swallows, forces a smile, turns on his boot heel and disappears.

❧ II ❧

AMANDA

Abby's sister Helen is awful, but she did me a favor. Mandy and I have been at an impasse over the past few days, and to be honest, I have no idea why she even wants us to keep living there. I've been horrible to her, and even the girls are sulking.

So when Helen called me and asked me if I would stay with Abby's family while she took her sister to Houston for a surprise packing trip, I pretended like it was an imposition.

But really, I'm delighted to be here.

Sure, it's configured a little differently than it was. I mean, for one thing, prior to the sale, the alien people moved all Jed's stuff out. I'm not sure where it all went, which is probably a pity. Mandy has the letters old Jed never sent her, of course, and I think our kids each picked a handful of things they liked, but most of that stuff—the accumulation of which took at least one lifetime—is just. . .gone.

Every day I move a little closer to obsolete as well, and that's a sobering thought.

But even without Abby, and even with the very Spartan furnishings—presumably Abby left it so spare to make space for the things she's in Houston at this moment packing to bring—it still feels more like home than Mandy's did. Actually, if I'm being honest, it feels more like home than any place I've ever lived, including the New York City apartment I literally furnished myself.

"Ooh," Maren's practically squealing as they walk up the drive from where the bus just dropped them. "Can I sleep in with you?"

Izzy shrugs. "Sure, if you want."

"What about me?" Emery asks. "Where can I sleep?"

"You go in with Whitney," Maren says. "You guys can play with Barbies." Maren's smirk isn't as subtle as she thinks she is.

Emery may be accustomed to Maren's snarky little digs, but Whitney's scowling like she's planning to knife her in the middle of the night. "We aren't babies, you know." Whitney's hands are on her hips, and one of her eyebrows is cocked. She looks exactly like a miniature of her mother when someone has displeased her.

"Babies play with rattles," Maren says. "I was suggesting Barbies."

Izzy laughs as the two of them walk up the steps and into the house. "Let's make some cookies—Mom found this new kind. She calls them Kentucky Butter Cake Cookies. You'll love them."

"Are they healthy?" Maren's become borderline obsessed with eating healthy and keeping her weight low.

Izzy scrunches her nose. "Sure."

"Great, then let's make them."

Butter Cake cookies are healthy? Maren's clearly not so bright. Either that, or she is more than happy to lie to herself.

But more concerning than her naiveté is the new pairing off thing they're doing. When we lived here before, Maren was always alone, and Izzy and Whitney and Emery were thick as thieves. I wonder what changed, and whether the little girls will be alright with it. Mostly, I'm worried that Maren will do something classically *Maren* and then Izzy will run back to the younger girls and leave my oldest daughter heartbroken.

I shake off my anxiety—that's an Abby kind of concern. I'm more of a *Lord of the Flies* style parent. I'm sure they'll work that out themselves, and if Maren gets dumped, well, it'll serve her right.

"Hey, Mom, can we go ride the horses?" Emery looks far less squashed by Izzy's defection than I expected, which is good. She's also had quite a few horseback lessons at this point. Plus, Whitney is quite good.

"If you let Whitney check your saddle and you stay in the pasture, that's fine."

The girls' voices go supersonic as they drop their bags in the dirt and jog toward the barn.

"Hey," I protest half-heartedly before giving up and walking inside. A little dirt won't hurt their schoolbags, right? Isn't that kind of the point of country life, anyway?

"Aunt Amanda." Gabe tugs on my wrist.

I didn't even realize he followed me inside. Actually, if I'm being honest, I didn't even check to make sure he made it off the bus. I'm clearly not a very good fill-in for his mother. "Gabe. What's up?" I think about crouching down to be closer to eye level for him, but that feels like it would be odd.

"When will my mom be back?" His eyes look both hopeful and anxious.

I've been there, buddy. "Well, she went to Houston with your Aunt Helen."

"So will she be back before dinner? Or after?"

I suppress a laugh. "She won't be back for a few days," I say. "That's why I'm here. Otherwise, Ethan could have kept an eye on you guys."

Gabe blinks once, then twice, and then suddenly, without any warning, bursts into tears. His entire face is red, and his breath is coming in gasping sobs. "But where will I sleep?"

"Where do you usually sleep?"

"Aunt Helen took my room," he barely manages to say. "And her stuff is *everywhere.*"

I quickly cross the family room to his door and swing it open. He's right. There's a bra slung over the lamp. Socks are strewn around the floor—and I've never seen her in anything but high heels. Why does she even *have* socks? There's makeup in various states of open and closed covering Gabe's desk. A pile of what I assume are dirty clothes are stuffed in the corner, and everywhere I look there's another unmatched high heel in a different color. There's a necklace hanging over the headboard of the bed, and when I walk toward the window, I step on a stray earring.

I back out again, slowly.

The severe, almost scary Helen is a complete slob. Why did she bring that many things for a week-long stay? And why didn't she take some of it with her to Houston? Is she planning on just being naked there?

"See?"

"Yes, sweetie, yes, I do see." I think about his concern—where will he sleep? "Where have you been sleeping?"

"In Mom's room."

Both our heads swivel slowly toward the door to the room Abby slept in for six months until we lost the ranch.

"That's Ethan's room now," Gabe reminds me.

Of course it is. Now that I'm not here, hogging half the space, Abby would have moved into the master suite that has its own bathroom. And that's where Gabe has been sleeping—sharing a bed with his mother, no doubt.

"Well, you can still sleep there," I say. "On a sleeping bag. How does that sound?"

When his tiny arms wrap around my waist and squeeze, something happens to my heart. It feels like it's expanding. "Thanks, Aunt Amanda."

I don't miss having to cut up food for little people, or help them dress, or deal with spilled food or sticky fingers, but I do miss the exuberant little-person hugs. Nothing else feels quite like them.

As soon as his concerns are resolved, Gabe pulls his coat back on and scampers out the door.

"Where are you going?" I call after him.

"I have to feed the goats," he says. "Be back later."

The goats. Why didn't I think of that? It's a good thing Abby's kids actually do their chores without being prompted, because I'm not entirely sure what things have to be done, especially not now that we've been gone.

Maybe I need to make a little sweep and make sure there's nothing obvious that needs to be done. I pull on

148

Abigail's 'barn coat' as she calls it, which is just code for a coat that can get dirty without causing concern. She always hangs it on a hook on the front porch, and she keeps her barn boots, which are perpetually mud encrusted, right beneath it. I slip my feet into her slightly-too-large boots too, and I clomp my way across the front yard toward the barn.

Kids are all over the place, including Izzy and Maren, who are not making cookies but are instead sitting on a tire swing dangling off the large front yard tree, chatting. It occurs to me that no one seemed to go inside and work on any homework. Is this normally what they do? Scatter when they get home and play?

"Hey," I shout. "Do any of you have homework?"

Maren and Emery ignore me, but Izzy and Whitney freeze and exchange some kind of glance from across the yard. Whitney's holding her horse and Emery's and she appears to be about ready to ride.

"What about Gabe? Where are the goats?"

Izzy points slowly toward the area behind the barn.

"We do have homework," Whitney says slowly. "But you said we could ride."

So it's my fault. Those little sneaks. For some reason, it makes me happy to see that they aren't exactly perfect. They're just as likely to skirt the rules as my kids, when their mother's not here. "As soon as you're done riding, you march inside and work on your homework." I spin in a circle. "That goes for all of you. I won't have Abby coming home and discovering that her kids are all failing because I was put in charge for a few days. Do you hear me?"

"What about us?" Maren asks. "You don't care if we fail?"

I roll my eyes and keep walking.

"Hey, Aunt Amanda." Ethan's rolling something into loops inside the barn. "Everything alright?"

"I was just. . ." I can't really say that I was circling around like a lost kitten, checking to see if everything was alright. I have no idea what any of the things in the barn are *for*, and no idea how I would figure out if something was wrong. "I'm looking for Gabe," I finish, lamely. "I wanted to see if he has homework."

"Probably." Ethan's grin is easy, and dimples pop up on his cheeks. "That kid's a terrible shirker."

"Am not," Gabe shouts from the back of the barn. "I'm feeding Hershey and Spot." He folds his arms. "They were really hungry."

Kevin walks through the back door of the barn, ruffling Gabe's hair as he passes. "Goats are always hungry, squirt. They'll eat almost anything, too."

"I'm not a shirt or a squirt," Gabe says. "I'm a hard worker."

"A squirt is an affectionate term," Ethan says. "Like when Dad used to call you booger. And I didn't call you a shirt. I said you're a *shirker*. It means someone who wants to get out of doing something."

"I don't get out of things," Gabe says. "I get in them."

"Like mud, it seems." Kevin tilts his head.

What's he talking about? I walk closer and realize that Gabe must have fallen in the goat pen, and it doesn't look like it's only mud. Chunks of darker brown ballish-shaped things are stuck to the back of his pants.

His school pants.

"I'm sure Hershey and Spot were happy to see you," I say. "But maybe we ought to go inside and get you cleaned up. I can make dinner, and you can take a bath and get into pajamas."

Gabe's lower lip is sticking out.

"I kind of need your help in there," I say in a quieter voice. "I don't even know where any of the bath stuff is, and I need someone to help me pick what to make for dinner."

He perks up at that. I may not be good at disciplining kids, but I know how to distract and redirect with the best of them. He trots inside, little chunks of stuff shedding from the back of his pants as he moves. With any luck, most of it will have fallen off by the time he reaches the front door.

"How's the new job going?" Kevin asks.

I cringe a little bit.

"That bad?"

"That new resort being built in Dutch John is taking all the contractors," I say. "I mean, working with Mandy's already no picnic—"

"Mandy?" Kevin's eyes squint up in confusion.

"Amanda Saddler," I say. "She offered to be called Mandy as a peace offering—we've been squabbling a bit, and now—"

"Cuz she gave the ranch to him?" Kevin points his thumb over his shoulder at Ethan.

Who looks really, really uncomfortable.

"You know what? It's all fine." I keep running my mouth without thinking. I'm such an idiot. If I'm not careful, my problem with Mandy will turn into a problem with Abby, and she didn't do anything wrong.

"You need contractors?" Kevin asks.

I hadn't even thought about Kevin. "You're busy with the ranch, obviously," I say.

"Not during the winter," he says. "Things are pretty slow right now—our slowest time."

"That's true," Ethan says. "You could totally pick up some extra work and I can finish the fencing myself."

"Are you sure?" Kevin looks giddy.

"Jeff too," Ethan says. "Now would be the perfect time."

"I would love that," I say. Maybe I could actually get some of these places finished and we can rent them or sell them as planned. "And if you know of anyone else who you think is reliable, send them my way, too."

"Will do." Kevin's smiling as I rush back to the house.

I'm smiling too, I realize, my heart already lighter, even if this isn't a long-term solution. I'm rummaging around in the fridge looking for a tomato to go with the nachos Gabe and I are making when my phone bings.

AS A THANK YOU. . . Helen's text makes no sense.

As a thank you, what?

But then I remember the crappy service we get here. She probably sent a photo and it's taking forever to come through. I wonder what it is. She seems pretty well off. Maybe she's gotten me some kind of gift in Houston. Or maybe she found some stuff at Abby's place they think I'll want.

Ten seconds later, when my phone buzzes again, I finally get an image.

Only, it's not the photo of a gift I'm expecting.

It's Eddy.

He has his arm slung around some woman with midnight hair that gleams like an obsidian wall, and he's holding a glass in his other hand. A foamy looking drink's sloshing over the edge of it.

I know it can't be this, but it sure looks like he's holding a beer and standing in a very friendly pose with his arm around some gorgeous woman in a silver sheath dress.

Adrenaline floods my body.

My hands shake.

I can feel the pulse beating in my temples.

How on earth is *this* a thank you? Or is Helen kidding? I nearly drop my phone in the process, but my fumbly fingers finally press talk and I hear the phone ring.

It keeps on ringing for a long time, and I brace myself to try and leave some kind of message for Abby's sister.

But at the last second, she picks up. "Hello?"

"What did you just send me?" I should try not to sound hostile, but it's hard.

"I'm sorry, should I not have sent it?" Helen clears her throat. "I'm the kind of person who always wants to know the truth, but if you're not. . ."

"Of course I want to know the truth," I practically spit. "But—"

Gabe's looking up at me, his large eyes wide, his mouth dangling open.

"But what?" Helen asks.

"Where did you get that?" I hiss softly. "How in the world is that a thank you?"

"Has Abigail told you what I do?" Helen's voice is smooth, unconcerned.

"You buy companies?" I hate how unsure I am.

"Something like that," she says. "I hear that you're buying houses and renovating them and flipping them."

"Something like that," I echo.

She laughs. "Touché. Well, as I'm sure you can understand, you can't buy a house and flip it unless you have a very good handle on what it will be worth in the end, what it will cost you to get it fixed up, and you're positive that you can buy it for a low enough price that you'll turn a profit."

"Okay."

"In my line of business, I use the very best investigators. It's an absolute requirement for what I do. Only, I'm in between jobs right now, so I figured I'd let them earn their salary doing other things."

"Spying on my boyfriend?"

"Looking into my sister's newfound friends and acquaintances," she says, as if it's the most reasonable thing in the world.

"Are you spying on Steve, too?"

She snorts. "Please."

I'll take that as a yes. "And you thought I'd like to know that my boyfriend is, what? Standing in some place that sells ginger ale, and talking to another woman?" I only manage to spit the words out through clenched teeth. I'm hoping she won't notice.

"If that's what you see when you look at that photo, then why are you so upset?"

I hate her. Abby's sister is the devil. No, the devil is powerful and important. She's the devil's consort—she wishes she mattered, but she doesn't. "Well, I appreciate your concern, but I'm sure Eddy's just fine."

"My investigators found out that he'd been enrolled in several different drug rehab programs. It stands to reason he's in AA, and if so, I'm not sure I'd be so confident if my boyfriend was standing in a bar. But I'm glad to hear you have that level of trust in him."

154

"I do."

"Wonderful. I'll be sure to keep any future information to myself."

"You don't have to do that," I say, ashamed, but desperate to not become a chump.

Helen's laughing when she hangs up.

I'm determined to ignore her photo and her innuendo, but I can't quite do it. I text Eddy about three minutes later.

HOW'S CALI?

He doesn't text back.

I slide the pan of chips and cheese and beans into the oven, and then I have nothing else to do. So I do what anyone would, and I text him again. HARD AT WORK? I'M WATCHING ABBY'S KIDS WHILE SHE PACKS UP THE HOUSE BACK IN HOUSTON.

Five minutes later, still nothing.

And that's when I do something really crazy.

I grab my bag that I set on Abby's bed. . .and I carry it right out the door. I drop it into the backseat of my car and march out to the barn. "Hey, Ethan? You in here?"

His head pops out from behind a stack of rectangular hay bales. "Everything alright?"

"You're eighteen," I say. "You're an adult."

His eyebrows draw together. "I am, yeah."

"And you're capable of keeping the kids alive and making sure they do their homework and eat, right?"

He blinks.

"You said winter's slower, and you had time, didn't you? Because I had an emergency come up, and. . ." I point back at my car. "I need to go somewhere."

155

"Go somewhere?" Ethan looks alarmed. "Is everything alright?"

"I just put a pan of nachos in the oven. They'll be ready in twenty minutes or so. Tomatoes and lettuce and ranch are already out on the counter. Gabe's in the bathtub and is ready to get out whenever. Can you hold things down until tomorrow night?"

"Yeah, sure, of course." He steps closer. "Are you alright? Is your family okay?"

"I sure hope so," I say.

And then I jump into my car and drive away. I call the airlines right away and manage to book a last-minute flight from Salt Lake to LA. But once that's done, the only thing I can think of is how Abby would not be leaving right now.

She's a balanced adult. She puts the kids first. She puts her job first. She would not be racing off, half-cocked, desperate to reassure herself that her boyfriend isn't drinking and smooching (or worse) some random woman in California.

But how well do I really know Eddy? And if Helen's right, and if I am a complete idiot, I want to know right away, before everyone else does. I want to be out in front of this disaster the way I wasn't with Paul. I can't go through that again—losing everything because I wasn't smart enough to check his investments or manage things without him.

I can't be a chump again.

I won't.

The street sign says I'm twelve miles away from Fort Bridger when I run out of gas.

Apparently in my desperation not to be an idiot, I didn't even notice that I was practically on empty. I'm sitting on the side of the road, crying, without enough cell phone reception to even call the airlines and cancel my exorbitantly expensive last-minute flight, when someone taps on my window.

I practically jump out of my skin.

"Are you alright—Amanda?" The man's face goes slack. "Is that really you? What are you doing here?"

It's David freaking Park. Of course it is.

The man is ruining my life, and he's there around every corner. "Go away."

"Is your car broken down?" He glances at the hood of the car, possibly searching for signs of an issue.

"Please just leave," I say.

"The sun's setting soon," he says. "I'm on my way back to Dutch John, but I can give you a ride—"

"I ran out of gas," I say. "It's not a big deal. I'll just walk down the road to Fort Bridger and buy some, okay?"

"Down the road?" He frowns. "It's at least ten miles. How about I take you down to get it?"

I throw my hands up in the air and finally stare right at him. "That won't help me. There's no way I'll make my flight by the time we drive down and get it and I drive back."

"Flight?"

God hates me. That's the only explanation I can think of in this moment. My boyfriend is doing who knows what with who knows who. My perfect sister-in-law's obnoxious older sister is the one who told me about it, so who knows who else is already aware. I just ditched the six children who were in my care to deal with my love life—my pathetic love life—and I didn't even notice I was out of gas.

And now, the final insult? The guy who has been pursuing me, the very man who is making my life suck more than anyone else right now, is on the front row to watch my humiliation.

"Please just go home."

"I'll be happy to drive you to the airport," he says. "It's not like I have anything else going on tonight."

He's kidding, surely.

But I'm desperate enough that I can't turn him down if he's not.

"What would I do with my car?"

"I can have one of my people bring gas tomorrow and drop it at your place, or at the airport, whichever you prefer," he says. "I really don't mind."

It's like he's an angel without wings. "What's the catch?" I ask.

He shrugs. "No catch."

I open the door, and poke him with my index finger. "No prying for information about my work projects, and no talking about yours."

"Done," David says.

Before I can reach back and get it, he's already snagged my bag. He tosses it into his Range Rover and gestures for me to get in. "Salt Lake airport, I assume?"

I nod.

He's true to his word for the entire two hours we're in the car. He sticks to neutral topics like music, food, and vacation destinations we like and dislike. He manages to make me laugh when he tells me about the turtle that bit his toe, and again when he describes the eagle who pooped on his head and the monkey that bit him.

"You don't seem to be at one with nature," I say.

"Maybe you should stick to more well-inhabited places when you travel."

He shrugs. "Maybe one day I'll have someone to travel with and I won't have to try so hard to find meaningful connection with the animals who clearly despise my intrusion."

"Oh, come on," I say. "I'm sure there are hundreds—no, thousands—of women who would love to travel with you."

David sighs. "But not the one I want."

"Hey, you promised—"

"Not to talk about work, and not to press you for details about your work," he says. "And I have kept those promises."

I suppose that's true.

"But I never promised not to flirt, and I certainly didn't promise not to pry."

"You've been so impressively polite up until now."

"We're close to the airport," he says. "I was nervous, but now I'm running out of time."

"Time for what?"

"To find out what the emergency is." He's grinning. "I mean, if your parents are sick or something, then I'm *so sorry*." He immediately sobers. "But if it's about *him*, then you know. I just don't want you to forget that there's this great guy back home, a guy who's willing to just drop everything and help you out when you run out of gas."

It is pretty lucky that he happened to be driving past when I ran out of gas.

Wait, lucky? Or creepy?

"How did you know it was me?"

His head whips sideways. "How did I know?"

I think back to the shock on his face when he saw my face, and the way he spluttered. He did seem genuinely shocked. And he does seem like the kind of person who would lend a hand to most anyone who was stranded. "Sorry, I'm a New Yorker. Paranoid is part of our nature."

"So it *is* about him," he says.

"What?" I ask. "Why do you say that?"

"You're deflecting." He shakes his head. "But in case you want to check, you can call the Lumber Supply in Fort Bridger. They're the only people in the area right now who have anything but pine, and there's no way I'm doing the entire resort with pine floors. Brian Bettin from purchasing would be happy to tell you how long I haggled with him, though I doubt he'll offer you the same price he agreed to supply for me."

"Ah." So it was just luck. "Well, I'm not going to tell you why I'm in a bind, and if that upsets you, tough cookies."

"Look, seeing as you're a New Yorker, you're probably wondering what my angle is." He glances sideways at me. "I bet you're wondering *why* I like you."

"No," I say. "I'm not."

"You're not?" He sounds completely disbelieving.

"I'm not," I say. "I know guys like you. You only want the red truck when someone else has it. Things have value only when they're in demand. It's pretty common with businessmen. If I'd been available when I went out for that date, you'd have lost interest immediately. But I wasn't, and that's why you became desperate to win me." I pin him with a stare. "It's not about me, and that's why you'll get nowhere."

He's quiet for a moment, following the signs to the

airport. It looks like I'll actually make my flight, miracle of miracles.

"That's not right," he says. "I can see why you'd think that, but it's not true. I *am* a businessman, and I have been for quite some time. I also have parents who have been pushing me to meet someone and get married for years. I'm Korean, after all. But if all I wanted was a good chase, I could find that elsewhere, believe me."

This should be good. "Then what is it?"

"You're one of the most beautiful women I've met, but you don't seem to know that, even though it's literally your job to post photos. You're *absent from* as many photos as you're present in on your account. That's rare for an influencer. You bring beauty to things around you, from your posts to the homes you remodel. You care for your children, but you don't change who you are to care for them and you don't pressure them to conform to what you want people to see. You're awesome in ways you don't even know that you are, and I find you refreshing."

They shouldn't matter—his words—but for some reason, they do. They're like a bucket of water dumped on a dying plant. They're lotion on dry and cracked hands. They're a balm to my soul.

"I have a boyfriend," I say, but my voice is way too small and way more unsure than I mean for it to be.

"I know you do." He stops the car in front of the airport drop-off. "But if he crashes and burns, I'd like you to know that I'm not here for the chase. I'm here for the catch." He turns toward me slowly, his dark eyes meeting mine and holding my gaze. "And I think you're worth the wait."

When I climb out of the car, my knees feel weak. Stupid knees.

"And Amanda?" David has climbed out of the car and is handing me my bag. "I know I promised not to talk about work on the way, but we're here." He looks right and then left. "It's not 'the way to the airport' anymore, right?"

I frown.

"Your friend Donna is working for me now, and we had an idea. I can offer you use of the guys I have contracted any time they have days off due to the schedule for half price. It was her idea, and it won't be as great as having first priority, but it should help you get things done. I also thought you ought to know that Donna's working with me, since you seemed so opposed."

"I can't believe—"

He holds up his hands. "Before you behead me, you should know that she called me. There was some kind of issue with her brother, I believe, and she had no job. I didn't badger her into coming to work for me, and we both want what's best for you. I'm not trying to run your business into the ground. Quite the opposite."

Nope, he's just busy saving another person who ran out of gas in her life—and together they're trying to think of ways to save me. I'm beginning to think David Park might be a guardian angel, or something. "Fine."

"So you're not mad?"

Not about that, anyway. "Thanks for the ride," I say.

And I mean it.

12

DONNA

Mr. Park wasn't kidding when he said he wanted a local with connections, but as soon as he discovered that I have reasonably competent organizational skills, he expanded my job description. I think if I were to write up my own job after only three days of work, I'd say I'm the catch-all girl.

Maybe the title for that is Mr. Park's personal assistant.

I pick up coffee. I make copies. I arrange things on his schedule. I set up meetings with people I know. I call people I don't and ask about things the project needs. I take notes for him in meetings. I follow up on things he makes comments about. Basically, if there's some way I can make his life easier, I do.

It's a lot more work than my last job, but true to his word pays much better, so I'm not exactly complaining. It doesn't leave me with much time to check my personal email or dink around online, though, so when I get a moment, I always pull up an internet browser and check in.

The email Abigail sent last night takes me off guard. I thought she was out of town—that's what Amanda said, that she was going to Houston early, as a surprise from her sister.

Dear Donna:

Your dad's family doctor has a clinic day tomorrow in Manila—I just heard back. If you have time to swing by, I'd love to get some information from him anticipatory to the upcoming deposition. I hate asking questions when I don't know what the answer will be. If you do manage to meet him, can you ask him about your dad's mental state around the time that new will was executed? We need to know whether he was inconsistent all the time, or whether clarity came and went. We also need to find out whether he would have declared him as incompetent officially at any point, and if so, when.

In other news, we already knew where one of the witnesses for the will was located. I believe you're friends with the woman's son, Will Earl. When I spoke to her, she indicated that she wasn't sure about the other two witnesses—she wasn't close to either of them. But I've confirmed that the second witness, a Jasmine Holden, is deceased. That only leaves one other witness. Unfortunately, I don't have any leads for Greg James, and there are dozens of them in Utah and Wyoming alone. So if you can ask around town, it would be wonderful if we could locate him. His testimony could make a difference for your case.

I hope you're doing well. I asked at the school and they said you'd left your job. Please call me if there's something I can do to help.

Abby

Left my job? They told her I'd 'left,' as in, I decided not to go anymore? That royally ticks me off. But maybe

164

it's for the best. It makes it sound like I'm in a better place by choice instead of happenstance. I suppose it only makes me look less pathetic, and that's probably not bad.

I wrack my brain to think of any way I could get over there, but I can't come up with anything. It's already two-forty-five, and his clinic hours end at five. Since I get off at the same time, and I'm thirty minutes from Manila, it's not going to happen.

In spite of my efforts to play it cool, a dejected sigh manages to escape.

"Is everything alright? That sigh didn't sound great."

"Oh, I'm fine." I make sure to smile brightly in case my peppy response didn't quite fool him.

He stands up and walks over to my desk, leaning casually on the corner. "You've been here three days and you've already organized the files, set my calendar in order, and lined up all the supplies that we were lacking for phase one. If you need to take off a little early to deal with something, please do."

I can hardly believe my ears. "Are you serious?"

"I don't run a sweatshop, Miss Ellingson." His half smile is adorable.

"I hardly think that expecting me to stay for a full workday would elevate you to sweatshop status," I say. "But I did have something come up."

"Can I ask what it is?" He sounds nervous, like he doesn't want to overstep. "You certainly don't need to share, but if there's something I can do to help. . ."

"Oh, believe me, you don't want to know."

"I think I do," he says. "In fact, I know I do."

"It's a little too Maury Povich for me to be sharing it with my boss."

His eyebrows rise. "Now I really want to know. I loved that show."

"How about I share the nickel version?" I ask. "You know I'm a local, but I went to school at Stanford."

"Wait, you did? When did you gradua—"

I shake my head. "I didn't." My voice is way too flat, but that can't be helped. "I got married instead and gave my last year's tuition to my ex-husband so he could start his new company."

David grimaces. "This sounds like a cautionary tale if ever I've heard one."

I shrug. "It worked out well enough—for him, anyway. But now I have no degree, and no husband, so yeah. Maybe not my best decision. Anyway, when I left for college, my parents told me they were going to pay for my schooling, but that was all the help I would get from them. The ranch and everything else would go to my brother Patrick when they passed away because I was taking my inheritance early."

David frowns. "I know Stanford's expensive, but that hardly seems fair."

"Well, with the time value of money and all that, that was their offer. In any case, when they died, I assumed it would be just as they'd said. I'd take nothing. They had a life insurance policy that Patrick said was in his name, and they left a ranch worth quite a chunk of money as well."

"Okay."

"Only, my friend Abby found—"

"The lawyer—Amanda's sister-in-law? That Abby?"

I nod. "She discovered that Mom and Dad redid their wills, so that whichever was the last to die would leave me half of the estate, in spite of what they'd said about leaving me nothing."

"Because your husband was a loser?" he asked. "Or because they had a change of heart?"

I shrug. "They liked my ex, or at least, they liked him well enough. I think maybe they just decided that it wasn't very fair to leave Patrick every dime just because I'd taken some at the earlier stage."

"That sounds like good news," he says.

"It would be, except that Patrick thought it was bad news. He knew about the will and wasn't going to show it to me. He's claiming Dad wasn't competent at the time it was executed."

David grabs a rolling office chair and pulls it over so he can sit. "I have a story for you—one I've never actually shared before."

A chill runs up my spine. My super hot, super smart, super rich boss is sharing stories with me. Secret stories.

"I have an older sister, and she's brilliant. Much smarter than I am. All she wanted to do was take over the family business, and she was absolutely suited to doing it."

This doesn't sound so bad. Yet. But it is ominous.

"I was about twelve when she graduated from college, ready to go into management and learn what it was all about."

"She's much older, then?"

David nods. "Almost ten years older than me, but she always had time to talk. She took me with her to events like basketball games and carnivals. She was a great sister."

I think back on my time with Patrick. He was only a few years older, and he never took me to a single thing.

"Dad gave her a job at the company, but not a very important one," David says. "And Mom started setting her up on dates. Lots and lots of dates. When she complained that they got in the way of her work, Dad threatened to fire her."

"That sucks."

"It did, yes." David smiles. "When she told him to go ahead and fire her, he did. He told her she could come back when she was ready to be married and not before."

"I don't get it," I say. "It's not the 1950s."

"In Korea, in some ways, it's kind of like that still. It's getting better, but not as quickly as I'd like."

"And?"

"They told her the company wasn't for her. It was for me. They told her that she was supposed to marry someone who would bring something to the table, someone with a family company of their own that aligned in interests with ours. They suggested she might help out with that company if she played her cards right."

"Whoa," I say. "That's downright lousy."

David nods. "That's when I left home to study abroad. Once I got to America, I wrote my parents and told them I would never come back unless my sister, as the CEO of our company, asked me to move back."

"What?"

He shrugs. "They were holding something for me that I didn't even want. Even if I had wanted it, she was older and she wanted it first, and what's more, she'd done the work to deserve it. They held out for almost a year, but eventually they realized that Da Eun and I were not going to budge. They finally gave in."

"But she's not the CEO yet?"

David laughs. "Oh, she is. She has been for years, but I also changed in that time. Now I like America, and I mean to stay. That's why I've taken over management of our US interests."

"Oh," I say. "Well, that's pretty impressive, too."

He shrugs. "That's not my point, though. I guess I'm telling you about that to say that I can't believe your brother is arguing the terms of the will. Wouldn't he be pleased that your parents decided to include you, especially since you're raising your son alone?" He bites his lip. "Did you get into an argument, maybe? Have you tried talking to him about it?"

Ah, poor David. He's such a good guy that he can't even comprehend the reality of my brother. "He feels justified," I say. "He was always promised everything because he stayed home and worked the ranch."

"Would you really take the ranch?"

I shake my head. "The life insurance policy's almost as large as the value of the ranch. He can keep the ranch, the cows, the equipment, the houses, all of it. I'd even be happy giving him some of the proceeds of the life insurance policy. Actually, he did offer to give me part of it." A hundred thousand bucks, anyway. But maybe I should just take him up on it. At least the arguing would be over, and it's more than I expected.

"Have you tried mediation?"

I shake my head. "Not yet, anyway. I do have a great lawyer, at least."

"What's going on today?"

"My dad's doctor is having a clinic day over in Manila," I say. "I'd love to go chat with him—we have a deposition set up in two weeks, and Abby likes to check in beforehand, but she's out of town. She asked me to talk to him instead, if I could."

"Oh, of course. Go ahead."

"Thanks," I say.

"If there's anything else I can do, anything at all, please tell me." He looks like he means it.

As it is, the doctor's locking the door when I arrive. I glance at my watch—it's more than an hour early.

"Hey there," I say. "Are you Dr. Vasut?"

He's wearing cowboy boots and carrying a briefcase. He looks like a strange mix of some kind of farmhand and an office worker. . .wearing a white coat. "And you are?" He glares at me suspiciously.

I wasn't expecting hostility. "I don't have an appointment, and I'm sorry. But I don't need any medical advice either. Actually, you treated my father."

His face shutters and he stomps past me, brushing me off. "I don't have time." He waves his hand through the air. "If you're really upset, find a lawyer."

"But I have a lawyer," I say. "That's the thing. She asked me to talk to you."

Now he's really moving fast. He's nearly to his truck.

"Wait," I say. "We have that deposition in a few weeks, and I'm supposed to find out what you remember."

"A deposition?" He pauses. He turns toward me slowly. "What's this about?"

"I'm filing a claim against my brother," I say. "My dad changed his will, and my brother refuses to acknowledge it."

"So you're not suing me?"

Why on earth would I sue—it hits me then. He's worried I'm upset with how my dad was treated. "Not at all. My father did pass, but it was no one's fault. We were perfectly happy with the care he received."

His shoulders relax and he smiles. "Well, then why don't you buy me a drink? There's got to be a bar around here, right?"

"There aren't exactly a lot of bars around—"

"There's a convenience store then, right?" He tosses his head. "You can buy me something and we can sit under a tree and talk."

In the middle of winter? Has he lost his mind? "Sure," I say. "I guess." I'm glad I brought mittens.

After we sit down with our beers, four more sitting next to us, Dr. Vasut pops his open and downs half of it in one go. "Ah," he sighs. "Now I'm prepared to talk." He looks pointedly at my beer, which I haven't even opened. I have to pick up Aiden soon—Will's mom is taking him until I find something better—and I can't start pounding beers.

"I have a son I need to pick up from school soon," I say.

He snatches the can from my hand. "That's a pity. More for me."

I am not really sure what to do with this guy. I really hope his drinking doesn't come up in the deposition. "Alright. Well, I'll try and be quick." I try to gather my scattered thoughts. "My dad was a big man with a shock of white hair, and he suffered from dementia and—"

"Wait, is your dad old Vern Ellingson?" He slaps his knee.

I nod, mutely.

"Are you his kid that went to Stanford?"

I can hardly believe my ears. "I am, yes."

"If I'm being honest, I thought maybe he was lying about that. Or confused."

"That's why I'm here. See, he executed a will." I explain the situation, and I mention the date. "I'm trying to figure out whether he might have been in his right mind when he executed the will. My brother is arguing that he wasn't."

"Your dad was in late stage dementia, young lady. Do you know what that means?"

All too well, in fact. "I cared for him the last five and a half months of his life."

He sighs. "You do know, then." He's surprisingly serious, all of a sudden. "But he had fairly frequent periods of something we call paradoxical lucidity. I actually submitted his case for a study they're conducting at Johns Hopkins. I would say that at least once a week, his wife reported that he'd have a period of lucidity that often lasted several hours. He'd know who he was, he'd ask about current events, and he'd be concerned about his children, his ranch, and his future."

Mom never told me any of that, but I saw some of it myself—like the day we went to the ER. "Okay."

"Your mom asked me if he was capable of making decisions in those periods of time," he says. "I told her he was. If she updated him on the things that had happened and how people were doing, then yes, he was perfectly capable of expressing to her what he wanted done for himself. I suggested she talk to him about possible funeral arrangements."

I should be delighted right now, but instead I find that I'm utterly drained—depressed, even. "Thank you," I say, standing without thinking. "That's what I needed to know."

"I'll tell them that during the deposition," he says. "Don't let that brother of yours bully you, you hear?"

I turn back toward him. "What do you mean?"

"Vern told me that he wasn't a very good father, and that his son was just like him. When he was in my office and he knew what was going on, he regretted how he treated you. I know he'd want you to fight for your share."

I nod in thanks and dart away, but not before Dr. Vasut sees me bawling like a baby.

❦ 13 ❧

ABIGAIL

Once I recover from my shock, I race out the door—only to be stopped by the not-smiling-proprietor. "You can't leave while wearing this," she says.

"I won't leave," I explain. "I just need to catch him, and I'll be right back in."

"This is a nine thousand dollar dress," she says. "You must remove it before you can exit."

My heart is pounding in my throat, but I do as she says.

The ties in the back I loved when I was putting it on feel like restraints. The delicate lace feels like it's mocking me. And the full skirt that I adored practically clutches at me as I step out of it.

I drag my pants and shirt on and race out the door.

"Your shirt's inside out," Helen rather unhelpfully shouts.

I don't care. I need to find Steve and explain.

But he's already long gone by the time I get outside.

No sign of his car, even. I duck back inside and grab my phone.

"Do you want the dress?" The woman asks, smiling again.

"What?"

"The dress?" She gestures.

Helen's hanging it carefully on the white satin-covered hanger and tucking it into the lace-trimmed bag it came in.

"Seeing as you didn't let me catch the groom, I'm not sure there's even going to be a wedding, lady. I'll get back to you."

Her smile melts again, and this time a frown replaces it. "You do that."

A nine-thousand dollar dress? She should be embarrassed to even have a dress that expensive. I definitely won't be in touch.

"Let's go," I say. I wait by Helen's car *forever* before she finally comes out.

"Where are we going, exactly?"

"To my house," I say.

"Did you forget?" Helen asks. "Your furniture is all gone—loaded into trucks. There's nothing in there anymore."

"Steve knows where it is," I say.

"He can hang out with the dust bunnies if he wants to," Helen says. "At least until my cleaning crew shows up tomorrow to eliminate them."

"I really do appreciate everything you've done for me," I say. "The movers, the cleaning crew, the packers, the wedding dress shopping."

"But you want me to shut up and drive?" She doesn't

even look angry. She's probably too busy silently gloating that we're fighting.

"Yes."

She does. In fact, I'm impressed with how quickly she gets us back to my house, and all without putting it into her GPS. Sometimes I forget she's a certified genius.

There's a car sitting in front of the house, and my heart hammers madly in my chest when I realize that. I leap from the front seat and race toward it—until I realize it's not Steve inside. It's Robert. And I've walked right into the quicksand. Before I can reverse, he notices the movement, turns around in his seat, and beams at me.

He leaps out of his car almost as fast as I just did. "Abby!"

I sigh.

"You're not here to see me," he realizes. Whatever else anyone says about Robert, he's always been quite bright.

"I had a fight with Steve," I blurt out.

I should not have said that.

He looks positively gleeful, but he tamps down on that quickly. "I'm so sorry to hear that. You thought he'd be here?"

I run a hand through my tousled hair. "I didn't know where he'd be. I hoped he'd be here and not at the airport."

"Right," Robert says. "But since he's not. . ."

I whip out my phone and call him again. It goes right to voicemail.

"His phone's turned off?"

"I messed up," I say. "And if he wasn't being such a

big baby, I could explain."

"Since you're not sure where else to go, maybe we could go to dinner?"

Helen's door opens and she steps out. "I would love that. I'm absolutely starving."

Robert's eyes slide sideways. "And you are—oh!" Recognition dawns. "Helen."

My sister gives a little half bow. "Nice to see you again, Robert. It's been a while, but you look just as handsome as ever."

Robert swallows, his Adam's apple bobbing slightly. "Same."

"People don't often call me handsome, but I'll take it." Helen slides back into her seat. "I'll drive."

Having been left not a single opening, I walk back and get into the front seat.

"What do you want to eat?" Robert asks.

"I *want* a burger and fries," Helen says. "But I *should* eat a salad or something."

"There's a Five Guys around the corner," Robert says. "Abby loves it."

I hate that he's answering for me, but it's not like I was about to suggest things myself. I'm too distracted and not at all hungry. While we drive to the red and white checkered burger joint—which Robert's right, I do love—I text Steve. The second he turns on his phone, I want him to know I have been looking for him.

I DON'T KNOW WHAT YOU HEARD, BUT I NEED TO EXPLAIN. PLEASE CALL ME. I'LL COME TO YOU. I TRIED MY OLD HOUSE, BUT YOU WEREN'T THERE. I DON'T KNOW WHERE ELSE TO LOOK. CALL ME.

I wait five minutes and then I text again.

CALL ME, PLEASE.

I force myself to put the phone in my purse and stop looking at it. He's either seen my messages and isn't answering, or he's turned his phone off. Additional messages will only make me look unhinged. And probably guilty, too. I'm not evil for having feelings or being honest about them.

When we walk inside the Five Guys, the smell of burgers and fries washes over me. I love their menu. Unlike most fast food places, it's unchanging. I've loved their burgers for more than a decade, and the only change to their menu was the addition of milkshakes, which was way overdue.

Because their menu is so simple, probably, the staff almost never makes any mistakes. My mouth salivates as I start to order my regular. "Little cheeseburger—"

"With lettuce, pickles, tomatoes, ketchup, and mustard," Robert says.

Helen's eyes widen and she glances at me sideways. "Is that right?"

I swallow and nod. "Thanks."

Robert orders his usual—the exact same as mine, but with mushrooms.

"Salted fries too," I say. "Does anyone else want any? What size should I order?"

"Count me out on fries," Helen says. "I shouldn't even have a burger."

"They have hotdogs," I say.

She shudders.

I don't really blame her for that. "And they have grilled cheese sandwiches."

"I'll just have a chocolate peanut butter shake," she finally says.

As if that's somehow better than eating a burger? I don't bother saying anything. When I try to pay, Robert's faster, practically hitting the lady at the register in the eye with his credit card.

"Thanks," I say.

"It's the least I could do," he says. "Congratulations are in order. I still can't believe you're engaged." His eyes dart down to my hand and freeze when they see the very large, very round diamond on my left hand. He swallows slowly.

Sometimes I react the very same way. After wearing the same, quite modest, wedding band for nearly twenty years, it's strange to be wearing a two and a half carat monster.

"I thought you hated round diamonds," he says. "Didn't you say they're boring?"

It's not hard to push past him and grab a booth. I'm not about to tell him that, unlike Nate, who helped me pick out a ring after we discovered I was pregnant, Steve surprised me. According to the jeweler, no other cut shines and sparkles quite as well, which is why they call the round stones "brilliant" cut. He picked it because no one sparkles quite like me.

"My opinions have changed," I say. "It happens."

"There's a first time for everything," Robert mutters.

Helen chortles.

"Oh, please." I fold my arms and lean back in the booth. "I change my mind all the time. I used to like bundt cakes, and now I don't."

"Burning out on a food because you eat too much of it isn't the same as changing your opinion."

"Oh, I think it is," I say.

"You still do that?"

Robert's eyes lock on Helen's like he's just realized something. "You knew her when she was small."

Helen smiles.

"What other things did she burn out on?"

"Let's see." Helen starts ticking things off on her fingers. "In no particular order: shrimp, Skittles, saltine crackers, chocolate—"

"Whoa! She used to like chocolate?"

Helen pats Robert's hand. "You have so many things to learn."

Thankfully they call our number, and I practically leap to my feet to retrieve the tray. I don't realize how starving I am until the first french fry's in my mouth. I have no idea how Helen's going to survive on just a shake. She's missing out on one of life's greatest joys. I eat the perfectly salty french fries, made with peanut oil, first. That's the key, we discovered. At first we thought maybe they made a deal with the devil, but it turns out it's just that peanut oil was *made* for frying long, skinny potato chunks.

I don't consume my burger right away, in spite of the protests from my belly. I have to wait for the heat of the patty to melt the cheese before the burger will be ready. But finally, it is ready, and I manage to eat the entire thing in two minutes flat. I always mean to savor it, but it never happens. No other place really compares to Five Guys when it comes to burgers.

Robert just finished his burger, too. He has a little speck of ketchup on the corner of his mouth, and a year ago, I'd have pointed it out. Six months ago, I probably would have, too. But not now.

He notices me looking at him, though. "When's the wedding?"

"This spring," I say.

"And you didn't tell me because we aren't working together anymore?" He looks hurt.

I feel bad about not telling him, really I do.

"She didn't tell anyone," Helen says. "Other than me and our parents. Believe me, we're shocked enough for everyone."

"Helen thinks it's too soon," I say. "She thinks I'm dishonoring Nate's memory."

Robert's mouth dangles open.

"I do *not* think that," Helen says. "I just happen to think that she's not ready, and that she's embarrassed to be moving to the middle of nowhere and marrying someone she just met."

"I'd be a major hypocrite to say you shouldn't have feelings for anyone else," Robert says. "But I won't pretend I'm not disappointed." He clears his throat. "Or surprised."

"Wait," Helen says. "Disappointed?" She glances from Robert to me and back again. "Did something *happen* between the two of you?"

Her acting is pretty decent—since I told her he liked me already.

Even so, I am not about to talk about that right here. Not in front of Robert. I could strangle her for practically forcing me to do it. Instead, I shake my head so hard my teeth practically rattle—maybe Robert will get the hint that I don't want to talk about it.

"I told Abby how I felt about her, and that it started way back in law school. I know I missed my window back then, but apparently it doesn't matter. I'm clearly not what she wants, then or now."

This has veered off the main road and right into the

intersection of Awkward and Uncomfortable. "Okay," I say. "Well, the wedding is set for May, and I'll be sure to send you an invite. Helen and I really ought to be looking for a hotel right now."

"I've already booked us one," Helen says. "Separate rooms, of course."

Thank goodness. That's one good thing about Helen —she has boundaries and almost never pretends that we're closer than we are.

"You could stay with me," Robert says. "I promise not to bite."

Helen snorts, and I try to kick her under the table.

"It's fine," I say. "I'd never want to impose like that."

Instead of arguing with me, Robert lets it go. That's how I know he's not going to press me, not about anything. Thank goodness. It allows me to preserve a sliver of our friendship, even after our awkward conversations and his confession and disappointment. We may not be working together anymore, but he's still probably my oldest friend. Even if I won't see him much anymore, I don't want things to be uncomfortable.

The kids still call him Uncle Robert.

We're finally piling back into Helen's rental car when my phone rings. As much as I'd rather not have this conversation while Robert and Helen are listening, there's no chance I'm going to avoid his call.

"Hey," I say.

"Okay." I always forget how low Steve's voice is. "I handled that badly."

I swallow. "I'm so sorry. It was just bad timing."

"I know," he says. "I believe you."

"If you had stuck around—"

"My ex used to talk about me behind my back all the

time," he says. "I can't even tell you the things I heard when I accidentally walked in on a conversation she was having."

I wrack my brain. Did I say anything bad about *him*? I can't think of a single bad thing I *would* say about him. I love him, truly, deep down in the bottom of my heart. Even the parts of me that feel guilty or nervous, those parts still really like him.

"But I've gone over what I heard in my mind a dozen times, and it's nothing like those times with her. You weren't even talking about *me*, you were talking about yourself."

I don't know what to say next, and that never happens to me.

"I'm already at the airport," he says. "I know that's stupid, but I just drove back on autopilot. Can we talk this over when you get back home?"

Home.

He's still referring to Manila as my home. That's something. "I really want to," I say. "I miss home. And you."

"Awww," Helen says. "That's sweet."

"Don't take this the wrong way," Steve says, "but I don't like your sister very much."

"That makes two of us," I say.

"See you tomorrow?"

"Absolutely," I say.

14

AMANDA

Once, when I was a freshman in high school, I stole my teacher's insulated mug. All of us were sure she was drinking vodka in there—she sipped on it like it contained the medicine she needed to recover from a terminal illness. With her glassy stares and her loopy and erratic responses, we did *not* believe her when she said it was lemon tea for her throat. I was pretty proud of myself for swiping it, but I discovered something that day.

Alcohol tastes disgusting—at least, to the uninitiated it certainly does.

I'm not sure if it was vodka or not, but it definitely wasn't tea.

I spat out the entire mouthful of whatever I triumphantly stole, regretting my decision immediately. I regretted it even more when my teacher threatened to send me to detention. All the triumphant jubilation of proving our hunch right evaporated in the face of her disapproval and annoyance.

I can't stop thinking about that experience over and

over as I pick up my bag from baggage claim. What exactly am I imagining will happen when I do reach Eddy? Is he going to be delighted that I've come out to criticize him for drinking? He's been sober for more than twenty years—who am I to tell my grown, adult boyfriend that he can't handle a drink or two? Maybe he can. It's not like I was around back then. I have no idea whether he's really an alcoholic or whether he was just unable to handle things like that when he was a teenager.

Do I really think he'll thank me for coming out and telling him I know what he's been up to? And if he *is* cheating on me as well, am I ready to deal with it? Do I want to break up with the first attractive, talented, smart guy I've dated in my life? What if he just got confused at the scope of what he's doing? Or what if it was an innocent gesture—maybe the woman was falling over or something. Her outfit probably was paired with very unsteady heels.

And maybe he was holding *her* drink!

But I can't get the image of him out of my mind. His arm was slung around another woman, his broad smile was warm and happy, and his hand was cradling a drink that sure looked like a lot of alcoholic beverages. Even when I try to shove the image away, it won't retreat nicely. Whether it's awkward or not, whether I regret coming for years, I am who I am. I couldn't have done any differently than I'm doing right now.

I do feel a little bad for ditching not only my kids, who would probably have been fine, but also Abby's. Should I have called Mandy at least? Why didn't I? Why *don't* I?

The simple answer is that I know she'll give me an

earful. Because I know I shouldn't have just left like I did.

That could be why I can barely sleep in the lousy hotel I manage to find near the airport. The next morning, after spending an embarrassing amount of time to make sure I look my best, I skip breakfast and hail a cab, practicing in my mind exactly how I'll greet Eddy. Sometimes I confront him right away, acting like a screaming fishwife. Other times I play things cool, simmering beneath the surface. But in every scenario, his guilty eyes widen and then drop to the ground.

He always knows he's been caught.

When I finally show up at his producer's studio address, my heart flips over in my chest, my pulse thumping loudly in my ears. Am I really here? Am I ready to do this? Should I really be confronting my boyfriend and asking him about his drinking. . .and that other woman?

I reach the front doors, beautiful glass doors that reach up, up, up, far above my head, and I freeze. The lettering on them is crisp and dark and contrasts perfectly with the sunny weather streaming through the panes. My hand trembles as it touches the heavy metal handle, and then I release it, turn on my heel, and walk back toward the curb.

This is not me.

Amanda doesn't confront people when she's upset. Amanda doesn't march into places and demand explanations. Amanda sneaks and suspects and side-eyes when she's unhappy. She waits and hopes and fears and doubts, but she doesn't accost and accuse.

That's much more of an Abby thing. The last time I tried to channel my inner Abby, I ended up with a bakery I didn't want. Or actually, even more recently than that, I figured I'd give that developer a piece of my mind, and I ended up face-to-face with David Park.

That didn't work out for me at all.

I'm about to turn around and sprint back to the airport when the door swings open, shoved outward by a tiny blonde woman. "Hello? Ma'am?" She can't weigh more than a hundred pounds, and fifteen of that is the nearly-white, bleached blonde hair piled into a carefully constructed messy bun on top of her head. "I just wanted to make sure the door wasn't locked."

I swallow. "Nope. It's not." But now I'm stuck.

"Were you looking for someone?"

I swallow again, even though my mouth is so dry that it's a useless gesture. Besides, even if it wasn't the Sahara in my mouth, it's not like a little extra spit would make my throat suddenly open up or would fill my brain with words that would make this less awkward. But swallowing and hoping inspiration will strike seems to be the only thing I can think to do. *What was I thinking, flying out here?*

"Amanda?" Eddy shoves past the waif at the door and walks out onto the sidewalk next to me. "It's really you!"

"Amanda?" the waif repeats. "Wait, is this your girlfriend, Eddy?"

She knows him. Of course she does. With his Adonis looks, I'm sure every woman who works for his label already knows him.

But unlike all my paranoid scenarios, Eddy doesn't look guilty in the slightest. No, he looks. . .delighted to see me. "I had no idea you were coming!" He keeps coming toward me, barreling my way practically. His hands circle my waist and he spins me in a giant circle, his mouth grinning so wide it looks like it might crack. There are crinkles around his eyes that I love, and his perfect, bright-white teeth are gleaming. "How did you know how badly I've missed you!?" His mouth covers mine before he's even set me down, and his arms pull me even closer, his grip tightening.

I forget why I came. I forget what I'm wearing. I forget what just happened and what time it is. All that exists are his lips against mine, his body pressed just where it should be, wrapped around me, keeping me safe.

Giggling. Snorts. Muttering sounds.

It finally hits me that we're kissing right on the street. I pat on his chest for a moment before he finally releases me. "You can't blame me for being happy to see you," he says.

In that moment, with his eyes drinking me in, I can't imagine how I ever doubted him. "I don't blame you," I whisper.

Catcalls behind us have Eddy rolling his eyes. "Let's go inside." He glances at his watch. "And I'm so sorry, but I'm booked for a solid four hours this morning."

Of course he is. "That's totally fine," I say. "I just wanted to surprise you."

His grin is lopsided. "It's the best surprise of my life." He presses a kiss to my forehead and drags me along behind him. "While I'm recording, Daniela can give you a rundown of things you can go and do. Nice restaurants, the closest beaches, whatever." Eddy pulls out his wallet and hands it to me. "Go shopping. Buy whatever you want, my treat." He grins again, this time at full wattage. "It's all on me. I'm just so happy you're here."

I swat his hand away. "Like I need you to pay."

He sighs. "Why did I know you'd say that?"

"Eddy," a woman calls from behind him.

I peek around his shoulder to see her. She's tall—almost as tall as Eddy—with deep red hair. Her skin is flawless, and her eyes are a startling green. Just like his. They'd make gorgeous children. I hate that I even had the thought—it's not like Eddy has ever said he wants kids—but I won't be having any more, and that woman looks like she easily could. She's got to be ten years younger than me.

"Twelve-thirty," Eddy says, his eyes trained on me. "I'll be out at twelve-thirty on the dot."

I can't help smiling back at him, but the second he disappears, my doubts return. That woman, the blonde, what did he say her name was? Daniela? She knew my name and that Eddy had a girlfriend, but what does that really mean? I continue to spin out for most of the morning.

I'm sitting on a bench in the sun, thinking about how much nicer it is here than back home in Utah. But then, instead of enjoying the sunshine and the perfect weather of California, I circle back to thinking about how much easier it is to take someone on a date here, to stroll arm in arm, and to stare into their eyes. It's not like you have to worry their eyelids will freeze shut or that some cow will need an emergency C-section at any moment.

That's when it hits me: I may not be made for a long distance relationship.

"Amanda?"

I whip around, and there he is again. Eddy. Beaming at me.

If he were a golden retriever, he'd be wagging his tail, that's how happy he looks. It's not the face of a cheater.

"How did you find me?"

"It's the closest beach to the studio." He shrugs. "I spent the first few days here too, every time we got a break." He drops onto the bench next to me and wraps one arm around my shoulders. "I could get used to this weather, that's for sure."

I freeze next to him.

"Of course." He points with his free hand. "A one bedroom in that building is four hundred and nineteen square feet. And it costs almost two million dollars." He smirks. "There's a lot of people who have gotten used to it."

"You're a big rock star now," I say as casually as I can. "That'll be a drop in the bucket for you soon."

He chuckles. "Ah, Amanda. Is that why you came?"

I can barely breathe. Does he realize I came because I suspected he'd found a girlfriend here?

"Were you really worried I'd buy a condo?"

I blink.

"Because I'm not that stupid. I wouldn't drop my entire advance on a down payment for some California condo. Not unless my girlfriend told me to, anyway."

"Which she most definitely is not."

"You don't love the land of silicon. . . everything?"

"Not particularly," I say. "But I do love seeing you." I shift so that I'm leaning against his side.

"Is that really why you came? You just missed me?"

"Of course." I lie so easily, so breezily, that I almost believe it myself. "How did you get out early?"

"I got all my songs done so perfectly that they let me leave half an hour before our time expired."

"So you're an overachiever here, too?"

"I had a pretty decent incentive," he says.

We spend the rest of the day walking in the surf, eating ice cream on benches, and snapping photos with seagulls swooping and waves crashing in the background.

"It's pretty nice that you're not rushing to edit and post these," Eddy says. "Or carefully ensuring that certain products are highlighted."

"Yeah," I say absently. "Or that your face isn't shown."

"I definitely don't miss that." He frowns. "But do you miss it?"

I shrug. "I still post things, for sponsors, even. I just don't feel like I *have* to do it anymore." I like how our hands swing between us as we walk.

"How's it going with Am—Mandy?"

"I can't quite keep it straight either." I sigh. "It's fine, but I can't seem to let it go."

"That she gave Abby the ranch?"

"I'm a terrible person," I say. "I know. It's just that I was never anyone's favorite, not for my entire life."

"You're *my* favorite." Eddy pulls me closer and looks into my eyes. "I mean it."

"Are you sure?" I ask. "You're surrounded by way hotter and way younger women out here."

He stops walking and tilts his head. "Is that why you came? You're worried?"

In spite of my best efforts, my voice hitches up a bit. "No. I just wanted to see your face."

"Amanda."

"Really," I say. "We're fine—I'm fine."

He squeezes my hand and starts walking again.

Crisis averted.

"How long are you here?" he asks.

"I have to go back tomorrow," I say. "I really shouldn't have come, but. . ."

"I'm glad you did." He points. "We should at least go into one store, because I need to get you a dress."

"A dress?" I quirk one eyebrow. "For what?"

"There's a party tonight," he says. "They're releasing our first music video."

"Oh," I say. "Okay."

I let him buy me a dress that costs *way* too much, and it feels nice. That's the only reason I don't curl up into a fetal ball when it's time to leave for the release party.

"I love having you here for this stuff," Eddy says.

"This stuff?"

"I've been forced to go to events at least half the nights I've been here, and going alone is a real drag."

I'll bet plenty of women would have been willing to help out there. I can't help scanning the glitterati for the woman in the photo Helen sent, but I haven't seen her yet. It's not like I'd forget that silhouette or her shining black hair.

Eddy introduces me to everyone without a hint of fear or trepidation. He's either utterly confident no one will spill his secret, or he has no secret to be afraid of—I wish I knew which. I'm introduced to the gorgeous redhead I saw earlier, who turns out to be his manager, and a leggy blonde whose name I've forgotten who does PR. I've been introduced to a dozen other singers and musicians and at least as many tech and industry people.

Still no sign of Miss Booby McDark Hair.

Did Helen photoshop the whole thing? I don't know whether to thank her since it's given me time with Eddy, or curse her for freaking me out. I imagine Abby won't easily forgive me for darting off in the middle of watching our children. But in typical Abby style, as long as no one's injured or maimed, she'll magnanimously let it go eventually, even if it was something she'd never have done in a million years.

Eddy squeezes my arm. "Look." He points.

I follow his directions, my eyes swiveling around and freezing about halfway to the place he pointed as they land on the woman he was canoodling with in the photo. Her hair is just as gorgeous in person. Her eyes, which were not even visible in the photo, are larger than anyone's eyes should be. She looks like an anime cartoon, with gravity-defying bosoms, overlarge eyeballs, and a tiny, full-lipped mouth.

I hate her.

"See?" Confident, gorgeous, talented Eddy sounds nervous for the first time since I arrived.

Did he see her, too?

I finally look where he's pointing, and I realize it's not at a person or a place. It's at a huge screen in the center of the venue. He's pointing because the music video is starting.

I knew that Eddy would be the central focus of the whole thing, but for some reason I thought the other band members would at least be visible. They look like a ghost band, visible only on the edges and in the background. Eddy's walking toward the camera in dark boots and jeans and a deep blue shirt—exactly what he was wearing in the photograph.

And then he's fighting with someone, throwing punches and taking them, too. Wow, they really made him look tough for a pretty boy. Is that a tattoo on his forearm?

I glance sideways.

"It's not real." He smirks and raises his arm to show me it's clear. "The designer, you met him, Kyle? He loves the bad boy look, apparently."

He nailed it, really. With Eddy's gorgeous face, a little bit of bad boy balances things out beautifully. "I wasn't worried."

I am such a liar.

And then, in the chorus, I see her. The woman with the ebony hair. Eddy slings an arm around her, and he's holding a drink. A foamy, golden-toned drink.

"That's not real either," Eddy says. "Trust me— they're very supportive of the fact that I'm in AA."

I'm going to shoot Helen. Right between the eyes. "Please," I say. "I'm the last person you need to tell about how things look on social media or on a video and how different it can be from real life."

If I were Pinocchio, my nose would be three feet long. But at least Eddy doesn't know how crazy I am.

Late that night, after Eddy's asleep, I text Donna. CAN YOU PICK ME UP TOMORROW?

WHAT TIME? Bless her for still being up.

I tell her, and thankfully, she says she can get me. Which means I got to see Eddy, and all is well, and I'm headed back home, with no one the wiser about my little freak out.

Except for Donna, and Helen, and Abby, and everyone else they may have told. I swear, if Helen's not gone when I get back, she's going to wish she was.

Donna can't pick me up. Her text messages roll in one after another when I turn my phone back on.

I'M SO SORRY, BUT I CAN'T PICK YOU UP. DRAMA WITH THE EX.

I KNOW IT'S FLAKY, BUT I'M NOT SURE WHAT TO DO.

I'm the last person who should be calling her flaky. It's going to be one expensive Uber, but it's not like I can fault her. I can't even bring myself to call Abigail. I'm too embarrassed that I ran out on her kids without a backward glance after one stupid text from her aggravating sister.

MAYBE I CAN FIND YOU A RIDE. I'LL SEE WHAT I CAN DO.

It's really my fault. What kind of person asks for favors from a single mom? I mean, honestly, I should've expected it would be too big an imposition for her to pick me up last minute. I only asked her because I know that Mandy and Abby will both be ticked, and I can't face them yet.

Miraculously, my bag wasn't lost on either end. No flights were delayed. I arrive right on time, and I'm tapping in my location and endpoint in the Uber app, bracing myself for the horrifying cost when someone calls my name.

"Amanda!"

My phone nearly slips from my fingers when I look up and meet David Park's eyes. "What are you doing here?"

"Donna asked me if I could give you a ride?" His charming grin is all innocence.

"I hate that you're her boss."

"So I should turn around, then? Just drive back?"

I glance down at my phone and practically gasp as the horrifyingly high fee pops up for my ride. "Uh, well. You are *already* here."

He looks like he knew all along that I'd never turn him down.

"But I insist on paying for your gas."

"I just filled up," he says. "And wouldn't you know it? They were running a promotion, and I was the one thousandth customer. My gas was free."

I roll my eyes.

"It's a ride," he says. "It's not like I'm taking you to a Broadway show and then to dinner at Ai Fiori."

Trust him to name my favorite restaurant in New York. I sigh. "More's the pity."

"Although I would be happy to—"

"Know when to stop," I say.

"I sense that it's time for me to stop," he says.

Before I can even grab it myself, he's swinging my

196

suitcase into the back of his SUV again. His shiny, black SUV that looks like it belongs on the streets of LA more than in the back roads of Wyoming or Utah. "This is a fancy car."

He cringes a bit as he climbs into the driver's seat. "It is? I was going for classy, but down-home."

I laugh. "Then you failed abysmally." I run my hands over the supple leather of the passenger seat, and then across the polished and shining finish on the wooden trim. "I doubt anyone would ever put Range Rover and down-home in the same sentence."

"That's where I went wrong." He sighs. "Well, maybe next time I'm attempting to assimilate with a local population, you can be my consultant."

I can't help smiling. He's not Eddy, but he's not Quasimodo either. "I appreciate you coming to my rescue. Again."

"You're welcome," he says.

"But if you think you're going to swoop in like this over and over and somehow worm your way—"

"I really hope that no one would ever put worm and David Park in the same sentence," he says.

"They wouldn't?" I raise my eyebrows. "Or you *wish* they wouldn't?"

"Ouch," he says. "You sure have that famous New York charm down pat."

"Actually, for a New Yorker, I'm pretty nice."

"Sadly, that's true." He's not laughing, but his eyes are crinkled at the corners.

"Not many people around here understand how kind I *am* compared to the people I've surrounded myself with for the last twenty years."

"You should be graded on a sliding scale," he says.

"I'll be sure to let the people I meet know. 'Amanda's really not that bad—for a New Yorker.'"

I frown.

"Oh, come on. You can smile. Actually, it was good to see you smiling again. The trouble in paradise must all be behind you."

"There was no trouble in—"

"Right," David says. "You didn't fly out there last minute because anything was wrong. I don't know what I was thinking." He shrugs. "Either way, I'm happy to see you smiling. Truly."

Before I can tell him to shove it, my phone rings. It's Eddy. I should have texted him to let him know that I made it.

"Not a word while I'm on the phone." I glare at David with my most serious look. The one that even Maren pays attention to...

He fake zips his lips and tosses the key over his shoulder.

"Hello?"

"Hey," Eddy says. "Donna texted and said she couldn't pick you up. She wanted to know if I had any ideas, and then I didn't hear from you—"

"It's fine." I am going to strangle Donna. "I found a ride, and I'm on my way. Easy flight."

"Oh, good," Eddy says. "I was worried."

What am I going to say when he asks who gave me a ride? My heart begins to race. Surely he'll remember the name David Park, even if I haven't told him that the person building the stupid resort near the Flaming Gorge is the same guy I went on that Bachelorette date with. It's not like I've been on many dates since Eddy and I started dating, so it's a memorable name.

Will he freak out?

"As long as you're alright, I'd better go," he says. "They're ready for me in the sound room."

"Right," I say, mostly relieved. "Of course."

"Did I mention it was great to see you?" He lowers his voice. "Because it was. Please surprise me again soon."

When he hangs up, I'm beaming.

"Yep, trouble in paradise is officially past," David says.

"It's not paradise," I say. "We're just a normal couple—"

"You're an influencer with a jaw-dropping face and a rock star experiencing a bizarre late-in-life revival. When I did a quick search on his name, all the girls were calling him 'hunky.'" He sighs. "Am I missing something? How are you a normal couple?"

"Fine." I shrug. "We're paradise."

"So why didn't you tell him who your ride was?" I hate how smug stupid David Park sounds. "I don't think anyone has told me to keep quiet while they took a phone call since I was a kid."

"He didn't have time," I lie. "I'd have told him if he wasn't in a rush."

"You'd have said, 'Hey, Eddy, the guy who picked me up from the airport was the guy I went on a date with last month'?"

I splutter. "No, but I'd have said your name. I'd have told him you're Donna's new boss and that when Donna had to bail, you filled in."

"Because I like you," David's voice is low. "I filled in because I'm hoping that perfect Eddy will screw up, and then I'll have a chance."

My hands tremble just a bit. "Don't."

"Fine, fine, I'm kidding."

He doesn't bring it up again for the rest of the ride, thankfully. And when he drops me at Amanda Saddler's house, my car is already there, waiting. "Hey." I point. "My car—"

"You gave me the key," he says. "I said I'd have one of my people fill it up and get it home."

"Actually, you said you could leave it at the airport." Why didn't he? I was so flustered I forgot to text and ask him to do just that.

"Even smart people say dumb things occasionally. After thinking about it, I realized I'd only get to see you again if it *wasn't* waiting for you there."

I turn back to him slowly. "Please tell me you didn't make Donna—"

He shakes his head with a smile. "Nope. I actually have more than one employee here, believe it or not."

"Thank you," I say, after I realize I've been a real brat. This man is busy, and I just imposed heavily, and he helped me out big time. "I really mean it."

He drops the keys in my open palm. "It's not like I even had to do anything," he says. "I just did what I said I'd do and—"

"Still. I appreciate it."

I've barely started to walk up the porch steps, dragging my bag behind me—David pulling away slowly—when I hear it. The screen door swings open, and I expect to see my kids' faces.

But it's Amanda Saddler's lined one that peers out. "You're back."

"I am," I say. "Are my kids—"

"Still at Abby's," she says.

"Oh," I say. "I'd better go—"

"Are we okay?" Mandy squints, but I don't feel like it's because the light is already low at four in the afternoon.

"What do you mean?" I ask, like I'm an idiot.

She cocks one eyebrow. "You know what I mean."

"We're fine." I purposely act like she's asking about the business. "In fact, I found some people to help get us through, until we can find more reliable contractors to replace the ones that jerk Mr. Park keeps stealing."

"That's not what—" Mandy straightens. "You found someone? Who?"

"Kevin and Jeff said that they can—"

Mandy's hand tightens on the screen door until her knuckles turn white. She's acting like she's not going to let me back into her house. "Jeff and Kevin? But Abby needs them."

Abby.

First Mandy buys Abby a ranch worth millions for no reason at all. Then our business is flailing, and she's worried about *Abby* again. Why is it always Abby? Why isn't she ever worried about me?

"Abby doesn't own them," I say. "Kevin said things are slow on the ranch during the winter, and he and Jeff would love some extra work. I figure they can help us—"

"As long as it doesn't leave Ethan and Abby in a bind," Mandy says.

"We're kind of in a bind right now," I say.

Mandy waves her hand through the air. "Our properties aren't going anywhere. If it takes us a little longer—"

"Do you think Donna feels that way, waiting to move in to her place? And isn't Abby waiting on an office, too? I mean, you'd think that she would *want* Kevin and Jeff to do extra work, so that she can have a real office and try and build her business here."

Mandy crosses her arms. "What's wrong, Amanda? Just put on your big girl panties and say it."

My big girl *what*?

"You're clearly upset with me."

"I'm tired," I say. "I just flew—"

"You're mad at me and you have been for weeks now."

"I met you first," I blurt out.

I wish I could yank the words back. I sound like an idiot.

Mandy laughs. A great big belly laugh. "You met me first?"

Why is that so funny?

"Did you call me? Am I like shotgun?"

It does sound a little ridiculous when she says it like that. "What I mean is that we were friends first. You and I bonded, or I thought we did."

"And?"

"And you bought a ranch for Abigail, but you didn't do anything for me."

"There it is," Mandy says. "That's your real beef."

"Puns?" I ask. "Really?"

Mandy slaps her knee. "Didn't even mean to—" She sighs. "Look. That gift had nothing to do with you."

"But it should have," I say. "My girls were mentioned in that bequest too, the one you said you were rectifying since Jed wasn't here."

"You didn't lift a single finger to help run that ranch," Mandy says. "And neither did your girls."

"But I was *there*," I say. "I actually was physically there more than Abby's family."

202

"And if I don't give you the prettiest balloon, the largest bouquet of flowers, and the most attention, does it mean that I don't love you more?" She arches one eyebrow imperiously.

"No," I say. But what I mean is *yes*. It feels like she loves Abby more.

"Then what?"

"Just forget it." I turn to leave.

"If you truly don't think that employing Kevin and Jeff is disloyal to your sister-in-law, then by all means, do it. They're fine boys, and I'm sure they'll do great work. But some things matter more than business. It took me years to learn that."

Some people matter more. That's what she means. I don't bother turning around. "Got it."

"Amanda, you need to grow up," Mandy says. "You're far too old to be acting like such a baby. The gifts I give someone are not a meter that shows how much I love them. I give people I care about the things they need or the things they deserve—it's not a contest."

The things they deserve.

Wow. Message received. Abby's deserving of more than I am. I find it rich that the woman who never got up the nerve to tell the man she loved that she liked him is lecturing *me* on growing up.

I'm literally fuming as I stalk through a pile of snow and mud to get to my car. I'm shaking, I'm so angry as I drive over to Abby's. Perfect, stupid Abby, whom everyone loves the most. Perfect Abby, who's been a widow for not even two full years, and already she's engaged again to Mr. Perfection himself. A horse trainer with visible abs who's also a freaking doctor. And a sister who stirs the pot and probably smiles while it boils over.

I do not slam my car into the back of Helen's ridiculously inappropriate-for-this-area sports car. I'm proud of myself for that. Not just because I'd end up taking a huge hit on my insurance, but because it means that I've calmed down. That's good. I definitely don't want to do anything rash.

"Mom!" Maren's standing near the front window and spotted me.

"Mom's here?" Emery's squeal makes me happy. At least someone other than David Park is happy I'm back.

When the door whips open, I expect to see Emery, or perhaps Abby. I brace myself for a scolding I know I deserve.

Only, Abby's not there.

"I wondered when you'd be back." I was not expecting Helen to answer the door. "Abby's meeting with a client." Helen scoffs. "If you can call him that."

"He's a client alright," Whitney says. "His wife died, and he's awful sad."

"His wife died?" In spite of my frustration, that gets my attention. "That is sad."

Helen shrugs. "She was eighty. He's eighty-one. I had a lot more pity for him before he spent forty minutes standing right where you are now, bawling."

It's almost comical, how exasperated she sounds.

"It was pretty annoying," Emery whispers. "I mean, I do feel bad for him, but get it together, dude."

A moment later, the door to the new addition opens and Abby walks out alongside a hunchbacked, white-haired older man who's wearing rumpled slacks and a faded grey polo shirt, his brown work coat still slung over his arm in spite of the way he's approaching the exit and all the freezing cold air.

He is, in fact, still crying.

You could not pay me enough to act as a grief counselor or a lawyer—but doing both? Abby is a saint.

Her eyes light up when she sees me and she waves, but the man is still talking, his arm clutching hers in a Kung Fu grip. I don't even try to interrupt as they shuffle past. I might get drawn in myself, like getting too near a black hole.

"You're back from Houston," I say. "And it looks like everyone is safe."

"No thanks to you." Helen's smirk is the most annoying thing about her. Worse even than her stupid, flashy car and her stylish but uptight clothing.

"I came to apologize to Abby for leaving so abruptly—"

"It was fine," Ethan says. "Mom really didn't need to have anyone else watch the kids. I can do it."

"I know you can," I say. "But you got stuck watching mine too, and I wouldn't have done it—"

"If it weren't a huge emergency," Ethan says. "I know. Mom knows that too, so don't worry. What exactly was wrong?"

I'm not about to tell him what really happened. I doubt he'd think a photo of Eddy with his arm around another woman constitutes just cause for ditching them.

But Helen's smirk reminds me that *she* already knows.

And I have no idea why she hasn't told them. Yet. "Helen, do you have a minute?"

She tosses her head and ducks into Abby's old room like she owns the place. Which only reminds me that I don't own any of it, and Abby does. I grit my teeth and follow her.

"What's up?"

I'm still struggling to process someone like her saying, *What's up?* Like she's a teenager. Or not as stiff as a cardboard cutout. "Er, I'm just trying to get a read on how much longer you'll be here, because—"

"Because you want me out so you can move back in?" She folds her arms and the corner of her mouth turns up in a knowing half-smile. "And you're wondering when I'll tell Abby that you completely abandoned her children and your own without a responsible adult to watch them over a *photo*?"

Okay, I was wrong. Her smirk isn't the worst thing about her. It's her superior attitude and the fact that she's basically blackmailing me. "That's not—"

"Abby told me that you're having trouble at Amanda Saddler's—that's the older woman you're staying with, right?" She leans against Abby's chest of drawers as if nothing in the world is wrong. "She said that you'd like to move back in here."

My mouth's dangling open. I close it.

"The thing is, I was planning to leave. In fact, I'm pretty sure Abby's been counting the days until I fly back home. I do have a big project waiting for me that will make me even richer than I already am." She uncrosses her arms and straightens. "But I already have more money than I could ever spend." Her smile is prac-tically wicked. "What I don't have plenty of is siblings. I only have one sister. So I'm afraid I'm going to have to disappoint you, dear, sweet, moochy Amanda." She steps toward me. "I'm not leaving anytime soon."

I hate her. More than caramels that taste great but pull out a filling. More than slick, invisible patches of ice that form on dark roads. More than hangnails that pull and pull and pull until they bleed all over your favorite blouse.

"If you're staying, we should get something clear." This time, I walk toward her. It brings me a ridiculous amount of joy when she stumbles back against that stupid piece of furniture. She's clearly not used to people fighting back. "Do not ever interfere with my relationship again."

"If you're talking about the photo I sent you of Eddy, I was only trying to help." She tilts her head slightly. "If I were you, I'd rather know the truth."

"The truth," I practically spit, "is that my boyfriend was filming a music video. The truth is that it was all an act, and you probably knew that, or your private investigator is a complete idiot."

"The real truth," Helen says softly, "is that you don't trust your boyfriend at all." The corners of her mouth turn up slightly. "You rushed off the second you got that photo because in your heart of hearts, you know that things with him won't last. You're waiting for the other shoe to drop, and your reaction to that photo was a lot more important than the photo itself."

I was wrong before.

I hate her more than I hate calories being listed on all snack foods. I hate her more than I hate that feeling when I wake up and realize I forgot to charge my phone. I hate her more than I hate people who suggest splitting the check evenly when we chose dramatically differently priced meals.

I hate her more than twenty-somethings who talk about how old they are.

"Helen, you're Abby's sister and I love Abby, so I'm not going to slap you or stomp on your foot or do any of the other nasty things I want to do right now, but I will say this. You don't have a boyfriend or a husband or any sort of happy significant other, so I'd prefer if you didn't offer me advice on mine."

I pivot and walk out as quickly as I can.

I practically trample Maren. "Mom, can we please go? I'm tired, and I have a project I need to finish."

The world has stopped spinning. Time has frozen.

Maren is asking to do schoolwork.

"Uh, okay."

Poor Abby's still stuck talking to the old guy when Emery and Maren and I finally head out. She waves again, but he either doesn't notice or he can't see well enough to know she's waving to a person who's leaving. Even odds on which.

I make a gesture for a phone with one hand and she nods wearily. Great. Now I'm just one more person in a line of people whom she has to deal with. I wonder if she's dreading calling me. I wonder whether she's thinking what a loser I am, and what a drain I've been on her life. She's probably mad at me for leaving, but can't bring herself to actually bawl me out for it.

Well, she may be annoyed with me for leaving her kids alone for a few nights, but everything turned out fine, just like I knew it would. Her perfect life, her perfect kids, her perfect fiancé, and her perfect wedding are still all intact. And her stupidly rich sister, who apparently has more money than she could ever spend, are all just fine, too.

It does occur to me to wonder, if Helen's that rich, why Abby needed Amanda Saddler to buy her a ranch. Why didn't she just call her sister? Are her parents loaded too? Is *Abby*? She never talks about money. For all I know, she's rich as Croesus as well.

I'm about to climb into my car when I notice Jeff and Kevin pulling into the drive. I should at least confirm that I'm not leaving Abby in the lurch. Then when Mandy asks, I can confidently say that I'm not being disloyal to her favorite person in the entire world.

"Hey, Kev," I say.

He trots across the drive until he's standing beside me. "Amanda. Everything okay?"

"I just wanted to make sure—we talked before about you and Jeff doing some work for me, but are you positive that it won't interfere with ranch stuff?"

"Actually." Kevin glances at Jeff.

Jeff looks at his shoes.

"We heard about a ranch that's going to be up for sale," Kevin says. "It's a town over and it's not in great shape, but we could afford it, maybe."

I blink. "You could afford—"

"If we make enough money," Kevin says. "The seller's going to keep running it for another year or two, but once we have enough for a down payment, they'll give us first crack at it."

"Oh."

"Now that we're not under contract to this place," Kevin says, "we could actually consider it."

And if I don't snatch them up, someone else will. David Park would take them in a heartbeat. They're smart, they're hard-working, they're skilled, and they're connected. "Well, I'd love to talk to you about a longer-term contract."

"We won't be cheap," Jeff says. "I mean, prices in the area have gone up lately."

I grimace. "I'm aware."

"We don't want to leave Abby and Ethan in a bind," Kevin says.

"But," Jeff says.

"She has Steve," I say.

And her rich sister. She can hire whomever she wants. Bring people over from the next town. Even if they have to pay far above average rates, they have a paid-off ranch. How bad can it be?

"Come over in the morning and we'll talk terms." It would be such a relief to have them for a year or even possibly two. "I'm excited to work with you."

16

DONNA

"Your son was already picked up." As usual, Alice's lipstick has hopped off her lips and is now smeared across her front teeth. But for once, I barely notice. Because I've just heard the words that every parent who has gone through a divorce dreads.

"Excuse me?"

The secretary at the elementary school blinks. "Was he not supposed to pick Aiden up today?"

My hands begin to tremble. A pounding starts at the base of my skull, like a toddler that's protesting bedtime by slamming his hand against the side of the crib.

"Donna? He just left, not even five minutes ago."

He's close. It takes time to make sure Aiden's buckled in. I don't even bother saying another word. I pivot on my heel and sprint out the door. My purse whams against my shoulder blade, and my feet slide in the slippery patches of snow littered all over the sidewalk.

But by the time I reach the parking lot, there's no

sign of Charlie or his Mercedes, if that's even what he still drives. Although, it's laughable, the thought that he might drive all the way out here. Regardless, there aren't even any cars he might rent in the parking lot. Everyone here drives work trucks or beat-up old cars like mine.

I've always hated the thought of Aiden going to his parents' house for a long weekend, but seeing as Charlie almost never comes to get him and usually passes on his weekends, I hadn't even considered that he might *steal* him on one of mine.

The rational part of my brain begins to turn over, like a car in the far-too-cold-early-morning air, and I realize that maybe it's a mix-up. Maybe Charles thought that this was his weekend. I dial his number and hit talk, suppressing my shudder at the prospect of having to interact with him.

He doesn't answer.

I have two choices here. I can call Steve's uncle, whom I've known almost my entire life, and if I'm hysterical enough, I'm positive he'll pursue Charlie himself. Or I can call my former in-laws and freak out, call Charles and freak out, and generally make it clear this was unacceptable and will never be repeated. Of course, letting them get away with something like this is a big problem—and that's assuming they're planning to return him on Sunday as usual. But pulling Charles over in front of Aiden and having him forcibly removed by the Sheriff seems equally bad.

But that scenario is bad for my *son*. That's the real difference. Not throwing a legal or law enforcement fit right now might make my life harder in the future, but my other option causes distress to my child, and I'd do anything to avoid that.

Which is why, instead of calling the Sheriff, I decide to go after him myself, in my crummy, beat-up old car. Luckily, stupid Charles had to stop for gas—and I catch him just down the road at one of only two gas stations in town. I'm pretty proud of myself for staying calm, for being prudent, and for not escalating this mess that Charles made.

"Mom!" Aiden waves at me from the back seat. "I don't have my suitcase." He points at his school backpack.

Charlie spins around, his eyes wide, his hand wrenching the gasoline dispenser from the car and shoving it back into the holder.

So much for the possibility of it being a mix-up.

I drop my voice to a whisper. "I didn't call the Sheriff, for Aiden's sake. Don't make me regret that."

"Mom's charity is hosting a Big Brothers Big Sisters of America dinner," Charles says. "She needs him there, and he'll have a great time. She was really upset when I told her I forgot to clear this weekend."

I pull my phone out of my pocket and wave it at him. "That's what this is for," I say. "You have to call me about this stuff. You did forget to clear it, and this is my weekend."

"But I've missed a bunch of weekends." Charles scowls. "And you'd have said no."

"At least you'd have discovered my answer before driving all the way out here," I say. "But—"

"Come on," he says. "It's always better to ask forgiveness than permission with you. You're like the great destroyer of all joy."

I wish that having the conversation turn in this

direction was a shock to me. "You cannot just take him," I say. "It's kidnapping."

"He's *my* kid," he shouts. "You have got to be—"

"We have a court order," I say. "And the very best thing you can do for me, and believe me when I say this, is violate that order like you tried to do today. You have no idea how fast my lawyer will get me sole custody, Charles. And that would make my life unbelievably easier."

"Your lawyer? The one who looks like Miss America—"

I shake my head. "Nope. You can keep your underhanded comments and jabs to yourself. I don't have to deal with them anymore. That's the beauty of divorce." I step a bit closer. "But one thing I won't budge on is this. You hand Aiden over to me *right this moment*, or I'll call the Sheriff, file a report, and submit your violation to the court and ask for a modification to the order." I fold my arms under my chest and assume my most adamant glare.

Charles rolls his eyes. "See? This is why I didn't call. It's not like I'm kidnapping him. I just want him to spend the weekend with his grandma. Is that really so bad?"

"It's not the activity you're taking him to, it's the way you're doing it," I say.

"*It's not the words you're saying, it's how you're saying them,*" he mimics. "Are you serious right now? Do you really think you're Doctor Phil?"

"Let him go." I hate the note of pleading in my tone.

"Or what? You'll really sic the cops on me? Does this backwater province really even have a Sheriff?" Charles leans against his car, obscuring Aiden's view of my face.

But when I twist my head to look at him, my adorable son looks distressed. In spite of my whispers, Charlie's yelling, so there's no way he can't tell we're fighting, which is exactly what I was trying to avoid by not calling the authorities. "I'll call Abby and the Sheriff so fast your head will spin—"

"And I'll tell them you said it was fine," he says. "And that you changed your mind because you got mad at me." I forgot how unbelievably smug he is when he starts to lie. "Who do you think they'll believe? My parents are impeccable members of the community and they'll back me up. They *heard* me talk to you about it on the phone last week."

Lying is practically breathing to him, and I have no doubt he'll do it. "So help me, if you don't—"

Charles straightens immediately, his eyes widening. "What's—"

"Let the kid go," a deep voice says from behind me.

I spin around faster than a teenager doing donuts on an icy parking lot.

Will doesn't look angry. He doesn't even look annoyed. He looks resigned and determined, and that might be scarier. "Right now." His huge boots make a crunching sound when he steps up next to me, so close to Charles he could reach across and pick him up by his shoulders.

Charles has always been good-looking in a business-slimy kind of way. He dresses well. He presents himself as impressively as possible, and most people are intimidated by him. But he's not a large guy, and he's never taken the time to build any kind of impressive physical strength. He's far too lazy for that.

Will could crush him with one blow.

It looks like Charlie knows it. "Who are you?"

"I'm a friend of Donna's, and when Alice told me—"

"Who the he—" Charles glances back at Aiden, as if just remembering he can probably hear us. "Who the heck is Alice?"

"Alice is the secretary at the kids' school. When Donna shot out of there like a bat out of. . .heck—" Will's eyes sparkle. "She called me. She thought I might be keen to lend a hand, and my hotel's right there." He points. "She knew I'd be close."

It's interesting he said *his* hotel. It's always been *his mom's* hotel when we've talked in the past. I suppose something about having another alpha male around brings out the fight in Will.

"Well, I'll have a few choice words for Alice when—"

Will steps closer—so close he can probably tell what kind of gum Charles is chewing. "You'll say nothing that isn't polite to Alice, and you'll release Donna's sweet son to her immediately." Will's voice drops to a deep, raspy whisper. "Or you'll book an appointment with a plastic surgeon to deal with the way I rearrange your face."

All the blood drains from Charlie's skin, but he's not quite ready to give up. "Have you ever heard of the word assault? If you so much as lay one finger on me, I promise, my lawyer will make sure that—"

"A jury of my peers," Will says with a smile. "That's who *my lawyer* would ensure made the decision about whether my actions were warranted. And I'd reckon they would think coming to Donna's aid in this set of circumstances was just fine." Will holds up his right hand and spreads his fingers right in front of Charles' face. "How about five fingers? I'll lay them just like this." He reaches for Charles.

And my cowardly ex shrieks like a little girl in a *Tom and Jerry* cartoon and squirms to the side. "Fine." He shakes his head. "You two are the reason I did what I did. Totally unreasonable. Thugs." He circles the car, his confidence growing as he moves out of proximity to Will.

"So you'll let him go?" Will asks.

"Yes," Charles says. "If you absolutely insist, then yes."

Will opens the passenger side door and slides inside, leaving the door hanging open.

"What are you doing?" Charles whips his door open and lowers his head to glare at Will.

"I'd hate to risk you hopping inside and locking your door—then we really would have to call the Sheriff, and my old pal Winston—he's a state trooper. Things could get. . .unpleasant."

"Aiden," Charles says. "Your mom says you can't come visit Grandma this weekend. She's being a real bi—"

Will clears his throat. "Your mom has—"

"Your mother can speak for herself." I open Aiden's door and wave him out. He grabs his backpack and hops out next to me. I gesture for him to walk toward the tree and he listens. "You two hold tight here for a moment. Can you do that?"

Will's grin is practically wicked.

Charles looks like a dog whose home has been stolen right out from under him. He can't decide whether to get into his car—sitting right by the awful and discon-certing Will, or whether to keep hovering beside his own rental. Seeing him this displaced feels very, very good to me.

But that's not what matters right now. I trot over to where Aiden's putting his backpack straps over his shoulders and crouch down in front of him. "Your dad and I had a misunderstanding. He has an event for your grandma that he wanted to take you to, but he didn't clear it with me first. Did he tell you about it?"

Aiden nods, his eyes nervous. I hate that my son is nervous.

"Were you excited to go?"

"I don't have a bag," he says. "And Dad's toothpaste is spicy."

"Minty," I correct without thinking.

"I don't like it," he says.

"But if you had your toothpaste and your stuff?" I raise my eyebrows. "Would you want to go?"

He glances back at Charles and then looks toward me, but he won't meet my eyes.

I lift his chin with my right hand. "There's no wrong answer, baby. If you want to go, just tell me."

"I don't want to make you sad."

I shake my head. "You won't. I promise."

His whisper is so much softer than mine was that there should be another word for it. "I do."

I force a smile. "Then you'll go, okay? Let's just go back by the hotel and grab your stuff." And now I'll be subjected to a rant by Charles about how I'm still in a hotel. I grit my teeth and walk back to the car. "So, I asked Aiden and he'd like to go." I fold my arms. "But he hates your toothpaste and he wants his things. So you'll wait here while I go grab his stuff."

Charles' mouth dangles open in a satisfying way. "What?"

"I said if you wait here, I'll go grab his things."

He straightens, his slender shoulders squaring. "You're letting him come? Really?"

"I asked *him*," I say. "Which is exactly what I would have done had you called like you should have."

Charles' eyes narrow and he looks at Will. "Oh. I get it."

Will stands up and leans against the top of the car so he's looking Charles in the eye. "What do you get?"

"You two must have plans this weekend, so you're happy to—"

"You're lucky we have a car between us." Will's drawl is slow, but brimming with hostility. "I'd break your jaw for that if it wouldn't upset Donna, and I'm not sure I'd have had time to think it through without the buffer."

Charles stumbles back a step, bumping into the gas pump.

"Will has nothing to do with this," I say. "I always want what's best for *Aiden*, and he wants to see your parents. It's that simple."

Even though I tell him it's not necessary, Will sticks around while I drive around the corner and park behind the hotel to grab Aiden's stuff. I take the chance to call my boss and ask him if one of our people can grab Amanda. He says he'll take care of it, thankfully. Because of stupid Charles, I'm way behind schedule. I fill a bag for Aiden quickly, but I can't exactly show up two minutes later, or Charles will immediately notice I'm still at the hotel. After a little bit of cooling my heels, I return, suitcase in hand.

Even with my forced delay, Charles looks around in alarm.

"That was fast. Where are you living now?"

"It's getting late," I say. "I'm guessing you have a flight to catch?"

"We do," he says. "Yes."

Even with Fridays off, flying out Thursday and back Sunday makes for a long weekend for a little guy. I press a kiss to Aiden's forehead and load him into the SUV myself. "Be good," I say.

Aiden just nods.

And then he's gone, and I'm sobbing. Will's arms wrap around me slowly, and I collapse against his chest. "I hate it," I say. "Even when there isn't all this drama, letting him go with *them* tears me up inside."

"I know." His huge hand cups the back of my head and pats me gently. "I know."

I'm not sure what I would have done if Will hadn't shown up, but it's really not fair of me to rely on him for stuff like this. "I'm sorry." That thought pulls me out of it. "I'll be fine. It was stupidly emotional—I can't believe he tried to just take him."

"He's a real piece of work."

I can't argue with that. "I picked a spectacularly awful husband." I shake my head. "What a disaster."

"At least you're done with him now."

"That's the thing." I sigh and start to separate myself from Will, in spite of how nice it feels to be held. "Thanks to Aiden, whom I love like nothing else in the world, I'll never be done."

Will releases me and shrugs. "One bullet and a shovel and—"

I shove his shoulder. "Don't even joke about that."

He rolls his eyes. "I'd never kill him. The worse he is, the more chances I have to show you how helpful I can be."

"I really appreciate you showing up," I say, "but Alice should *not* have called you."

"She was worried," he says. "She felt like it was her fault."

"I'm the one who listed Charles as one of the people who can pick him up," I say. "Since he lives in California, it never occurred to me that he'd just show up here."

"Now you know," he says.

"I sure do." I fish my keys out of my pocket. "Well."

"Do you need to go somewhere?" Will asks. "I'd be happy to buy you dinner."

"I shouldn't," I say.

"Why not?" Will asks. "Is there some long-standing rule that you never go on dates with men on Thursday nights?"

I cringe a little at the word *date*. "I've been single for like five minutes," I say.

"Closer to five *months*," he says. "But I get your point."

"It's just that—"

"No need for you to explain," he says. "I actually meant to come find you today either way." He shoves his hands into his pockets, and I don't blame him. It's getting colder by the minute, and the wind has picked up, too.

"Find me? Why?"

"I talked to Mom about the day she witnessed that will. She doesn't really know Greg—she rented him a room for a few months, though. He's not from here, and she couldn't remember why he was in town. She's also not sure why your parents asked him to be a witness. She didn't even know he knew them until that day."

That's not promising. I've never heard of Greg James in my life.

"But I've been asking around, and I have a lead. Mom thought she saw him talking with old Moses a few times, and I tracked him down and asked. Pete Moses said Greg James knew your mom because he had been doing some kind of work out at her place."

"Work? What kind of work?"

"That's what I wanted to know," Will says. "But Pete didn't remember. He said Greg did part-time work for him when he got sick, but only on his days off and only while he happened to be in town. He had a full time job that brought him here."

Pete Moses runs the local soil-testing lab. He'll check soil for farmers to tell them what fertilizer to use. He checks for ranchers to make sure their cows and horses are getting balanced diets and makes recommendations for hay and supplements. "So he's a chemist or something?"

"Pete said he was a geologist and he remembered one word, though it took him some time to recall it."

"What word?" Will's really milking this.

"Kinross, and get this. I looked it up, and there's a gold mining company called Kinross."

A what? Why on earth would Mom work with someone from a gold mining company? "I don't understand."

"Me either," Will says. "But I put in a call to Kinross and talked to a handful of people over there. I explained we're looking for someone named Greg James and that he knew your mother. They said they'd look into it and get back to me, and I guess we'll just have to wait."

A pang of guilt hits me. Will Earl is good-looking,

clearly competent, smarter than I realized, and hard-working. And for some reason, he's decided to help me —he's acting like he *likes* me.

He's way too good for me on paper, and it's only a matter of time before he realizes that. But setting that aside, there's no way I'd ever date a rancher. I left to begin with because I didn't want a life like Mom had. And that means that I shouldn't really rely on him, and I certainly can't let him spend all his free time doing things I could be doing for myself.

"I really appreciate what you've been doing—"

"For what it's worth, I also talked to my mom about your parents. She said that your dad was completely in his right mind the day he executed that will. He was sharp, and alert, and he didn't seem confused for a moment."

Which any judge will immediately discount as soon as Patrick explains I've been living with Mrs. Earl at her hotel and that her son and I are good friends. "Thanks." I bite my lip. "I just hope that if we find—no, when we find—this Greg James, he says the same thing."

"He will," he says. "I know it."

I wish I had his confidence. "Thanks again for your help," I say. "But I have some work to finish up."

"When you have more time, I'd love to hear about the new job."

Oh, man, I'm going to have to force some kind of awkward conversation with him. I just don't have the emotional space to deal with it right now. "For sure." I duck into my car and drive away—to his mother's hotel. Ugh.

But Will's not a creep. He doesn't follow me. He climbs into his enormous dually truck and drives the other direction. I breathe a sigh of relief. . .until I check my phone and notice I have a barrage of text messages from Charles.

The first one says, AIDEE SAYS YOU'RE STILL STAYING IN A HOTEL.

At least it looks like he's using voice-to-text. Aidee? Shouldn't his phone at least recognize his own kid's name?

HOW DO YOU THINK THE COURT WILL FEEL ABOUT YOU KEEPING OUR SON IN A HOTEL?

I'm itching to reply to that one. The court cares that he's fed, clean, and educated. I doubt they care much whether it's in a hotel room or a house.

The last one says, THE COURT VALUES STABILITY AND A SENSE OF SECURITY.

That's rich, coming from the person who literally just abducted him. I grab my bag and lug it into the hotel room. I wasn't lying about bringing my work home with me. David kindly lets me take off early to pick up Aiden when my sitter falls through, but I always make sure to finish up my workday from home.

I've just started going through the proposals when another message comes through. IF YOU CAN'T FIND A SUITABLE HOME IN THE NEXT TWO WEEKS, I'M GOING TO PETITION THE COURT FOR A CHANGE OF CIRCUMCISION.

I'm going to give him the benefit of the doubt and assume he meant to text a change of circumstance. He really shouldn't text while agitated, or while driving. But he's clearly upset, even though I just cut him a tremendous amount of slack. Trust Charles to repay my largesse with petulance.

I FOUND US A HOUSE. WE MOVE IN SOON.
I'LL SEND A PHOTO SHORTLY.

We may be a ways out from our move-in date, but at least the front looks picture perfect. I carefully stack the proposals again and begrudgingly head back out to my car. If I wait much longer, thanks to the lousy early sunset during the winter, I won't be able to get a photo. My poor old car chokes twice, but finally turns over again.

One more thing for the old to-do list: get my car checked out and tuned up so I don't get stranded again like I did with the stupid tire fiasco. Although, that worked out great for me. Will's cast-off tires are way nicer than the ones I had and he wouldn't even let me pay him for them.

A twinge of guilt hits me, but I shove it down. He insisted.

I'm pulling up in front of the precious little house when I notice a familiar vehicle in the driveway. It's certainly not a truck Charles is likely to forget either—the solid black dually that I saw not fifteen minutes ago. What on earth is Will Earl doing at this house? Before I muster up the courage to ask, I walk across the way to the driveway. If I take a photo from here, I should be able to capture the secure, solid, cute sense of this place without showing the truck that will make Charles flip out.

It takes a few photos before I manage it, but I'm happy with how they turn out. The shutters really pop in the low afternoon light, and the mountains in the distant background really frame it up in a picturesque way. I select the best one and send it to Charles. Let him chew on that.

I consider hopping in my car and skedaddling before Will even notices I'm here, but then my curiosity would eat me alive. I force my feet to move toward the front door, one miserable step at a time. But when I hear a loud banging, I race the rest of the way. What could possibly be—

The windows are cracked open, and once I get closer, I can smell why. The distinctive smell of mildew has mixed with the overwhelming scent of urine. It seems like the house was in worse shape than I realized. Someone has ripped up all the flooring, and Will's shoveling it into a wheelbarrow.

I'm at a loss on what the banging might be until—oh, there it is. Will has reached a spot where the floors weren't totally separated from the subfloor, and he pulls out a chisel and whams it with a sledgehammer until it comes off clean. Then he goes back to shoveling.

Even in the chilly winter air, sweat beads across his forehead. He wipes it away without a thought on the sleeve of his canvas coat and goes right back to shoveling. I should say something, but I'm not sure what to say.

Will helps out around the hotel regularly. He repairs things. He checks people in, covering for his mom when she's busy. He runs the ranch, or so she tells me. His dad checked out entirely a few years ago. I saw his auto shop —with a half dozen cars in varying stages of restoration. Some were up on blocks, some were almost fully restored. He shows up whenever I need him, and that's been far too often lately.

And now he's here, doing contract work for Amanda Saddler, apparently? Does he ever sleep? And why didn't he tell me he's working on the house? Why didn't

Amanda? When I asked her about progress, she told me they were running into trouble even finding contractors and then started ranting about my new boss. I was worried *nothing* had been done, but as I inch closer quietly, I can see that the floor demolition isn't even all of it. The electrical fixtures are down, and it looks like they've taken the kitchen cabinets out, though I can't see the entire kitchen from this angle.

If I circle around to the left and peek around the tree, I'll be able to see the far side of the kitchen and—

Will swears loudly.

It startles me, and I shriek and look around wildly for any sign of trouble.

"What are you doing here?" He's glaring at *me,* as if *I'm* the trouble.

"I—well, the thing is. . ." I'm not sure it's wise to explain that Charles is threatening me. Will was antagonistic enough before, and today's stunt was practically Charles' best behavior. I decide the best defense is a good offense. I straighten my shoulders and think, What Would Abby Do? It helps me inject my tone with a strong note of authority that I don't really feel. "What are *you* doing here?"

Will drops the shovel to the ground and leans against the handle. "I'm working."

I can see that, obviously. Now I feel idiotic. "But why?"

"Why?" He glances around like that's also obvious.

"I mean, why are *you* the one doing it? You don't work for Amanda Saddler, at least, not as far as I know."

Will looks like he bit into a sour plum. "I don't, no."

"Then why—"

"I didn't want to make you uncomfortable," he says,

227

"but Amanda's having trouble finding people right now and this project isn't at the top of the list."

"I heard."

"I also know that you're tired of being in a hotel. You looked so delighted when you saw the outside of this place and so disappointed when we walked inside."

Oh, no. Please, please tell me he's not here working, for free, to fix up a house Aiden and I will be renting. "Will."

He holds out his hand, and I can't help noticing how grimy it is. Somehow that makes it worse. "Don't fuss at me, okay?"

My mouth closes with a click.

"I know you aren't ready to date, and I'm terribly afraid that even if you were, you'd want nothing to do with me, just like back in high school."

His words make no sense. "In high school?"

"When I asked you to homecoming and you said no?"

Homecoming? It's like he's speaking Latin. "You never asked me to homecoming."

Will frowns. "I did."

"You did not. I'd remember that. I most certainly never told you no."

Will Earl was way, way, *way* cooler than I was during high school. He was like a brawny god, and he also happened to be the quarterback of the football team *and* the best basketball player at our school. We may never have been very competitive at sports, but within our small ecosystem, Will had much more notoriety for his sports talent than I did for being smart.

I would not have turned him down.

"The point is that I didn't tell you I was working

here because I didn't want you to know. I told Amanda I'd do it for free, to help her out for helping you out."

And I'm taking charity from him. Again. Without even knowing it. "I have a job," I say. "I'm making better money than I was before. I can afford to—"

"I want to do it," he says. "And this is the slow season for ranching, so I have time."

I want to argue with him, but he's right. I need this house, and the thought of no progress at all being made on it while I languish in a hotel room with Aiden is depressing. I can't keep relying on Will like I have been, but maybe since he's already started this project, I can stop right *after* he does this one last favor for me.

As I drive home, leaving Will to do disgusting work for no pay, I worry that I may be, in my own way, nearly as bad as Charlie. It's not a comforting thought.

17

ABIGAIL

Before moving out to live on a ranch, I took showers for granted.

They were nothing special—just water, hopefully heated water, that I used in combination with soap and shampoo to make sure I stayed clean. But now it seems like every day brings a new task that leaves me covered with ick.

When Steve said, "See you tomorrow," I kind of assumed that our flight back would be simple, and when I landed, I'd breeze my way over to his house. He'd swing me up in his arms, and we'd talk until things between us were fine again.

But life hits me like a two-by-four to the teeth the second we land.

"Mom!" Ethan sounds a little frantic when I pick up his phone call.

"Is everything alright?"

"So Aunt Amanda shot out here like a bat out of—"

"Language."

"There are bats in language? Is that even a place?" Ethan asks.

Apparently no matter how stressed he is, there's time to make jokes. "Something was wrong?"

"Aunt Amanda bailed, and that left me in charge, and no one freaking listens to me, little brats. It's really not my fault."

"Ethan, slow down and tell me what's going on."

"Whitney was moving the horses through into the barn, but she forgot to shut the gate. The cows got out, and—"

"Oh, no," I say. "Are they lost? Are any of them injured?"

"It took me almost two hours, but I got that disaster cleaned up," Ethan says.

Now I'm confused. "Okay."

"But in the process, we had another issue."

"What?"

"I just want to say that, for the record, it's not my fault."

"Right. Whitney's fault. Got it."

"When we were herding the cows back, some of them might have sort of run over some equipment we didn't realize was even there in the front, er, well, the side yard."

"Get to the point, Ethan." My head is starting to pound.

"It busted the sprinklers on the septic, which is bad, because apparently the tank was pretty full, and it warmed up here, which is nice, but the snow melting apparently fills the tanks more? Or that's what it says online."

"The septic has *sprinklers*?"

"They come on sometimes in that side yard by the barn."

I never noticed them.

"Apparently when it's overfull, it makes kind of a yucky smell."

"A smell that might have been covered by, say, the gazillion cows and all their poop over there?"

"Basically, we need to get the septic pumped. I already replaced the sprinklers, but it was too late."

"Too late?" I feel pretty ill at this point, and Helen is looking at me from the driver's seat like I've just told her I'm pregnant with Vin Diesel's baby.

"We didn't know anything was wrong until it backed up into the house."

I'm assuming that *it* is the septic sludge. Which means *poop* and other nasty fluids backed up into my house. My recently remodeled house.

Helen drops me off a block from the ranch. "I don't do poop." She doesn't budge, and I'm certainly not going to argue with her about it in the street. Luckily, Mandy has a septic guy who owes her a favor, so he rushes out to pump it for us. Unfortunately, it takes Ethan and me all day to clean up the mess. Around the time the kids are due home from school, I finally finish and take a shower.

It's the best shower of my entire life.

The second I step out of my room, clean and not stinking anymore, I prepare myself to welcome my kids home and then rush over to Steve's. I'm sure he's wondering what I'm up to, but I was not about to call him earlier, or he'd have insisted on coming to clean and scrub filth. After our last interaction, I think he's had about enough stinky misery to deal with from my end.

But instead of hugging my babies and preparing to talk to my fiancé, I'm waylaid. Again. There's a strange man waiting in my living room. He's small and so old that his back is a little bit bent. His hair is white, and he's wearing a heavy burlap work coat that almost everyone around here seems to have.

My kids are all sitting in the room, watching him. Helen must have gotten a text from Ethan saying the mess was cleaned up, because I notice that she's sitting in the front room as well, looking even more awkward than my kids. Instead of offering to take his coat or get him something to drink, Gabe's pelting the poor man with questions.

"What's your name?"

"Fred Eugene."

"How old are you?"

"Eighty-one."

Sheesh.

"Why are you here?"

I'm about to intervene, but before I can, the man bursts into tears, apparently because of something to do with Gabe's fairly obvious question.

"Sir?"

At the sound of an adult voice, he startles and stands up, brushing away the tears running down his softly wrinkled face. His dark brown eyes remind me of one of our sweetest cows—Mabel. "I'm sorry for coming here, to your home, but I wasn't sure what to do." He wrings his hands. "I asked around in town and they said you don't have an office yet."

An office? "Are you looking for a lawyer?"

He nods slowly.

"Okay," I say. "You're in the right place." I wave at the kiddos. "You guys can go."

They scatter like fleas on a dog that's being dipped, running right up the nose, before they realize they have nowhere to go. Ethan shoots out the door, but the others, Whitney and Gabe and Izzy, all wind up milling around in the kitchen.

"How about if Mr. Fred and I relocate to the game room and you guys can make dinner and watch a movie?"

Every single head bobs up and down enthusiastically, including Helen's.

"Sir." I point toward the hallway, and it takes a moment, but he finally understands that I'm directing him. Once we reach the game room, I close the door tightly, and gesture for one of the chairs on the back wall. "Please, sit. Tell me what's wrong." So I can get back to my regularly scheduled mess of a life.

"What's wrong?" His voice wobbles. "My wife died." He bursts into tears again.

Good heavens—that hits me like a kick to the shins. Suddenly, I'm tearing up as well. "I can certainly relate. My husband Nate passed away almost two years ago, now."

The man's mouth drops open. "But I heared you was marrying the horse doc."

I swallow. "I am, yes. You heard right." Apparently Helen was correct—people do judge. I'm going to cut him some slack, since he just lost his wife. "We met last summer, a little over a year after Nate passed."

The man frowns. "Well, I know I need a lawyer, but I don't know why or for what."

I sit down and spend the next few minutes explaining the probate laws to him. It's surprisingly hard to get the average person to focus long enough to make sense of how intestacy works, much less the process we'll need to follow with a will. He doesn't seem to be sure whether there is a will, or whether we'll be using intestacy laws.

"Do I really got to go through probate?" he asks. "I mean, we hardly got anything. A house that's little. Two cars and my pension."

"It really is the quickest way," I say. "And the inventory we'll need to put together for the probate will be exactly what you need for your estate tax return."

"Estate what?"

Oh, this poor guy. "Don't worry. I'll do everything that needs to be done." It takes a lot more talking but finally he's reassured enough to let me lead him out the door.

I'm a little shocked to see that Amanda's here—didn't she leave? But by the time we get outside, Mr. Fred Eugene has thought of a billion more questions. Amanda comes and I wave, but he doesn't take the hint. She hovers a bit, talks to Kevin and Jeff, even, and then she finally leaves while I'm still stuck answering his questions and comforting him. It takes us forever to work through everything in between so many bouts of sobbing that I almost start to get annoyed.

Yes, my husband died.

Yes, it wrecked me.

But I didn't slide along in a puddle of gloom, ruining the lives of everyone with whom I came into contact. I'm beginning to think Mr. Fred Eugene needs a good kick in the pants.

"Well, I best be getting on home," he finally says.

I don't shout for joy. I'm proud of that. "Probably a

good idea." I hope he doesn't catch a cold and follow his wife out. Although, he might prefer that, given the way he's been carrying on. "I'll be in touch."

The second he's gone, I shoot inside where Izzy has already made dinner. "Mom! You're finally back."

We're all taking our first bites after saying grace when my phone rings. I have no intention of answering it—unless it's Steve. When I check the screen, it's not. It's my other law client, Gillian. My pro bono client. I don't answer, but moments later, she texts me.

SOS!!! CALL RIGHT NOW.

For goodness' sake. I shovel a little food into my mouth—missing lunch while I was elbow deep in mucking out my house didn't add to my patience—and excuse myself.

"I thought you could work less now," Whitney says. "Why are you working more?"

Kids don't get it. "I have been working less," I say. "But I just came home from a trip and—"

"Ease up," Ethan says. "You of all people shouldn't hassle Mom. She spent all day long cleaning up the crap that you—"

I pick up my hand and he cuts off. "I'll be back in a minute. In the meantime, I'd like all of you to tell each of your siblings two things you love about them."

"I love this game," Gabe says.

That makes one of them. Everyone else is groaning.

"But Mom, your two things are always the best ones," Gabe says. "And if you're not here—"

"I'll share mine when I get back."

Turns out, Gillian's version of SOS and mine aren't quite the same. The IRS assigned her informal review date, and she wanted to talk about what that meant. The good news is that it was quick—the bad news is that my kids are all done eating by the time I return. I'm working my way into the kitchen to help Whitney with dishes when my phone rings *again*.

This time, it's Donna. "Hello?" In spite of my best efforts, a clear note of frustration is present.

"Is this a bad time?" Donna asks.

"I have four kids." I sigh. "It's always a bad time."

She laughs. "I only have one, but I can relate."

"Is everything okay? Did you get ahold of that physician?"

"I did." Donna relays some of what he said—all good news as far as I can tell—and then inexplicably starts sobbing. I swear, it's like the day of unfettered weeping today.

"What's wrong?" I don't really want to know, because I'm a bad person. But I don't *want* to be a bad person, so I make myself repeat it with a little more sincerity. "Donna? What's going on?"

"First, I lost my job." She hiccups.

"But you found a new one, right?"

"Yes, but I'm still in a hotel. And stupid Charlie says I have a week before he files for a modification. And Patrick flumbubber. . ." At this point I can no longer make out any of the words she's saying.

"Flumbubber?" I echo. "Donna, I am so sorry. Listen, we will sort through all of this, I swear."

"But you can't fix it!" she wails.

Oh, dear. "I find that when you make a list and then address each issue one at a time, things become much more manageable."

"Can you just be my spirit animal?"

"Donna, I spent eight hours today scrubbing human

237

feces off the floors and floorboards of my house. I doubt you really want to channel your inner Abigail right now."

That grabs her attention. "Abby! Why didn't you call me?"

Because unlike everyone else I know, I deal with my crap myself. But I don't say that. "I had it under control," I say. "But now, let's make your list."

Once she calms down a little, the list isn't that bad. She has a missing witness, a brother we already knew was an unbelievable jerk, and no house to mollify her ex, but one in the works, at least.

"First, on the Charles issue, don't worry. No court would even grant a modification this close to the initial hearing because the father isn't satisfied with the four walls, bathroom, and bed you're providing for your child. He's healthy, he's well, and he's going to school every day. So set that aside. I suspect most of his vitriol stems from his feelings of inadequacy following his run-in with Will, but if it continues or worsens, a sharply written letter from me should curb his plans. If that doesn't work, even most idiotic lawyers will tell him that's not enough. I'd say go ahead and let him waste his money."

"Really?"

"Absolutely," I say. "Now, on to the issue of the witness."

"Will's actually looking into it, so I'm hoping to hear something soon."

"Okay, well, if we don't find him quickly, let me know. I have some excellent contacts that do great digging, so that, combined with his name and the reference to whatever Kinross is, should be enough to track him down."

"Thank you."

"It's literally my job," I say.

"But what magic can you work about the house?"

"Correct me if I'm wrong," I say, "but I think you're already *working* the magic you need." I can't quite keep the innuendo out of my voice.

"What?" She sounds uncomfortable now.

"Didn't you say *Will* was already working on the house?"

"Abigail!"

"What?" I sigh. "If I've learned anything since Nate died, it's to let people who want to do nice things do them."

"I can't encourage him," she says.

"Why the heck not?" I make another list. "He's hot. He's kind. He's a good person. *And he likes you.* What's wrong with letting an old friend lend a very capable hand?"

"I don't like him," she says. "I like my boss."

"Your boss?" I nearly choke. "The guy who liked Amanda? The one from her Bachelorette thing?"

The silence is rather telling.

"Look, can I call you back tomorrow? I just got back, and maybe we should get lunch or something. It sounds like I'm missing some context information."

"Good idea," she says. "Let's do that."

And I'm finally off the phone and can head over to Steve's place to talk. Finally. I hate the weird place we left things, and it's been making me uneasy for more than twenty-four hours, now.

I kiss Gabe on the forehead and check his teeth. I hug Whitney and Izzy. I give Ethan a list of tasks, and I'm walking out the door when I pull up short. Because Kevin and Jeff are standing on the front porch, looking nervous and itchy. Kevin's pinching the brim of his worn cowboy hat in his hands over and over. Jeff's scuffing his boot against the same spot on the floorboards of the porch as if he thinks there's something stuck that should be removed.

Only the spot looks just fine.

"Hey guys." I don't groan. I don't shout. I don't gnash my teeth. "Is something wrong?"

"Well." Kevin frowns.

"Oh, no," I say, panicking. "Please tell me the septic didn't back up into your—"

Jeff waves his hands at me. "Nothing like that, no. Our septic's different and it's fine."

I sigh. "Thank goodness. I cannot handle any more garbage today."

Kevin scrunches his nose and looks at the ground.

Jeff inhales and then his words all tumble out in a jumble. "The thing is, we got this great chance and we had to take it."

"Excuse me?" I have no idea what's going on.

"Amanda needs people to work on her remodels, and that jerk over in Dutch John is taking all her people," Kevin says. "She's desperate, and we don't have a contract with you, and the one we had with Jed is void now, so we decided to help her out."

"Oh." His words finally register. "You're leaving." That's why they're so nervous.

Kevin swallows, his Adam's apple bobbing. "Yes, ma'am."

He has never called me ma'am in his life.

"Sorry to leave you in the lurch," Jeff says. "But we got some friends we could refer you to, and you can call us whenever you have questions or need a hand."

A two-by-four to the mouth might have been slow

playing my day today. Returning home feels a bit more like a sledgehammer to the nose. "Of course," I say. "I appreciate all the help you've already given us."

I ought to hunt down Ethan and give him the news. He's the one it affects more than anyone else, but I can't bring myself to do it. I just can't. It's too much in one day, and I need to see Steve like I need to breathe. What do I need to say to make them go away?

"Okay, well, I guess we'll head back to the house."

Whoa, what are they going to do about that? It's a perk of this job. I guess that's a question for another day. "Alright. Thanks for telling me right away. And send me the information on the people you think might be looking for work." Though with this scrambling going on for contractors, I'm guessing these people are either going to be really pricey or not very competent.

I can't worry about that right now.

Once they've turned around, I resume my path toward my car. But again, two steps from my car, someone calls my name.

"What now?" I spin around, my eyes flashing, my hands clenching the keys.

"Are you alright?" Helen looks genuinely concerned. "Today felt like a documentary on Animal Planet, only you were a gazelle and your friends were a pack of lions."

It felt a little like that, too. "It's kind of my job, though," I defend. "My friends and other random people, they all come to me to fix their problems, and some days that feels more exhausting than others."

Helen's boots crunch on the crusted patches of snow as she walks toward me, slowly. "Do you know what your issue always was?"

I don't think I have the patience to have someone else bite a chunk out of me today. "Helen—"

"It's also your greatest strength."

Well now I can't beg off. She's dangled that like a carrot in front of me—the promise of a compliment from the never-positive-about-anything Helen. "What?"

"I think an outside observer would say that you lost pretty much every argument we ever had growing up— not just between you and me, but ones with you and Dad, you and Mom, you name it. You always lost. You went on to become a very successful attorney, so why didn't you ever win while you were at home?"

I was wrong. There's no compliment coming. She duped me again. "I need to go," I say. "You can criticize me when I get back."

"Because every single person in our family is a taker. Uncle Carl. Mom. Dad. Me. But not you. You're a giver, Abs. You give and give and give, and right now, you've surrounded yourself with a whole pack of takers. Leaving home was the best thing you could ever have done for yourself—not staying nearby at Stanford. Not continuing to attempt to get Mom and Dad's approval. You quit the game, and that's how you won. But I'm worried you're signing up for another unbeatable scenario."

"Steve's not a taker," I say. "And that's where I'm going. That man has given and given and given to everyone in his life, including his scummy ex-wife and his newly-discovered daughter." As I say the words, I realize how true they are. He has been patient with me. He has helped and guided and supported me at every step. Our only hiccups have been me dealing with my past, and Steve having to split his focus in too many directions. "I have to go."

This time, I ignore her protests and her naysaying and her predictions, and I climb into my car and drive away. When I pull into Steve's driveway, I realize that I didn't even take the time to tell him I was coming. I haven't checked in with him all day. I have no idea if he's even going to be home. I don't know whether he'll be happy to see me or whether I'm walking into a fight.

But the second my car pulls up in front of his house, the front door swings open and Steve trots out. "Abby!"

His smile is as broad as his shoulders, and that's saying something. Even though it's cold, he didn't take the time to grab a coat. He must have seen my car and run for the door. His long-sleeved blue shirt clings to his pecs and lean abs. His eyes match it perfectly. He's not beautiful like Eddy, but he's rugged and he's sharp, and he's brilliant.

And he's mine.

It's the first time I've thought that about a person since. . .well, since Nate died. Nate had been mine for so long that I didn't think I'd ever really claim another person.

Popular culture tells us that it's wrong to say a person *belongs to you*. They're people. You can't own them.

But when you love someone and they love you back, it does feel like you belong to each other. Owning something is nice because it gives you a sense of security. It gives you a sense of peace in the face of the perilous unknown lurking around the corner of literally every second. I haven't felt much security or peace since Nate's cancer diagnosis.

And sometimes it feels like every single day brings yet another sledgehammer to the face. Today has certainly brought more than its fair share of hits. But

Steve's like a security blanket for me. He is there for me, and I'm here for him. He'll smile at me at the end of the day, no matter how long, and he'll work with me on repairing the sledgehammer damage.

I am not alone.

Something about that thought makes tears well up in my eyes. One of them rolls down my cheek as I climb out of the car, and poor, devilishly handsome, barefoot Steve races toward me as soon as he sees it.

"What's wrong?" His arms wrap around my waist and drag me to him. Even if the snow has melted, his feet must be freezing from the intermittent icy patches on the pavement. There's no way the salt scattered on the ground doesn't hurt, but he pays no attention to any of it. Because Helen's wrong.

I'm not surrounded by takers. My kids give. My fiancé gives. I'm not a bottomless well that's never filled. I'm surrounded by people who help me, too. Today was a long day, but I'm in a good place.

As I'm having those thoughts, Steve's arms shift. His hands slide, and his fingers splay, and suddenly, I'm shifting and lifting and floating. He bumps the door with his hip, slamming it shut. And then he carries me across the entryway into his house. "It was freezing out there. You can tell me more about who I need to kill now that we're inside."

I swat his shoulder. "You're a doctor. You took an oath to do no harm."

"I'm pretty sure that's not the only thing that should keep me from killing someone." He drops his voice to a whisper, the scruff from his face brushing my cheek, and the soft heat of his breath fanning over my mouth. "But as a doctor, I could do it quickly, efficiently, and leave no trace."

A shiver runs up my spine. I know he's kidding, but it's still unbelievably hot that he'd even imply that he'd do that for me. He walks into the family room, still carrying me like I weigh nothing. I most certainly do not weigh nothing, but feeling that way is. . .nice. It's almost like I'm living a fantasy. Not many women my age get to do this—experience love again. Meet a brilliant, hard-working guy who loves kids and has a six-pack. Be carried up steps into a house and set down gently on a sofa.

The same man brushes his hand against the curve of my jaw and presses his fingers against my trembling bottom lip. Without having endured great sorrow in my life, I wouldn't be here either. If I could do it over again, I'd spare Nate's life. And since it was outside of my hands, I refuse to regret living fully.

"I love you," I say simply. "And I'm sorry."

"I adore you," Steve whispers. "And I was the one at fault, not you. You were just honest about how you feel, and I've always told you that was fine. I've always said I was okay with it."

"It doesn't mean it won't ever hurt you," I whisper.

He stares into my eyes like he's studying for an exam. "I dream of you, you know. Every night. I think of you constantly when I'm awake. The last twenty-four hours, after I ran off like a moron, were absolutely horrible." He presses a kiss against my temple and then another against my forehead. "You were right to let me stew in it for a bit, but please forgive me."

"I wasn't letting you stew," I say, "I swear. Today has been a mess."

His brow furrows. "What's wrong? I can help. Why didn't you call?"

I shake my head and smooth his brow with two fingers. "The only help I need is for you to forgive me." I stare right back into his eyes, and something inside me swoons. My heart flutters and stutters. My hand lifts up to cup his jaw, reveling in its square shape and its bristly feel. "Somehow, even after having the most miserable day I've had in a long time, I knew it would be safe to come here."

"I'll always be safe," he promises. "And after we're married, you won't need to come here anymore—you'll already be here."

The idea of living with Steve shorts my brain— somehow even though I'd agreed to marry him, I hadn't thought about living with him. I spent a few days here when the kids were sick. He took care of all of us, and he did it generously. I felt safe, and I wasn't alone, and that in and of itself was like emotional porn for me.

But his words sink in, and something hits me.

"Wait, here?"

His head dips, his lips finally covering mine. "Mm."

I'm almost lost to his smell, his feel, and his taste. It's a good place to be lost. He shifts me a bit, making room for himself beside me, and I'm glad, not for the first time, that his couch is wide—roomy enough for two. But that's like a kick to the shins again. The kick I needed to escape the magic amnesia of being kissed by him.

Here.

I'll already be here, he said. At *his* house. But I just got the Birch Creek Ranch back. And I can't very well leave Ethan there to manage an entire ranch alone. He's an adult, yes, but he's not *really* an adult.

It's hard, but I pull back from Steve.

When something in his chest rumbles and he shifts to move toward me, I press one hand against the smooth, narrow divide between his pecs. That's almost my undoing. The man has a seriously beautiful torso.

I shake my head. "You said 'here.'"

He grunts.

"Steve."

He blinks and shifts. "I did. Whatever I said, though, I'm sorry. I didn't mean it."

I laugh. "Steve!"

"What?" He smiles. "You can't blame me for losing all sense around my fiancée, can you?"

I don't blame him, but as much as I want to sink back into that oblivion, I won't be able to. Not until we've worked this out. "Do you really think we'll all move here after the wedding?"

"Well." Steve runs his hand through his hair absently. "Not Ethan, probably. That's one of the reasons he needed the truck, obviously."

"Right before I came here, as the culmination of the crap things that happened to me today, Kevin and Jeff informed me that Amanda hired them out from under our nose to go to work for her full time."

Steve sits up straighter. "She can't do that. They signed a contract for a year. You have until May at least."

I shake my head ruefully. "They did, but that agreement wasn't made with us. And when the ranch sold, their obligation ended."

He swears under his breath. "I'm sorry."

"I can't leave the ranch," I say. "I can't leave Ethan alone."

"It's five minutes away, though," Steve says. "He wouldn't really be *alone*, alone."

"Steve." I put a hand on his arm, my fingers curling around his taut muscle. "Come on."

"I have animals, Abby. I know you want to help Ethan, but—"

"He's the reason I'm here," I say, "and we have barns and sheds and plenty of space on the ranch for all your animals."

His laugh isn't mirthful. "Those are not barns. They're. . ." He trails off, clearly unsure what to call our barns that aren't up to his standards, other than a barn, I guess.

"I know it's a step down for you," I say. "But compromises must be made."

"By compromises, you mean I have to abandon my perfect set up and go live at crazy old Jed's house." He huffs. "You don't even like the house."

"But the cows on property have to be watched. We can't just ditch them, and I won't leave Ethan alone. I feel like you're not listening."

"You're overprotective, and I usually don't mind," he says. "But Ethan's eighteen and he's a mature eighteen. He might even *want* to live—"

"You think he'll want to be abandoned? The kid whose dad died less than two years ago will want to run a ranch all alone in a place he's never been with no one he loves or knows on the property with him? What if he's injured? What if he gets kicked by a cow, or—"

"Abby, we can find more ranch hands, obviously."

I twist around and shove to my feet. "I can't do this right now."

"Do what?" Steve stands up too. "Talk to me."

"Fight," I say simply. "I don't have the energy to fight tonight."

Coming here was supposed to heal me. It was supposed to recharge me. Steve was supposed to be my safe place, my comfort, and my support. Now it feels like the same sledgehammer from earlier today just knocked that support out at the knees.

"Abby, I don't want to fight either." He reaches for me, but I dart out of his grasp.

"No," I say. "You can't touch me. That's not fair."

His eyes light up. "It's not fair?"

"I have children, Steve. You know that. You always have."

"But they come first," he says. "Not me, the kids."

My nostrils flare, and I fume. "I was a mother before I met you."

"And you'll be a mother long after I'm gone. Is that it?"

I can't believe he's jealous of my kids.

"Did you even consider moving here for a moment? Or will it always be Abby's way or the highway?"

I pivot on my heel and walk out. I wasn't kidding—no emotional space for arguing, not right now. I worry that he'll chase me out, but I shouldn't have. Steve is always there when I have a problem, but he's never been one to hound me. He simply stands in the doorway, a troubled look on his face, while I walk out to my car and drive away.

18

AMANDA

The kids' bus has barely rolled past our house, and I haven't even had a cup of coffee when Abby knocks on my front door. Er, Mandy's front door. Either way, I'm totally unprepared. Showing up on someone else's front porch is *not* something I'd ever have done, but it is a pretty classic Abby move. She always confronts things head on.

Perhaps I should've been expecting her.

"Good morning," I say lamely.

She presses her lips together. "You ditched my kids after telling Helen you'd watch over things, and then you snaked Jeff and Kevin without even telling me about it."

"No small talk," I say. "Okay."

"Did you really want to chat about how the snow has melted?" she asks. "I thought you might have something else to say to me, something more substantial."

"I hope Steve's ready for this." I gesture at her. "You're a real treat."

Abby's fists tighten into hard balls and I recall, belatedly, that she does a lot of kickboxing. I take a step back to give her a moment to think before acting.

"I'm not going to hit you." She scowls. "No matter how badly you need a good lashing, I think we've missed the window where something like that might help."

I'm floored. In all the years I've known her, I've never seen Abby attack like this. I might even be proud of her, if I weren't the person on the receiving end. "Maybe I do need a spanking," I admit.

"How about this instead?" She leans toward me, rocking forward onto the balls of her feet. "No matter when Helen leaves, you're not welcome in my house."

"Helen?" My voice is horribly shrill. "Your sister's the actual devil. Did you know she sent me a photo of Eddy? It's her fault I left, so you really ought to be shouting at her."

"That's why you left? Because of a *photo* sent to you by someone you barely know?" Abby looks floored.

"Eddy had his arm around some woman and a drink in his hand." Did Helen really not tell her anything?

Her nostrils flare and her eyes spark. "I assumed you at least had a pressing matter—sick parents or a friend in dire need. I thought the only way you'd abandon not only *my* kids, but *yours*, was for something life-threatening. Are you really that deficient a mother?"

Did she really just call me *deficient*? "My kids are just fine," I say. "In fact, when I got back, Maren asked to head to our house right away so she could get to work on a school project."

"Really?" Abby folds her arms. "For what class? Did you watch her do it when you got home? Or maybe even help her with it?"

I throw my hands up in the air. "Does it matter?"

251

"She lied to you," Abby says. "And you're too oblivious to even notice. She wanted to leave because she'd lied to Izzy, and she had picked on Whitney and Emery, which resulted in Whitney and Emery fighting, and subsequently, Whitney ran away from home, which inadvertently let the cows out, and that ended with busted septic sprinklers, and then a septic tank that backed up into my house." Her lips press together and she glares. "How much of that did you know? Or did you possibly not even question the bizarre statement from your non-school interested daughter about wanting to go home to work on a school assignment?"

"You weren't there either." I put my hands on my hips. I'm sick and tired of her always being the goddess of everything. She can't possibly be positive that things went down just like that. "Maren's doing way better, and for all we know, one of your perfect children caused all those problems." It's not super likely, but it *could* be true.

"Look, Helen meddles," Abby says. "I'll give you that. She's terrible about it, and it's a frustration I've dealt with for decades. If you'd called me about it, or if you'd called Eddy before abruptly racing off to California, which I'm assuming is where you went, maybe I wouldn't have had to spend all day up to my elbows in—you know what? It doesn't matter, and clearly you don't care. Luckily I've raised my children well, and they took care of each other as well as they could. They also took care of *your* children, which none of us received so much as a thank you for. And at the end of the day, no one was injured, so it could have been far worse."

"Even if they had been, you've got Steve right there to take care of it."

"Do I?"

What's she saying?

Her lips twist. "Figure out your living situation on your own, Amanda, but I'm not shocked you're not getting along with Mandy. And don't be surprised when no one else wants someone like you around, either. The only person who can fix that is the one having issues with everyone else."

She's marching back to her car so fast that I barely have time to process the sting of her words before she's closing the door and slamming her car into reverse.

"Still planning to move out?" Mandy asks behind me. "Because I have a really spacious tent I'd be willing to rent to you. Course, I mean to charge you double the market rate."

I close the door and turn around. Mandy's leaning against the wall, her arms crossed and her eyes glittering.

"And what's the market rate on a tent rental?" I know my snark isn't helping, but it just slips out, like a wounded animal snarling. Does she really need to pile on? Clearly she just heard what Abigail said to me.

"You just couldn't help yourself, huh?" Mandy shakes her head. "I warned you that taking Kevin and Jeff was a bad idea."

"She barely even mentioned that. And they need the money that they'll earn while working for us." I lift my chin. "I'm helping them, so Abby can be as upset as she'd like, but I'm not the villain here, and—"

"If my neighbor and I both need a new fence along our shared property line," Mandy says, "I can simply put up whatever I want, however I want to do it, and send them a bill for half. Or I can contact them before doing anything and ask them what they'd like to do. After we agreed on the best way to solve the problem, ting the cost. Which do you think is more likely to result in their actually paying me for half of that fence?"

"Obviously talking to the neighbor is the right answer." I'm not a moron.

"Often it's not about what's done, but it's about how you go about doing it."

I roll my eyes. "I'm not stupid."

She snorts. "All evidence to the contrary."

"What's with everyone today?"

She holds up one finger and shakes it at me. "When parents discipline their children, they don't do it because they hate them. They do it because they *love* them, Amanda. You think I'm being rude, and you think Abby attacked you just now. I can tell by the flush in your skin and by the set of your jaw. You have your metaphorical dukes up, ready to defend yourself. If you'd drop your guard, you might realize that you've been attacking everyone around you, and we're about done letting you maul us."

"Me?" I splutter. "I'm not attacking anyone. I'm simply dealing with the issues that arise in my life in the most expeditious way. No one accused Donna of betraying us when she took the job working for that awful David Park."

"Donna lost her job thanks to her brother," Mandy says. "You really think these situations are the same?"

"I think you're so busy being on Abby's side that you don't even bother stepping back to consider if what I did was really that terrible. It's not like I blackmailed them. They're big boys, and they chose to come work for us. If it hadn't been for David Park and his stupid retreat, we wouldn't need them. It's multifactorial, and no one seems to even consider that."

"Do you know that Abby didn't even mention Jeff and Kevin more than once? You're fixated on that, because it's the only part of the last few days that you've got any kind of justification for, even though we both know it's not why you hired them. You did it because you felt guilty, or because you were ticked, or because you're really just that selfish, and I'm not sure which is the worst."

"Why are you talking about them, then?" I ask. "You're the one who's fixated."

"That fence analogy was because instead of abandoning the kids to go haring off over a photo, you should have called me. Or Abby. Or Donna. Or Eddy. Literally *anyone* instead of just bolting. The fact that there's more than one epic lack of judgment that shows your total selfishness is impressive, really."

It feels like she slapped me. She barely knows me—and she knows my kids even less than Abby does. "You should close your mouth right now. None of this is any of your business."

"Your problem, Amanda Brooks, is that you're a coward," Mandy says. "You're afraid to discipline Maren. You're afraid to apologize to Abby. You're terrified that Eddy might leave you. That's why you rushed out there because of a single photo. Your fear's going to wreck the life you've begun to create for yourself if you can't get over it."

"That's rich," I say. "The woman who didn't tell her neighbor she liked him for sixty plus years is lecturing me on fear."

She flinches. "It's people who have suffered trauma

themselves that can most easily recognize it in others," Mandy says. "I wish I'd had someone to shake me before it was too late."

"I should be thanking you, then?" I ask. "For shaking me?"

"Oh, I know you won't," Mandy says. "But you should. Just like you should've gotten on your knees and begged for forgiveness from that loyal, hard-working, brilliant sister-in-law of yours. You wronged her not once, but twice, and instead of apologizing, you mocked her without having any idea what's going on in her life— or your own either, apparently."

What's going on in her life? I pause for a moment. Is something happening with Abby?

Mandy shakes her head. "A school project."

Anger flares again. She thinks it's *funny* that I trusted my daughter? If she were a mother, she'd understand that's what mothers do. They back up their kids. Even though I'm ticked, I keep circling back around to what she said. "Is something going on with Abby?"

"She just left her job," Mandy says.

I roll my eyes. "So did I."

"And you have a better job working with me," she says. "What does Abby have?"

I hadn't thought about that, really. "She's a lawyer."

"Without any clients in a strange place where she knows no one. Do you think she's making the same money, now? Or even anything close?"

"You just gave her a ranch," I say. "You think she's stressed over money?"

"I don't know," Mandy says. "Planning a wedding's stressful too, and as you pointed out, her sister's not easy to deal with. Did it occur to you that the same Helen who sent you that disturbing photo might be causing her distress too?"

"But it's *her* sister."

"And you're her sister-in-law, are you not?"

I'm about done with dickering back and forth. "I've got a meeting with Kevin this morning," I say. "We're going over the property priority and our labor needs. Are you coming to that, or will you be too busy criticizing me to provide helpful input?"

"I can't deal with you right now, either," Mandy says. "I'll be happy to attend meetings with you again, but not until after you've apologized to Abby."

"Are you really making our partnership contingent on my doing whatever you say I have to do in my private life?"

Mandy purses her lips. "Abigail Brooks is our legal counsel. I can't have a partner who isn't able to work with her. There. Is that a business-enough reason for you?"

"Why did I think this job would be any different from working for Lololime? You're dictating to me the same way they did."

Mandy sucks air through her teeth and then shoves away from the wall. "You're like a wild animal that's been injured, thrashing around with no thought or understanding, so I'm going to walk away. I'm doing this because I love you, so you try and remember that." She pushes past me and out the door.

The second she leaves, I sink to the floor, my feet shooting straight out in front of me.

Abby's mad because I screwed her. I ditched her kids and mine, all because I didn't trust Eddy. Then when I got back, instead of apologizing to her, I got upset at everything she had in her life from her rich family, to her fiancé, to her angelic kids, and I stole her ranch hands to. . .what? Why did I do that? I mean, we do need them, and they are happy to be making more money. But isn't that exactly what I'm upset at David Park for doing to me? Stealing locals to meet his ends without concern for what other projects are going on locally?

But I'm wrong to be upset in the David Park situation—it's business, and he's not actually wronging me. Doesn't that mean that Abby's wrong here?

Often it's not about what's done, but it's about how you go about doing it.

Stupid Mandy and her condescending platitudes. Curse her for always being right. She and Abby should start a club and then they can vote to kick me out. I start to cry then, tears rolling down my face.

"Mom?"

I nearly jump out of my skin.

"Maren?" I swipe at my tears and shove myself upright. "What are you doing here? I saw the bus leave more than half an hour ago."

She gulps.

"How did you miss it?" I'm sure Abby would have been up before her kids, making a nutritious breakfast and then combing their hair and tying their shoes each morning, but mine have always gotten themselves ready. It's better for them—they learn self-sufficiency.

But they also scare the bejeebers out of me sometimes.

"I was up too late working on a project and slept through my alarm."

Working on a project? Alarm bells go off in my head.

"Emery usually wakes you up, right? Doesn't she typically chuck pillows at you until you get up?"

"Yeah," Maren says. "Just not this morning, I guess."

I wonder whether Emery's mad at her and really didn't try to wake her, or whether Maren's just lying. "What's this big project you've been working on?"

Maren plops down at the kitchen table and rests her head against her hand.

"Is everything okay?"

Her head whips around. "Why? Did you want to give me some awful advice so I can have no friends just like you?"

My eyes widen and adrenaline floods my body. I leap to my feet. "How dare you speak to me that way?"

Maren rolls her eyes. "Where do you think I learned it?"

My hand's itching to slap her. "You don't talk to Aunt Abby like that."

"She never talks to me like that, either." She shrugs and grabs the loose Pop Tart in its silvery package on the corner of the table. Emery's such a lightweight she can't even finish a package of Pop Tarts.

"Do not throw that kind of thing back at me," I say. "You can't blame me for your behavior."

Maren shoves a chunk of pink frosted Pop Tart in her mouth, speaking as she chews. "Alright, Mom. Dazzle me with your advice, you know, amazing suggestions from the woman who was just sobbing on the floor alone."

She's attacking me to divert attention from her problem. Focus on the issue. "What's wrong?"

"I had a group project," she says. "We had to take

political themes and put them to a rap and make a music video."

See? There really was a school project.

"This girl in my group, Avery, wrote the words, and I was supposed to do the videos. Tuck was supposed to put the clips together and master it all."

"Okay."

"Only, I picked that because Izzy said she could help. She said she'd either do it, or she would coach me through it. Then she got all weird and wouldn't." She shrugs. "So I didn't do it."

Just like that? She just didn't do it? "What do you mean she got all weird?"

Maren rolls her eyes. "She sounded really stupid when she did it, and I told her that and she quit."

"You told her that she sounded stupid? When she was doing a rap for you with the words one of your friends made up?"

"She kept trying to change them," Maren says. "And when I wouldn't let her, she got an attitude. Like, it wasn't even her project. It was mine."

"When is this due?"

Maren looks sideways. "Today."

I glance at my clock. "As in, school just started an hour ago, and you're not there, with your group assignment that's due?"

"Tuck's freaking out about it, and so is Avery. They're such babies."

They're likely stuck taking a zero thanks to my kid. "That's your plan? Just don't go?" I'm a complete and total moron. Why didn't I ask more questions when she said she had a project yesterday?

"Look, I'm sick today, okay? If you back me up, then there's nothing they can do. They'll have to take it late."

I think that the worst thing about this entire mess may be that it never even occurred to her that I might not go along with this horrible plan. "Get your jacket." I stand up.

"No."

"Get it now," I say. "You're not sick, and we're going to school, right now."

19

AMANDA

By the time I turned eleven and started the sixth grade, we had moved twenty-three times. I only knew that because Mom had a little dreamcatcher that hung from the rearview mirror of her beat-up old Taurus, and every time a child was born, she carved a notch. And every time our family moved, she sliced a line. You could literally read the story of our family around the edge of the dreamcatcher.

Notch. My brother Xavier.

Three lines.

Notch. My brother Peter.

Five lines.

Notch. Me.

Then so many lines it took me three tries to count them all. Fifteen in total, by the time I thought to count. Fifteen plus eight is twenty-three. I could remember the number because when I told her that's how many times we'd moved, Mom said that's how old she was when she gave birth to me. I thought that seemed awfully old.

That was about a month before the first time that I

didn't *want* to move. See, for the first time ever, I had a real friend at school. Her name was Heather. She was as normal as we were strange. She wore bows in her hair every day. Her mother made her lunch with the same exact things every single day. And she dropped her off in her shiny, sleek car every morning and picked her up every afternoon. Heather said I was her favorite person in the world. She even gave me a necklace at school that very day that was half of a heart, all jagged on one side. It was the nicest gift anyone had ever given me.

The bus dumped us on the corner and I skipped home, eager to show Mom and Dad my prize, but before I could say a word, Dad shouted, "Get your crap in a bag. Time to bounce."

That's what he said every single time it was time to go—it meant that he'd been caught stealing from his boss and we had to leave. Only, that day, I didn't want to go. I tried crying. I tried begging. I even offered to trade my dad anything of mine he wanted.

"You ain't got nothing anybody wants," he said.

So when everyone else was getting their most prized possessions in grocery sacks and brown paper bags, I decided to sneak out of my house and start walking to Heather's. Most kids wouldn't try to walk more than five miles on their own, but I wasn't most kids.

I knew where the Randalls' was, and I knew how to get there. It was just a matter of walking it without getting caught by my parents. I knew they'd look for me at least for a while, but I figured they'd give up quick.

Then I could live with Heather. Maybe her mom would let me say I was her sister. I had enough clothes until I grew again, and then I could show them how Mom taught me to snag things from unattended washers and dryers so I wouldn't cost them nothing. I'd gotten some really nice stuff that way.

But Mom and Dad didn't give up on me like I thought. They combed the streets for hours. Long enough that Dad got caught by the cops and went to prison for a year.

It wasn't a good year.

That year, when Mom was stuck with us, waiting on Dad to get out, and no one had a job to make any money, that's the worst year of my life. It's also the year I learned that when it's time to run, sticking around only makes things way worse for everyone.

Facing up to the consequences of your actions is a nice idea, but in practice it sucks. As an adult, it made me way more cautious about making sure I never wound up like Dad, on the wrong side of things, in a situation where I could be chucked into jail, for instance. But it also gave me a healthy understanding of why people run.

Only, I don't want that for my girls. Watching Maren essentially run away and stick her head in the sand on this group project made me realize that my inattention might be almost as bad as Mom and Dad's obnoxious irresponsibility and deceit.

Or at least, I'm teaching Maren the things I never wanted her to learn. I can tell from the look on her face that she has no intention of listening to me.

"If you don't go get your booksack and change, I'll haul you to school in those pajamas." I eye her up and down, conveying my disgust at that thought with a curled lip.

Maren arches one eyebrow. "You're kidding."

"I most certainly am not. You are going to march into school and explain to your teacher that you failed to complete your part of the assignment. Then you'll explain that it wasn't Avery or Tuck's fault, and you'll throw yourself on his mercy."

"No way."

"What we will not do is call in sick when you're fine, and you certainly will not sit here and insult me while doing it."

"Mom, you can't make me do that. We'll all get a zero," she says. "I didn't mean to insult you. It's just that you're the best. Everyone else would have to lie to their moms, because they don't get it, but you're always on my side." She beams. "Now can I call in sick?"

I snag her jacket off the floor by the sofa—how has Mandy not kicked us out yet?—and toss it at Maren's head. "Fine. You want to do things the hard way? March."

"I haven't even brushed my teeth," Maren wails.

"Tough cookies—er, Pop Tarts," I say. "Now, go."

I'm honestly a little shocked that it works. I expected her to physically collapse, and I'm not positive that I could physically drag her to the car.

I don't think she really thought I'd drive all the way to the school.

"Mom!" She actually spasms around like she's having a toddler temper tantrum when we arrive, her hair spazzing around along with her arms and legs. "You can't be serious. I can't go in there, and certainly not like *this*."

"Ah, but I am. Let's go." Because I may be unable to face up to my limitations and errors, and I may be every bit the coward that Mandy says I am, but I'm not about to turn my daughter into the same cracked person that I am.

It's an awkward forty-five minutes, but we work past

265

it. Her teacher immediately tells her teammates that their grade isn't tied to hers. Then he asks to see what Maren actually filmed—and says it's not bad. He lets Tuck master it in class, and they submit the project for a low B.

It could have gone way worse.

Although, I doubt Maren will ever live down the fact that I hauled her to school in her plaid flannel pajamas.

After we're done, I collapse into the driver's seat and slump over the wheel for at least ten minutes, imagining how it would go if I were to force myself to do what I just made Maren do: talk to my teacher. Abby is way scarier than Mr. Geisler, and she's also not obligated to treat me kindly as part of her job. I want to drive to her house and beg for her forgiveness, but I can't quite bring myself to do it.

What if she tells me to jump in a lake? What if I can't fix what I broke?

I drive home instead, preparing myself for a day of bawling in my pajamas. My phone rings as I'm parking, and I realize I have about ten missed calls.

All of them are from Kevin.

"Hello?"

"Amanda?" Kevin's angry. "We've been waiting on you for almost an hour. Are you alright?"

"I'm fine," I say. "I had an emergency with my kid. Let's meet tomorrow morning. Is that okay?"

"Fine." He hangs up.

And I'm off to an auspicious start with the new employees I stole. Fantastic. Maybe they can walk next door and tell Abby what a craptastic human I am. The three of them could probably fill a punch bowl with stories of how Amanda has let them down.

Except Abby would never allow something like that. That kind of behavior might knock her crown askew.

I review all the ways in which Mandy's right about my cowardice on the way home. I hated my marriage with Paul, but I just sat in it, being miserable. Then when he died, I should have gone out and looked for a job, but I knew they'd just reject me. I lucked into the social media stuff, or I'd likely have had to crawl home to my very not wealthy or classy parents to beg for help. That would have been worse than a dog eating its own vomit.

Then after we came out here, I just sort of sat around, waiting for Abby to do everything. I only came because I was afraid if I didn't, I might not get the Lololime account. And then once I started dating Eddy, I never confronted my boss. I kept it a secret. And once Eddy and I were out in the open, I knew I didn't want him to leave, but instead of telling him that, I kept quiet. And once I got that photo of him, I didn't call and ask what was going on. I flew out like a lunatic and then didn't even come clean about why I went. Then I slunk home and refused to apologize for my delinquency to my perfect sister-in-law.

Abby's so perfect that she's forgiven me over and over in the past, but everyone has a limit. What if I've finally reached it?

And without someone to kick me out of the house and load me into the car, how can I possibly overcome my cowardice?

I pull into Mandy's driveway, making the bend right in front of her place and nearly plowing into a tiny Toyota Camry. "What the heck?" I shove my car into park and hop out. I peer at the little car, wracking my brain for anything else I may have set up today and forgotten about.

I can't think of a single thing. Maybe someone's here for Mandy. Maybe it's a delivery person? I look around, but don't see anyone. If it wasn't someone we know, Roscoe should be freaking out.

Where is he?

Could whoever it is already be. . .inside? If so, that's creepy. I climb the stairs slowly, my heart racing just a bit.

"Hello?" I call out.

No response. My hand's trembling when I unlock the door—which *was* still locked—and turn the knob.

Eddy's standing in the entryway, beaming at me. His dark hair cascades over his forehead, occluding one bright green eye just enough to make him look roguish.

"What are you doing here?" I race toward him, spreading my arms wide.

He picks me up and spins me round and round, lowering me slowly so that my lips fall down right over his. "Surprised?"

His hands at my waist. His hair brushing against my forehead. His lips against mine. The best feeling in the entire world. But I have too many questions to sink too deeply yet.

"You were recording," I say. "How did you leave?"

"I've always been an overachiever," he says. "Did I tell you I was number two in my class in vet school?"

"Several times." I can't help my smile. He's too cute. "Are you saying that—"

"I already had so many songs written—and they approved twelve of them before I agreed to do this whole thing. Actually, if they hadn't offered to let me do this mostly how I want and approved the songs I'd already written, I'd never have considered it in the first place."

"What does that mean?"

"I'm done recording," he says. "Since we recorded most tracks together as a band, the production should be a breeze, too."

I can hardly believe what he's saying. "How long are you off for, then?"

"They booked a full month for recording in case we needed it, but I got it done in two weeks, because I'm a professional. Did I mention how much easier it is to handle all this as an adult? Not even comparable."

Without even thinking, I start clapping. "So you'll be here for more than two weeks? Is that right?"

He sighs. "Not exactly."

"No? Wait, why not?"

"You know there was a lot of publicity, thanks to you and all your posts when it came out about who I was, and there were even more when they discovered that I'd been wrongly accused."

I don't like where this seems to be going. "Okay."

"Well, the studio wasn't sure quite what to expect, so they set up a fairly basic tour at mid-range venues."

"Sure," I say. "I mean, you haven't performed in more than twenty years."

"They're all sold out."

"Oh."

"And they had another artist whose. . .let's just say her tour has not been going well. She made some remarks about that political—"

"No." I shake my head. "You should get your time

off. They have to produce the album, and they have to make the physical copies."

"Most people buy music online these days, and their turnaround to those platforms is days."

"What?" It feels like I'm being cheated.

"This is good news. They were able to salvage the bookings that fell apart after that media fiasco and they posted it as a surprise announcement that those tickets they had sold could be converted to a concert for me, *or* they could return them and they'd open the unsold tickets up for any of my fans to buy."

"How long do you have, then?"

"The single they released has been doing really well, and they want us back right away to get ready for a show late next week."

Of course I'm delighted for his success. Mostly. But what's he saying? He gets a few days? "So you have. . ."

"I have to leave tomorrow night," he says. "Do you have any free time between now and then?"

"I have to meet with Kevin and Jeff in the morning," I say. "But otherwise, I think I can make room."

"Great," he says. "And if that meeting's not until tomorrow, then let's get lunch."

"Wait, how did you get in?"

"You always leave the back door open."

Roscoe wags his tail and licks Eddy's hand. "I assumed that my dog would keep bad guys away." I narrow my eyes. "Guess I was wrong."

Eddy tugs me close again. "You like bad boys."

Too bad he's right. My life would be much easier if he wasn't. When he kisses me, I forget all about the miserable day I've had. I forget about Maren and Abby and Mandy and all that exists is Eddy and me and the heat between us.

Until Eddy releases me.

That's not like him.

"Hungry," he says. "I skipped breakfast for this flight, and then drove straight here to surprise you."

Right. "Lunch," I say. "We should go get lunch."

"I mean, I'm hungry for all kinds of things." Eddy bites his lip. "But food first." His dreamy grin always slays me.

"It's unfair that you're so beautiful," I complain.

"I've been thinking of adding a scar here." He drags a finger down his cheek. "You know, make me look a little more rugged, a little more legit."

I roll my eyes. "Don't you dare ruin what God gave you."

"Not to argue with you," he says, "but I'm pretty sure my mom and dad are the ones—"

I slap at his shoulder, but he catches my hand and drags me toward the front door. "Let's take my car," I say. "Yours looks like it would be downright dangerous if it snows. Plus it really doesn't fit your image."

He smirks. "Last-minute options are pretty limited."

"Maybe you could have switched to your truck before coming here."

"I thought about it," Eddy says. "But I couldn't wait."

That warms my heart. "Alright, sweet talker, let's go get food."

Brownings is just opening when we arrive.

"Look who it is!" Greta Davis gives me a hard time about giving up on Double or Nothing, but she loves Eddy so much that she always treats me really well. "Our local rock star."

Eddy beams. "Any chance we could get a table?"

She looks around at the empty room. "Take your pick, early bird."

He grabs my hand and drags me to the corner. "Secluded." He sits across from me and stares into my eyes. "That's always best."

"Yes, you're practically alone in here. Don't mind me. . ." Greta laughs and offers us menus.

"Please," Eddy says. "I leave for not even two weeks and you think I've forgotten the menu? It's not the Cheesecake Factory. I think I can remember my options."

"The Cheesecake Factory?" Greta frowns. "We don't even have cheesecake."

He laughs. "You have their specific cheesecake on your menu. Did you think I forgot that part?"

"But in this case," I say, "he's making a joke about their menu being as long as a book. It's got to be twenty pages. I bet even the chefs don't have it memorized."

Greta drops a menu anyway. "In case the smart aleck decides he might have gotten our menu confused with the other fancy ones he's been reading lately, here." She spins around to leave.

I love Greta. I think it may be the bright red hair, but her personality is very zingy. Even with grey streaks earned by many years here on Earth, she's still spicy.

"Not so fast." Eddy folds his hands across his stomach and cocks his head sideways. "I'm starving. I'll have the prime rib sandwich and a slice of cheesecake."

Greta turns back slowly and eyes Eddy from his head, all the way down, stopping at his belt buckle. "You really think, when you're about to go on tour, that it's a good time to eat extra desserts and cheese-laden sandwiches?"

"Isn't that almost the healthiest thing on your menu?" I ask.

Greta glares.

"Not including the cheesecake, obviously," I say.

"I skipped breakfast," Eddy says, "if that helps."

Her scowl dissolves into the smile she was using it to cover. "I'll get it right out, but don't go packing on the pounds now that you're representing Manila out there in the big wide world, you hear?"

"Yes ma'am." Eddy salutes.

"For you?"

"I'll take the grilled ham and cheese, not grilled, with extra tomatoes."

"If it's not grilled, it's not—" Greta snaps her mouth closed. "Sometimes I forget that not all of us are beyond paying attention to what we eat." She winks. "One plain ham sandwich with extra tomatoes, coming right up."

"It really is better grilled," Eddy says.

I'm preparing my argument to defend my poor attacked sandwich when the door jingles. I don't pay much attention to the new diners, since I rarely know anyone, even in a town this size. I just haven't been here long enough yet to need to greet every local who waltzes in like everyone else does.

But Eddy swivels around out of habit, I assume.

And when David Park meets his eyes, David freezes. "You're here."

Eddy frowns, his beautiful features clouding with confusion. "Who are you?"

I shake my head at David, knowing Eddy's too distracted to notice, but David either doesn't see me, or he isn't sure what shaking my head means. "I'm David Park. I'm building a resort over in Dutch John, right on the Flaming Gorge."

Greta's sister Linda brushes her apron down, probably just having tied it on, and points at the table next to ours. "Did you want to sit here?"

It's only then, thanks to the distraction, that I notice that Donna came in with David.

"Sit with us," Eddy says. "It feels like I haven't seen Donna in forever."

"It has been a while." Donna shoots an apologetic look my direction before sitting down. Arguing with Eddy would be rude, and Donna has apparently moved past her days of being horrible, dang her.

"I hear you lost your job," Eddy says.

"My brother's a snake," she says.

"I could have told you that." Eddy leans back in his chair. "But why do you look familiar?"

David sits next to me and turns to face me. "Do you follow Amanda's social?"

"Of course." Eddy frowns, his dark brows drawing together.

"You probably remember me from that." His eyes shift to mine. "Looks like you guys worked everything out."

"Worked out. . ." Eddy leans toward us. "What's he talking about?"

"Nothing," I say. But it's clear from Eddy's face that he's not going to let it go. "David gave me a ride to the airport when I came to see you, because my car ran out of gas."

"You ran out of gas?" Eddy blinks. "I had no idea."

David shoots me a strange look, but he's bright. It

looks like he's catching on. "Yes, I'm just glad you got the car recovered and whatnot."

"I did, thanks."

"Actually, Amanda hasn't mentioned you to me at all," Eddy says. "Not since that date she had to go on to cover our relationship."

David's lips purse.

"He's the one who's stealing all my contractors," I say. "I'm still a little miffed at Donna for going to work for the enemy."

"The enemy?" Eddy looks between David and me. "You look a little too friendly to call him an enemy."

"I keep telling her that it's just business."

"It's personal to me," I say.

"You two sound like Meg Ryan and Tom Hanks in *You've Got Mail*," Donna says.

"Don't they end up together?" Eddy narrows his eyes.

Greta shows up then, thankfully, lowering a tray with Eddy's sandwich and mine. "Here you go. I'm assuming you want the cheesecake last."

"Cheesecake?" David raises his eyebrows. "At lunch?"

"It's for Eddy," I say. "He likes to enjoy every meal."

"Smart man," David says. "Other than the fact that he left his girlfriend out here, alone."

Eddy's about to take a bite of his sandwich, but he drops it back on his plate instead.

But before he can say anything, David continues, "If I wasn't around, she might have to rely on someone nefarious to give her rides when she runs out of gas."

"Okay," I say. "Very funny. I'm sure you and Donna are here to talk about work stuff, though. I feel terrible that you felt obligated to sit with us. Feel free to. . ." I make a shooing motion with my hands.

Of course, David doesn't budge.

Greta's watching us like we're a tennis match, her head shifting back and forth between the speakers, entirely quiet. But she seizes the opportunity with the lull. "Can I take your order?" She's holding her pencil above her notepad, like she's a reporter or something.

"I'll have a cheeseburger and fries," Donna says.

"Same," David says. "With ketchup and mustard, no mayo."

Greta nods and heads for the kitchen. I wish I could grab onto her leg like a baby koala and just ride her calf to freedom.

"So you don't like mayo, huh?" Eddy asks. "That's pretty unAmerican."

"Is it?" David asks. "Amanda doesn't like mayo either."

I can't handle this. It's giving me an ulcer. I was *jealous* when Abby had Steve and Robert both chasing her. I'm clearly too stupid to live. "I bet you two would be happier sitting over there." I point at the opposite side of the smallish dining room. "Then our chitchat won't bother you."

"We came over to meet with a carpenter," Donna says. "We just thought we'd grab food before we drove back."

"I think this is a great chance for us to get to know each other," Eddy says.

"It's not like you need to know David," I say. "I mean, when would you ever see him? By the time you're done with your tour, he'll probably be gone, working on some new project in some far-flung location."

"Gone where?" Eddy asks. "Where's home for you?"

"I love America," David says, "for the record. And I

have no plans to leave this area any time soon. I was thinking I'd buy a house close to here so I can spend a lot of the year nearby. It's always a good idea to keep an eye on the management team, even once the initial build is done."

He has got to be kidding.

"Management?"

"David runs his family's American business operations," Donna says. "He grew up in Korea but moved here for high school, and then he went to college at Stanford."

Eddy looks like someone slapped him, his eyes angry and his cheeks pink.

Donna sounds like a grandmother doting on her favorite grandson. "He also speaks fluent Korean and English."

"German, too," David says.

Shut up, you idiot. It's my fault for not telling Eddy that David was here and that I had seen him. Even so, David and Donna are both making it worse. And for the first time, I realize how cute their names sound.

"David and Donna," I say. "Even your names go together well."

Donna covers her grin with her napkin, but I'm hoping that at least Eddy saw it.

"Only, Donna's not the girl I like." David's practically turned sideways in his chair, staring right at me when he says it. "Plus, that's a little like monochrome clothing, isn't it? Couples shouldn't have names that start with the same letter. I think I'd prefer dating someone with a name that starts with a vowel, maybe." His bemused expression is pissing me off.

I've never seen Eddy eat so fast in my life. He had

been saying that he was starving, but when he stands up and chucks a wad of bills on the table, I'm pretty sure that's not the reason he bolted his food. "Let's go."

"Hundreds?" David lifts both eyebrows as his eyes track toward Eddy slowly. "Impressive."

"Can we not do this?" I beg.

"Do what?" Eddy asks. "Because I'm about one inch from punching this idiot in the face."

Okay. "That's exactly the kind of thing I was hoping to avoid."

"Were you?" Eddy's eyes are hurt when they meet mine. "Because it sounds like you two have gotten pretty close, which is news to me."

I stand up, a little annoyed now with his insinuation. "He gave me a *ride* when I was stuck on the side of the road, en route to see *you*."

"I'd think you'd have mentioned something about such a good Samaritan when you arrived," Eddy says. "I wonder why you didn't."

I shrug. "Maybe I was too busy gawking at the lady you shot that music video with. You two looked pretty cozy."

"We should move," Donna whispers.

"Oh, I don't think so," David says. "This is the best thing that has happened to me this week." He crosses his arms and leans back so he can see my face as well as Eddy's.

"Keep pushing, loser," Eddy says.

"Loser?" David stands up then. "I've been called some pretty creative things since moving to America. My English wasn't always the best, and that made it easy for bullies to be boorish. But even then, no one called

278

me a *loser*." He still doesn't look upset. He's utterly calm —not even annoyed.

"No one?" Eddy asks. "Really?"

David shrugs. "Losers don't own companies worth half a billion dollars."

Eddy blinks. "What on earth are you doing out here?"

"The same thing I do everywhere I go." Without even looking at his wallet, David pulls some bills out and drops them on the table. He smiles then, only it doesn't reach his eyes. "Whatever I want." He catches my eye and winks, and then walks out *before* Eddy. His food hasn't even come yet.

Donna stands and then sits down. "I'm not sure what to do."

"You can walk to your hotel from here, right?" I ask.

"But I still have half a work day, and my car's at the office."

"You should go," Eddy says.

She shoots out, leaving me alone with Eddy.

Before he can say anything, Greta shows up with two burgers.

"Don't ask," Eddy says.

He barely speaks five words the entire drive back to Mandy's. Once we arrive, I shove the car into park and turn to face him. "What? Just say it."

"What do you want me to say?"

"I have no idea what you're thinking," I say, "but I know it's nothing good."

He's going to yell about David. Or he'll be angry that I didn't mention he had moved here. It's fine though, because obviously I just didn't think it mattered. He's surrounded by women all day and all night in California.

His voice is both measured and soft when he finally does speak, his hands resting quietly on his knees. "Why did you really come to see me?"

Okay, that's a question I didn't expect. It takes me a moment to figure out what to say. "Why are you asking me that?"

"He said you ran out of gas."

"I did."

"Someone who's planning a surprise trip doesn't run out of gas. *Adults* do not run out of gas. Only someone in a very big hurry—someone who's not thinking about things calmly—runs out of gas."

I can't even argue with him. It's true. "Helen sent me a photo—"

"Who on earth is Helen?" He closes his eyes. "It's like I leave for two weeks and there's some kind of fruit basket turnover."

"Huh?"

"It's an old game we used to play on the trampoline. You'd say 'fruit basket turnover' and everyone had to get up and bounce around—you never heard of it?"

I shake my head.

"Well, it's a total reset. I've lived here most of my life with people I've known just as long. But now I'm gone for two weeks and there's some crazy rich guy throwing money around."

I don't mention the hundreds of dollars he dropped to try and impress David.

"And some woman named Helen, apparently, who is sending photographs to people."

"Helen is Abby's sister, and she came to celebrate the wedding, or that's her story. She's a real piece of work, though. She's rich, rude, and so snooty you wouldn't believe me."

"She sent you a photo of what?"

"Of you," I admit. "Your arm was draped around someone and you were holding a drink in your hand."

His brows draw together. "You thought I was cheating on you?"

"I was worried you were drinking." I can barely force myself to admit it. "But it would have sucked if you were cheating, too. I felt like if one was true, the other might be more likely."

He climbs out of the car and starts to circle it like a lion looking for a gazelle. I let him do it a few times before I climb out, too.

"How long are we going to be running in circles out here?"

"You said I could go." He stops and waves his hands in my face. "You told me you thought it was a good idea, this tour."

"A good idea?" I practically choke. "I didn't want you to resent me, so I didn't tell you how much it would suck, but I *never* said it was a good idea. You chose to leave, and you didn't even seem to notice how devastated I was by your decision."

"I'm not a mind reader, Amanda. You can't *feel* things and assume I'll intuit them. That may work with Abby because soul sisters have a connection or whatever, but that's not me. I'm a dimwitted musician who does better with animals than people."

"You seemed to be doing fine with the people in California," I say. "Especially the ones with boobs."

He shoves his hands into his pockets. "Is that really what you think?"

"I don't know," I say. "It's been a really long, really miserable two weeks."

"Because of me?" he asks. "Or other stuff?"

"Little of Column A, little of Column B."

He freezes then, his eyes studying my face. "It's hard, the distance. I'm not good at it, and you haven't even been able to talk to me much because of my schedule. Plus, if you tell me about things that aren't going well, I'll just be stressed because I can't help. So you keep everything to yourself, and that makes you mad at me."

"Not mad." My voice is small. Too small. I muster up my strength. "I'm not mad." I'm scared. Mandy nailed it. I'm scared that I'm not good enough for him, and that deep down, he knows it. He'll find someone better in California, and even if he comes back, we'll still die on the vine.

"You never told me you wanted me to stay," he says. "I didn't think you cared that much."

If I tell him how badly I'm struggling right now, I look like an incompetent mess who can't survive without him. How in the world could he be *more* interested in someone who falls apart when left on her own? "Of course I care," I say, "but I really am doing fine."

"Don't open any more photos people send you." He steps closer, and he pulls his hands out of his pockets. "And if you do, call and ask me about them. Don't spin out."

"Okay."

"And don't go on any more dates, fake or otherwise."

"I have zero interest in Mr. Park, while Donna is head over heels. Trust me, he's annoying, but there's nothing to worry about there."

His lower jaw juts out in a caveman-like expression that I inexplicably love. "That guy pisses me off."

"He was actively trying. He has nothing to lose," I say. "He's just picking at you to see if he can make you flinch."

"I hate it."

"Clearly," I say. "And I'm so sorry I didn't tell you about him giving me a ride."

"Or being around here at all," he says.

"But it wasn't like I had something to hide. I just didn't want to have it out with you over the phone."

He sighs, and slings one arm around my shoulders. "Let's not spend any more time arguing. I hate that even more than David stinking Park."

I'm terribly relieved that our argument is past, but I can't help worrying that I did it again—took the coward's path. I should have told him how much I wish he was coming home for real, not for a measly 36 hours. Because even if he's done recording, he has months left of his tour, and we barely survived two weeks.

❧ 20 ❧

DONNA

The knock at the door startles me. Hardly anyone knows I'm here, and very few of those people would feel comfortable knocking on a hotel room door. Even Abigail calls or texts me when she's coming over.

"Hello?"

"It's me," Will says.

And I'm wrapped in a towel. "Hang on," I say. "I'm getting ready for work."

"No rush," he says. "But I have news."

I hope it's good news. Please, let it be good news. I throw on clothing and run a comb through my hair, barely remembering to swipe on some deodorant.

When I open my door, Will's standing patiently, leaning against the wall. He's not a shiny, flashy business-man, not even close. He's wearing faded jeans, a plaid shirt, and a heavy grey work coat with cowboy boots.

But the most defining element is definitely his dark felt cowboy hat.

"Sorry you had to wait," I say.

"Not your fault," Will says. "I should've texted first."

"I'm glad you caught me. I'd have left for work if you were a few minutes later." I wave him inside. There's nowhere to sit but the bed with my luggage covering both chairs, so I go ahead and wave him over to it. At least I made it this morning.

"The gold people called back. They told me that they can't divulge anything at all, because they can only talk to the owner of the property."

"What?" I want to break something. "But we need to find their employee in order to work out the proper owner."

"I explained that," Will says. "The woman I spoke with is named Nikki. She said if you can send her a copy of your dad's death certificate and the will, she can talk to you as a possible heir."

"I have those as email attachments. Abby needed them for the court already."

He shows me the email address of this Nikki lady, and I forward the documents over.

"It's a quarter till nine," I say. "Think I can call yet?"

Will shrugs, so I dial.

Their message system says they don't open until nine. Which means I just have to sit and wait. "I could call them on the way to work."

"I guess," Will says.

But of course he wants to hear what happens—and seeing as he did most of the legwork to get this information, it would be pretty rude of me to ditch him on the two-yard line.

But I do need to get to work. David's nice, but that doesn't really excuse tardiness. I fire off a quick text. ESTATE MATTER CAME UP. BE A FEW

MINUTES LATE. NO MEETINGS UNTIL 11 TODAY.

"What do you like about that guy?" Will asks.

I can hardly believe what I'm hearing. "Huh?"

"We have a few minutes to kill before the gold place opens," Will says. "And your face lights up whenever you talk about him or text him or call him, and I'm old enough to know what that means."

"My face does not light up," I say.

"I may not have a college degree," Will says, "and I may not be a business mogul, but I could be awarded a PhD at interpreting your facial expressions."

I bump his knee with mine. "Come on."

But he's deadly earnest. "When a problem crops up, you do this cringey thing where your right eye squints more than your left."

"I don't."

He plows ahead as if I never questioned him at all. "When you're surprised, unlike most people whose mouths drop open and their eyes widen, you hiss and then clamp down, your lips tightening, your eyes half closing."

Because if I shouted or jumped up and down or squealed, Dad would beat me for interrupting whatever he was watching on television. That doesn't feel like something I should explain.

"And when something great happens, like Aiden gets picked to play the turkey in the Thanksgiving play, your lips rumple and you look sideways."

"What?"

"You do something like that whenever you talk about your boss. Your eyes go soft and shift to the side, and you sigh."

"My boss has a major crush on Amanda. He *moved here*, no, wait, he started to build a retreat here because he wanted an excuse to be around her."

"But she has a boyfriend, and his feelings have nothing to do with how you feel."

"Look," I say. "It's time. I can call." I've never been more delighted to dial a phone number in my life. I should just tell Will that I like David—he doesn't have a chance because I like someone else. But for some reason, the thought of telling Will that I like my boss makes me feel uneasy.

"You've reached the Rocky Mountain Office of Kinross, Nikki speaking."

"Hey, Nikki," I say. "This is Donna Ellingson. I understand that you spoke with Will Earl and are expecting my call?"

"Your dad died and your brother's trying to steal the estate? Yes, and that guy calling for you, is he your husband?"

Ah, Will. "No, he's a friend."

"Oh, lordy, well, he sounds like a stone cold fox. So if he's ever in my neck of the woods, you let him know—"

"Where is your neck of the woods, exactly?" I ask.

"I work in Reno, but we have projects all over this region. Our biggest ones are in Bald Mountain and Round Mountain, but Greg James—" She makes a choking sound. "By golly, I nearly told you everything."

"But you can tell me," I say. "I sent you the papers Will said you needed."

"You did?" She giggles. "Hang on." There's some clicking, and the whole time I wait, the woman's breathing into the phone like a three-year-old talking to his grandparents, but finally she exhales gustily. "There it is."

"So you were saying? Greg?"

"He went out to your town out there, because one of our competitors did some research showing that there should be a nice bunch of veins out your way."

"And?" I ask. "Was there?"

"I hate having to tell people this. It always feels like I'm informing them that they didn't pass a test or something."

I take that as a no.

"Your parents were disappointed, too. I remember your dad kept shouting at some woman and saying how it wasn't going to work."

"Shouting at some woman?" I ask.

"Yeah, he yelled her name so much, I think I even doodled it on the notes. Hang on." She rummages around. "Yeah, right here. He was shouting at some woman named Amelia."

My heart sinks. "My *dad* was shouting at her? Are you sure?"

"We'd only have spoken to the property owner," she says.

Of course, Patrick would totally lie about it if he had to. "And you told him that you *didn't* find gold?"

"I did, yes," she says. "He was especially disappointed because the veins we did find were so close."

My blood runs cold. I've always wanted to know why Patrick wanted Abby's ranch, and now I have a very strong suspicion. "Was the gold found on Jedediah Brooks' land?"

"I'm not allowed to talk about—"

"Of course not," I say. "Right. I know." But I can't

think of anyone else in the world who would have found gold and done nothing, and it would explain Patrick's underhanded tricks and desperation to buy that ranch.

"Is that all you needed?" she asks, clearly impatient to get back to her normal workday.

"Actually, Greg James must have gotten along pretty well with my parents, because he acted as a witness to my dad's will before he left town. Is there any chance we could get ahold of him?"

"He's in the office today, I think," she says. "Hang on."

After a few beeps, a man picks up. "Hello?"

"Greg James?"

"Speaking."

I explain who I am and what I'm after, and he grunts. "That's me. I remember doing that for your dad and mom."

"And would you mind testifying about it?"

"Lady, I'm in Reno, Nevada. I can't go back to your tiny little town for something like this. They said it's a self-proving something or other and I'd never have to."

"A self-proving affidavit," I say. I only know because Abby just explained it to me. It means that portion of the will is notarized, so the witnesses aren't required to show up and testify. The notary stands as evidence that they believed what they signed. Even so, the court some-times ignores it without more. "My lawyer said you wouldn't have to come. Writing a statement and getting it signed and witnessed would be enough. It's also called an affidavit. My lawyer said she could talk to you and draft up a document and you could just modify whatever you needed to and sign it."

"Fine," he says. "I can do that."

289

"Thank goodness." I'm just relieved he's not going to contradict Mrs. Earl's testimony.

"I do have a question, though. Does it matter that about five minutes after signing the will, your dad was screaming about a baby crying and your mom poisoning him?"

"What?"

"He was totally lucid during the signing, but then your mom got up to go to the bathroom. By the time she came back, he was glaring at everyone. When she asked him why, he said he was sick of the baby."

"Some babies can be annoying," I say a little sheepishly.

"There wasn't a baby, though, and a few minutes later, he practically hurled your mom across the law office. He said she was poisoning him with arsenic."

Maybe we can leave all that off the affidavit. It's really hard not to groan. "Well, you'll have to decide what exactly you want to say, but I'll talk to my lawyer about that and see what she thinks. Unlike most lawyers, she's very honest."

"That's a shame for you," he says.

No kidding. "She makes up for it by being brilliant."

"I'm sorry about all this," he says. "I hope it works out."

I hang up.

"That conversation was a roller coaster," Will says.

"I have to get to work," I say. "Did you get all that, though?"

"Your volume is turned up so loud that I could hear most all of it."

"That's Aiden's fault. He talks to his dad sometimes, and he always turns it up louder and louder."

"I'll have to thank him later." Will's grin is so boyishly charming that I find myself smiling back at him. "I thought you'd be bummed."

"I am," I remind myself.

"First no gold, and then the witness that seemed so promising might be a landmine."

"Not only that," I say, "but Patrick was dying to get his hands on Abby's ranch, and now I think I know why."

"You think that's where they found gold?"

I shrug. "Where else could it be?"

"If so, he really is underhanded. Instead of telling the new heirs, he hides it and tries to force them into selling it to him for a rock-bottom price?"

That only makes me more certain. "I really have to go to work, but maybe I can meet Abby for lunch and catch her up."

I call her on the way to the office, but she's busy during lunch. "I could meet you after work."

"Sure," I say. "I just suggested lunch so I wouldn't be cutting into your Steve time."

I wonder after I hang up whether I imagined it, the snorting noise she made when I said that. Surely I did.

When I reach her house that evening, Aiden disappears like a teenager asked to do the dishes, and Abby ushers me into her new game room. "Sorry this isn't much of an office."

"Please," I say. I don't care where we are, how professional it looks, or how many Lego towers decorate the shelves. I jump right into the story about finding Mr. James.

"Will is a good friend," Abby says.

"Stop."

She shrugs. "If you say so."

"I appreciate all his help for sure," I say. "And that's all."

"You didn't say why your mom and dad knew an engineer who worked for a gold mining company," Abby says.

"That's because I figured I'd save the good part for last." I pause for dramatic effect. "I found out why Patrick wanted this ranch so badly."

Abby stares at me blankly.

"They found gold here," I say. "I'm sure of it."

"Here?" She frowns. "That can't be right."

"Why else would my brother go to such great lengths to try and buy it from you? It wasn't like he really needed more land to manage."

"Maybe he wanted to flip it. You know, get a great deal from the alien life foundation and then—"

"Nikki said that one of our neighbors found gold. That's why my parents had him come out, and the time it took him to find the gold in our area is the reason why he was around long enough that they asked him to witness the will."

"I can't call this Kinross group or whatever until tomorrow," she says.

I nod.

"Well, I suppose we'll find out then."

"Call me first thing." I scribble down Nikki's information. "And email her your deed or whatever first. She won't talk to you without it."

"The good news is that, in light of all Patrick's behavior, I think we should add a claim for damages for bad faith."

"What does that mean?"

"It means you could be awarded the entire estate.

The will has what's known as a no-contest clause. If triggered, he'd take nothing at all."

"But aren't we the ones contesting the will?"

"It's not contesting a will that was fraudulently or improperly made that triggers it," Abby says. "It's contesting a will when you knew it was valid, and that's what we're going to claim he did. Between the doctor's statement and the deposition, I think we can prove it."

I mull over Abby's new position on my way back home. Aiden is humming some song from the radio in the back, and it's especially funny to hear him singing about how he can't be stopped—since he is less than four feet tall.

But the more I think about Abby's plan to take every dime, the more uncomfortable I feel about it. How are we at this place? Why can't Patrick and I work this out? Without planning to, my car's suddenly driving to his place.

"Stay in the car," I say when I arrive. "Mom will be right back."

"Why are we here?" he asks. "Uncle Patrick always yells at you."

I sigh. "I'm hoping to change that, okay? It won't take long."

Amelia answers the door, and she looks glassy-eyed to me. She must have had one too many glasses of wine. I really hope Patrick hasn't been drinking. If so, I should just turn around now.

"Donna." My brother shoves his wife behind him like I might maul her otherwise. "Why are you here?"

"You're my brother," I say. "Do I need a reason to be here?"

"You aren't welcome," he says. "I figured you knew that."

"My lawyer thinks we'll win all of this." I look to the right, and then I turn to the left. "She thinks that because of your documented bad faith, I'll win the ranch and the life insurance both. You'd be left with nothing."

Patrick's jaw clenches, and he lunges toward me. His wife must have grabbed his shirt. That's the only explanation for why he jerks back. Undeterred, he shouts, "Get out."

"You should probably leave," Amelia says softly from behind him. "It's been a long day."

"It's been a long month," I say. "A long year."

Amelia looks like she agrees. Patrick still looks livid, a vein popping out in his forehead.

"I wanted to extend my own offer. We can end all this nastiness right now. Just keep the ranch and give me the life insurance. I'll even let you keep a hundred thousand of the life insurance. That way you can set up a college fund for Beth."

"Go to h—"

Amelia must do more than tug on his shirt this time. Patrick practically topples backward.

"Think about it," I say. "Because I've found Greg James. He's preparing an affidavit. I found Dad's doctor, who also supports his ability to execute a will, and you know Mrs. Earl's on my side."

"How many people did you have to sleep with," Patrick asks, "to get that money?" His lip curls. "If it was just the doctor and that Greg person, you must be worth quite a lot."

"You're worse than Dad," I say. And I mean it.

"Oh, I forgot about that dopey Will Earl. That's why

his mom's helping, isn't it? She thinks you might end up with her son? But we both know that won't happen. He'll sleep with you, but he'd never marry trash like you."

"You embarrass me," I say. "I only came over tonight because I felt bad for you. But with the way you've been treating me, when you lose everything, I'll let you sleep on the street. You belong there."

Patrick's fist connects with my cheek so fast that I don't even brace for the blow. I should have, but. . .

He has never hit me before.

I said he was worse than Dad, but I didn't really mean it. Not until that moment. My own brother. And my first thought as I crumple is, *Poor Amelia.*

My vision isn't working quite right, but I hear a sound that strikes terror into my very soul. My darling little son is shrieking, and the sound is getting closer. He leaps over me and lands on Patrick like a koala bear attacking a gorilla.

I blink and blink to clear my vision and force myself to stand. Years of dealing with Dad's bad temper has prepared me for this moment. But Patrick merely looks shocked. He makes no attempt to protect himself from the Tasmanian devil attacking him with milling arms and thrashing legs.

Aiden's shouting and his face is bright red. As I manage to focus a little better, I realize that my darling baby is bawling. Tears are rolling down Aiden's face as he hits his uncle to try and protect me.

"Aiden, sweetie. I'm fine. Let's go."

But my words aren't registering at all. In the end, I have to pry him off of Patrick, his fists still rhythmically whamming against Patrick's chest. Finally, when he sees my face, it snaps him out of it and he smiles. "Mom, I'll keep you safe. You'll see."

My heart breaks a little bit. "I know, baby. I know."

It takes me almost an hour to get him calmed down and tucked into bed. But once that's done, I finally have the peace of mind to call Steve.

"Donna?"

Clearly I don't call him much. "I have a favor to ask."

I tell him what happened, and he stays calm. That's the benefit to having a friend who's an ER doc. He's seen it all, so nothing causes him to freak out.

"You really ought to go into the ER," he says. "A record from there—"

"I won't leave Aiden," I insist. "It would be great if you could come here, take photos, and be ready to give Abby an affidavit."

"But Patrick knows I'm dating your lawyer, so that'll undercut—"

"We'll have photos and my testimony," I say. "It'll be enough if I decide to press charges."

"If?" Steve clears his throat.

"Stop," I say. "I know all about this. I grew up with it. I'm not some shrinking—"

"It's precisely because you grew up with it that—"

"I'm a victim," I say, "but I'm also a warrior. Right now, come and do what you can, and I will absolutely mitigate the impact of any trauma on my son. Okay?"

He sighs, but he listens. A few minutes later, he shows up.

"I half expected Abigail to arrive with you," I say. "Bazooka in hand, waving it around, prepared to blow Patrick to bits."

Steve snorts. "Yeah, well, she probably would have come if we were talking right now."

That surprises me more than Patrick's punch to my face. "You aren't *talking*?"

As he examines me, he explains about Helen and her constant interference and his overreaction in Houston to Abby's confession.

"Her husband *died*, Steve," I say. "Of course she wakes up in a panic, worried she's doing the wrong thing. I'm surprised she's not *more* broken than she is."

"I know."

"This is all your fault."

His tone is sharp. "I know." But his eyes are soft. "But when she came over to talk about it, it was fine. We moved past it. Only, then I mentioned that I can't wait to have her come live in the same house as me, and—"

"Come live?" I raise both eyebrows. "As in, she's the one moving?"

"Why is that so wrong?"

I cringe. "She has four kids, Steve. She's moved three times in the last year. She just sold the house she built with her husband that her kids *grew up* in. You don't think that you should have asked her where she wanted to live. . .and listened?"

"I'm always listening to her," he says. "I always give her what she wants, but I have my barn. It's not as lucrative as my job at the ER, but the horse training is who I *am*. If I don't have that—"

I shake my head.

He keeps arguing.

I just keep shaking my head.

"What?"

"You're a moron."

"Why? What now?"

"You think you can't train horses at her place?"

"There's no round pen, and—"

"Steve Archer, are you the best horse trainer in Utah because your stalls are pretty? Is it because of your stupid round pen?"

"No." He looks at his feet.

That means he gets it. Finally. He's as bullheaded as Abby's cattle sometimes. "You can fix this, right?"

"I sure hope so." He straightens. "But why do you care so much?"

"Because if you two superhumans can't make things work, what hope is there for the rest of us?"

ABIGAIL

Helen's on a conference call, practically yelling. Even though she's in the room we converted from garage space, I can hear her in my bedroom. I pick up my phone and notice that Steve has now called me eleven times.

I need to call him back. I want to call him back.

But I'm still upset, and I never ask important questions of someone unless I already know the answer. It feels like our next conversation will be full of important questions, none of which I know the answer to right now.

I worry he'll get tired of calling and just show up. I text him quickly to head that off at the pass. LET'S TALK TONIGHT. TOO MANY WORK THINGS TO DEAL WITH.

He stops calling after that.

It's a relief, and also, confusingly, a little disappointing. I'm officially acting like an adolescent. I want space, but I want him to not want to give it to me. I want him to call, but I don't answer when he does.

I always assumed teenagers and young adults acted erratically because their brains were still developing, but now I wonder whether it's something else entirely. Once something has been decided, we settle in. I'm having the spaghetti for dinner. Okay, that's alright. I like spaghetti. I would, at that point, start thinking of good side dishes to pair with it.

But if, instead of choosing that as the main course, I'm offered a long list of all the things I love to eat and I have to choose just one? Then doubt rears its ugly head. Same thing if it was a list of things I hate—the discomfort comes in the uncertainty.

Is the spaghetti better? Or will I stain my blouse? Or even if it won't be too messy, will it be too acidic? Could it cause heartburn? Perhaps something gentler would be better. Or would that be boring?

Except instead of choosing between pasta and steak, my current gambit of decisions requires me to examine my inner motivations and desires and compare those to the things I *ought* to want and figure out how they can best coexist.

No wonder I'm acting infantile.

Lucky for me, I actually *have* a few work tasks to accomplish to give myself a reprieve. I whip my laptop open and shoot a copy of the deed for this property to the woman Donna told me about, the gold company's secretary. I draft a quick email to accompany it, asking her to call me with any information she may have about the existence or lack thereof of gold on our property.

Then I decide I ought to, while I have some momentum, prepare the motion for summary judgment on Donna's case. The more quickly we can get things resolved, the better for her. Honestly, it's what's best for her brother, too. The more quickly we resolve the estate, the better all around.

Eliminate uncertainty. That's my new motto.

The motion goes together quickly, probably because I'm really good at drafting and even better at summary judgment arguments. The criteria are all so clean and clear, not like real life usually at all. I'm hunting through my email to gather the attachments for it, and I pull up the property title search on the ranch. Normal due diligence is boring, but when you don't do it, it always comes back to bite you. I click on the attachment, prepared to copy it into the right file, when I pull up short.

I've been so distracted the past week that when this came back, I didn't even check it. Donna told me the ranch her family owns has been paid off for two generations. Of course the title was clear—I knew it would be.

Except, it's not.

Right there in plain black and white is a lien against the property, in Donna's father's name, for *a million dollars*. The value of the property based on the estimate I had a realtor prepare is right around two million dollars, including the two houses, barn, and storage building. The corresponding life insurance policy her parents have maintained was for a million and a half dollars. It's pretty common for parents to take out a life insurance property in a substantial sum when they want to compensate two siblings but preserve the value of a ranch, and the existence of the life insurance policy was one of my points of evidence in the motion for summary judgment.

Only, that doesn't track if the life insurance policy barely covers the loan amount.

If they needed money, why not cash out the life insurance policy? It was whole life, which is like a glorified savings fund. Canceling the policy and taking the cash value would have been much easier than taking out a mortgage.

Most importantly, where did the money *go* if the land was previously paid off? What did Mr. Ellingson do with it? The loan began just after Donna's mother passed, according to the registered lien.

I call Donna immediately.

"A loan?" she says. "Are you sure that's right?"

"I've already emailed you the document. I wish I'd opened it three days ago, but—"

"There can't be a loan. I helped Patrick go over the estate when Mom passed, and they owned it free and clear. Dad couldn't have. . . Wait. When did you say Dad took out the loan?"

I zoom in on the document. "It was recorded a year and a half ago. A few months after your mother passed."

"Dad wasn't competent then," Donna says. "At least, not most of the time. That was more than a year after the will Patrick's questioning was executed."

"Correct me if I'm wrong, but your brother Patrick had a power of attorney."

"You think he took out the loan in Dad's name?"

Unfortunately, that's exactly what I think.

"But that means he might *need* the life insurance," Donna says. "Because there's no way anyone can pay off that size mortgage and live off the proceeds of running the ranch. At least, there's no way Amelia could. She likes nice things."

"What if he did that on purpose?" I ask. "Maybe he

took out that note and set that money aside, so that he could tell you he had to have the policy proceeds?"

"He's not that sly," she says. "He's been hiding the fact that there was a loan, and with Patrick there's only one reason he'd do that."

"What?"

"He doesn't want me to know why he took out that loan." She pauses. "Which means he needed that money for something badly."

"We need to be able to prove to the court that he took out that loan on your dad's behalf and used the money on himself. Then this case becomes a slam dunk."

"A slam dunk on paper," Donna says. "But how would I ever collect?"

That is the issue, yeah. If Patrick stole that money and spent it, instead of stashing it somewhere. . .the odds of ever collecting it aren't great. "You could still force the sale on the ranch, take the proceeds after the mortgage is repaid, and then take the life insurance. You're still looking at two and a half million, and Patrick gets what he deserves: nothing."

"I'd feel pretty bad about that," Donna says. "He'd be penniless."

"He got a million dollars eighteen months ago," I say. "And he lied about everything, including the will, the loan, all of it. I don't feel bad for him in the slightest."

Not ten seconds after I hang up with Donna, my cell phone rings.

"Hello?"

"Abigail Brooks?"

"Speaking," I say.

"My name's Nikki. I'm calling from—"

"Ah, the gold company, right?"

She clears her throat. "This seems to be my week to break bad news to people, but I regret to say that your land also had no gold located on it, at least not in any substantial quantities."

I'm glad I didn't mention the possibility to Ethan. Kids are extra prone to falling into the depths of despair about things like this. It's hardly disappointing to me. I only heard about the possibility for the first time yesterday. "But Donna seemed to think that a neighbor—"

"We are certainly not at liberty to disclose information about other property owners," she says. "But I will say that we did identify gold in significant quantities on a property in the area, and the owner was unwilling to take steps to extricate it. If you were to discover who it was and convince them otherwise, we'd be very grateful."

"It would be way easier if I had any idea who it might be," I say.

"Would it help if I said that the property was north of yours?"

North? I tap my lip. "It might at that."

The second I'm off the phone with her, I hop in my car and drive next door. My heart races a bit, thinking about my disastrous trip over here before, but when I arrive, Amanda's car isn't parked out front.

Only Mandy's is.

An alarming thought occurs to me. In my life, Helen's making me insane so I'm avoiding her as much as possible. Steve and I are arguing, so I screen his calls. And Amanda and I fought, so I'm actively nervous to see her.

The common denominator in all of these is *me*.

Does that mean that I'm the problem? And if I am, what should I do about it?

"You ever going to get out of that car, cupcake?" Mandy's leaning against a support beam on her porch, her pig making tiny circles back near the doorway. He hates the cold. But when I open my door, Roscoe sees me and races over to collect his obligatory pets and licks. Pets by me, licks by him. I don't mind it over the summer, but my hands are already cold.

"Amanda's not here?"

Mandy frowns. "You two still fighting?"

I swallow. "I came to talk to you about something."

"Then do it," she says.

I cross to the porch. "Outside?"

She laughs. "Oh, fine. You can come inside."

Once we're seated in the family room, she even offers me a warm drink. Perhaps she's not as angry at me as Amanda is. "I won't take all day," I say. "I have a lot of work to do myself."

"Amanda's struggling," Mandy says. "I know it sounds like I'm making excuses for her, and I know she's been struggling often, but just know that she's more hurt than she is angry. She knows she's wrong, but it's hard for her to admit it, especially to you."

"What does that mean, especially to me?"

"You're Mary freaking Poppins," Mandy says. "You're Gandalf the Grey. You can do no wrong."

"I have no idea what you're saying. I'm certainly not a British nanny with a flying umbrella or a wizard in Middle Earth."

Mandy snorts. "You're Practically Perfect in Every Way, though. Even *you* can't argue that's not true."

Ah, the irony. "It feels like everyone I know would disagree with you today."

305

"Your kids?" She raises her eyebrows. "Would they disagree?"

"My kids love me," I say. "We're doing fine."

"You're fighting with Steve, then?" Her eyes are shrewd, and they see more than I wish they would.

I don't say anything, but I think my compressed lips give me away.

"That was inevitable, you know. You're both accustomed to having your own way, and merging two lives is always messy."

I think about what she's saying. Is she right? Is the discord between Steve and me just the natural unhappiness that ensues whenever two people have to mush their lives together? We are both older, and we are both set in our ways.

"And the Amanda thing? I already told her this, but she was to blame there, not you."

It's like someone wrapped me in a warm blanket and hugged me, and I didn't even know how badly I needed it, how much the unhappiness was making me doubt myself, until I start to sob.

"Oh, no," Mandy says. "Not you, too."

Amanda was crying? That helps me get things under control. "Is she alright?"

"Having Eddy gone has been hard on her, and me giving you the ranch was even harder."

"Why did you do it?" I've been dying to know, but when I asked before she just said she was correcting the injustice that was done to us.

"Why'd I give you a ranch, or why'd I give Amanda the shaft?" She arches one eyebrow. "Surely you know the answer to both."

"You said it was to fix what Jed did, but Amanda's kids are Jed's grandneices as well."

"They don't want that cattle ranch," Mandy says. "And they don't need it either."

"But Amanda interprets the whole thing to mean that you think we're more deserving."

"Of that working ranch?" She laughs. "You are. She didn't lift a dang finger."

Now she sounds like Ethan. "But she did help out with the kids while Ethan and I took care of things, and she did—"

Mandy throws her hands up. "I love Amanda, but loving someone means you want them to heal from their trauma. Trust me when I tell you that Amanda won't be shafted, but she needs to learn what it means to love someone. Love isn't about demands and fifty-fifty splits and fairness, and you don't find joy in life by exacting justice."

I think about what she's saying, and I wonder how someone so smart managed to miss out on loving the person who lived right next door. Are we all really the most blind about our own life?

"What did you want?" she asks. "You didn't come here to grill me about Amanda. Is this about the office? Because I think you should revisit the first one. I know it's a mess, but—"

"Can you even find people to get any work on new offices done right now?"

Mandy frowns. "It has been a bit of a backlog, I'm not going to lie. That's why Amanda went after Kevin and Jeff." She throws her hands up in the air. "Which I told her I am not supportive of, for the record. No good ever came from stealing from family."

"They might have been hired by that guy over in Dutch John if they didn't come work for you." I hate to lose them, and I'm worried about Ethan, but it wasn't realistic to expect them to stay when their contract lapsed. "I'm stressed about that, and frustrated, but I'm not freaking out."

"That's good, and I know it's not ideal, but it may be a few months before we have the manpower to renovate Double or Nothing or overhaul the post-office-turned-secondhand-store."

I sigh. "At least I have the addition we built that's in pretty good shape—I can keep using that as long as I have to, I guess. It's making me into a crazy person, but at least I have a door I can close to keep the kids out when I'm talking to clients."

"That's why you came?" Mandy asks. "To try and get a timeline on the office situation?"

"No," I say. "In fact, what I came to ask may seem like it's out of left field a bit."

Mandy frowns. "What is it?"

"A lady on the phone today told me that we don't have gold on our land. She said their geologist found gold somewhere close, but it wasn't on our ranch. I think Patrick Ellingson thought it was on our land, and that he had a reason to believe it was." I look at her questioningly. "You wouldn't know anything about that, would you, neighbor?"

"Patrick Ellingson is a greedy, stupid, and arrogant man." She smirks. "But I do know something about gold around these parts."

"Are you really not going to tell me?"

"If you swear not to mention a word to anyone else, then I will."

❧ 22 ❧

ABIGAIL

"**I**f you swear not to mention a word to anyone else, then I will."

I cover my mouth and hold up one hand like I'm taking an oath.

"As your client, I'm asserting privilege on this. Got it?"

I nod.

"That busybody thought he was still on Jed's land when he traipsed right over on mine. I most certainly didn't give him permission to search over here, and when he found gold, he told Jed where it was, and that moron realized the guy's mistake."

"So Jed did want to find gold?"

Mandy laughs. "He always thought his good luck was right around the corner. He's the one that brought them here in the first place."

"The gold company?"

"Of course." She points behind her. "That stream that runs down behind my land cuts through my gold vein, and it hauled just enough down to Jed's for him to find it. But that geologist figured out right quick where it came from and came knocking on my door."

"So it *is* your gold, but you don't care?"

"Do you know how they mine gold, missy?" She shakes her head. "It's messy, and people would be all up in here, blowing holes and digging up mounds, and jolly well ruining the whole place." She shudders. "No thanks."

"But it's selling for more than—"

"Do I seem like someone who's hurting for money?" Mandy sighs. "When I was a kid, I thought the worst thing in the world was being poor. I made it my life's goal to get rich, and I did it. But that's when I discovered that I'd found fool's gold. Being rich wasn't what I thought. There's always risk in life, and there's never a guarantee of nothing."

"So Jed must have told his friend, Patrick's father, and—"

"Vern was an even bigger idiot than his son," Mandy says. "He'd surely have been just as excited."

"Wow," I say. "Just, wow." My phone bings, and it's a message from Gillian about the meeting with the IRS.

"With your busy workload, I assume you can't go to lunch right now?"

"Sadly, no," I say. "I have something to get to right away, in fact."

"But you'll be free by two-thirty for the pep rally, right? Amanda can't go, and neither can I. Maren'll be sad if no one goes to watch her cheer. She's leading that new one, the one with the pyramid."

Two-thirty. I could probably get there in time, and then I could give my kids a ride home. "Amanda can't go?" I can't deal with seeing her quite yet, even if she is hurting. Even if I know that I need to let it go.

Mandy shakes her head.

"Thanks for telling me. I'll try and make it."

By the time I get back to my house, still shocked to discover that Mandy's sitting on a mountain of gold and doesn't care, I'm ready to dive into the actual work demanding my attention. But I can't.

Not because of Helen, which I might expect as an interference. No, her car is surprisingly absent from our front drive. But a little old Lincoln Town Car is in its usual place, and Mr. Fred Eugene is sitting on the hood, looking depressed. I'm beginning to think it may be his only setting.

"Mrs. Brooks?" He lights up a bit when he sees me. "I got some strange mail and I thought you could help me figure out what it is."

Good grief. "Alright, Mr. Eugene. Why don't we go inside and I'll take a look."

The entire way from his car to my porch, I'm terrified he'll slip and break his hip, and then. . .but I guess I'm his lawyer. It's unlikely he'd be able to find someone else around here to sue me, right? Even so, I really need to get an office. I can't keep having people showing up at my house at all hours, but with the combination of explosive growth and a tiny town, there's not much I can do about it.

Once we get inside and I take a look at the mail, it's immediately obvious what it is. "This is a bill for a safety deposit box," I say.

"A safety deposit box?" He scratches his head. "Why would she have one of those?"

I shrug. "Could be for anything. Did she have jewelry

she didn't want to keep at the house?" That's the number one reason the older people I've helped before have gotten one. I don't really understand it, but I think it's a generational thing. "Or maybe she kept important documents there."

He laughs. "We didn't have anything important, other than our marriage certificate and our birth certificates, and I have those."

"Well, I'm not sure, but if you take this bill to the bank mentioned along with the letters testamentary I'll grab in a week or so, they'll happily show you the contents."

He droops like a flower in the hot sun. "I'm not sure I can do it."

"But Mr. Eugene—"

"Could you come with me?"

If someone had told me that Fred would be capable of making puppy eyes, I'd have called them a liar. But he does. He looks like the cutest old-man-Shar-Pei I've ever seen. It's not possible to resist that kind of pathetic need. "Alright," I say. "I should be able to get the letters testamentary early next week. I can go with you after that."

He beams at me for a moment, presumably until the news that his wife passed occurs to him again. Then he sinks back to the depths of miserable despair. I remember this phase—the everything-hurts-and-nothing-is-worth-it phase. Luckily for me, it lasted less than a week. I moved on to the bouts-of-uncontrollable-sorrow-interspersed-with-normal-life phase rather quickly. Maybe it's my personality, or perhaps it was my age, but it seems like Mr. Eugene is in no hurry to reach anything that approximates normal life.

I barely get him back in his car and puttering out of the driveway in time to handle the IRS and still make it to Maren's pep rally. I even remember to text Emery and Izzy so they won't get on the bus to come home.

I'm standing near the basketball bleachers, watching them get ready to cheer for about thirty seconds before Amanda shows up. Her face when she sees me is absolutely priceless. She looks like someone just yanked down her pants and exposed her backside to the entire school.

At least that rat Mandy sold us both out with her shameless lying.

"Hi," Amanda says.

I force a smile and turn back to watch Maren. I know I need to apologize for attacking her, but I'm just not ready. I do what I always do in these types of situations. I go over in my mind the reasons I was wrong to try and let go of my anger.

Mandy met Amanda first, she developed that friendship, and then I'm the one who benefitted. I lost us the ranch, essentially, because I was gone longer, and I was the legal counsel who failed, and then my shortcomings were rewarded by a fairy godmother Amanda found. I'd probably be upset about it, too. I'm not sure quite what lesson Mandy's trying to teach her, but it seems like a hard one to process. And Amanda has never been one who gracefully learns lessons. That's just not her strong suit.

But she'd have my back in a knife fight, even if it was the very worst kind, the ones that happen on social media. She's also funny, self-deprecating, hard-working in her own way, tenacious, and she does a much better job of letting things go in her parenting and in life than I do.

Plus, out of the brothers, I had a great husband and she got the pile of moldy junk.

And from the little bit I've heard, my parents (as flawed as they are) were basically on par with Mother Teresa compared to hers. And, her boyfriend is gone. That's the biggest stress currently, I imagine. I've been fighting with Steve and he's right here in Manila.

But on top of all the rest, she's not someone who does well with not being the prettiest, the most successful, and the most admired person in the room. So being next to me when I'm preparing for a wedding when I've been widowed for less time. . .

I say the one thing I know will break through to her. "Steve and I had a huge fight. Actually, it's our first fight ever, and I blame Helen." It's a cheap shot, probably, bonding over the shared frustration with a member of my family, but it's real, and I think she'll feel that.

Her eyes widen, and she walks past the two people between us and wraps her arms around me. "I'm sorry I've been such a horrid sister lately."

I didn't realize how much I needed the hug until my heart contracts. Not the one that pumps blood through my body, but the heart that reacts when one of my kids is in trouble, or when Steve looks at me like he's never seen anyone else quite as beautiful. For the first time in days, it's easier to breathe.

The media puts all its emphasis on love stories, but they miss some of the most important things in life. It's not only our romantic relationships that sustain us in life's dips and valleys. It's also friends and family, and when things aren't right with them, everything else feels askew.

When she finally releases me, tear tracks are clear on her cheeks.

The people around us start to cheer, and we both turn immediately toward the gym and start to clap right along with them. When Maren's eyes scan the audience, I'm pretty sure she can't tell we missed that cheer.

Both of us make darn sure to pay close attention the rest of the time. But when it ends and everyone else is milling around, Amanda turns nervous eyes my direction. "I'm so sorry, Abby. I was wrong, and then I was wrong again, and when you showed up, I just doubled down. It's a bad habit."

"Are you okay?"

She looks down at her hands. "Not really. It feels like everything is unraveling right now, and I could really use a girls' night and a case of wine." Her laugh feels forced.

"What can I do?"

She shakes her head. "Nothing. Just listen, and don't hate me for letting you down again." She swipes at her cheeks. "You drew the short straw when it came to sisters, I guess. As much as I hate Helen, I feel like she might actually be better than me. At least she doesn't ditch your kids."

"Ethan's eighteen," I say. "And Izzy acts like she's forty years old."

We both laugh at that one.

"But seriously, they were all fine. I wish you'd called and told me what was going on, though. I can't give you lousy advice if you don't even ask for it."

"Your advice is always good," she says. "Too good,

sometimes. When I want to wallow, hearing from Mary Poppins can be a little demoralizing."

"What's with people calling me that today?"

"Mandy calls you that all the time. You didn't know?" Amanda laughs. "I swear, that woman is too much."

"She is unique." I think about her ignoring the discovery of gold on her ranch. "There's no one quite like her, and she still surprises me. I pride myself on having insight into people, but I regularly wind up shocked when she opens her mouth."

"Mandy's furious with me for hiring Jeff and Kevin. She wanted to fire them."

"Did I mention how sage her advice is?" My half smile's almost genuine.

"I'm sorry I stole them," she says. "I will give them back if you're panicked. You might have to pay them a little bit more than you were, but I'm sure if I talk to them, we can get them to stay."

"If it wasn't you, it would have been someone else," I say. "I realized that once I got a little further away from it. They're too talented and too ambitious to stay as ranch hands when the market is heating up in tiny Manila, and I consider it lucky we had them on our side so long. But now that the contract they signed with Jed is gone, nothing really held them to us except their own generosity."

"How about we split them?" Amanda says. "There's no reason you can't have them for things like trail rides and branding and calving. It might delay our work by a tiny bit, but not by much. And I want to make things right."

"Alright." I think about it. "Here's my counter offer. We get five hours a week of consult time, and then access for special events, which we'll pay them for at your standard rate."

Amanda smiles. "As their boss, I accept. Only, since we stole them, we'll pay."

"That's a relief."

"Are you kidding? I think Mandy was going to kick me out. And fire them. You way underplayed that."

I snap my fingers. "Dangit! There's nothing I hate more than losing a negotiation."

Amanda laughs.

"You two are talking again?" Maren's staring at her mom.

Amanda slings an arm around my shoulder. "Girl, please. Sisters fight, but they always get over it."

Maren arches one eyebrow. "You were bawling on the floor in your pajamas."

"Shut your face," Amanda says.

In her patented move, Maren rolls her eyes and snorts at the same time. "Whatever." But when she walks away, she doesn't quite hide her smile.

Sometimes I forget how many people take their cues from our behavior. I really need to do a better job of acting like an adult, even when my feelings get hurt.

"What are you going to do about Steve?" Amanda asks. "Because if you don't patch that up quick, I might have some 'mysterious injuries' that require me to go to the ER for—" She shimmies with a goofy smile on her face. "—*treatment*."

I can't help laughing. "Yeah, right."

"Oh, don't be so sure I'm kidding. Eddy's not around anymore, and about ten seconds before you snatched him up, I saw Steve mowing his lawn and mwraow." She makes a clawing motion. "I mean, holy cats, he is in good shape."

I can't argue with her there. "I am so going to put the kibosh on his bare-chested mowing after we get married."

"Do you have to?" Amanda's shoulders slump. "You ought to at least give us single girls something to look forward to. It's not like I drove by ten times or anything." She's smiling when she glances at me sideways. "Just four."

"Amanda."

"Okay, fine. Five."

"Stop."

"I'm serious this time, though—what are you going to do?"

"We'll get past it, I'm sure."

"Right? If you can forgive me for abandoning your kids and then insulting you when you called me on it, you can get over anything."

She sounds so positive that I really wish I was that sure myself. I mean, I want to get past it, but Steve sounded serious when he said that with me, things are always my way or the highway. If he really thinks that, we have more problems than where we'll cohabitate after the ceremony.

"Go see him." Amanda bumps me with her hip. "I'll take all the kids home."

"Really?" I ask. "What if Helen sends you another photo?" I widen my eyes.

"Stop."

"Go." She nudges me again, but this time it's with her hand against my shoulder. "You know you want to."

She's right. I do.

But when I get to his place, I can't find him anywhere. I check the barn, his house, and even walk around the property for a bit. After fifteen minutes, I give up. I really do have too many things going on to just sit around here waiting for him to show up, and texting him feels a little. . .I don't know. Pathetic. I'm ready to apologize, I think, but I'm not prepared to sit around all day waiting for him to do it.

When I reach my house, there's an extra car in the drive, parked right alongside Helen's. At first I wonder if maybe Steve inexplicably bought a high-end sedan, but then the front door opens and I see them.

It's like that split second before a car accident, when you realize something terrible is about to happen, but you know that there's not a single thing you can do to stop it. That's how I feel in this moment.

"Mom? What are you doing here?"

I really hope that didn't sound like I just said *I hate that you're here. You weren't invited.* But I fear she can read the subtext in my tone as easily as she'd read a complicated academic paper.

"Darling," my mother says. "What a *quaint* little place you have here."

Because her subtext is like a billboard ad. She may as well shout, "Your house sucks and you're a huge failure."

"Thanks, Mom." Just like when I was ten, I can't bring myself to admit that I hear her insult loud and clear.

"Are you coming inside?" My dad's wearing a full-length black wool coat inside the house, but he's still got his arms crossed and he's brushing at his arms as if he's freezing to death.

"Of course," I say.

I can't help myself—I walk inside like I'm headed for my own funeral. "Helen." I catch her gaze, my eyes flashing with suppressed fury. "Is this where you went?"

"They wanted to surprise you," she says. "Wasn't that sweet?"

I scrunch my nose. "Like a potato," I say.

"Do you mean a yam?" Mom asks.

"Nope," I say. "I meant what I said."

Mom frowns.

Dad shuffles toward the kitchen. "We had to come, to show you all the mounds of crap your mom's been saving."

"Excuse me?" I ask.

Mom grabs my arm. Other mothers might bother with pleasantries, or even a hug for the daughter they haven't seen in over a year. Not mine. She simply snatches my arm and tugs me across my own family room toward the kitchen table. "You need new drapes, by the way. You'll have to add that to your wedding registry. I think your aunt Janet will—"

"Mom, we aren't doing a registry," I say. "If I want drapes, I'll buy them."

"Maybe Helen could—"

"I don't need Helen to buy them, Mom. If I want something new, I can buy it myself."

"Your sister makes quite a lot of money, you know," Mom says.

I can't quite help how flat my tone is. "I'm well aware. In fact, I heard she got a screaming deal on a money bin last week."

"What now?" Dad asks.

"You know, like Scrooge McDuck had in *Duck Tales*," I say. "With the crazy inflation lately, she's converting

320

her assets to gold coins, and she wants to learn to swim in them. I hear it's amazing for your complexion, and toning your arms."

Mom stares at me for a full twenty seconds. Then she just shakes her head and points at the table. "You're lucky I took the semester off, you know. I was supposed to be researching, but I have assistants who are reasonably competent. That gave me time for this."

I finally focus on the area that was formerly my kitchen table and now resembles what I imagine it would look like if a bridal shop and a floral shop had a baby and it puked in my house.

"What on earth is all this?"

Mom starts reaching for things. She thrusts a wad of flowers at me. "What kind of floral scheme are you thinking?"

"Scheme?"

"You know, what's your cohesive theme? What do you want to say with the flowers?"

"Flowers don't talk, Mom." I think she may have been spending a little too much time on her research.

"If you haven't decided that yet, it's fine. We can take it back a step. What are your colors?"

"Mom, I don't have to—"

"I know what you're going to say," she says. "I agree that you shouldn't spend a lavish amount of money on this wedding. But your sister has generously offered to pay for—"

"Mom!"

Her mouth drops and her eyes widen and she eyes me like I just suggested we purchase indentured servants to staff the wedding dinner.

Why does this happen every single time she comes?

I'm a forty-year-old woman, almost, and she still ignores me. "I don't need help with any of this. Not in selecting it, and not in paying for it. I'm more than capable of doing both myself. In fact, it won't be that long before I'm helping my child plan his or her wedding."

Mom's hands move over the things on the table frenetically. "Where did I put those swatches for the—"

"Did you hear me?" I ask.

She straightens and meets my eyes. "I did, but seeing as you didn't let me be involved at all last time, and since Helen doesn't appear to ever plan to get married, this may be my *only* chance to help."

I sigh. "Okay, Mom. Show me what you have."

Which is why I'm hunched over a pile of junk I don't care about when the door opens. "Grandma and Grandpa are here, kids," I say over my shoulder, mustering as much excitement as I can possibly manage. Which isn't much.

"Grandma and Grandpa?" The deep voice definitely doesn't belong to any of my children.

I turn to look at Steve, shocked he just showed up unannounced after our strained interactions since the fight. He's wearing his normal uniform of faded jeans, worn boots, and a soft plaid shirt covered by a dark canvas jacket. And like most days, he's covered with a spattering of mud. Looks like he came straight here from working a horse.

"Who is this?" Mom raises one eyebrow in disapproval. "He didn't even knock." The distaste on her face is so strong that it could probably strip paint.

"Yes, Abigail, why did this man just stomp into your home?" Dad edges closer, as if he might in any world, no, in any *dimension*, be able to do anything other than theorize Steve into submission.

"This man stomped into my house because he's my fiancé, I say."

"Right," Steve says. "I'll be living in this house, soon." His eyes are soft. Pleading.

"You must be kidding." Mom turns to look at Helen and me at the same time, purposefully excluding Steve. "This mountain man? That's really who you picked to follow Nate?"

"You hated Nate," I remind her.

"He was growing on me."

"After twenty years," I say, "he was finally *growing on you*? How exciting to hear. I bet he's dancing up in heaven."

Steve uses his left heel to pop off his right boot, and then slowly tugs the remaining boot off as well. Then he crosses the room in his socks with Helen, my mom, and my dad all glaring at him. Without missing a beat, he slings one arm over my shoulders. "Can you believe I managed to convince her to marry me?" He shakes his head. "I must be pretty good at persuading people, at least, right?"

Mom covers her nose as if he smells, and it's the last straw for me. I tried, I really did, but I'm too old for this kind of thing.

"You know, Mom, the one thing you didn't ask me about with regard to wedding plans?"

"What's that?" Mom appears to be actually listening, so I have high hopes that this will strike a chord.

"Whether you were invited."

She blinks.

"And maybe you should have asked."

She frowns.

"Because you're not. And furthermore, I'm going to have to ask you and Dad to leave."

"Leave where?" Mom's brow furrows.

"My house. You're welcome to come back when you're able to be civil to me and to the man I love. Until then, don't bother calling me either." I turn another ninety degrees and glare at my sister. "And you. I don't need your money, your superiority, or your terrible and officious help. You go with them."

When they all just stare at me, shocked, I clap. Mom and Helen both startle at the sound.

"You may not think Steve looks promising," I say, "but among his other charms, his uncle happens to be the local Sheriff. And if you don't leave, I'll give him a call and ask him to pay us a visit and remove you himself."

♌ 23 ♓

AMANDA

Eddy's only been gone for a day, but when he texts me, NOT LOOKING FORWARD TO TRAVELING AROUND FOR THE NEXT FOUR MONTHS, my heart drops.

Neither am I. Actually, I hate the idea of him hopping all over the country without me. I MISS YOU ALREADY.

I MISSED YOU WHEN I BOARDED THE PLANE. BUT AT LEAST THE TOUR TICKETS ARE SELLING.

Yeah, yeah. I should be happy for him. I know he was worried his fame was a flash in the pan and listeners wouldn't care. But apparently nostalgia combined with a pretty face is a pretty strong pull.

How fabulous.

I mean, I *am* happy. But it's hard to take a lot of people flirting with and lusting after my boyfriend. He's *mine*, and I don't like to share.

"You busy?" Mandy asks.

I spin around.

She's standing in the doorway holding a list. "You have a minute?"

Apparently we're starting our workday at seven fourteen in the morning, now. "Sure."

"You went to the Greta Lane site yesterday?"

I follow her into the family room as she asks me a handful of things about the work Kevin and Jeff have managed to get started at all three of our top priority sites, including the house she's planning to rent to Donna.

"I know it won't be our most lucrative turnover, but we need to make sure it's getting done," she says. "Donna's stuck at a hotel until it's ready, and once we get that critical list complete, a lot of which that sweet boy started, she can move in. Get the court off her back."

"Wait." I sit down on the sofa and set my notes on the coffee table. "Is the court involved?"

"Not yet," Mandy says. "But if her ex has his way, they will be, apparently. She's been really stressed about it."

"I haven't really felt lucky about my husband passing away over the past four plus years, but sometimes I forget that it could have been worse in many ways."

"No matter how bad things are," Mandy says, "they can always get worse."

That's not a very comforting thought.

"No one else is looking after that girl, so you and I need to." She perches on the edge of the armchair next to me.

"*That girl* is nearly the same age as me," I point out. "And I don't hear you worrying that no one's looking after me." I made myself a promise not to bring up the ranch again, but it's hard. At least I didn't specifically mention it.

"Abby's looking after you," she says. "And of course I am, too."

"Huh." I'm not sure what else to say. It doesn't *feel* like she's looking after me.

"Why do you think I gave Abby that ranch, when all I gave you was a gift card to Nordstrom?"

"You knew I liked to shop?"

"I'm actually asking whether you have any idea what I was thinking."

"I thought we had a bond," I say. "I thought you liked me the best."

"And did you want to run a ranch?" She arches one eyebrow. "Is that the problem? You wanted to be moving hay and fixing fences and getting ready for the calves that'll be coming before too long?"

"You know I didn't want to do any of that."

"I needed to clean up Jed's mess," she says. "The one good thing about the court ruling as it did is that they didn't drive a bigger wedge between you and Abby. You didn't want that ranch—you just wanted your half of the value of it. Having a mortgage on it would cripple that poor boy who has no idea what he's doing yet."

"I get it," I say. "You're a guardian angel, and I didn't need saving or whatever."

"I thought you liked working with me. Wasn't it nice of me to give you a job?"

"Was it?" I ask. "You said you needed my help. Was that a lie? Is all of this just you doing me a favor?"

She sighs.

"Why are you asking me all these questions?" I ask. "If you want to tell me what I did wrong and why I got a five hundred dollar gift card and they got a two million dollar ranch, then just do it. If not, then stop twisting the knife."

"I won't be around that much longer, you know," Mandy says.

Something about the way she says that makes the blood in my veins run cold. "What does that mean?"

She shrugs. "Nothing dire, and I'm not hiding secret news or anything that's stupidly dramatic. But about a decade ago, my friends started dying. Not just an isolated person I knew who had a heart attack, but most of them, one at a time, like dominos someone stacked too close."

I hadn't even thought about that. Other than me and Abby, I wasn't really sure she *had* any friends. "Have you lost people you were close to?"

"Of course, you ninny. Lots of them, starting with my parents. But that's not my point. My point isn't that my loved ones have passed—you knew that already, because Jed just died. My point is that when your death gets close, you start thinking about what you'll leave behind when you do go."

"Like your house, you mean?" I ask. "Or do you mean your money?"

"People worry about houses and money and cars while they're young. Those things matter when it feels like you'll have loads of time yet to drive and live and spend. At my age, you start thinking about the legacy of your life. *What will people remember about me?* That sort of thing."

"Okay."

Mandy stands up and brushes off her pants. "They

328

start thinking about how the people they care about will do when they aren't around to lend a hand."

Is she talking about me?

"The reason—"

My phone rings, and it's Jeff. I hold up one finger to tell her I'll be quick. "Yeah? What do you need?"

"The inspector said they want the approval for—"

"The state inspector?" Mandy practically yells. I'm surprised she could understand him.

Note to self, she can still hear pretty well.

"They'll want that one with the seal I showed you," she says. "It's in the filing cabinet, in the Yarborough Way file."

I moosh the cell phone between my ear and my shoulder and trot around the corner to the office. I nearly drop my cell phone in the process of getting the dumb, heavy metal slider shifted over so the drawer will open, and then the files are so overstuffed into the cabinet that pulling the right one out dislodges three others. Papers go flying all over the place. "Hang on, Jeff. I'll take a photo of this and send it to you, okay? Let me know if that's not what he needs."

A few moments later, he sends back a thumbs-up emoji, so I take that to mean we're good.

Mandy was saying *the reason*. I wonder if she was about to tell me why she gave Abby the ranch. Why did he have to call *right then*? With my luck, even if he hadn't called right then, it would turn out she was really only going to tell me the reason she hates drinking milk or something.

"What happened in here?" She's standing in the doorway, looking around the room with a concerned look on her face. "What did those files ever do to you?"

"You need another cabinet," I say. "Or you need to get rid of some of these files. I pulled out the one we needed and all these just hopped out at the same time like it was a prison break."

She taps her lip. "I've been thinking it was time to go through and get rid of the old stuff that's no longer necessary."

I bend over to pick the piles of paper up, barely paying attention to what they are, except to try and sort them into the right folder. Luckily, she's not fancy with the titles. If I can find the address of the property on the paperwork, it's almost always the same as the file name.

Except this one is addressed to *her* house, and the company is Kinross Gold. "Hey, what's this?" I start to scan the letter without really considering it.

Dear Ms. Amanda Saddler,

We're delighted to inform you that our geologist located a rich vein of gold on your property. We're prepared to make you a very competitive offer to purchase your land, or we would be willing to consider a royalty share agreement in which you maintain ownership, but we buy the mineral rights and extricate the gold.

Before I can read any more, Mandy snatches the letter out of my hands and crumples it up. "You can't just go around reading whatever you'd like." She scowls. "Did Abby tell you to look for this?"

"*Abby?*"

"Did I stutter?" She huffs. "I didn't think she'd violate—"

"I'm still not even sure what *this* is," I say. "But Abby didn't breathe a word—" The words of the letter begin to sink into my shocked brain. A rich vein of gold. Our geologist located. "There's gold on your land?"

Mandy's lips flatten.

"Why would you hide that? Or did you sell part of it? Is that how you got the money to start up your real estate—"

"None of this is any of your business," she says. "You need to worry less about gold and prying into other people's lives and think more about what you want with *your* life. What really matters in life is spending time with the people you love."

It seems like a strange thing to say, coming from a woman who lives alone and had no children and never even told her neighbor that she liked him. I don't have the energy or the desire to argue with her anymore, though. "You're right," I say. "It's none of my business."

I spend the next few hours focused on our business, driving to two of the sites, meeting with suppliers, and then interviewing a few guys Kevin found. One of them looks great, one of them looks unreliable, and the third looks like he found him in an orange jumpsuit, fresh out of lockdown. But our options are extremely limited. "If you're okay with supervising them, I'll hire them all."

Beggars can't be choosers and right now, we're definitely beggars. Let's just hope he learned how to run a decent drain line when he was in prison getting those fascinating neck and face tattoos.

By the time I finish with my checklist of tasks for today, I barely have time to make it to the school before the girls are out. If I was late, they'd double freak out because today is horseback lesson day.

"Did you bring our snacks?" Emery asks.

"And the water bottles?" Maren arches one eyebrow. "Last time you forgot the water bottles."

"Are you still fighting with Aunt Abby?" Emery asks. "Because I don't want to go if you are."

"You two know that I can't talk when you don't give me time to respond, right?"

"Did you?" Maren asks.

"I didn't forget the water bottles."

"I mean, did you make up with her? I saw you talking during my pep rally."

"We're fine," I say. "Sometimes grownups fight, but they get over it."

"Did you really just say that? We're not five," Maren says. "You don't have to call yourself a *grownup*."

What was that Mandy was saying about spending time with loved ones? Mine are jerks. "I brought apple slices and Z-Bars, but I'm not sure you really deserve them."

"Sorry, Mom," Emery quickly says. "And thank you."

"Yeah, thanks," Maren says.

It's not lost on me that she didn't apologize, but I'm not surprised either. Emery's apologies feel reflex-like, as if her knee-jerk reaction is to apologize. Maren's on the opposite end of the spectrum, where pulling an apology out of her is like removing a wisdom tooth with no anesthesia. And it never really sounds quite right, even when you do.

The next half hour, once we reach Steve's, is boring. Abby's not even there—work stuff, maybe? Ethan drops his siblings off, and it's some kind of flurry of grooming and strapping saddles on all the many horses. Four girls and four horses might not seem like a lot, but it's tiring.

"Ethan doesn't do these lessons anymore?" I ask.

Whitney rolls her eyes. "He does them at different

332

times now, while we're at school. He said there's too much chaos for us to take a lesson together."

As I watch them take the lesson, I kind of get where he's coming from. Honestly, I know Maren's only taking lessons so she can connect with her sister and cousins, but she ought to be taking them at a different time I think, and maybe Emery, too.

Abby's girls are racing around at double the speed of mine, and they can do any pattern Steve assigns them. Mine, on the other hand, look like bumblebees who drank too much rotten apple juice and can't move in a straight line.

I pity their horses.

"You can't yank like that," Steve says for the third time. "If you do it again, I'm going to revoke your driver's license."

Maren can't quite suppress her smile.

Abby's lucky. For a guy who didn't have any kids of his own—er, not until very recently, anyway—he has a way with them. He's correcting them firmly, but also in a light way so that they don't get overly upset.

As I watch my kids learning, flailing and regrouping, and by the end of the lesson, actually getting the walking-in-a-circle correct, which I know is probably kind of pathetic, but honestly feels like a coup, I *get* it.

The reason it sucks that Eddy's on tour is that he's not around.

And you don't have your kids' trust and earn the love of your family members by being a good person. You don't earn it by making a lot of money, either, or Paul would have been very beloved before he died and his aggressive options ruined us all.

No, you earn trust and affection and faith by being

there. By cheering. By giving rides. By seeing the losses and the wins and loving them no matter which one they're racking up at the time. You don't grow closer to someone unless you do the time to support them in their accomplishments and their failures.

And even success doesn't mean much unless you've worked to achieve it.

The reason I care about their being able to make a circle is that I saw how hard it was for them to finally do it. When they're eating dinner tonight, we'll tell Mandy how it went, Maren poking fun at Emery, and Emery reminding Maren that her circle looked more like a tampon than a toilet paper roll, and it won't be epic or earth-shattering or life-altering.

But it will be one more small step away from Eddy.

A million of those small steps are going to happen in the next few months, and he knew that, and he chose to take them anyway. He picked his music, and not us.

And that hurts with every baby step.

❄ 24 ❄

DONNA

Forty-seven minutes isn't that long. You can barely watch two episodes of *Friends* in that timeframe. When I lived in California, if my commute to work had been forty-seven minutes, it would have been shorter than most of my friends'.

But here, where everything is accessible within a few moments and the town doesn't even boast a stoplight, it feels like I'm light years away from my home when I'm working forty-seven minutes away in Dutch John. Their kids are bussed here to our schools, it's true, but I don't think I realized quite how far they had to go every day until I was making the drive myself.

It's making me wonder whether renting a house in Manila is the best plan. My biggest concern is how far Aiden is from me while I'm at work. After all, it's not like I have a spouse close who can just run over and check on him if something goes wrong. And I'm so far away that I can't use my lunch break to attend school functions, either.

"Hey, Donna, did you see the bill from the electrician?" David Park breezes in with some work-related question and no chitchat at all, every single time. He's always doing something, and the second he's done, he races to the next task like he's a thoroughbred on a track.

Even though he's all about the work, he still makes my heart pick up speed.

"It's here." I hand it to him. "And I have a stack of messages." I lift a pile of sheets and wave them at him.

He cringes. "Do I even want to call those people back?"

"How should I know?" I ask. "I'm not your secretary."

His head whips sideways and our eyes meet.

I laugh.

He shakes his head. "You still get me more often than I'd like to admit."

I don't think he's used to people giving him a hard time. "Your mom called," I say. "Her English is pretty good."

"Liar," he says. "There's a reason they sent me here. My parents both think they're great, but they've memorized entire sound sets for each phrase. It's pretty horrible trying to parse through what they're saying most of the time."

I chuckle. "They miss you, or so your mother says."

"Don't be fooled." He points at me as he backs away. "They want grandchildren. That's not the same thing."

My phone rings, and I answer without thinking. "Park Hyun Capital and Development, Donna speaking."

"Donna?"

"Yes, that's me."

"It's Alice," she says. "From the elementary."

Formerly my counterpart, before I was fired. "Oh, hey," I say. "Please tell me I didn't forget a half day." My forced laugh sounds stupid, even to me.

"The thing is, there's been an accident."

My heart stops.

And I realize that forty-seven minutes isn't long, it's a lifetime. I'm forty-seven minutes away from my baby, and there's literally nothing I can do from here. Once I finally recover my ability to breathe, I gasp. "What?" I clear my throat. "What happened?"

"He was playing on the swings with another little boy, Gabe Brooks, and they were talking about what superhero they wanted to be."

"Is Gabe alright?"

"He's fine, but apparently Aiden said he wanted to be Superman and he jumped off the swings to prove it. He landed wrong, and I think he broke his leg. It's bent strange, and he won't stop screaming."

My heart twists up like a pretzel. "I'll leave right now."

"How long will it take for you to get here?" she asks. "Because once you get here, you'll just need to turn around and head for the ER, right? Is there someone closer you could call? If you give me permission, they can get him for you."

Yes, that's the smart thing. Even if he wants me, even if he'd be happier with me, our priority has to be getting him in for treatment as soon as possible. "I'll leave right now, and I'll start calling people who might be able to bring him to me."

"You have to give me authorization to release him,"

she says. "Usually we'd want it in writing, but since it's an emergency. . ."

"Abigail Brooks," I say without thinking. "Amanda Brooks. Steve Archer. Amanda Saddler. Mrs. Earl." I pause and then just push past my reticence for the same reason I can authorize over the phone. It's an emergency. "Will Earl."

"They're all cleared to pick him up?"

"Yes, and if one of them can grab him, I'll just meet them at the hospital."

Abby, Amanda, and Steve don't answer.

Amanda Saddler's in Green River already, so she's even farther from him than I am.

I call Will, but he doesn't answer, either. I text him the same thing I sent Amanda and Abigail. AIDEN BROKE HIS LEG AT THE SCHOOL. I'M AT WORK. CAN YOU PICK HIM UP AND MEET ME IN GREEN RIVER? IF SO, I CAN DRIVE STRAIGHT THERE.

I call his mom next, and she doesn't answer her cell phone. But she does pick up on the hotel line, with a very beleaguered tone. "Can you hold for just a moment?"

"Uh, sure," I say. "But I was calling to ask a favor."

"Donna?"

"It sounds like you're super busy," I say. "I'll just try calling Will again."

"He's in the last few minutes of his car auction thing," she says. "He won't answer. Do you need something?"

"You're swamped?"

"Huge group just showed up to check in, and they're all complaining already."

I don't think a few minutes will really change anything substantial for Aiden. I'm just being an overwrought mother. "It's fine," I force myself to say.

"I'll call you right back when I get them settled."

I'm in my car, buckled and putting it into gear when I decide I should call the front desk again. I'm worried that Aiden might be bleeding internally or something. What if he, I don't know, passes out? Maybe we should call an ambulance. It's times like these that I hate small towns.

"Hello?" Alice sounds totally normal.

"It's Donna. How's Aiden?"

"I'm not sure," she says.

"*How can you not be sure?*" My voice has hit supersonic, but I can't bring myself to care.

"He's not here," she says. "He just left."

"*Left!?*"

"Donna, you told me I could release him if—"

"Who was it?" I ask. "Who picked him up?"

"Will Earl," she says. "Carried him out like he weighed nothing, and he had Aiden making jokes and laughing on his way out."

Making jokes? "About what?"

"Heck if I know. Something about Legos and Pokémon having babies."

"Thanks," I say. "I'll call Will." But when I check my phone, I've already got a text.

ON MY WAY TO GREEN RIVER. SEE YOU IN THE ER. An image pops up right beneath it of Will and Aiden's faces smooshed together, both of them throwing thumbs-ups in my direction. LITTLE GUY IS GOING TO BE JUST FINE. DON'T PANIC.

For the first time since Alice's call, I can breathe.

I want to call, but he's driving. The last thing I need to do now is cause an accident because I'm still fretting. I make myself focus on getting to Green River as fast as humanly possible, even if Will is going to be at least twenty minutes ahead of me because of my stupid remote location.

When I finally reach the ER, I rush inside.

"You must be Donna," the lady at the desk says. "You look exactly like your boyfriend said you would. He's so cute with your son, by the way. I totally thought it was his dad until your son corrected me."

I open my mouth to explain, but then it occurs to me. . .Will is really good-looking. If I tell her he's *not* my boyfriend, who knows how much attention that might send our direction. Nurses, techs, all of them a distraction from Aiden's care. Better to leave it alone. "Thanks."

But what she said keeps bugging me.

I'm following her down the hall, and I can't quite help myself. "What did he say I'd look like?"

"Frightened and worried, with your eyes looking everywhere at the same time." Her smile is soft. "He said you'd have wisps coming out of your high ponytail, because that's what you wear for work, but that your lipstick would look perfect, like an actress on a movie screen."

"That's—"

"And he said that you'd be wearing something that would be appropriate for a law office, but that you'd have some kind of cute details that gave you personality, like a bow on your earrings or flowers on your high heels."

As my black high heels with a tiny pink butterfly

click against the tile, my irritation rises. "Why did he spend so long chatting when Aiden's got a broken leg?"

She shrugs. "We were waiting for them to take him back, and when he was talking about you, your son smiled more."

"Oh."

"But my favorite part was when he said you had the most beautiful smile in the world." She grins. "Your son nodded his head and said, 'Mom's not happy that much, but when she is, the world has more sunshine.'"

Aiden thinks I'm not happy very often?

"Don't worry, though, your boyfriend told him he'd make sure you're happy a lot more now." She waves me closer. "It was the cutest thing I'd ever seen. A boyfriend *that* hot who talks about me like that?" She sighs. "I'd give my right arm."

"Are we almost to the room?" I've had about as much of this as I can take.

"Oh, right there." She points. "They're right inside."

I worry that Will overheard her gushing, but when I turn the corner, the doc's already inside, talking to Aiden.

"—that hurt?"

"Ow!"

Every muscle in my body contracts when Aiden shouts. "Hey," I say.

Will makes a fist and grimaces and shakes his hand in front of Aiden. "We got this, right?"

Aiden's mouth twists and he nods.

"I was checking to see exactly where to get the X-rays." The doctor spins around, his glasses sliding down his nose a bit. "It's a little uncomfortable, but your son has been a champ."

"Thanks," I say. "How much more do you need to do?"

"I'm done with that part," he says. "They'll take him back in a moment."

"Then what?"

"Depends on what they show," he says. "If it's misaligned, or if there are fragments, he'll need surgery."

"Which is fine," Will says. "Because then you'll have a really cool scar, too."

"Just like yours." Aiden beams at Will.

"Like yours?" What's he talking about?

Will stands up and lifts his shirt up with one hand, pulling the waist of his jeans down with the other. I ought to object, but my heart is hammering too fast to do anything except inhale sharply. I'm sure there's probably a scar somewhere, but I can barely make my brain work.

His stomach looks like it should be on a billboard ad —washboard, dark skin, practically glistening. How is he *that* tan at the end of January? And there's just the tiniest trail of dark hair visible right underneath his belly button.

"Last year Mister Will got kicked by a cow," Aiden says. "A chunk of its hoof got stuck in his belly."

That wakes me up. "What?"

Will drops his shirt and shrugs. "Ranch life."

"His story sounds so cool." Aiden looks glum. "Mine is stupid. I just fell off a swing."

"That's not how I heard it," Will says. "The word on the street is that you were flying *so high* in the sky that your friend Gabe couldn't even come close to matching you. He cried and begged for you to stop or to slow down, but speed swingers can't be contained. When the

342

chain popped though, you were ejected, and the ground couldn't withstand the magnificence of your landing. So your leg gave way."

The ground couldn't withstand the magnificence? What the heck is he saying?

But Aiden's laughing. "I think the ground beat me."

"We'll get it next time," Will says.

There are some things a mother simply can't do. The entire drive here, I was worried. My baby was hurt and he couldn't hold my hand. Who would wipe away his tears? But thanks to Will, there aren't any tears. He's been modeling himself after someone who gets hooves lodged in his stomach and keeps on trucking.

I suppose things could be way worse.

When they arrive to take Aiden back for the X-ray, something occurs to me. "Hey, your mom said you didn't answer the phone because you were in the middle of your auction for that car you've wanted forever."

He shrugs. "It's not like my mom knows everything that's happening in my life."

"So it wasn't today?" What a relief.

"Oh, it was."

I swallow. "You can leave right now. Maybe you'll—"

Will wraps an arm around my shoulders. "The sale would have happened while I was driving to the school to grab Aiden."

"Oh, no," I say. "I'm so sorry. I shouldn't have called."

"What I meant was that my mom has no idea what matters to me, not that I'm upset about missing it."

I freeze.

Will turns slowly, his face hovering over mine. "I don't care about that car, not if Aiden's in trouble. Not if you need me."

343

"But you said you'd been trying to get one for years."

"Not as long as I've been trying to get you." His head lowers slowly toward mine, his deep eyes intent.

My heart has fled the scene. My brain is blank. This isn't what I want, and I know that, and I've told him, but he doesn't seem to be listening. And my mouth isn't working well enough to remind him.

"Alright." The doctor drops a chart on a table behind us.

I leap away from Will so quickly that I bang my head on some kind of metal arm. "Ow."

"Careful there, Mrs. Ellingson. You'll want to avoid becoming my next patient if at all possible, because I think your son might have a bit of a rough go for the next few weeks. He's going to need a few pins and a pretty long cast."

"Oh, no."

"The good news is that it will heal cleanly and he's expected to make a full recovery. No restrictions expected."

"But—"

"You will want some help getting him hauled around for the first few weeks, preferably someone strong who won't struggle lifting and carrying him."

"I'd be happy to—"

I reach out to block Will and my hand presses against the place on his torso where his chest meets his abs. My fingers can feel each and every ridge of his stomach and his chest feels even better. Once again, my mind goes utterly blank. My hand shifts just a little, the tips of my fingers curling around the edges of the line between his abs. Holy Hannah. How in the world does he have the time to—

"Great. Well, you two seem a little busy." The doctor's laughing at me.

I snatch my hand back, swallowing so that I can figure out how to talk with such a dry mouth. "I won't need help. I'm strong and healthy. I can lift him myself for whatever he needs."

"He'll be unwieldy with the cast, and—"

I wave my hands in the air, careful not to get anywhere near Will Earl. "It's fine. I said it's fine."

"Alright." The doc pushes his glasses up again. "Whatever you want."

That's the problem. I *want* Will Earl, because, well. That part is obvious. But this time around, I'm not settling on anything at all. If I ever date someone again, it's going to be someone who is perfect on all fronts. Someone like David Park. I knew when I left home that I didn't want to marry a local, small-town guy. The fact that I got confused and married a jerk doesn't mean I need to make high-school-Donna's dreams crumble in misery.

No, Will Earl is definitely wrong for me.

I'm just confused right now because it's a period of high stress. I'll be fine by tomorrow.

❧ 25 ❧

DONNA

I haven't had my hair done in months, so when Abigail suggests that we spend our Saturday at a salon she's heard good things about in Vernal, I practically squeal with joy. Aiden is once again with his father—who had all kinds of threats for me when he found out about Aiden's leg—and I should feel nervous about it, but at least his grandparents are pretty good about following medical rules and making sure he eats and whatnot.

"This is not exactly what I'd call girl talk," Abby says while our hair is processing, "but we do need to go over the motion for summary judgment and make sure you agree with my positions and claims." She hands me a thick stack of paper held together by a single shiny staple in the top left corner.

"Is this so you can expense our trip?"

"Think that'll work?" she asks.

I shrug. "You're the lawyer."

"I doubt it," she says. "But I bet I can bill you for the time I'm spending in this salon chair."

I laugh. "What is that, exactly?"

"It's a motion for summary judgment on your brother's will contest. If the court finds that it's clear and makes sense, it should resolve the entire thing without the need for a trial. It's a process the court encourages if there aren't material questions of fact that still need to be resolved. In this case, I think we have enough evidence to do it."

I knew Abigail was brilliant, but as I scan the motion for summary judgment she's put together, I can hardly believe it. "You did this. . .while managing Amanda's drama and your own wedding and the ranch?"

Abigail leans toward me, her expression bemused. "I didn't handle things with Amanda very well—maybe you weren't listening. And as for the motion, this is literally my job. It would be like someone being shocked that Amanda can snap a decent photo and edit it properly, or that you can organize the things David needs to arrange the construction of his new resort."

"How's the wedding going?" I ask.

She shrugs. "It's back on track, finally. My sister kind of derailed it when she showed up, but she crossed a big line, and I finally sent her packing."

I can barely believe what I heard. "You did what?"

She sighs. "I'd been longing to do it since she arrived, all judgmental and rude about my decision. None of them were kind or understanding about Steve, and they just made me feel bad about my life."

"Sounds like my family, exactly," I say.

"When Helen didn't get what she wanted, she called in the cavalry, and within minutes of my parents' arrival, they were critical, aggressive, and just all-around belligerent. I had to deal with it when I was younger, and it made me feel like a miserable loser. Well, I'm almost forty, and I'm too old to take abuse like that anymore."

"And when you told them to go, they just went?"

She licks her lips and presses them flat. "Not exactly."

"Ooh," I ask. "What happened?"

"They resisted, of course." Her hairdresser comes back and starts to check her foils. "And I told them if they didn't go, I'd call the Sheriff and have them tossed out."

"You didn't."

"They didn't believe me at first, but when Steve backed up my story that he's related to the Sheriff, they grumbled and put on a big show, but they did finally leave."

"I can't believe it," I say. "You really are horrifying."

She doesn't laugh like I hoped she would. Mostly, she just looks tired. "Are you prepared, Donna?" she asks. "Going up against your family is draining and scary."

The papers in my lap grow somehow heavier. I decided not to tell Abby about Patrick hitting me, because I couldn't bring myself to testify against him, not while I'm also suing him for the estate he thought was rightfully his. If I'm being honest, I feel a little bad about taking it in the first place. My parents always *told* me it was for him. They said that I'd given up on my part when I decided to go to Stanford. I never thought it was entirely fair, but it was a deal I agreed to go along with and I accepted.

Before I've figured out how to answer, my lady also arrives, checking the progress on my hair. "You two ready to be shampooed?"

Both of us agree, and we're off, to have our necks

brutally abused by a stone sink that wants nothing but to torture us.

"Why don't they make neck pads for these or something?" I ask.

"I've been wondering that for years," Abby says. "We should patent one. We'd make a killing."

The hairdressers don't look like they love us, but I suppose I can't blame them. We're first-time customers, and we've spent the entire time talking to one another and not to them. "Sorry, guys."

They both assure us they don't mind, and we spend the rest of the time telling them about our kids and how we became friends, etc. It's not until we're walking out the door, with much nicer hair, that Abby says, "You didn't answer my question."

"Huh?"

She pats her large purse that now contains the motion again. "Are you ready for me to file this? Because it's going to bring things to a head, and if the court doesn't accept it, the trial will start soon after."

I inhale and exhale. I think about Patrick and how he treated me for the past year, how he's treated me recently. It may not have been what our parents said they'd do for years and years, but I think that they came around near the end of their lives to the belief that they'd made the wrong decision. I understand how it might be hard for Patrick to accept, but he's gone beyond difficulty in accepting change and broken laws. He even hit me—and I still struggle to wrap my head around the transformation. He went from a little boy who hid under the table with me when Dad raged, to an adult who punched me in the face.

But that nastiness inside him only makes me more

prepared to advocate for myself. If my family doesn't have any regard for me or any desire to keep me safe, why shouldn't I take the entire inheritance? Abby's not lying. Her motion tells the truth.

"Do it," I say. "Do you think there's a good chance we'll win?"

"Honestly," she says. "I don't know how we'd lose the trial. He'd have to be sleeping with the judge for them not to rule in our favor after this mound of evidence."

"Was it really necessary to go into his unfair dealings with the ranch?" I wince. "I mean, I know it personally affected you, and I'm sorry to even ask it, but it feels like we're piling that on for no reason."

Abby opens the car door and motions for me to get inside. She slings her bag in the back seat, buckles, and once I've buckled too, she meets my eyes. "I said we'd almost certainly win the *trial*. A motion for summary judgment is a little different. They're hard to win. They were created to prevent the pendency of frivolous claims. As you know, we've also brought a claim against his lawyer, and although we haven't pursued criminal measures, it could result in him being disbarred. Our charges are significant, and in order to tell the entire story from a factual and evidence perspective, it was necessary. But I understand having second thoughts about wrecking your family relationship. So if you want to pull the plug or soften the whole thing, now's the time to do it."

I shake my head. The time to have done that was last week, or better yet, last month, and it's not my fault that we're moving ahead like this, prepared to take everything from him.

It's Patrick's.

After I drop Abby at her place, instead of feeling a sense of peace and safety from having the moral high ground, I just feel lousy.

Really lousy.

My dad was the real problem. He beat us both. He crushed us both. Whenever we'd try to band together, to buoy one another up, Dad would slam us both so hard that we would stop worrying about helping anyone and think only about ourselves.

And the more I think about it, the more I worry that the whole "trade your Stanford education for your inheritance" thing was just another power play to drive us apart. Whenever I came home, he'd use it to both tear me down—since I didn't finish—and simultaneously make Patrick feel awful by repeating over and over that he never got into college. When my brother offered me that deal, maybe I should have negotiated. His actions were horrible. There's no doubt about that, but I haven't spent much time wondering why a man who hasn't ever hit anyone, as far as I know, would do it now.

I wish I could talk to him, but I don't have the courage to call him, and I'm certainly not showing up on his doorstep again. I get in my car, prepared to try and. . .I don't know. Call Amelia and see if she might meet me? But when I start driving, that's not where I go. Somehow, without thinking, I wind up at the closest bar. It's not like alcohol will fix anything, as I discovered the last time I came here, but I'm not an alcoholic. I don't have to get drunk.

And sometimes a few drinks just make me feel better. I could really use that right now. So before I have time to think about it, I go inside.

I'm not sure how many drinks I've had when Will

texts me. Certainly not very many. Nothing like last time, when I barely remember him coming to pick me up. None of the letters and numbers on my cell phone are blurring together, for one.

YOU BUSY? he asks.

NOT REALLY, I text back. JUST DRINKING.

WHERE?

WHERE DO YOU THINK?

Ah, Will. Here, surrounded by strangers, loosened up a bit by liquid truth, I admit it to myself. He's hot, he's much kinder than I expected, and I want to date him. But I know it's a terrible idea, and I'm proud of myself for holding the line.

I made a mistake last time—distracted by the shininess of my family-money boyfriend. I won't do something stupid like that again. Charlie wasn't a horrible person because he had been raised in the city, or because he was well educated. That was incidental. With someone like David Park in my life every day, I know that rich people are just as likely to be good as anyone else. He may not like me, but I'll meet someone like him who does, if I'm patient enough.

I won't settle.

I whip out my phone, an idea occurring to my rather buzzy mind. I should text David. Maybe he'll want to come get a drink, and it would be a good chance for him to see me outside of work and realize I'm not just a model employee.

I'm also a woman.

My fingers are hovering over the keys while I ponder what to say when someone says my name.

"Donna."

It's a deep voice. It makes a shiver run down my

spine and heat pool in my belly. I turn around slowly, excited that David came *without* me even texting. Only, it's not David. The voice that called to me, the voice that I'm craving, doesn't belong to my boss.

It's Will Earl.

His jacket's open, and he's wearing a dark blue t-shirt underneath. It clings to him like it's made of old school Saran Wrap. You know, the kind that stuck to things in all the wrong places? Except these don't look wrong, but I know they are. Even so, I can't seem to look anywhere other than his chest.

He's walking toward me. I know, because his chest keeps getting closer and closer.

I hold out my hand, not sure exactly what I'm intending, but I know I need to stop him from taking over. Only, he doesn't stop when his body reaches my hand. He keeps moving, and my elbow buckles. My fingers splay across his pecs, and they're even harder and less yielding than I remembered.

I can't help my sigh, or the caress I give as my hand moves down his midsection.

"Okay," he says. "Time for you to go home."

His arms wrap around my waist and suddenly, I'm being lifted, spun around, and set on a course away from the bar. I'm not even done with my drink. I open my mouth to object and realize that somehow, I did finish it. "I haven't paid," I say. "You can't just march me out of here."

He chucks a pile of cash on the bar and waves at the bartender. "I'm taking her."

The tall, gangly guy in his twenties nods like that makes perfect sense.

I hate him. He's got no loyalty. "Will Earl," I say as

angrily as I can. Only, instead of angry, it almost sounds breathy.

Through some kind of miracle, he actually stops. His hands shift a little, both of them almost meeting around the front of my stomach. His face is above me, but near my ear. "What?" His breath washes over me, minty and warm.

It sends another shiver down my spine. I swallow. "You can't just come here and take me away. I don't belong to you."

I can hear the smile in his voice. "Say that again."

"I don't belong to you." I try to turn, but his hands won't let me.

"Let's talk outside," he says. "I promise I will not, nor would I ever, force you into my car or anywhere else, but I think the cool air will do you some good."

I think about arguing, but I realize that what he said is true. He's much stronger than I am. He's much more sober too, but I believe him when he says he won't really force me to go anywhere I don't want to go.

When we walk outside, the cool air hits me like an ice water attack. The swirling feelings inside of me, the hazy want and desire that have been warring with my irritation at his manhandling, all evaporate.

I'm being a buzzed idiot. Will's helping me. I doubt his hands around my waist mean anything at all. He's just guiding me out because that's what a friend should do. "Thanks."

He releases me, and I turn to face him. "I wasn't paying attention, and I think I drank more than I should have."

"You shouldn't go drink alone," he says. "It's easy to lose track, and that bar's not full of boys-next-door." He snorts. "Or maybe it is, but you'd be surprised how many of them are perverts."

"Are you a pervert, Will?" I lift my eyes to his.

"I care about you," he says. "I didn't think we'd have this conversation here or now, but I'm not sure how much longer I can wait."

Any words I meant to say lodge in my throat.

"I like you," he says. "I've liked you for a really long time. I asked you to homecoming when we were in high school, our senior year, and when you never replied to me—"

I shake my head. "What are you talking about? You said that before and I forgot about it with all the mess with Charles, but—"

"I delivered two dozen roses," he says. "And a gift card for a hundred dollars to TJ Maxx. The card had a horrible poem I wrote written inside, which I still regret, but I thought the idea of asking you to the dance and giving you a way to shop for a dress was a good one."

No way. "You didn't."

Will frowns. "I left it on your porch. Did you think it was from someone else?"

"My brother did what you're describing, exactly that, when he asked Jamie." Of course, now that I'm saying it, I'm wondering how I could have been stupid enough to believe it was true. My brother wasn't someone to get roses, much less a gift card he'd have to drive to another city to procure.

Which means that even back then, I'm the moron. Me and Jamie, both.

"I think Patrick ruined that," I say. "And I'm sorry."

"That makes a lot more sense," Will says. "I figured

you'd at least have mentioned it, but when I asked you about it. . ."

A fuzzy scene rises up in my memory.

Will was in his football practice gear with his mouth guard dangling down in front of his chest. "Hey, Dee," he said. "Done any shopping lately?" His All-American grin was in full force, his white teeth shining, his sweaty hair falling down across his forehead.

I had thought he was mocking me back then. I'd worn the exact same shirt almost once a week for more than two years. "Shut up."

He frowned at my hostility, his beautiful, bright eyes darkening. "So that's a no, then?"

I thought he was really mean, at the time, mocking me and then doubling down. I had no idea he was taking my defensive words as a rejection to his generous invitation.

When I look up into his eyes, he's utterly still. "I don't want there to be any confusion this time." He swallows. "Donna Ellingson, the first day I saw you after you came back to town, my heart practically exploded in my chest. When I asked around and they told me you were getting a divorce, I couldn't believe I might have another chance. And the more time I spend with you, the more I wish that you'd given me a shot years ago. I would have spared you all the pain and all the misery if I could. I'd still do anything I could to make you smile."

"Will."

He shakes his head, and his hands clench at his side. "Just let me finish."

I nod.

"You think you don't want a rancher, because the only two ranchers you ever knew were filthy, selfish sacks of crap who abused you. But I swear, we're not all like that. I'm a simple man, and you're brilliant. I never went to college, and you went to the nicest school on this side of the country. I do work harder than anyone you know, and I'm as reliable as the tides. If you just give me a chance, I'll prove it to you, every single day."

My heart is the one that's close to exploding. I've seen that he's loyal. He's been there every single time I've needed him, and he's never even flung the inconvenience I've caused him back at me, like Charlie always did. He's not simple, either. He's talented, and he's devoted, and he's kind.

And he loves Aiden.

I can see it—that can't be faked. Not in front of someone who has become a human lie detector by living with a charlatan for years.

But he's right that I don't want a rancher. If I started dating him, it would feel like settling. It would feel like, because of Charlie, my chances were all shot, like he said. Instead of coming back here, recouping for a bit and going back out into the world to kick butt and take names, it would feel like I came back and withered.

I can't have that. Not for me, and not for Charlie. "But Will, the thing is—"

"'But Will.'" He sighs. "I guess that's my answer, but. . ." He looks around at the empty parking lot, and he looks back at me, clearly calculating something. "I can't just walk away. Not yet."

Before I can tell him that my answer's never going to change, his hands circle my waist again. He tugs me toward him slowly, giving me plenty of time to protest, giving me time to stop him.

As much as I know I should—I don't.

I think I kissed him here before, when I'd had way too much to drink. Just another one of the times this man saved me. But I don't remember it, and every part of me *wants* that memory. Even if I can't end up with him, even if I won't surrender my dreams of the future like that, I can at least have this moment in time.

When his head begins to lower toward mine, when his intense, soul-searching eyes meet mine, I don't look away or pull away or shove backward.

I welcome him.

My hands slide upward, starting with his abs that I so love to touch, and moving up slowly, one glorious inch at a time, until they wrap around his neck and cup his jaw, shifting against his slightly bristly skin. "Kiss me," I say, my voice low.

And I mean it.

His mouth isn't slow then, and his hands aren't soft. His lips claim mine, the pressure insistent, the pace fast. The electricity I'd only felt before as a shiver up my spine is turned all the way up, the breaker completely thrown.

The feeling when our lips meet is like a live wire sparking over a river of water.

It's an explosion across the sky.

A river of fire flooding my veins.

I'm not sure how long we stand there, our arms entwined and our bodies pressed tightly together, but finally I remember who I am and what I want and I force myself to stumble apart from him.

"I'm so sorry, Will. But this time, I got the message, and my answer is the same."

It hurt a lot less before, when I didn't know what I was turning down.

❧ 26 ❧

ABIGAIL

After Nate died, as long as I was busy, I kept my head above water. It was the quiet moments that threatened to drown me.

It's much harder to tread water than it is to swim.

I thought that, once I started to heal from the loss, once I stopped fearing the quiet moments, once I began to look back on our two decades together with more fondness than pain, I was in the clear. It didn't occur to me that the same pain, or something very similar, could happen because of discord with my family.

When I left home to go to Princeton, my parents were upset. My sister had followed in their footsteps and waltzed right into the spot they made sure was available for her at Stanford. I knew I couldn't do that. I wouldn't have excelled in that situation, watched and poked and prodded by my parents.

I'd have imploded.

But no one even considered when I left that I might never return to their embrace. They assumed I'd go to Stanford for graduate school. And when I decided to go

Harvard for law school, they thought I'd take the bar and find a job in the Los Angeles area, at least.

Because it was an incremental set of steps, one after another, each made after consideration and great contemplation, they never freaked out on me. Nothing was ever brought to a head. When we were together, I would quietly cower and duck my head, and then once they left, I'd do as I felt I ought to do. The fallout always happened over the phone or, in a worst-case scenario, during a short trip they made to fuss at me. Nothing had ever gone the way their recent visit went.

Because young Abby would never have dared to act the way I did this time.

I thought it would feel empowering, like I was merely a fledgling, and now I'm a full-blown dragon, capable of defending my own lair.

Instead, in the quiet moments, I feel gutted.

In fact, it feels like I'm broken all over again.

I'm sure that with time, I'll heal just as I did after Nate's death. The big difference between the two is that cancer stole Nate from me, but the rift with my family was torn wide open by me. It was the collateral damage inflicted by my own desire to defend myself for once.

As a reasoning adult, I understand that I was doing it to protect my entire family. I was in the right, and that sense of justice keeps me moving. It just doesn't negate the pain. To avoid thinking about it, I've been doing a lot of swimming lately to keep busy. I can't really do water-treading at all—no quiet reflection for me.

"Mrs. Brooks?" The bank manager's smile is so fake that I have trouble looking directly at it.

"Yes?"

"You and your client can follow me and I'll show you to the lockboxes."

I still can't believe that Mr. Eugene really needed me to come with him to access a lock box. The manager's wording registers with me slowly. "Wait. Did you say *boxes*?" I ask. "Plural?"

He shuffles along behind me, still looking a bit like a wilted flower. His head is bowed, his shoulders are slumped, and it looks like we're marching to his arraignment or something instead of into the center of a bank where he'll be doing a routine part of his job.

As if it takes him a moment to understand my question, he stops a beat or two after I ask. Then he turns back toward me, slowly. "There are two boxes that were being rented by Mrs. Eugene. You weren't aware of that?"

"We only got a bill for one," I say.

He nods. "Well, that's because the bill is generated automatically by the system. They'll always be invoiced one year after they were first created."

"So there are two?" I turn toward Mr. Eugene. "Any idea why she might have had more than one?"

He shrugs, his eyes just as mournful as ever.

"Well, maybe you can figure it out today. Here you are." The bank manager points. "This and this are the two boxes. We've opened them for you, and you can carry them into that room there." He points the opposite direction at a small room with a counter and two benches. "It locks from the inside, if you need privacy, and you can put the blinds down as well."

"That won't be necessary," I say. "But thank you."

Since I'm concerned that Mr. Eugene might actually collapse under the weight of the boxes, I reach for both of them. They're surprisingly heavy, and I end up taking just one of them to the breakaway room. "What's in these?" I glance at the bank manager as I emerge for the second box.

He shrugs. "They are quite large. Your client's wife rented the largest boxes we had."

I lug the second one into the room as well, legitimately worried that the unreinforced counter won't hold the weight of both, but it does, at least, for now.

"If that's all you need?" The manager looks like a kid being held back in the principal's office on the last day of school.

I wave him off and he shoots out, grateful to escape what is clearly going to be an exciting moment of exploration with my sad sack client. Unfortunately, Mr. Eugene isn't someone who does things quickly, so this isn't going to be fast.

I open the first box, and although I was prepared for most anything, its contents shock even me. Six large gold bars are stacked inside it, each of them stamped as one kilo. No wonder it was heavy. There's close to fifteen pounds of precious metal in brick form. Next to the gold bars is a stack of old and heavy-looking jewelry.

"Did you know your wife had gold bars?" I force my eyes away from the gold bars and toward Mr. Eugene.

He shakes his head slowly. "Why would she have those?"

I carefully remove the jewelry, which he insists he's never seen, and the gold bars, and arrange them in a line. Underneath the stack of pirate-looking treasure, there's also a stack of papers.

"This is a deed to some real property in Texas," I say. "West Texas."

"Real property?" He clears his throat. "Is there fake property?"

I suppress my smirk. "It's a legal term. It means real estate, as opposed to say, a car, or stock in a company, which is also 'property' under the law."

His brows furrow. "Oh." He brightens immediately. "Oh! I really should have remembered this. Dolores lost her aunt a few years ago, and since Aunt Irma had no children, she left everything to Dolores."

"This aunt had property in Texas?"

"That's where her family is from."

I filter through a whole stack, including stocks and bonds certificates that look to be close to fifty years old. There's also three hundred and some odd thousand dollars in cash. I cringe to think how much it has depreciated while sitting in this box.

When we open the other box, it also has land—two parcels, actually, also both in Texas. One in West Texas, one in East Texas. There are also five gold bars, and although there's no jewelry, there's six hundred thousand and change in cash.

"And this second box?" I gesture at the contents. "She didn't mention any of this to you either?" I can't believe it.

"She had an uncle die a year after her aunt," he says. "I guess she just took his stuff too and put it all in here."

"The deeds have been transferred into her name," I say. "It wasn't like it just went in here. She thought about all of this, and met with some kind of lawyer to handle it all. I wonder why she kept them here." And why he didn't know anything about it.

He looks at his shoes. "She did ask if we wanted to look at a different house a few years back, or perhaps consider moving to a different town, but I told her I liked where we were. We have a great view of the mountains."

I have no idea what kind of marriage they had, that he had no idea she had eleven gold bars, three pieces of land, and almost a million in cash and not only did she not use any of it, she didn't even tell him about it. Or if she did, he wasn't paying attention. "Alright, well, we'll need to—"

"I brought some papers," he says. "I figured I'd show them to you after we got this done, but maybe they're related to some of this."

"Papers?"

He crumples inward a bit. "I know I keep bothering you with this stuff, and I'm sorry, but it's really confusing. The statements came in the mail, and they have a lot of numbers on them. I didn't even realize we had them, but there was a whole stack of them, unopened, in a box in the closet."

Heavenly days. What now? At least I don't have to feel bad about charging him for my services anymore. "Alright. Let's leave these gold bars and jewelry in the lockboxes for now, but we can take the deeds and stock certificates and cash and sort through this back home."

It takes a few moments, but I finally convince him to deposit the cash into an account with the bank. The idea of driving him home with a million dollars in cash feels like the beginning of a bad horror movie. I can just see him featuring in a newspaper headline tomorrow morning.

OLD MAN MURDERED IN HOME. NO LEADS ON MOTIVE.

Until his attorney calls and explains she left him at

home with a huge wad of cash. I wonder how quickly they'd clap me in cuffs. Sheesh.

"Do you want to add it to the account your wife had already opened?" the bank manager asks.

I can't help it. My hands pop up to my hips. "You knew there was an account here in her name? And you knew we thought there was only one safety deposit box, and you didn't think to mention it until we asked to open a new one?" What the heck kind of people run this bank?

He shrugs. "I assumed you knew."

I roll my eyes. What a liar. "We'd like to open a new account in my client's name and deposit this cash into it. And as the signatory individual on the lock boxes, he can do that. We'd also like to formally request all the records on the existing checking and savings account."

"He's named on the account already," he says, "and it was created with a right of survivorship, so technically it's already his."

At least his wife doesn't appear to have been doing anything nefarious—he's just monumentally out of the loop. I think maybe he was honestly just entirely disinterested in wealth. I might not have believed until meeting him that there are people for whom money just does not matter, but apparently it's true.

We go through the baffling paperwork he mentioned while we wait for the manager to clean things up, and I shouldn't be surprised, but somehow I still am.

"These are royalty statements," I say. "Your wife has been receiving payments for the removal of crude oil from her land in Texas. There are operating oil wells on both of the West Texas properties right now. Did you really not know?"

He shakes his head slowly.

The bank manager brings me the current account statement and some printouts on the history showing when the account was created—six years ago. There are nine million dollars in his account currently. Most of the large deposits began two years ago, and the only cash sweeps that have happened have been to the IRS.

I do some quick calculations. Gold. Cash. Checking account. "Fred, you're currently in possession of some ten and a half million dollars, and that doesn't include the land value, the future income from the oil reserves, or the stock or jewelry, which I haven't yet been able to look into."

He frowns. "Excuse me?"

"You're worth more than ten million dollars, sir. You're extremely wealthy."

By the time we get back to Manila and I drop him off, he still looks like he was struck in the face with a stray baseball. "Once I've discovered more about these stock certificates and the jewelry, I'll be in touch."

He nods.

I hope he's alright, but I can't just sit with him all day. Although, I suppose he could afford to pay me to do just that. It's so strange. The little man who shuffled into my house not long ago is actually a multi-millionaire. Who'd have thought? Certainly not him.

When I get home, I barely have time to get dinner started before the kids escape the bus. Surprisingly, Ethan follows them inside. "You're done with the fences?" I ask.

"Mom, I finished them last week."

"What have you been doing out there?" I ask.

"Buff came to check the calves today." His bemused

expression makes me happy sad. Sad, because my little boy is growing up, and happy because he's competent and responsible, and I'm delighted to see it.

"And how are they?"

"Everyone looks like they're doing well. Two sets of twins, which is kind of fun and a little nerve-wracking."

"What's for dinner?" Gabe asks.

"I made chili." I point at the pot. "It just needs to simmer for a bit. And I just put the cornbread in, so it'll be out in time to cool down before dinnertime. Who has homework?"

Gabe drops his backpack on the floor. Whitney flings hers into her room and takes off her coat. Her shoes, she just flips wherever they land in a classic Whitney move. And Izzy sets her things by the door and practically jogs into the kitchen.

"Mom," Izzy says. "You've been working a lot, which is great, since it's a new job. And when you aren't working, you're planning wedding details. We're glad things are moving along. But."

"You aren't spending any time with Steve," Ethan says. "He was grumbling about it at the girls' last lesson."

"It's a lot to manage," I say, "between kids and work and—"

"We know," Izzy says. "So we're giving you the afternoon off. Drive over there and just do whatever he's doing. Ethan made sure he's not working."

"You're. . .what?"

"I'll take care of dinner," Izzy says.

"And I'll feed the animals," Whitney says. "I've been practicing."

"Because I can feed the goats and the chickens," Gabe says.

"But no more chucking handfuls of mealworms all over," Izzy says. "Those are expensive."

"They make the chickens like me," Gabe says. "And you don't even pay for them." He sticks out his tongue.

"Okay," I say. "How about no more than two handfuls of mealworms?"

"Mom?" Izzy says.

"What?"

"We've got this. Just go."

"You realize that I like spending time—"

Ethan circles around behind me and puts his hand on my lower back. He snatches my jacket off the back of the sofa and gently herds me toward the door. "You love us, we're special, that will never change, we know."

I snap my mouth closed. It almost sounds like he's mocking me.

"We're not making fun of you, Mom," Ethan says, as if he can read my mind.

Perhaps it's more that I always share everything I'm thinking and they're now in tune with my thoughts. That's a horrifying thought. "But if—"

"If lightning strikes the hay and the barn catches fire," Ethan says, "we'll call you. Right after calling the fire department."

"And if Whitney falls and cracks her head open," Izzy says, "we'll call you. Right after calling Steve." Her eyes are sparkling.

"And if Gabe bites me again," Whitney says, "I won't call you. I'll just punch him."

"What?" I look around at the other kids' reactions to see if she's kidding.

"You said you weren't going to tell her that," Gabe says. "I want my Pokémon cards back."

"What on earth is he talking—"

"Later." Ethan's shoving me faster. "You can get to the bottom of the great Pokémon trade and bite cover-up later. I promise it will keep."

I suppress my laugh. "Fine, but don't think I'll forget about it."

Gabe scowls at Whitney. "If you hadn't knocked over my—"

But Ethan's handing my purse through the doorway and closing the door, leaving me to stand on my front porch alone.

I blink once or twice and decide they're probably right. With all the client mess, and the family drama, and the wedding details, I've been neglecting my own fiancé. He hasn't complained, but probably only because he didn't want to add to my stress. I stop overthinking things, which is hard for me, and I drive down the road to Steve's.

When I arrive, there's another car there. A small, shiny blue Toyota. There's a woman standing in the front yard, pointing at things and talking to him, holding a clipboard.

I haven't seen someone use a clipboard since I signed up for a gym membership a decade ago, but they are a little behind the times here.

"Hello?" I close the door and walk toward them.

Steve's face lights up when he sees me, but then he glances at the woman and semi-cringes. Who *is* she?

"Hello." The woman's a little stiff when she turns, like she's one-quarter plastic and can't easily move like a human. I'm pretty sure there aren't prototypes for AI robots yet, but if there were. . . "My name is Linda Larson." The smile she plasters

369

on her face looks familiar, but I can't place quite why.

This poor woman has a first and last name that start with the same letter? "Um, I'm Abigail Brooks."

"This is my fiancée," Steve says.

"Oh." Her eyes widen, but nothing else crinkles or wrinkles at all, as if her entire face has been frozen with four hundred units of Botox. "How wonderful. He's told me so many wonderful things about you. So you'll soon be Abigail Archer."

Ohmyword. For the first time, it occurs to me how terribly corny my name will be when I take Steve's last name. It's worse than Linda Larson. I do my best not to cringe. "Uh, yeah."

She's still smiling, and it finally hits me why I think it looks familiar. My grandma gave me several china dolls when I was young, and my mom wouldn't let me throw them away. They would stare at me every night from the top shelf of my bookcase, their dead-eyed smiles mocking me.

Linda's smile looks just like that.

Steve sighs. "Linda's a real estate agent from Green River whom a friend referred me to."

"A what?" I don't understand.

"I think a little gem like this will sell awfully quick," she says.

Sell. Wait. Steve's selling his house?

"Did you need anything else from me?" Steve asks.

"Nope. Once I get that signed contract, I'll send someone to take photos. If you can make the changes we discussed, we'll be all set to get that listing live before spring hits."

"Great." He shifts toward her car, and she heads over and gets in.

She waves at me once before leaving, her expression still creepy as all get out.

"You're selling the house?"

Steve shakes his head. "You always ruin my surprises."

"What other surprises have I ever ruined?"

"You came out and caught me ten days before I meant to propose." He's grumbling, but it's the kind of complaining he does when it rains and he has to shut off the sprinklers, or when someone spills water on the floor he was about to mop.

He's not really upset.

"You can't sell your house," I say.

Steve closes the space between us and pulls me toward him for a hug. The words he whispers near my ear are calm, soft, and utterly sure. "I can do whatever I need to do to make my *wife* happy." He squeezes me. "And I will. I'm sorry I got upset before, but I promise that this old dog will do everything he can to learn new tricks."

I pull away, looking him in the eyes. "No, I mean, I don't want you to sell it."

"What?"

"Ethan will want his own space one day," I say. "He needs our help now, but he won't always. And your place is perfect for you, for the horses, and even eventually, for the kids. Plus, you don't care about the house, so I can do literally anything I want to it."

"I don't follow."

"I haven't talked to Ethan, but I had an idea. For the first year or two, you come live with us. You'll have to drive to and from your barn to care for animals, but you have Javier to help you out, and he does most of the everyday feeding and stall cleaning anyway."

"Okay."

"During that year or two, you let me spend anything I want making the house exactly how I want it to be."

He smiles at me, his one dimple showing up clearly.

"And then once we're sure Ethan can manage things, we move everyone else over to your newly refurbished place, and we just check in on Ethan to make sure he's doing alright."

"You'd do that?" he asks.

"Gladly," I say. "I feel like that's a compromise that will be hard on both of us in some ways, but also perfect in lots of others."

"I think it'll be way less stressful than selling," he says.

"Did you hear that I'd be spending copious amounts of money mucking around in your home?"

"What changes do you plan to make to the barn?" he asks.

I shrug. "None."

"Then we're good. I actually have a decent amount of money. I've been single for a long time, and other than horses, I don't spend it on anything. Mostly I make money off of them, so we're good."

"Are we really good?" I ask.

Steve takes my hand and tugs me toward his front porch. The sun's starting to drop lower in the sky, and the air's getting chillier too. Even with my coat on, I shiver. He sits on the porch swing and pulls me down next to him, wrapping an arm around my shoulders.

"You did a huge thing when Helen brought your

parents here, kicking them out. Telling them off." He presses a kiss to my forehead. "I can't tell you how much I appreciated that you defended me, truly."

"It's fine," I say. "They've run me over and criticized me and made me feel small my entire life."

"I can't condone that kind of thing from them, of course," he says, "but family is complicated, and I just wanted to say that if you're happy with how it went down, then so am I. But if you're not, I'm a big boy. I don't actually need you to throw people out because they might hurt my feelings."

"They were—"

He presses a finger to my lips. "I know who you are, and I know that the most controlling, most powerful force in your heart is your loyalty. It fills me with joy to know that, outside of your kids, I'm right up there at the top. But they can mock me, and they can disparage me, and they can make me grovel too, and I don't actually care."

I open my mouth and he moves his finger out of the way and kisses me.

He only pulls back far enough to speak, so his words cascade over my face like caresses. "If you want them at the wedding, if you want them to come visit regularly, or if you want them to move out here, I will grit my teeth and smile and you won't hear a single word of complaint from me. Because you defended me first, and I know where I stand."

"Thank you," I say.

"You've been struggling with it," he says. "I can see it."

"I've never fit in with them," I say. "They've never

been proud of anything I've done or any of the choices I've made."

"But they're still your family, and only you can decide whether having them at the wedding will make you happier or more upset. But once you make up your mind, I'm right there with you, writing a check, or forcing a smile, or whatever else you may need."

And that, in a nutshell, is why Steve and me work. He cares enough about me to do things he doesn't want to do, and I care enough about him to do the same. "It's not my way or the highway," I whisper.

He gently presses his outside arm against the side of my head until it rests against his shoulder. "I didn't claim that I never say idiotic things." He sighs. "But I promise I'll apologize for them, and I am sorry for that one."

"I promise I'll accept your apologies, but I don't promise not to bring the stupid things you say up over and over. Forever."

He laughs.

And we spend the rest of our date hammering out the remaining details of the wedding *we* want, without regard to anyone else at all.

❦ 27 ❧

AMANDA

I should not be here. I feel like a complete and total idiot. I worked late every single night last week so that I could, what? Rush off to California again and surprise Eddy by going to his second concert? I mean, after the fiasco of my last trip, he's going to think I'm here to check up on him again.

Am I?

If I'm being honest with myself, maybe. I mean, I don't want to be here for that. I want to celebrate his success and be proud of his accomplishments. I want to be his adoring fan and his biggest supporter. But I'm worried that that's all a front for my strongest feelings: jealousy and fear.

I hate it.

But I'm learning that being honest with myself is the only way for me to avoid doing something entirely insane. I didn't know how much of my damage from the past would wind up front and center when I started dating someone I really cared about. I just hope Eddy will continue to be patient with me.

It would help if I could stop letting my crazy dangle out in the open like an unsightly skin tag.

I don't tell anyone who I am. I simply present my ticket and go into the venue when it opens. It's not a huge stadium like the time I saw U2, but it's not a rundown club, either. I'd guess it's got between fifteen hundred and two thousand seats—and it looks nice. Very art deco.

"Is it your first time at the Wiltern?" the guy next to me asks. He's wearing a very stylish outfit, including a dark scarf and shiny leather shoes.

I nod. "Yep. I take it that you've been here before."

He gestures for me to go ahead first. "I'm at the end." He points at the chair near the edge of the row.

"I'm G28," I say.

"Right here." He points three seats over. "I come pretty often. I like live music, but I hate fighting my way through tens of thousands of people." He smiles. "Plus, I live two blocks from here. So I keep an eye on the artists coming and buy tickets for anything that looks interesting."

"And you thought the Eddy Dutton Band looked interesting?"

"I loved his music when I was a kid, and I'm a nostalgic kind of guy. Plus, I like his new song," he says. "I think it's cool that he finally got cleared after all these years."

"It's pretty awful that his old label basically framed him." I can't keep from doing a little prying to see what a typical fan thinks about the whole thing.

He shrugs. "Who knows what really happened or how it went down, but second chances don't come often in life. I'm glad he's getting his."

"I wonder whether he's nervous, performing again after all this time."

"I'm sure he's a little nervous," he says, "but performers usually love it, and I hear it's like riding a bike."

"Guess we'll find out."

More people show up on the row then, filtering into their seats. It feels like it takes forever, but it's really no more than about thirty minutes before Eddy and his band come on stage. I'm surprised to see that his drummer is a woman, and she's a really pretty woman at that.

Her hair's done in twisty, wild-looking dreadlocks, several of which are pink, and she's wearing huge black boots, but her dark dramatic makeup perfectly offsets her feminine, petal-pink babydoll dress. She can't be more than mid-twenties.

I'm guessing Eddy's going to say a few words, since he's approaching the microphone, but before he touches it, the drummer starts playing, and two or three beats later, everyone else joins in. I love the keyboard—that's one of my favorite things that rock bands layer in.

Eddy's wearing dark jeans and cowboy boots, which I think is a smart nod on the stylist's part to his country background, and a dark green button-down shirt. I'm sure if I had a better seat, I'd be able to tell that it makes his eyes pop even more than usual. He looks utterly at home, and although he's playing one of his new songs and very few people here have heard it, they seem to be nodding along.

"He's so hot," the lady next to me says. "Can you believe he's forty?"

"That just means he'll *know what he's doing* instead of fumbling around." She giggles.

Both of the twenty-somethings laugh.

I think about their commentary on his age. It's really unfair that women are considered old at forty, and men are considered 'seasoned,' but that's not a battle I could possibly win today.

In fact, for the rest of the show, I try my best *not* to listen to what anyone is saying. I try to just enjoy the fact that he looks comfortable up there, comfortable and happy. I'm pretty impressed by how much the audience appears to be enjoying the show. It could definitely have gone much, much worse.

After it's over, I debate my options. I could call or text him, obviously, and tell him I'm here. That would make things much easier for me, but it would also eliminate any hope I have of surprising him. I decide that, although it might be harder, I'd like to try and sneak back to say hello. As a bonus, I'll get to see how he looks in his element. I love seeing people who are good at something do it, and the idea of watching him giving the rest of his band notes on the performance is appealing to me.

Do they do that? The lead singer and front man, telling the others what to do? How to try harder, or where they were overdoing? If so, I'm going to have him tell that little drummer girl to wear more clothes and stop mock-flirting during the performance.

Although, I suppose the men here at the show probably enjoyed having some female eye candy. And if that kind of girl is what Eddy wants, he'll certainly have his pick of them over the next few months. The concert is packed full of women who look as good or better than the edgy drummer, all of them sighing and making googly eyes in his direction.

"Ma'am, you can't come back here," a man in a black shirt and black pants tells me, when I try to brush past him and through a door marked BACKSTAGE.

"I know it's your job," I say, "to keep people out, but I'm Eddy's girlfriend."

He chuckles. "Nice try."

I whip out my phone and pull up an image from my Insta account. "Except, I actually am. I came to surprise him. It's not like he's, like, Garth Brooks or Eminem, or someone. I swear, this isn't some kind of game. Look."

The man glares at me at first, but finally, after patiently waiting and refusing to stand down, he glances at my phone. That's when I have him, I know. Once they acknowledge that you might be right, you've already won. "See?" I tap the screen. "This is clearly him." I shift my finger over and tap my own face. "And this is me." I spin the phone back a bit and push my face in front of his. "I'm her." I point again.

He glances around as if to check whether his boss might see him breaking protocol—as if they don't literally do this sort of thing all the time—and he waves me past. "I never saw you."

"Right," I say. "You never did."

Most of the people in the venue are either streaming down the exit aisles and stairs, or they're already gone, so it's not like I'm here the second the concert ended, but I didn't dawdle either. I can hear people talking as they pack things up. For the first time, it occurs to me that I might have missed them. What if someone else does all the grunt work, and he just breezes right out?

Instead of strolling down the hall in my Miu Miu

379

moto boots, I start to jog. I'm not panicking, but my plan to surprise him could totally backfire if he's gone.

But then I hear his voice, and I make a sharp turn toward it. I nearly faceplant into a door, but at the last possible second, my hand connects with the knob and I manage to wrench it open.

And I essentially fling-fall through it, into the room beyond.

Where the stupid drummer is up on her tiptoes, kissing Eddy.

I swear, loudly. And then I spin around on my chunky and luckily almost flat heel and race back out the way I entered. Gracelessly. Speedily. And without much of a plan.

I'm nearly past the bouncer who tried to stop this catastrophe from happening when I hear him. "Amanda!"

My heart races, thinking of any possible explanation for why that woman in a little pink babydoll dress would be pressed against him like that, or how he could love me and be here, doing that with her. But either I'm too stupid, or he's too sly, because I can't think of a single thing that would excuse it. Not from any angle.

Which means any interaction we have right now is going to be really, really bad. As upset and disappointed and angry as I am, I'm not ready for that. Not yet.

"Amanda! Wait." He's nearly reached me, so if I don't turn around and face him, he'll touch me. He'll grab my hand or my arm or something, and I can't bear it.

"No." I stop and turn around slowly, flinging my hands up into the air, palms out. "Don't come closer."

"It's not what you think," he says. "Jaclyn—"

"She was brushing an eyelash off your cheek?" I ask.

"She was checking to see if your breath was fresh?" The rage is building inside of me. "Or maybe she wanted to see whether your flossers work, or if she should keep using the string kind that's cheaper."

"She kissed me," he says. "I shoved her away, before I knew you were there."

"And I just happened to arrive at the *very second* that something like this happened?" It's too unbelievable for words. I'm such a moron—even if it's true, even if she was pursuing him and he shut her down, I can only imagine how often this is happening from all sides for me to barge in on it, and how often it will continue to happen from here on out.

"I already asked my manager to replace her," he says. "Twice. She's been unprofessional before, but she said a talented, reliable drummer is hard to find, and that they're all a little crazy."

"I can't do this," I say.

He follows me again, obnoxiously, his voice a little wildly desperate. "Can't do what?" He steps closer. Too close. "Amanda, talk to me. Please."

The bouncer's eyes are wide as he watches me stalk past. His mouth actually drops open as Eddy chases me. I hate that even with our photo shoved in his face, he still doubted me.

That may be the root of the problem. I'm reasonably good-looking, but Eddy's an up-and-coming rock star who's drop-dead gorgeous. We're not well matched, and we never have been. The small town muffled our disparity, but it's glaringly apparent to literally everyone here.

And now we're not even in the same time zone, nor will we be for months to come. In his line of work, his manager's right. They can't go around firing everyone who thinks he's attractive and acts inappropriately. There will be all sorts of beautiful and crazy people flinging themselves in his direction.

I don't stop walking until we push past the doors and onto the street. The throngs of people milling around look downright shocked when we emerge. I stick out my hand and wave it around to try and hail a cab.

"Are you saying you can't talk to me right now? You're too upset, or. . ."

I glare at him. "Or what, Eddy? What else could, 'I can't do this' mean?"

He swallows.

"Because that other meaning? The one where we don't talk anymore *ever*, that's the one I meant." As if I'm actually on the set of a film or something, a cab pulls up at that very moment. It doesn't even feel real, because I'm definitely the kind of girl who says a big dramatic thing and then stands there, staring at the guy for another four or five minutes, giving up and commenting on the weather and the local sports team while I wait and wait for transportation that will whisk me away—only it never quite shows.

But this time, the time my heart is shattered and I wish there was more time for him to convince me not to go, the enchanted pumpkin miraculously appears.

"Airport," I say as I'm climbing into the back of the cab.

"It's because of that Park guy, isn't it?" Eddy asks. "Did you come here looking for an excuse to dump me?"

I hope that my disgust is plain on my face. "If that's what you need to think to sleep at night, go ahead."

And then I'm gone. Before I can even properly react to his childish accusation. Before I can really process what happened. I flew out here to try and connect with Eddy, and to try and tell him how hard this has all been on me. I wanted to try and come up with some kind of plan to talk, to work our way through this, no matter how hard it will be.

But I was afraid there wasn't enough left to save.

And now, we've broken up.

I'm at the airport when I realize that I left my bag at the venue's coat check. I'm such an idiot. No one answers when I call over there, and I'm finally stuck texting Eddy to have him collect it for me and have his manager ship it home.

He texts me a dozen more times, asking me to call him. Begging me to answer the phone. And then, as I'm boarding my plane, I get a video. It's grainy, and it's small, and my finger hovers over the button to just delete it without watching.

But *she's* in it, with her stupid tulle skirt and tiny, boob-framing top, and before I can think hard about it, I'm clicking to enlarge the dumb thing and then I'm hitting play. It's clearly security footage Eddy made some poor security man hand over to him. The fact that he's sending it at all means he was clearly telling the truth—nothing happened, or at least, not on his side.

"It went so well," she's saying in an irritatingly juvenile tone. "I can't believe you still won't go celebrate. I mean, come oooon."

"I don't drink, Jaclyn," he says. "I've told you that a dozen times at least."

"It's a stupid rule," she says.

"I'm in AA," he says. "It's not a rule. It's the only way I survive life. It's who I am."

"No, it's a rule you had shoved at you when you were

a kid. I read the articles. You're not a kid anymore. You're a man, and I swear, you can control yourself. I have faith in you."

"Just stop." He's brusque, and he's firm.

But she isn't convinced. "Wait."

He pauses, his back to her, his shoulders stiff. "What?"

"Your girlfriend," she says. "The old lady?"

Eddy whips around like a snake ready to strike. "Don't ever call her that again. In fact, never mention her."

"Are you embarrassed?" I can't see her face from this angle, but I can hear the catty smile in her tone.

"The only reason Amanda's not here, ripping your throat out for being a brat, is that she's at home, watching her beautiful children. What you call old, I call experienced. What you call lady, I call Madonna. You have no idea what you're talking about, so just shut up already."

"You really miss her." She sighs, all the flirt and fight going out of her. "I didn't really want to believe it, but do you really love her?"

Eddy sighs. "I've said that a million times."

She steps toward him. "It must be so hard to be apart like this."

I have to give her credit. She does not give up easily. But Eddy's a moron for letting his guard down, thinking she's finally gotten it. "It is."

"Has she been as lonely as you are?"

"She's got friends there," he says. "And some guy is chasing her, so before you call her old, you should know that very few women are as amazing or as desirable as my girlfriend."

"I'm sure." She's practically purring, and now Eddy has stopped all his hostility entirely, thinking she's switched off.

He's right about one thing. If I'd been there earlier, I'd have strangled her.

"I hope she knows what she has." She reaches up and strokes Eddy's hair.

"Stop." He knocks her hand away.

"Oh." She freezes. "It's—there's something there." She reaches for his hair again, but her arms snake around and grab his face. And then she's up on her tiptoes, locking lips with my boyfriend, which is just when—

And there's the crash when I fall into the room, and at the same time, Eddy's shoving her away.

The video cuts—which is fine. He was chasing me immediately after, so it's not like there was something else he could be hiding.

I'm not surprised at what I saw. I knew he wouldn't lie to me right there, right in the middle of it all going down. If he'd liked her, he wouldn't have needed to chase me. But it does confirm the other thing I already knew.

Months of this stretches before us, at least.

Maybe much longer.

The people who envy women with gorgeous boyfriends are missing something big. It's exhausting to have a super hot boyfriend. Everyone wants him, and no one thinks you deserve him. If I could get just a mostly hot boyfriend, that would actually be way better. Someone like Abby's fiancé. Broad shoulders and a ruggedly handsome face are more than enough for me.

Eddy's traffic-stopping face is more trouble than it's worth. Although, I suppose now that's not true.

It's not anything to me anymore.

I think about it all the way home, and I can't tell if I'm just numb, or if I've been preparing myself for this, but I'm not nearly as devastated as I expected to be. I'm fine to walk and talk and answer questions. I navigate the airport, and since I didn't leave my purse with my keys behind, I even manage to find my car in the wee hours of the morning and drive home.

I arrive right around dawn.

Mandy is, of course, already up, sipping her morning coffee and watching the sunrise, so she knows the second I pull into the drive.

Her brow's furrowed, her eyes troubled. "What happened?"

"Nothing good," I say. "Or, I don't know. Maybe it's better this happened quickly instead of a year from now. Or even more. I mean, I'm not on Death's door, but I'm not exactly young either. I shouldn't be wasting time."

"Come now," Mandy says. "Let's not talk about Death's door. I prefer to call it the long walk back home."

"I caught him," I say. "Pink-tulle handed." Her jokes about dying are almost as funny as my jokes about being dumped.

"I don't follow," she says.

"He was kissing some woman when I got there—actually, not some woman. The drummer."

"I don't believe you," Mandy says. "He wouldn't do that. I've seen how that man looks at you, and I've known him his entire life. He's never looked at anyone that way before."

"I just can't do it," I say. "I can't. I'm going to spend my life alone, just like you."

"You listen here," she says. "You're an idiot if you

think—" She stumbles forward, clutching the nearest support column on her porch, but her hands can't support her weight and she tumbles forward.

If I hadn't been there to catch her, I'm not sure what would have happened. She's not heavy, but she's not light, either. It takes me a painfully long time to lug her to my car, and all the while she's barely drawing in breaths next to me. I could call an ambulance, but I'm sure I'll be faster.

I don't bother waking the girls or even calling them. They're not expecting me home today, and I don't have time. I hop in the car and floor it the entire way to the ER in Green River.

The ambulance bay has a truck in it, no lights or sirens running, when I arrive, so I just pull up alongside it. "I need help," I shout.

"What happened to your mother?" the man in the white uniform asks.

"She collapsed," I say. "She was fine one moment, and then the next, she just fell over."

The next twelve hours are some of the most frightening of my life. I talk to a dozen different professionals, from nurses, to techs, to radiologists, and finally, a cardiologist.

"I'm sorry this has been such a long day," he says. "But I wanted to update you on your mother."

I never bothered correcting them. What's the point? They might have kicked me out if I had.

"You probably know that the heart has several different arteries and veins that connect right there where it pumps blood."

I didn't, but I nod anyway. It seems like the right thing to do.

"Mrs. Saddler had three significant blockages that we were able to identify. The first was in her leg, and the other two are near her heart. We were able to place a very small stent in her leg following an angioplasty, and we were able to clear the blockage on one side of her heart and place a stent there as well. But the blockage that was the least severe, we didn't touch for now. She needs to regain her strength before we tackle that last one."

"Regain her strength?" I ask. "What does that even mean?"

"For a while now, her body has been getting far less blood than it needed. Any small thing could have pushed her over. As a result of that, and the trauma of this recent procedure, she needs a break. She'll be doing much better than before, now that two of the three problem areas have improved, but she'll need to pace herself, and someone needs to keep an eye on her."

I've never known Mandy to pace herself. Not even once. "When can I see her?"

"I'll have someone take you back now."

I sit with her until she wakes up. She's pretty groggy, but in true Amanda Saddler fashion, within a few hours, she's ordering everyone around and arguing with me about the treatment plan. "This place is very poorly run," she says. "And there's no way that I'm getting the other stent placed in eight weeks."

"Keep arguing, and I'll call Abby," I say.

"No." She claws at my hand, but it's so weak it makes me want to cry. "You can't."

"Why not?" I ask. "She'll be furious if I don't, and you'd better believe she's not going to just stand here while you tell the doctors what you will and won't do." I can't help my smile. "She might even get you declared legally incompetent so we can make all your medical decisions. That would be fun."

"You can't tell anyone about this," Mandy says, "especially Abby. It's because of her that I want to wait longer than eight weeks. I'm a bridesmaid at her wedding, and I'm not doing a risky procedure right before and missing it."

"It's not risky," I say.

"Anything involving the heart is risky, and those doctors can just wait to cut into me until it's more convenient."

"What's this nonsense?" The same tall, thin cardiologist who spoke to me earlier breezes into the room. "I'm happy to see you sitting up and talking," he says. "But I don't like patients dictating medicine. It's like inpatients running an asylum."

"Your job," Mandy says, "is to get me patched up so I can live my life, right?"

"It is," he agrees. "But if I can't get you patched up. . . you won't have a life left to live."

He's clever, this guy.

"Ha," Mandy says. "I know what you're trying to do there, but you can't scare me. I know that you have no idea, every time you go in for one of these things, what's going to happen. How many of my friends do you think have died? I'm sure you know the leading cause of death in America."

"Heart disease," he says. "But—"

"But, nothing. My friends have systematically put all your children through school and probably paid for a beach house and a yacht. That's fine, and I'm grateful for your hard work and dedication, but I'm not paying for your next vacation home until after I've gone to my friend's wedding."

"This is not a hill to die on," I say. "If we let him choose—"

"Pardon me," she says, "but that's exactly what it is. It's my hill, and I can choose when to risk death and how long to wait before risking it."

Finally, after a few more back and forth attempts, the poor cardiologist throws his hands into the air. "Fine. We'll delay an extra month so that you can attend your wedding. But absolutely no dancing, and no significant exertion of any kind."

Mandy beams. "Fine."

The doc has been gone less than ten seconds when she turns to me. "Now, tell me again what stupid thing you did that caused me to have the heart attack in the first place? I've had this sinking feeling for a long time now that you dumped that fine boyfriend of yours. Tell me I'm wrong."

I turn toward her heart monitor nervously.

"Don't look at that. Look at me."

I do.

"You're an idiot, Amanda Brooks. I'd better tell you this now, because I don't know how long I have, and I'm apparently an idiot, too."

I blink.

"I gave Abby that ranch because I love you *more*. And selfishly, I wanted to know whether you loved me, too."

I am so confused.

"Think about dogs. Why do they love us?"

I have no idea. "Well, it's a bad analogy for you, because Roscoe just decided to adore you. But most dogs love their people because they give them treats and food. If another person came along, with a steak in hand, that dog would abandon the first owner immediately to grab the steak."

"You gave Abby the ranch because you thought if you gave me something, I'd run away after someone else?"

"Not quite." She leans back against her pillows, her face pale.

"Let's talk about this later," I say. "There's no rush."

She laughs. "Speak for yourself, you adolescent. I'm almost out of time."

"That is *not* what the doc said," I say. "He—"

"I wanted you to love me even though I *didn't* give you a thing," she says. "And I'm so stupid. It took me this long to realize that I already know that you do."

I lean forward to hug her, but she's connected to an oxygen cannula, and an IV, and there are wires for monitors everywhere. "I don't know how to hug you right now, but if I could, I would."

"I'm sorry," Mandy says. "I shouldn't have been testing you."

"It's my fault that I failed," I say. "It wasn't because I would only love you if you gave me something."

"I know," Mandy says. "It hurt you, because you thought I didn't care about you as much as I care about Abby."

"Exactly," I say. "That's it."

"We're both morons," Mandy says. "Maybe that's why we're perfect for each other."

"They've been calling you my mom all day," I say.

"Well, if your mother's someone who wants to take care of you, and thinks about bonking you on the head

391

when you do something stupid, then they're calling me the right thing."

"I never bonk my kids."

"You don't do it enough," she says. "I agree."

"That's not what—"

"I probably ought to tell you that I wrote a new will a few weeks ago," she says. "I'm leaving everything to you, you ninny. You're the daughter I never had but always wanted. Only prettier, and smarter, and more talented."

Now I feel pretty idiotic, but also very, very loved.

28

DONNA

A bigail files the Motion for Summary Judgment, but thanks to our rural setting, the hearing date is set for almost a month out. And then that hearing gets delayed because the judge gets the flu.

That bumps us another whole month.

But at least right after the first hearing is canceled, we're finally able to move into the new house. The floors are done, and the lights and water work, so that's something. If I have a regular headache from the sound of late night tile cutting, well, at least I'm not in a hotel. I've been slowly but surely buying little pieces of furniture as I find them online or in Facebook Marketplace in reasonably close areas.

My job marches along too, moving closer to completion on the main retreat building, and Aiden's doing well in school, his cast off and life mostly back to normal, thankfully. My life is exactly what I wanted. Even the persistent Will has finally given up. No more texts, no more calls, just like I wanted.

I didn't expect to miss hearing from him quite so much.

But I'm still pretty sure I was right. Aiden disagrees, regularly asking when Mr. Will can come and play. That always stings a little. I can't bring myself to tell him that Mr. Will isn't coming over anymore because I told him not to. . .

Abby's wedding's around the corner, and even though she's insisting that she doesn't want a bridal shower or a bachelorette party, I feel like we ought to do something. I pick up my phone and call Amanda. "Hey!"

"You've been busy over there," Amanda says. "I drove past the resort site the other day, and it's all framed up. Roof was going on."

"That part happens really fast," I say. "It's all the details that eat you alive."

"Tell me about it," she says. "I'm the one in charge of all those details around here."

"Speaking of details," I say, "I wanted to see what we're doing about Abby."

"Doing?" Amanda sounds strange, like her voice is just a little too high. "What do you mean?"

"Her wedding is almost here."

"Believe me, I know. I'm running out of time."

"Time for what?" I ask.

"What are *you* calling about?" she asks.

Now I'm really suspicious. "Is there some kind of bachelorette party I wasn't invited to? Did I do something to tick her off?"

"What?" Amanda laughs. "Nothing like that. I've been working with Steve and Mandy to coordinate a top-secret project and we're down to the wire. That's all."

"Huh. Okay. Well, if you need help, let me know. But I wanted to see if we're really not going to do a shower for her?"

"What did you have in mind?"

"I'm not sure," I say. "Maybe a joint bachelorette party and bridal shower thing?"

Amanda makes a hmm sound. "That's not a terrible idea. Can you imagine how horrified she'd be if we gave her lingerie? I can almost see her eyes bulging out of her head right now."

"Oh my word, yes," I say. "That would be hilarious, as long as we don't invite Mandy."

"Are you kidding? She'd be the one giving her the most inappropriate stuff."

I realize she's right. "Alright, so if I set something up, you'll go?"

"You bet," Amanda says. "I can't believe we're less than a month until the wedding."

"I still need to find a date to the wedding," I say, just as David Park walks into the office. I can feel the heat rising in my cheeks. I drop my voice to a whisper. "I'd better go."

"Did you hear back from the sheetrock guys?" David asks. "Or set up a time for the inspector to come?"

"Yes to both," I say, "and the flooring samples are in the corner." I point.

"Perfect."

I've been working on trying to get my courage up for weeks, and now that he heard me basically say it, I decide it's now or never. "Hey, so, my friend's wedding is in a few weeks," I say. "The weekend after our press conference."

David's face turns toward me, his dark eyes meeting mine. "Your lawyer friend who's marrying the doctor."

"Right," I say. "Abigail. And I don't have a date yet, so I thought maybe—" The pained look on his face is answer enough, but I can't just give up mid-sentence, right? Isn't that more pathetic? "I was, well, I need to, erm, find a dress."

His shoulders relax, and he exhales. "You need to get off early today? Of course you can. Go right ahead. And if you're headed into town anyway and don't mind going to Vernal, you could check on that shipment that we're supposed to be getting from Lumber Liquidators."

"Right," I say. "Of course."

"What kind of gift should I look for?" he asks. "For this Abigail person?"

My heart skips a beat. "Present?"

"I might have mentioned last week that I'd be happy to take your friend Amanda, you know, when I bumped into her at Brownings. She didn't say I *could* be her date, but she didn't say I couldn't, and I figure that's a decent start."

"Oh." Why did I think he'd given up on her? Now that she and Eddy are broken up, of course he's probably doubled down. I think I just hoped he had quit trying, since it's been almost two months and there's been no progress.

"I haven't been too aggressive," he says as if he can sense what I'm thinking. "I didn't want her to reject me just because she was upset about her breakup. But I think two months is plenty of time to let her breathe, don't you?"

"Mm."

"I mean, if I wait much longer, someone else will scoop her up."

"Right." I can barely speak. I need to get out of here.

Once I've been driving down the road for a few moments, I expect to be bawling. I figured that, without the need to preserve appearances, I'd collapse. Only, I don't.

I'm fine.

Why am I not devastated to hear that David Park may be going on a date with Amanda? I should want to scratch her face off. But actually, I kind of hope he makes her happy. She's been unbearably depressed since she broke up with Eddy. Every time I see someone sharing his songs on social, or someone around here mentions him, I cringe a little. I'm glad his tour is going so well, and I'm happy that he's got a second chance, but I think the price for it was way too high.

I was never part of his fan club, but now I think Eddy Dutton is an epic moron.

And if David Park can make Amanda happy, then I wish him well with it. But why do I wish him well? I've had a crush on him for months, now.

Haven't I?

Or was he just a conveniently safe person to like? Someone who doesn't like me back and won't be here for much longer, assuming all goes well?

What's wrong with me?

Nothing a little shopping won't improve, or at least, I hope so. I call Mandy. "Do you have a dress for the wedding yet?"

"I'll be in a bridesmaid dress," she says. "Just like you, idiot."

"For the ceremony," I say. "But what about for the party afterward?"

"We wear the same thing, then," she says.

"Are you sure?" I haven't been to a wedding in a while. "Well, then do you want to go shopping with me down in Vernal for a gift for Steve and Abby?"

"I've got that handled," she says. "You're behind, dewdrop."

I barely avoid swearing under my breath. "Fine."

"You want a shopping buddy, though?" she asks. "If you swing by and pick me up, we can head down to Vernal together."

"Am I that obvious?"

"Even a blind, deaf idiot would know you don't want to go alone."

"Guilty," I agree.

A few minutes later, we're en route.

"So what did you get her?" I ask. "A set of silverware? A tea service?"

Mandy eyes me with scorn. "Do I look like I'd buy her forks? Really?"

I shrug. "What do you get the woman who has everything?"

"Something she doesn't have, obviously."

"But you already gave her a ranch. What could possibly top that?"

"You'll have to wait and be surprised along with everyone else at the wedding," she says. "It's my very first time to be asked to be a bridesmaid, and I'm excited."

"Fine, keep your secret. I was just trying to figure out an appropriate price point."

"You can't judge based on me. I've got a limited

amount of time to be here and plenty of money to burn."

"Did I mention that my birthday's coming up?" I ask.

She cackles. I love her cackle.

"Are you taking a date?"

"Me?" This time when she laughs, it's more like a series of hoots than a cackle. "No way. What about you? I bet that Will Earl looks delicious in a tux."

"I haven't heard from him lately," I admit. "I might have told him pretty clearly that *we're* not going to happen."

Her mouth dangles open. "Are we talking about the same person? Broad-shouldered, smoldering eyes, football legend, rancher Will? Mom owns the hotel on Main?"

I grit my teeth. "Yes."

"But. . .why would you do that?"

I keep my hands on the steering wheel and force myself to look straight ahead. I don't need her to judge me. *I'm* already judging me plenty. "I thought I liked someone else."

"And you've just now realized that you don't? Are you serious?"

I shrug.

"How are three women who are so smart all so gosh darn stupid?"

"Three women? Abby's fairly self-aware."

"Compared to you and Amanda, she is."

I laugh. "What did Amanda do?"

"She dumped Eddy. You know as well as I do how stupid that was."

"I'm not sure. He cheated on her," I say.

The sound Mandy makes is like a wood chipper. "Did not."

"What?" I blink. "She heavily implied—"

"That girl is a mess. He most certainly did *not* cheat on her, but his dumb banjo player, or piano player, or drummer or something kissed *him*, and it happened to be right when Amanda walked backstage, and she thinks that kind of thing will just happen over and over."

I think about Eddy's face and his musical talent. "I'm sure it would have—or, you know, is happening right now."

"You think she did the right thing, then?" Mandy's eye roll might flip my car. "You're both morons."

"But the decision is made," I say, mostly talking about Amanda. "It's not like she can just go back in time and say something different."

"You can't make life decisions based on fear," Mandy says. "She broke up with him so she wouldn't have to suffer while he was on tour. So you know what she's been doing the last two months?"

"Working hard so she won't think about it?" I mean, that's what *I've* been doing.

"She has been focusing on work," Mandy says. "But she's also been obsessively scanning anything and everything about Edward Dutton online."

That seems. . .healthy. "I'm sure some of that will die down—"

"When he comes back home and she bumps into him at the True Value? Or maybe when he records his next album or starts dating someone new."

I wince. "There aren't any easy answers with this stuff."

Mandy beans me on the head with her purse.

"Hey," I shout. "I'm driving. I could have swerved off the road."

"You didn't," Mandy says. "And maybe that knocked some sense into you. There are *very easy* answers that you two are too stupid to see. She needs to call or fly or ride her bike or bum rides to wherever Eddy is and beg him to take her back. Then she needs to start trusting in herself and in him so that she won't be miserable all the time."

"You're making it sound like this was all her fault—"

"It *is* all her fault, you idiot," Mandy says. "You think it's up to Eddy? She can't believe he will love her until she learns to love herself."

"That sounds like something you'd find on a fortune cookie."

"The fact that that kind of thing is written inside of delicious cookies doesn't make it any less true," Mandy says. "And you." She exhales heavily. "Don't even get me started on you. You need to—"

"Crawl to Will Earl and tell him. . .what? That I want to. . .date?"

"I was going to say ride a tricycle over there, but sure. Crawling is fine, too, and there's a certain poetic justice to it."

"I can't do it," I say. "Telling him I was wrong? Asking for a do-over? It's too embarrassing. I told him I knew my mind."

"Which clearly you didn't."

"No, I didn't," I say. "Does that make you happy? I blew it. Again."

"Admitting it is the first step," Mandy says. "I never made it past that, you know."

I think about what Amanda and Abby told me about

how she was in love with Jed. She's never brought it up to me before, but it's pretty tragic, honestly. Especially knowing that he loved her back. "You know that what happened with you and Jed is rare, right? Odds are good that in my case, he's not also pining."

"I watched him last week. He was cleaning windows on his mother's hotel."

"Okay."

"He cleaned the same one three times, without even moving over."

"That's hardly conclusive evidence of anything," I say.

"That boy is distracted," she says. "And I think it's because he's still upset about you turning him down."

Sheer conjecture, or possibly wishful thinking.

"When did he tell you how he felt?" she asks.

I tell her the date.

Her grin couldn't be more self-satisfied. "Do you know how much work he did on that house you're in? He spent night after night over there, and he didn't stop until two weeks *after* you turned him down."

I can't get that thought out of my head. Not during the rest of the drive. Not while we're shopping. Not when I finally settle for buying Steve and Abby horse head bookends.

"Yes, I know it's a dumb gift," I say. "But she likes books, and they like horses."

"I didn't say anything," Mandy says. "Although, it's true, my gift is way, way better."

She's such a brat.

But even though my heart is lighter on the way home, I still can't stop thinking about what she said. He worked for *two weeks* after I turned him down? Why would he do that? Maybe he felt he had to keep going until the part he started was done. He is someone who finishes what he starts.

On the other hand, what if she's right? What if he does still like me? After I put Aiden to bed, my phone mocks me. His number is right there, saved like magic. All it would take is the touch of a button.

I resist.

Then I resist some more.

But just before nine o'clock, which is my own personal line-which-must-never-be-crossed for late night calling, I pick it up. My fingers tremble as I press each button to bring up his name. And then I press talk.

The green phone icon shows up, blinking, indicating that the call is trying to connect.

It's real. I'm calling Will.

He picks up on the third ring. "Hello?"

"Hey, Will," I say. "It's me, Donna." Of course he knows it's me. It's his cell phone, so unless he deleted my number, he knew when he hit talk who he'd be talking to.

"I know," he says, so neutrally that I can't interpret a single thing from his inflection.

"I, um, well, this is kind of a strange call." I want to tell him I was wrong. I want to ask him if he's moved on, and whether he still wants to date me, and whether he's still thinking about that kiss. I want to beg him not to be mad at me. I want to tell him that I'm broken, and it's nothing personal.

I just wasn't ready.

"It's strange? Why?" He sounds confused. I don't blame him.

"No, I mean, I'm sorry."

"You're sorry?"

"I'm calling because. . ." No words come out. Come on, brain, *engage*!

"Because?"

"I need a date to Abby's wedding." Those particular words tumble out in a rush. "I thought you might be willing to—"

"I'm sorry," he says, "but I've already got a date to the wedding." Then he hangs up.

29

AMANDA

Abigail is *not* at her house when she said she would be. I call her for the third time.

"Hello?" Her voice is muffled, and there's some kind of strange noise in the background I don't recognize.

"Where are you?" I ask.

"Oh, no." She swears under her breath. "We were supposed to go together to pick up the party favors."

"Is everything alright?" None of her kids know where she is, which is uncommon. She's usually taken out a banner ad telling them how to reach her when she's not at home. It feels like they usually know every single thing that's going on. They're the most coordinated family I've ever met.

"I mean, it will be," she says. "Can you go without me?"

"That's a bad idea." Not because I can't pick up the box of cowboy boot Christmas tree ornaments that say Abby and Steve and the wedding date alone, but because that's not really what we were supposed to be doing at all.

"The thing is, Steve got this call from a friend, and there was this horse that had been so badly neglected—"

"You're bailing on me for a *horse*?"

"Well, kind of," she says. "If you saw her, you would get it. She's got that skinny-fat belly that they get when they haven't eaten well. You can see her ribs, but—"

"Are you saying Steve can't handle this horse himself?"

"I'll be fine," I hear Steve say. "Just go."

"But I'm a mess," she says. "I'm so dirty and sweaty right now. You'd have to wait for me to shower and change."

My voice is flat, but I force the words out without being terse. "I'll wait."

"I'm sorry," she says.

I should've told Steve. The only way, with those two, to be sure something like this won't happen, is to let the non-participating partner know what's going on. That's my fault, I guess.

I start calling people immediately. Greta from Brownings is understanding, as always. "It's fine," she says. "That'll give us a little more time to finish with the lights and flowers."

Donna actually sounds relieved. "I had a work thing run late, so it's better, really."

Mandy's the only one who's annoyed. "Because of a *horse*? They're not even married yet, and she's already as bad as Steve. I'm starving."

"Eat a banana," I say. "Better for your heart than anything they'll have at Brownings."

"I hate bananas."

406

I can't help my smile. "You said you were hungry."

She makes a sound like a leaking gasket and then hangs up.

Since I have a little time, I decide to stop by the True Value and grab an actual gift bag for my present. The pink and black Victoria's Secret bag kind of gives the contents away, and I'd rather surprise her. I'm on my knees, rummaging around in the pile that happens to be on the very bottom shelf for a bag that doesn't have a teddy bear or a baby carriage on it—the selection in Manila always leaves a little something to be desired—when I hear a familiar voice.

"You're a hard woman to find lately."

I freeze and turn around slowly, my head twisted but the rest of my body still on all fours. Certainly not my finest pose. "David?"

"I've been casually trying to bump into you everywhere for almost two weeks now."

Trying to bump into me? What's he talking about? I straighten up and turn around. "Why?"

"What are you doing, anyway?"

I lower my voice to a whisper. If I've learned anything in the past year, it's that with small towns, you never know who might be listening. "I'm hosting a surprise bridal shower tonight, and I need a gift bag."

"Oh." He bumps the pile with his toe. "Didn't want to imply anything with this one?" A bag with a baby bottle and a pink rattle on it slides off onto the floor.

"Exactly," I say. "But why have you been looking for me? You have my number."

He clears his throat. "It would have seemed a lot more casual if I'd been able to just happen to be seated at the next table, but I've been eating lunch in Manila

407

every day and. . ." He spreads his hands out in front of him. "No luck."

"I'm not eating out much lately." I don't mention that I no longer have many people to eat with. Donna works with him, Mandy's on a very special diet, and Abby's too busy with the wedding. Without a boyfriend, I mostly eat at home or order takeout.

"The thing is, I hear you have a wedding coming up." He leans over, plucks a black and white bag out of the pile, and hands it to me. "That's usually something you'd take a date to, no?"

I swallow.

"I know you and Eddy broke up." He doesn't sound like he's gloating. He's not even smiling—he looks almost sympathetic. "If it's not too early, I wanted to offer to be your date. I promise not to be even one percent creepy."

I think it over. A smart, rich, handsome man wants to take me? I mean, I don't like him, but if I wasn't all cracked and broken inside, I might. Plus, I don't think Eddy will be back in time for the wedding, but just in case he is, I'll look way better if I manage to have a date. "I'm still pretty wrecked," I warn.

He shrugs. "No strings. Seriously."

"Well." At least I'd have someone to sit next to for the photos, and someone to fetch me beverages, and someone to laugh at my lame jokes. "Alright."

With the wattage of his smile, I regret my decision immediately.

"You're sure you won't read into this?" I ask. "Because I'm really not—"

His hand touches my wrist. "I won't read anything into it, I swear."

I nod. "Alright. I'm a bridesmaid, so I'll be wearing purple, er, lavender, technically."

"Should I get a purple tie?" He grins.

"I'll pick one out," I say. "Can't have people thinking we're *too* matchy-matchy."

He shrugs. "I'm fine with it if you are."

It would be nice, to sink backward into dating him, like falling against a pile of sofas. Bam, insta-boyfriend. David thinks that's what he wants, but I doubt it's the truth. If he really wanted that, he wouldn't have been able to politely wait two months before bumping into me. But I don't bother arguing. "Thanks."

"Thanks?" He grimaces. "That's not exactly what I was hoping you'd say after agreeing to let me take you."

"You've saved me, you big strong hunk of a man." I wink melodramatically. "Is that better?"

He snorts. "A little, maybe."

"Great, well, I'd better go buy this or I'll be late."

"Text me with any details," he says. "And I'll see you around."

Luckily, Abby doesn't take nearly as long to get ready as I would in her place, and she's cleaned up and ready to go when I reach her house. She's wearing jeans and a plain white t-shirt when I pick her up. I consider suggesting she change, but with her, that would be all it took to tip her off.

"Will they still be open?" she asks.

"I called. They'll hold them for us."

"I hope they look alright," she says. "Because we don't really have time to do anything else if they don't."

"I'm sure they'll be fine," I say. "Don't stress."

When we pull into the Brownings parking lot, Abby

glances at her watch. "I don't think we have time to eat. Didn't you say it closes at seven?"

"I'll just grab something to go," I say. "I already called the shop owner, so she'll wait if she has to."

Abby bites her lip, but doesn't argue.

I go inside, make sure everyone is ready, which they are, and then text her. THERE'S A NEW CLIENT IN HERE WHO HAS A QUESTION. SHE KNOWS WE'RE IN A HURRY. IT'LL ONLY TAKE A MOMENT.

She's wearing her game face when she strides into the restaurant, but when she sees us all gathered in the front of the restaurant, her mouth curls up into a grin. "What's going on?"

"Surprise," Donna says. "We couldn't let you get married without any kind of celebration."

"And we didn't think you'd like topless men," Greta says.

"Plus, we were pretty sure no one we found around here would look better than the groom." Linda hoots. "I mean, I'm not saying anything here, but we're all ready for that grass to start growing again."

All the ladies hoot and holler this time. I don't really blame them—Steve looks *good* out there, mowing his lawn.

Venetia glares at Linda. "You changed his diapers."

Linda shrugs. "That was a *looong* time ago. I can barely remember it."

"Come on in and eat," Mandy says. "I'm starving."

We're nearly done with dinner when Helen walks through the front door, her mother at her side. I doubt many of the other ladies recognize them, and the convivial jokes and talking continue, but Abby freezes.

Her head whips toward mine. "Did you invite them?" she hisses.

I lick my lips and nod. "But I didn't think they'd actually come."

She sighs, stands up, and walks toward the front to greet them. Before I can say another word, the three of them disappear out the front door and into the night.

❦ 30 ❦

ABIGAIL

For the past two months, Helen has either called or texted me daily. At first, I ignored her. After all, she brought Mom and Dad, and she had to know they wouldn't be kind.

Yes, they were supposed to come to visit eventually, but she expedited the whole thing, and instead of preparing them to like Steve, to accept my move, and to support me in my new job, she brought them here like a big old can of gasoline to try and burn this move and this life and this impending wedding down to a pile of smoking slag.

She did hire movers to make my departure from Houston smoother. She also bought me an absolutely breathtaking gown, in spite of my insistence that I didn't want her to do it.

But ever since she sold her first company, money has been Helen's way of getting whatever she wanted. After I ignored a solid week of phone calls and texts, she texted that she was coming to visit. She would arrive the very next day to ensure that I was alive, unless I replied.

I texted her back: ALIVE.

She didn't press. But the next day, she called and texted again. I ignored both attempts to reach out, growing more and more irritated by her persistence. Judging by her incomparable success in the business world, Helen has been tenacious about business matters for a long time. But of course, I've never before witnessed her expend quite this much energy toward any sort of relationship.

In spite of myself, I was impressed and a little touched.

"Are you ever going to answer her?" Ethan asked, peering over my shoulder.

"Eavesdropping is rude," I said.

"What is an eave, anyway?" He shrugged.

"It's the part of the building—"

"Oh," Ethan said. "I don't actually care. That was just my way of redirecting you to avoid a lecture, which incidentally is the same thing you just did, only in your case, it was to avoid answering my question about Aunt Helen."

"It's none of your business what I do with my sister," I said.

"Only, it's a little inconsistent," he said. "You're always telling us how we have to forgive our siblings, even when they've dumped a box of Legos in our room, or when they've accidentally deleted the document we spent four hours typing that's due the next morning for a college assignment, for instance."

"Those are very specific examples," I said. "Holding a grudge?"

"I'm just doing what I learned from my *mom*." He smiled and walked away.

I was actually proud of him, and also very frustrated by his perception. The next day, I answered Helen's phone call. "What?"

"No, I think the word you're looking for is *hello*," she said.

"Right," I said. "Hello. Now, what do you want?"

"To be invited to my sister's wedding," she said. "And to be forgiven."

"People are usually forgiven after they apologize," I said, "and you have not, notably, done that."

"An apology only rings true when the person did something wrong," she said. "If I said, 'sorry you were upset,' that's not a real apology. That's me saying I'm sorry that *you* overreacted."

"Then why don't you apologize for what you did?"

"For trying to help my sister see what I thought was right? For spending my time and money to do things I thought would improve her life?"

"If you wanted to lose weight—"

"Which I don't," Helen said.

"But if you did," I said. "If you wanted to lose weight, would you look for a trainer who was thin, or someone who was heavy?"

"I suppose I'd ask someone who was thin." She's smart. She had to see where I was going.

"Your life sucks, Helen. Sure, you're rich, but you're one of the most unhappy people I know. So if you want me to forgive you from mucking with my life, maybe stop trying to convince me that you know best. You don't."

She was quiet for a few moments, and then she hung up.

She didn't call me back, but she kept texting. None

414

of her texts were apologies, but they didn't stop, even when I ignored them. And they never threatened to just show up, either.

That's why I'm so surprised when she and Mom walk though the door of Brownings. Even if Amanda told her I was having a party, and even if she's decided she could finally bring herself to apologize, why now? Why come in the middle of a party my local friends and family are throwing? Is she trying to wreck another important thing for me?

"What do you want?" I don't beat around the bush. "I've got friends in there and family too, and I can't spend all night out here, arguing with either of you."

"I don't want to argue." Mom zips her coat up even higher, practically strangling herself.

"That's a first." I cross my arms. "You could've called, you know. It would have saved you the hassle of traveling to such a remote location, and it would have let me have a fun night instead of a tiring one."

Mom's chin lifts. "I tried calling."

She called me exactly twice in two months.

"Why did you come?" I ask again.

Helen lifts her arms, both of which are holding a bag. "We have presents."

"My friends are in there," I say. "My family—"

"Yes." Mom's nose scrunches up. "You said that, although who you could possibly classify as your family in there is debatable. I didn't see anyone I know."

"Family isn't only the people related to you by blood," I say. "You choose a spouse—a partner. And it took me years, but I realized you can choose your other family relationships too. They're just the people you've trusted to be a part of your life, and the people who consistently bring you joy or ease your pain. You're none of those things." Saying that actually hurts me a little bit, but it's time for me to stop letting them harm me.

"I'm sorry you felt bad," Mom says.

Helen cringes. At least she's bright enough to hear it.

"But you have to admit—"

"Nope," I say. "I don't. I don't have to admit anything. And you can turn around and head home, unless you're ready to say you're sorry without qualifying that you're apologizing for *my* feelings."

"I'm sorry *I* didn't support you," Helen whispers. "I'm sorry *I* didn't listen."

Mom's head swivels toward her, her eyes as wide as an owl at midnight.

"Steve's a good man, and clearly you and your kids are happy here. You're right. I'm not happy."

"You were just named as one of the ten richest women under fifty," Mom says. "And you were on Forbes' Most Eligible Bachelorette list."

"None of which means anything," Helen says. "I'm all alone, every night. Just like you and Dad."

"We're never alone," Mom says. "We're always together."

"Even when you're together, you're alone," Helen says. "You're smart enough to know what I mean."

"You may come inside." I gesture at the door.

Helen and Mom both start toward it.

I grab Mom's arm. "Not you. You can go back to whatever hotel you're planning to stay at tonight."

"I was going to stay with you and see my grand-children."

I laugh. "Think again."

She swallows, her lips compressed, her hands curling

around her slacks and wadding them into balls. "I shouldn't have made fun of your fiancé."

I put one hand on my hip.

Helen turns back, her mouth slightly open, her right eyebrow arched, as if she's witnessing a miracle. In some ways, she is.

"And?"

"I'm sorry."

"For what?" I'm pressing my luck, but I can't help it.

"That I didn't celebrate what you were happy about?" She's made it into a question, which is pretty annoying, but it's progress. Huge progress. I decide to take it.

I wave her past. "Go ahead. But if you so much as—"

She beams. "Best behavior."

That's what I'm worried about. "Nothing offensive. Nothing at all."

Of course, when we go inside, that's when Amanda and Donna stand up and announce that it's time to open presents. Gift opening is traditionally *not* my mother's finest moment. She always has some kind of comment on everything, and it's never considerate. It usually makes the giver feel like a complete and total moron.

And that's when it's *her* birthday, so presumably, it's her friends and family giving the presents.

At my parties, she's literally been known to send people home in tears. I glance at Helen, who's not doing a great job at suppressing a smile. I point at her and purse my lips, trying to signal that it's her job to keep Mom muzzled.

She sighs, rolls her eyes, and nods.

"Here, open mine first," Donna says.

A bright green bag with plenty of white tissue paper is passed over. I tug the tissue out and pull out a tall, black book. It's thin, and to be honest, it looks like a menu for a restaurant. I look a little closer and realize the print at the bottom says *Menu: In Bed*.

Oh, no.

"What is it?" Mandy asks.

"It's a book." I slam it shut and practically drop it next to my chair.

Amanda scoops it back up. "It's a *challenge* book," she says. "It has lots of different things you can do—"

"Alright," I say. "Who else brought something?"

Donna's frowning, and she and Amanda share a look.

"Amanda has something." Greta points. "Right there."

I reach for it.

Amanda snatches her black and white bag away so fast it nearly breaks one of my fingernails. "Later," she hisses. "You can open mine later."

Mandy practically chucks hers at me. "Open mine, then."

It's a large enough box that if Amanda didn't have quick reflexes, it might have taken my head off. Once it's squarely in front of me, I split the box open and stare at the pile of things. No option but to pull them out one at a time.

A pair of fluffy, hot pink slippers are on top.

"Mraow," Mandy says.

Couldn't Mom and Helen have come an hour later? Why doesn't my life ever work that way?

Next is a beautifully wrapped box of lotion. "Thank you," I say. "It's so dry here compared to Houston that I go through lotion like crazy."

"That's not lotion." Mandy's eyes sparkle.

I look closer and realize it's *massage oil*. "Right. Well,

thanks." I can't even look at my mother. At least she's not saying anything. I pull out a pair of lacy white under-wear. "Uh, great."

"Turn it over," Mandy says.

Across the bottom, it reads: Mrs. Archer. For some reason, it makes me laugh. Pretty soon, everyone in the room is howling with me. And when I turn sideways, I realize the strangest thing of all.

My mom is laughing, too.

By the time I pull out the card at the bottom of the box (thank goodness!) and open it, I'm a little less concerned about Mom's head exploding so I read it aloud. "A one-year subscription to the lingerie of the month club."

Mandy slaps the table. "Because most gifts are only for the honeymoon, but this is the one that keeps on giving." She cackles, and I stop worrying about whether my mother will have an aneurysm and die. If she does, well, it's not my fault. It's *Mandy's*.

Besides, this is my bridal shower, a party I didn't ask for, but my friends are throwing for me anyway. I'm not going to let her ruin it. I can barely believe it, but my mom and Helen manage to keep their mouths closed through a dozen other gifts.

And then Helen hands me one. "Here."

"No way," I say. "You already paid for my dress and my move."

She pushes the small box my direction again. "Then consider this an apology gift."

I take it. "Fine. I can't argue with that." I unwrap it carefully, revealing the bright blue of a Tiffany's box. I should have assumed. When I open the lid on a heavy box that's far too large for a ring, a simple necklace, or even earrings, I gasp.

It's the Elsa Peretti gold cuff I love—Amanda must have told her. It's wide, and it's irregular—wide on one side, but narrowing a bit across the wrist, like it's made of melting wax. It's also engraved on top to read H loves A.

Helen's big on spending her way out of trouble, but she had to talk to Amanda about what I might like, and then she had to ask them to engrave something meaningful. It's the message more than the gift that makes me cry.

Helen loves Abigail.

For the first time in a while, I think that maybe she does.

"Well, now I can't give you mine," Mom says. "Not after this. I knew I should have gone first."

"It's fine, Mom," I say. "You don't need to give me anything."

"Just take it." She thrusts a box my direction.

I unwrap it rotely, preparing myself for something strange that I won't understand. In all the years I've been alive, I have never gotten a gift from my mother that I actually wanted. Lately she's just sent me a fruit subscription box. At least that's something she knows the kids will eat. I doubt I do much better with her, to be honest. We just don't get one another very well.

So when I open the box and it's a t-shirt that says *Princeton*, I'm not exactly surprised that I have no idea what she's thinking. "Uh, thanks. Were you in New Jersey recently?"

She shakes her head, and then she slowly unzips her coat. Underneath, she's wearing a shirt that reads: Proud of my Princeton Grad. It even has a cheesy graduation cap graphic hanging askew on the capital letter P.

My eyes well with tears. My throat closes off. And suddenly, I'm bawling like a baby. I'm thirty-nine years old the first time my mother ever tells me she's proud of me. But it happened.

Even more than the validation I feel, my mother finally took the time to try and give me a gift that will make *me* happy instead of giving me one she thinks I should like. Arms wrap around me then, and part of me desperately hopes they're my mom's, but of course I know they aren't. People don't change that much in one day. I'm already shocked at the progress she made.

But a hug from Amanda, and then another from a probably jealous Helen, is also good.

Perhaps it's the lawyer in me, but I usually try to avoid any sort of situation I can't control. It's safer, it's cleaner, and it's just more enjoyable. But sometimes the surprises in life can bring us a lot of joy.

"Thanks for the party." Then I turn toward Helen. "And thanks for coming even if I didn't make you feel super welcome. I love you all."

And I mean it.

❦ 31 ❦

ABIGAIL

The first time I got married, things were rushed because I'd just found out I was pregnant. My dress was an empire cut so I wouldn't have to let it out three times in the month it took us to prepare. And I was afraid to say no to anything my mom or my soon-to-be-mother-in-law asked for because I felt like I was in the wrong.

Now that I'm thirty-nine, and I've stood up to my mother, and I have four headstrong children of my own, I'm getting exactly the wedding I want. I refuse to compromise on anything.

But I still have trouble saying no, apparently.

"You'll have to be really quick," I say. "I'm getting married this afternoon and—" But Mr. Eugene has already hung up. Perhaps when I said be quick, he literally thought I meant he should hang up on me mid-sentence and rush to his car. He is very literal.

In support of that hypothesis, he shows up at my house less than eleven minutes later. At first, I don't realize it's him. Gone is the twelve-year-old Lincoln Town Car.

I have to do a double take, but sure enough, it's him climbing out of the *passenger* side of a shiny white BMW five series. Hunched shoulders, button-down single-color dress shirt, slacks that are just a touch too short, and little brown wingtips—he looks almost the same as before, except that everything he's wearing looks brand new.

And for the first time ever, he's not alone. I was so distracted by the changes I'm late at studying the biggest one: a woman who's probably in her fifties with smooth, newscaster hair, a sleek business suit, and four inch pumps circles the car and takes his arm.

Did he hire a personal assistant? Or maybe he finally took my advice and found an accountant. Either way, hopefully I won't have to hold his hand quite so much any more.

It's not until he waves that I notice another few things. Mr. Fred Eugene, serially depressed widower, is beaming. There's a spring in his step. And he meets my gaze openly. "I'm so glad you could meet with us."

I mouth the word "us" silently. I really had no idea he might show up less than a week after I last saw him using words like "us" and "glad." You don't use "us" for an accountant, do you?

"And who is this?" I ask.

The woman holds out her free hand to shake, but I notice that she does not relinquish Mr. Eugene's hand to do it. "I'm Brooke, Freddy's fiancée."

I nearly swallow my own tongue. *Freddy? Like he's five?* "His, uh, wow. That's—"

"Very exciting," she says. "I know."

I was going to say *fast*, but I nod along as if I was merely excited. "And are you here to talk about the terms of a prenuptial agreement?"

If looks could maim, I'd be missing an eye and possibly an arm. "Of course not. We have no doubts, do we Freddy?"

I throw up a little bit in my mouth. "What's the rush, then?"

Brooke points at the porch. "Could we go inside?"

"Of course." I walk with them to the front door and then allow Fred to shuffle ahead, since he's well acquainted with the location of the game room, which has been my *de facto* office for months now, thanks to all the construction roadblocks the growth in the area has caused.

Once Brooke and Fred are seated, she smiles. "Fred's understanding was that this whole probate process was supposed to take around two months, but it's been more than three now, and things still aren't resolved." She leans forward, her brows drawing together. "We're concerned that you're dragging it out to increase your fee."

I do not come off the sofa and deliver a roundhouse to her face.

I'm proud of that.

"To increase my fee?" I do, however, stand up. "I'm getting *married* today," I say. "My wedding is in a few hours. Your soulmate here has had me accompany him to the bank on several occasions, and to numerous other places, doing things a lawyer should not have to do. Now that he has *you,* I'm sure that will no longer be necessary." I turn to Mr. Eugene. "But surely he can attest that

I have, at no point, suggested that I do even one minute of work he did not specifically request for me to do."

"You did say it would take two months," Mr. Eugene says, staring at his shoes the entire time.

"That was an estimate I gave in our very first client meeting that even then I told you was contingent on the court's schedule. You had also told me at that time that you had two cars, a home, and a pension. Now your estate is worth more than twenty-four million dollars, and the inventory is much more complicated. We're still waiting on the final appraisal of the second producing oil interest, but once we have that, we should be able to file it with the court and finalize things."

"It's just that, until it's done, Mr. Eugene doesn't have full access to his funds."

I frown. "Several million dollars is in a joint account that had a right of survivorship and he can use it now. Are you saying he needs more than three and a half million dollars? For what?" My hand is now itching to call Steve's uncle.

Brooke stands, too. "Your bills, for one—"

"My last invoice was for just under four thousand dollars," I say. "Does not compute."

"We're doing just fine," Mr. Eugene says. "I don't need more money. We just wanted to check in on the progress for the inventory."

"We'll let you get ready for your wedding now." Brooke snatches at Mr. Eugene's arm. "We have a busy day as well. We're going to see our granddaughter's school play."

Our granddaughter? They've known one another for a week, and she's calling her granddaughter 'our' granddaughter? This woman is a piece of work. "Have fun," I say.

But as I watch them shuffle out, I keep a careful eye on Mr. Eugene. Brooke may be domineering and grasping, but she seems to be polite to him. He is beaming at her. He looks genuinely happy.

And that's the first time I've seen him happy. . .ever. Maybe it's not up to me to judge how he chooses to spend the fortune life has blessed him with. I hope it brings him lasting joy for whatever time he has left, and that Brooke is a better person than she seemed from our brief interaction.

"Mom?" Ethan's already in his tux. "Whoa, you're still wearing jeans."

"I certainly am," I say. "We won't be leaving here for at least forty-five more minutes, and I don't plan to put my dress on until we reach Steve's place."

"I guess if I had a white tux, I'd be more nervous about putting it on early." He smiles. "Did you ever even imagine all this dirt and dust back in Houston? Sometimes it feels like all it takes is to walk outside and we're covered in grime."

"Living out here is definitely different," I say. "But you're the one who insisted on it."

"True," Ethan says. "I felt pretty bad about it for a while, but it seems like you're a lot happier here."

I hug my son—who's now as big as his father was. "I am." Looking back at our time in Houston after Nate's passing feels like staring down a long, dark hallway. "We needed to get out of there, but we just didn't know it." I glance at my watch—my makeup is done, but I still have a few things left. "I better run and curl my hair."

"Mom?" Izzy sounds panicked, but all I can see is her

426

nose and one eye. At least she's put on her mascara already. She learned to do it herself last week, and it takes her more than fifteen minutes.

"Yeah?"

"I need help."

Ethan's shaking his head and there's a glint in his eye. "You can't catch a break, can you? Not even on your wedding day."

I shrug. "I'm a mom today, and I'll still be a mom tomorrow."

"It would be nice if, just for today, you could just be a bride, though, wouldn't it?"

Sometimes I wish I could get a time-out from it, but that's not how it works. "I never regret having you guys. Never."

"Mom!" Izzy's not calming down, so that's my cue to scoot over.

I tap once on her door and then slide inside. She's sitting on the floor—the wood floor—in her underwear, bawling. Her silver dress is in a puddle next to her.

"Um."

She looks up at me, and I realize it would have been better if she *hadn't* already put on mascara. But she's such a cute little raccoon.

My heart contracts in a way that only a mother's can. "What's going on?"

"I got—" She hiccups, loudly. Then she starts crying again.

She's trying to tamp down on the sobs, but it appears to have really taken hold. I wrap my arm around her shoulders. "You don't look sick, so I'm sure everything will be alright. Why don't you tell me what's wrong. What did you get?"

"My period," she wails.

Oh. Of all the days for my darling teenage daughter to start her period for the first time, my wedding day would *not* have been my choice either. Which is why I should have expected it. I can't help laughing.

"This isn't funny!" She swipes at her eyes. "It got on the dress. The dress!" Her anxiety's fighting her complete and total misery and they're both getting all tangled up in tears and general histrionics.

I squeeze her shoulders. "Izzy. Calm down! Women have dealt with this for hundreds, no, what am I saying? Thousands of years. It's really fine. Exciting, even. It may be bad timing, but trust me. We've got this."

I walk her through the logistics, and then we talk damage control. I take a look at her dress, and she's right. "There's no way to clean this up quickly." I glance at the clock again. "Not if we want it to be dry, which I think we do."

She laughs this time. "We do." Her face is still red and tear-streaked, but the puffiness is already receding as the sobs finally wind down. But then, as if this just occurred to her, they ramp back up. "I'm going to miss my own mother's wedding!"

I grab her hand to make sure she's listening. "I'm going to make a suggestion. Let's see if we can find a dress in my closet that will work as a substitute."

She frowns. "None of your dresses will fit me, and even if they did, you don't have a silver one."

"Well, aren't you Miss Negativity. How do you know what dresses I have?"

"I have eyes, Mom."

"I have dresses in my closet from high school." I stand up. "Let's just go take a look."

We get her cleaned up first, and I walk her through the basics of her new and exciting situation. Then she pulls on yoga pants and a t-shirt and follows me into my room where I start rummaging. I'm the kind of person who absolutely loves dresses and buys them all the time, but since I wear suits for work, mostly, and I am now living on a ranch, most of them have become closet dust collectors. "Ah-ha!" I hoist the dress I was thinking of into the air and wave it at Izzy.

"That's not silver," she says.

"It's purple and silver, which are my colors."

She frowns.

"Well, we aren't going to find something exactly the same, obviously, but this will work. And beyond that, it's my wedding, and it's a small wedding, and you're not bridesmaids. You and your sister, Emery and Maren, you're my flower girls. So you'll look fine in the photos, especially if we stick you *between* the bridesmaids in purple and the flower girls in silver."

"It'll be kind of like I'm both?" She arches one eyebrow in a move I know she stole from me.

"Yes," I say. "Sure."

It takes a few pins and a bit of maneuvering, but we get her all cleaned, prepped, and polished, and we even redo her makeup.

"Perfect," I say. "No one will ever know." If I hurry, I can pull the top part of my hair back into a knot and curl the bottom and some wispy pieces around my face. That might even look better than what I had planned.

"Mom?" As Izzy leaves, Gabe enters, his entire face turned downward, like he's being pulled more aggressively by gravity than the rest of us.

"What's up, little man?" I hope he can't hear the

brusque note in my tone. I'm trying to be a good mom, but my emotional fuel for that is quickly draining. "What's wrong?"

His sad little eyes look up toward mine, and his lips tremble. "I'm really happy about getting a new dad, but I'm worried I'll forget my real dad."

My heart sinks. Why is this all coming to a head today? Because today is *the* day it happens. I sigh and sit on the edge of my bed. I pat the spot next to me.

It makes me a little sad how easily he's able to trot over and hop up onto it.

"You will forget your real dad," I say softly. "It really stinks, but I bet you've already forgotten a lot. It's kind of the nature of being so young."

"I'm not young," he says. "I'm almost eight."

I don't explain that seven is kind of the definition of young. It won't make any more sense to him now than it would have a year ago—after all, he can reach cabinets now. He can brush his own teeth. There are so many things he can do right now that he couldn't do six months back. It's impossible for him *not* to feel like he's big.

"What I mean is, you're going to forget things about Dad, and that's okay. It just happens. Did you know I'm already forgetting things about him, too?"

This was clearly the wrong thing to say, because his sad face crinkles up into absolute distress and tears start flying out of his face almost horizontally, defying my knowledge of physics, like he's an actual cartoon character.

He's still small enough that I can drag him up onto my lap, but only just. I rock him for a moment. "The

430

good news is that I do remember a lot more than you, and so does Ethan. So does Izzy."

"Not Whitney?"

Whitney's so close to his age that I bet she's feeling the same way. "I'm not sure, but I do know that I and Ethan and Izzy, we like talking about Dad. We'll do it with you as much as you want." An idea occurs to me. "You know I've made all those photo albums over the years."

He nods, his crying winding down into something more like regular sobs.

"How about if I go through those, and I use them to think of any stories that have to do with you and Dad? Then I can write those down. Would that help?"

He blinks and wipes at his face. "Maybe."

"You know, in some ways, forgetting is how our body lets us heal from the trauma of loss."

Gabe has no idea what I'm saying.

"When we lose someone, at first, it feels like we've lost an arm or a leg. We feel like we can barely move. We wonder if we should even keep on living."

His eyes widen.

"But as time passes, we remember the good things. The hard things and the bad things kind of fade. And when even the good things get fuzzy, our heart doesn't hurt as much about the fact that they can't be with us."

"That makes me more sad." His lip's trembling again.

"But you know what? Having Steve here won't make it any worse, I promise. He won't ever tell you not to talk about your dad, and he will always be happy to read you stories or listen to the ones you recall."

"Do you think Dad's happy, up in heaven? Or is he mad that you're getting married?"

That question knocks me back a bit. "Happy?" I try to imagine big-hearted Nate up in heaven, sitting on a cloud, looking down at the day I'm having today. I think he'd be laughing, honestly.

But in the end, I think he'd be happy. "I do."

"Would he like Mr. Steve?"

This time, the tears are popping out of my eyes. "I think he would, yeah."

"So do I." Gabe smiles. "You can't cry. You're getting married, Mom."

"So I am." I inhale deeply and run my fingers under my eyes to wipe away the moisture. "I think your dad's biggest wish would be that we'd be happy, even though he can't be here to make sure we are. I think he wants us healthy, which Steve will help with, too."

"Yeah, cuz he's a doctor."

"Right." I tap his nose. "But I also think he'll be delighted that I've found someone his kids like and someone who really loves you guys."

"Do you think he does love me?" Gabe's back to slumped shoulders. "Or do you think he wishes that he could marry you without all of us to pester him?"

"Your brother Ethan's the one who's always saying you're a pest, not Mr. Steve. I think he is much, much happier here in our house with us, and I think I'm only a part of that joy." I lower my voice. "I think he fell in love with all of us at the same time."

After another few moments of snuggling, Gabe hops off my lap. "I'm sorry I made you cry, Mom."

"You didn't," I say. "And I love you."

"I know."

I glance at my watch. "But I'd better get things

moving, because otherwise I'll be late for my own wedding."

"I'll go get my suit on." Gabe dashes from the room.

"Ethan!" I shout as loudly as I can, but he's not far.

His head appears in my doorway moments later. "Yeah?"

"Can you make sure that—"

"Gabe's buttons line up and he can find his tie?"

I nod.

He throws me a thumbs-up. "I'm on it."

I'm definitely out of time to curl my hair. I don't even have time to pull it into any kind of twist. I barely have time to swipe on a little extra deodorant and grab my dress and my turquoise and gold cowboy boots. Oh, and my pearls. I'm pulling them from my jewelry box when I hear the sniffle behind me.

I spin around, my dress in a huge white bag over one arm, my boots and pearls in my other hand, and I realize the noise came from Whitney.

At least she's in her dress. Does it make me a terrible mother to think that? She's done her own hair, and it's. . .unique. She's twisted it into a knot behind her head—a ponytail she twirled into a ball, no doubt—and she's wearing both a headband *and* a bow on top of the knot that's so large I can see it from the front.

It's also bright yellow.

"Is everything okay?"

She spreads her hands down her skirt, smoothing it, and twirls for me. She moves surprisingly well in wedges for a girl her age. I wish the little silver sparkle heels didn't look quite so cute, actually. It makes her look much older than ten.

"You look great," I say. "Though I might just—" I

drop my shoes and necklace on the edge of the bed and reach out and tug the yellow bow off the back of her head. "This is a little overpowering. I think the headband is perfect by itself." At least it's purple and has flowers.

"I wasn't sure about that," she says, "but I thought the yellow might stand out against the silver, like silver and gold."

I set my dress on the bed, too, and then I crouch down in front of her. "Are you alright?"

She nods, her eyes somber.

"Why did you come in here?"

"Izzy and you had all that time, doing whatever or talking. And then you and Gabe did, too, and I heard you crying *and* laughing."

She's jealous. I should have known. If I pay one child a compliment, the other three become nearly apoplectic that I haven't petted them and told them how wonderful they are, too. I should be annoyed, since it is my wedding day, but I'm not. I tug her close and wrap her in a tight hug. "You are adorable and I love you. You know that, right?"

I can feel her nod against my shoulder.

"Izzy had a problem, and Gabe was sad. Are you sad?"

She shakes her head but doesn't pull away.

"If you aren't sad, and you aren't worried, I'm going to go ahead and do this." I pull back and kiss her forehead. "And then we're going to get loaded in the car. Okay?"

She swallows slowly, and nods. I can tell she's still a little disappointed.

"How about this?"

Her eyes light up with hope.

"Since you're the youngest of the girls, why don't you walk at the front of the line when the flowers girls enter? We can do it by birth order and put you first."

"Oh," she says. "Good idea."

I text Steve as we load up. BUMPY MORNING OVER HERE. FINALLY ON OUR WAY OVER. SORRY WE'RE A LITTLE LATE.

When we reach his house, he's already waiting outside. I'm worried he'll have tight eyes—Nate always would when things went off schedule.

Maybe it's the emergency room doctor in him, or maybe it's the country boy. I'm not sure. Either way, he's totally calm, and when he smiles, there's nothing but happiness in his face at the sight of me. He looks amazing in his dark but perfectly faded jeans, his nicest pair of recently buffed cowboy boots, a silver vest, and a dark suit coat with a purple tie. The little white wild-flowers in his pocket look perfect, but the thing that ties it all together is his tan felt cowboy hat.

"You can change inside." He points. "I think the guests are all around back, and they're ready to go." Before I can even reply, he turns toward my army of children. "Hey, guys! Are you ready for a lifetime of sleepovers?"

Izzy starts laughing. Gabe just nods. And Ethan's whoop makes Whitney jump.

"The party's just starting." Steve looks like he really means it.

"Can I bring my Legos?" Gabe lifts a honeydew melon-sized bag into the air. "In case it gets boring?"

Steve laughs. "Of course you can."

"But you might lose some," I say. "If you're okay with

that, then. . ."

Gabe's eyes widen and he stuffs the bag back into the corner of the car. "Never mind."

Steve shepherds the kids toward the back of his house, and I go inside and change as quickly as I can. By the time I'm wearing my dress, my boots, and my pearls, I'm worried the horses will be antsy and the people annoyed.

But when I walk around the corner, Steve has the wagons all lined up. A few of his friends own draft horses, and they volunteered to drive their teams so our entire ceremony will be vehicle free. Since I'm marrying a horse trainer and Steve apparently broke three of the drafts, it felt right. And my fiancé's holding the reins for both Leo and Farrah. Someone, probably not Steve since his braiding is embarrassingly bad, braided Leo's mane, weaving tiny bunches of white yarrow into it.

It looks like something out of a storybook.

No one plays the wedding march as I walk toward my future husband, and that's okay. There are only a hundred or so guests here—mostly our close friends and family. Steve helps me swing up onto Leo, which is normally easy, but when I'm wearing a dress this puffy and Leo's bareback, it feels like quite a feat. Once I'm up, Steve swings up onto Farrah's back with ease, and he circles us around to face the guests.

"Thanks for coming," he says, his voice loud and strong. "We can't say how excited we are that you could make it." He tips his hat to the bright blue wagon at the front and the man shakes his reins, cueing the huge draft horses to start moving.

Steve and I take the lead, walking toward the meadow where we had our picnic on that first real, no kids, no community events date. As we push into the clearing, I'm struck by just how perfect it is. The bright orangey-red Indian paintbrush and white yarrow cover the field, with the exception of the area we cleared. Steve set up a nice white tent and had chairs lined up in rows underneath. There's a gorgeous white dais at the front, with big vases of Indian paintbrush and daisies running up either side.

We walk our horses to the front. Neither of them spooks, neither of them even fidgets. There's a nice, refreshing breeze, but it's a sunny, beautiful day. For this area and this timeframe, we're darned lucky. They even wait patiently for all the guests to climb out of the wagons and find seats.

Of course, before the pastor begins the ceremony, it starts to rain.

ABIGAIL

Ll the guests are already ensconced under the tent, which is fortuitous. My photographer starts snapping photos as quickly as possible, presumably desperate to take at least a few where I don't look like a drowned rat.

As if my thoughts about the safety of the wedding guests inspired it, a lively breeze turns into gusting wind, and even the guests are getting soaked.

"Um, do you want me to proceed?" the pastor asks. "Or?"

"What do you want to do?" Steve's voice is calm, and his eyes are attentive.

"Let's have the wedding," I say. "I don't care about the rain."

Steve ties the horses under a nearby tree, letting them eat a little bit while we have the ceremony, and everyone shifts a bit to let us stand under the edge of the tent. It doesn't help much, but at least it feels like we're less wet.

The pastor's address is a little rushed, perhaps, and

he doesn't pontificate about the beauty of marriage for very long, but once he's done, he does give us a chance to share our vows. I glance back at the guests. "Should we skip this part?"

Ethan's sitting on the far end, and his hair is plastered flat with rain, but he shakes his head. "We want to hear it. We're already wet, so who cares about a little more?"

"Exactly," Mandy says. "Say all that mushy stuff as loudly as you can."

"Then I'll go first," Steve says. "I'm not much for words, you know. I say as few as I can at the hospital, and my co-workers at my other job don't talk much." He means the horses, of course.

The guests, wet and miserable as they are, still chuckle as they get it.

"From the moment I saw you, Abigail, I knew I wanted you in my life. You were bright and shiny and sharp, but you also managed to be kind, and considerate, and a terrifying weapon to bring justice into the world."

"Terrifying?" I ask.

"Hey," he says. "It's my turn. You'll get yours in a minute, counselor."

That earns him another round of laughter.

"But in the entire time I was pursuing you and trying to convince you to make the biggest mistake of your life, I never really thought you'd pick me. I was damaged goods—divorced, single at almost forty, and I lived in a tiny town you didn't plan to live in for very long."

I reach for his hand, and he takes mine in his large one.

"What I didn't realize at first is that you were feeling some of the same things. You told me, if you remember,

439

that you were broken, and that you weren't ready to date, and that you had lots of children, and you were too much to handle."

I don't specifically recall saying any of that, but it sounds true.

"That's when I realized that marriage isn't about two perfect people finding each other. It's not even about two puzzle pieces fitting together flawlessly. It's more like two people who both heal one another's broken parts. What I do all day at work? I patch people up and medicate their imbalances."

Medicate their imbalances? I'm trying not to cringe, but. . .

Steve laughs. "I said I'm not much for the talking, but that's what we do, isn't it? And sure, there are bumps." He looks up at the rain with a beleaguered expression on his face. "And there are setbacks." He shakes his head, spraying water outward. "But my life is so much sunnier with you in it, so I don't mind when it rains. I promise you today, that no matter the bumps, no matter the setbacks, no matter the downpours, we'll plow ahead together, like we are today. I'll be by your side, and we'll ruin our brand new leather saddles at the same time."

"Speak for yourself," I say. "I'm riding bareback."

Another round of laughter—tempered a bit by my actual dismay that the rain is ruining his saddle.

"Is it my turn now?" I ask.

He nods, beaming.

"I had a very nice set of vows written," I say. "And not a one of them had anything to do with obeying you, so get ready for that."

He laughs. "I wouldn't have dreamed of you saying that."

"But as we stand here, a surprise rainstorm drenching us, I think about the morning that preceded this wedding."

I look out at the guests.

"My kids were nervous this morning. Both Steve and I are getting married for the second time, and neither of us is traveling light in terms of baggage."

I manage to create a few chuckles of my own.

"Most of you know that Steve's the best horse trainer around here. When he gets a new animal, he doesn't expect them to have no injuries, no constraints, or no vices. He rides them where they are, dealing with the issues as they arise. He's always done the same for me. In fact, I think the day I realized I loved him was the day we spent cleaning up puke together, in the middle of a huge blizzard."

Some laughter, but a lot more shocked faces.

"Life isn't always easy, and for my kiddos." I make sure they're all paying attention by looking from one to the next. "You need to find someone to marry who will be just as steady and strong in the mishaps of life. And you need to find someone who will laugh about them with you, and not spend all their energy lamenting what went wrong."

I turn back to Steve.

"I spent so much time with my kids this morning that I ran out of time to curl my hair. And guess what? It would have been totally wasted, even if I had. I could be really upset right now, but here's my vow. Instead of freaking out when things go wrong, I'll try to look at the good things instead. And I'll always try to spend my energy and time with you on the things that matter most —you, the kids, and our future."

And just like that, the rain stops and the sun comes out.

"I think this is a great sign," the pastor says. "I've rarely seen a couple better prepared to endure the storms of life."

"Endure?" Steve laughs. "I'd say that we'll triumph over the storms."

So would I.

❦ 33 ❦

AMANDA

If today had been my wedding, I'd be in tears right now.

That ceremony was a dumpster fire, or I guess it was the opposite of that, since it was a total downpour. I'm hoping the reception goes much more smoothly. Luckily, they scheduled an hour between the ceremony and the reception during which time the bride and groom were meant to be taking photos. Practically, it's become a window for the rest of us to change into non-water-soaked clothes. Lucky for David, even though he's staying in Dutch John, we're headed that direction for the reception anyway, so we both get the chance to change. In fact, he's staying at the resort where Abby's reception is located, which makes his change the easiest one.

And so far, he has been entirely true to his word. He didn't bat an eye when I told him he'd be escorting me and both my daughters. He's not clingy, he's not pressuring me about anything, and it is nice to have someone on whose arm I can hang.

"I hope that tux isn't a rental," I say after he emerges from his room in a suit. "I doubt they'll give you your deposit back."

"Yeah, it looked pretty bad," Maren says. "Sorry."

"Maybe you could dry it," Emery says.

"You guys thought it might be a rental?" He laughs. "It's not."

I should have known. No one could look quite that good in a tux that wasn't made for them. He's not as beautiful as Eddy, but he's awfully sharp-looking all the same. "You might still be a touch overdressed, though."

"I haven't been here long enough to have bought cowboy formal clothing yet," he says. "Sorry."

"I think we'll survive," I say.

Once we walk into the reception hall, I take one look around and realize that he's almost the only person here who didn't get the jeans and sport coat memo. Even Steve's dad, who moved to a much bigger city, reverted to the exact right attire when he came back.

David gestures at the barn decor and the other guests who are mostly wearing cowboy boots. "Maybe if my performance tonight is good enough, you'll pay me back by taking me shopping so I can blend in better."

Maren and Emery disappear immediately, running off to sit by their cousins. I snag a place at a table near the edge of the room.

"Well, at least there's that guy." I bob my head at the other youngish guy in a suit who's sitting one table over. It looks like he's Helen's date.

David grits his teeth. "Don't compare me to him."

"Do you dislike him?" I ask. "How can you? You haven't even met."

"Oh, I know Kyle Saunders."

I turn around in my chair to get a better look. Helen's date isn't especially tall, but he's taller than she is. He's not amazing-looking either, but he's not *un*attractive. Mostly, when I look at him, I sense. . .sharpness. He's like a well-honed blade, or a predator looking for dinner. He's looking at Helen now, listening to something she's saying, and he's amused, at least.

Maybe that means we're all safe. For now.

"How do you know him?" All kinds of questions vie for space in my brain. "Is he a bad guy? How do you think Helen knows him?"

"I know him from school," David says. "And I have no idea how Helen knows him. Is that her?" He's eyeing Helen, alright.

I hadn't given Abby's sister enough credit before. She was always wearing something very fastidious, very professional. But seeing her in an evening gown is different. I had no idea she was quite as thin as she was, or that she was quite so well endowed in spite of it. After assessing her appearance, I expected David to be gaping at her.

But instead, he's glaring.

"That's Abby's sister," I say. "Maybe tone down the death glare."

"Abby's sister?" David blinks. "Well, that's unfortunate. Someone should warn her—maybe she was set up and doesn't know what he's like. Because anyone who would knowingly date someone like Kyle Saunders isn't entirely human."

I can't help myself. I poke the bear. "He's not that bad looking."

And I'm richly rewarded. David actually splutters. "Not bad—he's the devil himself."

"What exactly has he done to deserve that name?"

"Let's review." David holds out one hand, only his index finger extended. "In school, he blackmailed the board members to have the valedictorian kicked out so he could graduate first in our class."

I frown.

He holds out his middle finger as well. "And then in graduate school, he slept with not one, but two female professors when his grades weren't what he wanted."

"Wait, that works for guys?"

"Apparently." He holds up a third finger. "And then after we graduated, he forced the founding family out of a large company and took it over, subsequently eliminating a pension fund to get a bonus for himself." He throws his hands up in the air. "He has destroyed countless failing companies, leaving hundreds of thousands unemployed, all so he could sell off their parts for a profit."

I blink.

"Kyle cares only about Kyle, and trust me. You want *nothing* to do with him. His most universal policy is scorched earth."

"Wow, tell me what you really think," I say.

David's gaze snaps back to mine. "Sorry. We're here for a wedding. But if you get a chance to warn Abby's sister, I would."

"Actually, they sound kind of perfect for each other," I say. "From what Abby's told me, Helen's something of a business piranha. She gobbles up companies and—"

"Wait, is Abby's sister named Helen *Fisher*?"

"Yeah, that's her maiden name. Her parents are both professors at Stanford—"

"And that's where Helen went to school." David shakes his head. "Holy moly, I can't believe that's her." He looks me dead in the eyes. "They do deserve each other. From what you've said of Abby, and what Donna has said too, it's a miracle she and Helen came from the same parents."

"Her parents are pieces of work," I say. "Really. It's a testament to Abby's goodness that she made it out of that home as generous as she is."

Abigail picks that moment to appear, no longer in her waterlogged wedding gown, but looking as cute as ever in an eggplant purple, Audrey Hepburn style, A-line midi dress. Her hair has that fluffy shine you only get right after blow-drying it. Steve's wearing something that looks very similar to what he had on before, but I guess he didn't have an extra purple vest hanging around. They look absolutely adorable, and I'm not the only one who starts clapping.

"Thanks for being patient, everyone," Abby says. "I think it's time for food."

There are plenty of hoots and hollers at that, and one thing that everyone here is always happy to eat is barbecue. Steve must've guided Abby on that one, because I really don't see her as a pulled pork sandwich kind of gal. I'm not a huge fan either, but at least with the coleslaw on the sandwich like Abby eats hers, it's edible.

I'm wiping barbecue sauce off the corners of my mouth when the door behind us bangs open. I might not have even noticed, but several people turn to look at me, and one of them is Mandy. She clears her throat, and her eyes cut behind me toward the door.

In movies, this type of thing always happens in slow motion, like the entire room stops and the viewer can focus on the big entrance. But in actuality, David keeps telling the story he was in the middle of, about how his childhood dog was adorable and kind and sweet, but he also kept pooping in his dad's shoes, because his dad was the puppy's competition for his mother's time.

It's a funny story, but I completely stop listening the second I lock eyes with Eddy.

It's not just my ears that stop working. My heart stops beating. My body starts sweating, like, everywhere. Why didn't it occur to me that he might be here? His tour ended yesterday. Steve's his friend, and Abby is, too.

But wouldn't they have warned me if he was coming?

"Sorry I'm late," he says, scanning the room. "You have no idea how many flights got delayed and then canceled thanks to that dumb storm up north."

"I'd guess the people up north are less flippant about it," David says. "At least, the ones sitting under piles of snow so heavy they're breaking their roofs and damaging their pipes."

Eddy's eyes practically crackle. "I can't tell you how happy I am to see you again. Donald, was it?"

David puts his arm around the back of my chair. "I didn't expect you would care whether you saw me or not."

I still can't seem to move. Or speak.

"Amanda," Eddy says. "Can we talk?" He jabs a thumb over his shoulder. "Outside?"

"We're at her sister's wedding," David says. "Is this really a great time to drag her off?"

"It's the first time I've been *home* in months," Eddy says. "So, yeah. It's a great time."

"She doesn't look that happy to go with you," David says.

"You haven't let her say a word," someone at another table says.

My eyes search the room, and I realize that everyone is watching. That's the joy of a small town, I suppose. They all know Eddy and I were dating, and they all know we broke up when he left on tour. But it wasn't a local who interjected himself into the conversation.

It was that Kyle guy Helen brought.

"This isn't any of your business," David says.

"Actually, I think someone should be saying that to you," Kyle says. "I hear you're the third wheel on this racetrack."

David stands up. "You don't know anything about the people here or my date tonight."

I don't blame David for trying to stick up for me. In fact, he hasn't been super possessive, and he knows the Eddy thing wrecked me. It makes sense that he'd try to defend me. I think all in all, he's been pretty great about every bit of it.

But I want to talk to Eddy.

And I want to hide behind David.

It's like when you really want to try the zipline your kids begged you to take them to, but the longer you wait on the platform a million feet in the air, the more nervous you get and the more you think you might puke and you just want to crawl down and never go up any ladders ever again.

I feel just like that.

David and Kyle are now shouting at each other.

David's saying something about the unconscionable way Kyle does business. Kyle's laughing at how disappointed David's parents must be that they've raised a monumental failure.

"Amanda." Eddy's voice is low. "Please?"

I make the tactical error of meeting his eyes, and then I'm a goner. When you've cared deeply for someone and they ask you for something small, you do it. Or at least, I do.

I nod.

And we slip out the door while the two business guys wreck Abby's wedding. I do feel bad about that, especially since one of them is my date. But I'm too splintery inside right now to do anything about it.

"I'm sorry," Eddy says. "When you left, I wanted to drop out of the tour. I called my manager and told him I was done."

My heart's beating a ridiculously staccato rhythm in my chest right now.

"He sent me a bill that represented what I'd owe if I canceled the contract. It's more than I could pay in five years. Maybe ten."

"I wish I was one of those women who could shout at you right now," I say. "But I'm too pragmatic. I'd never have let you break your contract. We're too old to shout and scream and throw fits because real world things are hard. But you didn't call. You didn't tell me you even wanted to make it work."

"I did call," Eddy says. "Several times."

"You never left a message." He never flew out, either. He must have had at least a day or two off to come out. Although, this is a pretty inaccessible place.

"Would it have worked if I had?" Eddy asks. "Or would it just have kicked up more drama for both of us?"

"I guess we'll never know, since you gave up." I hate how bitter I sound, but I can't help how I feel.

Eddy frowns. "Do you know what it's like to be on tour?"

I can imagine, I think. "That's how I felt when my husband died," I say. "Emotionally wrung out. Hollow. Exhausted. Drained to the point of no return. And scared, too."

He snorts. "Yes. Like that."

"Was it worth it?" I suppose I do have a little melodrama left in me. "Was being on tour again everything you hoped it would be?"

"No." He shakes his head. "It was a big mistake. I wish I'd turned them down. Everything—the adoration of fans, the climbing the charts, the interviews and hoopla, it all felt empty."

That feels good to hear, which means I'm a pretty bad person. "I'm sorry."

"I'm sorry," he says. "Actually, that's not right. I'm devastated. I'm shredded. I've thought about nothing but you. I've done nothing but regret my decision for months."

"It's been hard on me, too."

"Looks like it." He glances back over his shoulder at the door into the reception hall.

"No," I say. "Don't do that."

"I'm sorry," he says. "I haven't been here, but I swear I've imagined it every single night, that guy doing his best to *console* you. All I wanted to do when I saw him was beat the ever-loving tar out of him, but I was civil. You have no idea how hard that was."

My hands fly to my hips. "Are you wanting me to pat you on the back here? You didn't *punch* someone like a *caveman*, someone who did nothing wrong, someone who is escorting me here to be polite, someone I'm out with for the very first time so I won't be all alone at a very public function. Bravo."

"It's your first date?" His hopeful, puppy-like expression infuriates me.

"What do you want, Eddy?"

"I want—" He chokes off and reaches into his pocket. Then he drops to one knee. "Not another single person tried to do anything inappropriate the entire tour. Do you know why?"

What's he doing?

"Because I told them I was *engaged*. I told my manager we weren't ready to announce it yet, because we didn't want to overshadow the focus of the tour, but everyone knew. They knew that no one else had any kind of chance. The problem wasn't that I was far from you, it's that we made the mistake of going into that without a more significant commitment. Something people hear and say, *oh! They're together, together. Not just casually dating.*" He opens the ring box. "I knew from the first moment I said it that it's what I wanted. I was terrified of commitment, you know. My parents are miserable; they've always been miserable. But with you, I'm nothing but happy. Or, you know, I was, before I got stupid and went on tour." He shakes the box so I will look down at it. "Marry me?"

If he had proposed months back, before all this happened, before our breakup, I'd have said yes. I think I would have. It would've been fast. It would've been hasty, even, but I was head over heels. We were as solid as Abby and Steve, I thought. I knew that whatever came at us, be it rain, or a surprise child he didn't realize he had, we'd face it together.

But we didn't.

When things got hard, we both bailed. I ran away, and Eddy let me.

I shake my head. "I can't."

And then I walk inside, back to my date.

It's easier than it should be. And it's harder. I feel numb, like I'm not part of my own life. Like I'm walking around in a daze, speaking and laughing and smiling like a robot while I'm dead inside.

The rest of the night passes in a blur, mostly. Someone obviously intervened with David and Kyle, because they're still glaring at one another, but no one's shouting. Actually, most of the people in the room are dancing.

"Everything alright?" Mandy hisses. "What did Mr. Animal Doctor have to say for himself?"

I shake my head. "Later."

"Will he rip my head off if we dance?" David reaches for my hand.

I let him take it. There's peace and quiet to be had with David at my side. He doesn't tangle me up and cause my insides to feel like a poorly blended smoothie. "I'll risk it if you will."

David's smile is reassuring. He's not scared of Eddy. It won't matter anyway. Eddy's going to disappear any minute. That's what we do. Except, he doesn't. When the dance ends, I notice that Eddy's sitting on the other end of the room, staring at me.

Donna reaches our table seconds later. "Can I borrow him?" She points at David.

"Go ahead," I say. "He's an excellent dancer."

"I'm sure he is," she says. "And that's just what I need."

I notice that Will is out on the dance floor right now, leading some thin brunette around—and then things click. That's the single mom Eddy brought to the fourth of July barbecue—or at least, I thought they were together then. She managed his shows when he was just a local singer and guitarist.

I wonder if Donna's trying to make him jealous. Seeing as she didn't come with a date, I bet that's going to be hard to do.

"What did he say?" Mandy hops two chairs over until she's right by me. "Don't hold out on me."

"How's your heart?" I can't help my sly half-smile.

"Ticker's fine." She thumps her chest. "Now stop delaying."

"He proposed."

Mandy whistles and shakes her head. "That boy swings for the fences."

"Grand gestures are dumb," I say. "He wasn't here when I needed him."

"He's responsible and wouldn't duck out on what he'd pledged," she says.

"Whose side are you on?"

"I'm always on yours," she says. "But you want that boy, and you're just being bull-headed."

"David has been—"

"*Boring*," she says. "That's what Mr. I'm So Handsome and Generous in Business has been." She yawns, and I honestly can't tell whether it's real or not.

But it makes me yawn, too.

I notice Eddy yawns across the room as well. I shouldn't be paying attention to him. I really shouldn't.

"Other than the fight he instigated with that other suit, he's a yawn fest."

"I'm glad that calmed down."

"Trust me, you don't want to date a guy who shows more fire and temper about some other man than he does over you."

To be fair, I think David's trying to be calm around me because he *does* care. But it's pointless arguing with Mandy.

"I had an idea," Mandy says. "Being here, at this resort, that's what gave it to me."

"What's that?"

"My old house—you like it? Or no?"

That's quite a change of subject. "Well, I think—"

"When I die would you want to keep living there?"

I turn until my chair is facing her fully. "Amanda Saddler, do not talk to me about dying or—"

She waves me off. "Stop. I'm fine right now, but one day it's going to happen, and I'm asking if you'll want to stay there, or if you'll want to move out."

"I don't know." But I think about it, and I realize that even in the six months we've been there, we've made as many happy memories as we've ever made anywhere. It took some time, but it finally feels like home. "I think I'd remodel a few things, but I'd keep it."

"What if we cleared out the area just past it—out beyond my garden. We could get rid of that old barn, clear the thicket, and then we could. . . build our own resort."

"Are you hearing yourself?" I ask. "We're standing in a resort right now, and David's building one—"

"This is a resort that caters to fishermen and hikers and whatnot. David's is for highfalutin rich people. I'm talking about a retreat for women, like you and me. Women who are tired—no, exhausted. Women who want a break—maybe they want to bring their kids. It would be women and children only, though. No men allowed."

I think about it.

"We'd have crafts and games for the kids," she says. "We'd have relaxation and therapy and group games and activities for the mothers. They'd have some time together, but plenty of time apart to decompress, to work through things, and to recover from whatever brings them here."

"What would we call it?" I feel like the name is the first thing that colors your impression of a place. It would have to be something good.

"Saddler Ranch?" she asks. "We could even have some horses for people who like to burn huge piles of money and get dumped in the dirt."

I laugh. That's about right—horses never appealed to me much, either. But Saddler Ranch is what she's always called her place. I think we need something that has meaning to people in all walks of life.

"What about Strike Gold?" I ask. "We could have gold panning for one thing, and we know they'd find some." I can't help my smile. "Actually that could be a fun selling point. Women could have the chance to pan or mine or find enough money to pay for their stay."

"But what does—"

"We've been taught that you strike gold when you meet a man who will take care of you, who will love you, right? But what if we teach them that the real overlooked gold in our lives is our family? And our friends. Meaningful friendships are being overlooked because the world tells us that romance is all that matters." I lean closer to her, too excited to be more calm. "We teach women to love themselves and one another, and only then will they be ready to find love anyway."

Mandy's face breaks into a smile. "That is what killed you and Eddy. You can't love someone else until you really love yourself."

Like a strike to the brain, what she said hits me with a thousand volts. She's right. Eddy and I didn't work because I didn't have enough faith in myself to trust that he really cared about me. And I didn't trust myself to survive him being gone.

David's back before I can try to articulate my epiphany, and we dance again. But before Abby and Steve even cut the cake, the music cuts off and the newlywed couple rushes toward the door.

"Hey," I shout. "What's going on?"

"Emergency at home." Abby turns and gestures for me to come closer. "All you single ladies, get over here."

She turns back toward the door, and without really waiting at all, she chucks the wedding bouquet right at me.

And I watch as it lands at my feet on the ground.

Donna snatches it up and tosses it in the air. "Wahoo. Did you see that?" Her eyes sparkle. "It just flew right to me."

I laugh along with everyone else. "Clearly, it's fate."

"Did you really hate the idea that much?" Eddy's voice is soft at my ear.

I close my eyes, but I also shake my head just a bit. "No, I didn't *hate* it, Eddy. It's just not right."

"Not right?" he asks. "Or not right *now*?"

"I don't know yet," I say.

"I'm not going anywhere, not again," he says. "I intend to show you that even if it's not right *now*, it will be. I really hope that it will be."

So do I.

DONNA

This wedding has been a disaster, start to finish. If I were Abby, I'd be worried it was a sign of impending doom, or some kind of evidence that the powers-that-be didn't bless my union. For her, I guess it's just another Saturday.

She and Steve look as happy as can be.

Most people are almost done eating, but a few are going back for one more round. The dance floor's clear, and a band starts to play. Meanwhile, I think I'm the only person here, other than Amanda Saddler, who doesn't have a date.

"Hey, girl, you could sit by me." She pats the chair next to her.

I watch as Will and Rebecca, a barrel racer who has always lorded her skill on horseback over everyone else, move onto the dance floor. I force my eyes away, and turn to face the person who's actually talking to me. "Why? Do I look like a harbinger of misery, standing over here by myself in the corner?"

"No," she says. "You look lovely. But your glaring's a little obvious."

Glaring? Staring, maybe, but I'm not glaring. "I still can't believe Will brought Rebecca. How old is she?"

Mandy squints. "You know her, clearly."

"I mean, she was a *freshman* when we were seniors."

She blinks. "So she's. . .what? Three years younger than you two?"

I fold my arms. "She has a kid."

"Hello kettle," Mandy says. "My name's pot. Nice to meet you."

"I mean, I know I have a kid too," I say. "But I was married to the father."

Amanda Saddler's voice carries its signature rasp and an extra helping of dry sarcasm when she says, "And that went really well, so I'd definitely brag about it."

I drop into the chair next to her and put my chin down on my arms. "Fine. Rebecca's nice, and funny, and kind, and her boobs are three years perkier than mine. I'm just being a brat because I can't believe I was so stupid that I missed my shot."

"Did you ever even call him?" Mandy arches one eyebrow.

"I *did*," I say. "And I asked him to be *my* date to this, and he turned me down."

"Ouch." She sighs. "Well, I guess maybe you did miss your chance. That stinks."

"I'm not sure how much longer I can just sit here and watch them canoodling on the dance floor," I say.

"Canoodling?" Mandy snorts. "How old *are* you? Maybe she is thirty years younger than you are, because you sound like my mother."

460

I ignore her. "I need to manufacture an emergency or something."

As if I've conjured it, Eddy breezes through the front door and almost the entire room falls quiet while he tries to talk to Amanda and David argues with him. Then some guy sitting by Helen starts arguing with David. *This* is why people come to weddings. Not to get rained on during the ceremony or to get free barbecue sandwiches.

No, we come for the drama.

Amanda Saddler and I both lean forward in our chairs.

"This isn't any of your business," David Park says, clearly furious with Helen's date.

"Actually, I think someone should be saying that to you," the flinty-eyed man says. "I hear you're the third wheel on this racetrack." Helen's date is remarkably well-informed for someone who doesn't live around here.

David stands up. "You don't know anything about the people here, or my date tonight."

"And yet I still seem to know more than you," the flinty-eyed guy says. "It's the one constant with you—I'll always outdo you. No matter the circumstance."

"You two are well-matched," David says, glancing from Helen to the guy and back again. "I can't believe I had no idea that Helen *Fisher* is Abigail's sister." He shakes his head. "The Chop Shop Queen of Harvard Business School."

"I've never done anything illegal," Helen says.

"Nothing you've been caught for, anyway," David says.

"You should watch your mouth," the flinty-eyed guy says. "Antagonize me any more and I'll run another of

461

your crappy little businesses into the ground, just for fun."

"Ooh, this is getting good," I whisper.

And that's when I notice that Amanda Saddler's no longer sitting next to me. She's walking toward the front of the room at the same time that Steve's grabbing the microphone from the stand.

"Attention," Steve says. "Miss Amanda Saddler, whom most of you know and love, collaborated with me to prepare a special gift for my lovely wife."

What's going on?

Mandy snatches the microphone from him. "I'm sure none of you have forgotten that the reason we're here today is to celebrate the wedding of Steve Archer and Abigail Brooks." She scowls at David and Kyle, both of whom immediately sit down. She forces an unconvincing smile.

"Did you bring the photos?" Steve whispers, but he's close enough to the microphone that we can all hear.

"Of course I did," Mandy hisses. "What kind of idiot would forget the most important part?"

"Where are they?" Steve asks.

Mandy points at the back wall, which is empty of anything at all, and where there are most certainly no pictures.

"Um." Steve's nose scrunches and he cocks his head a little to the side.

"Holden," Mandy shouts.

The lights in the front of the room dim, and an image is projected on the bright white wall. It's a photo of Amanda Brooks' failed cookie shop. It says, "Double or Nothing Bakery" right on the front in plain letters.

"Most of you know that Abby's best friend Amanda started a cookie shop here last year."

Abby's standing just at the foot of the stage, watching the image with curiosity.

"Come on up here." Mandy waves.

Abby marches up the steps, a quizzical look on her face.

"You may as well have a front row seat." Mandy cackles.

"My darling wife is a lawyer—in case you hadn't heard—and she gave up her fancy job when she decided to marry me. For months now, she's been working out of her home. With four kids, that hasn't always been easy. But with all the robust business coming into the area, we've had trouble finding contractors to make the necessary modifications to any of the local storefronts."

"So I had an idea," Mandy says.

"Actually, it was *my* idea," Steve says.

"We've worked much better together than it seems like we would based on tonight," Mandy says.

"We took this store, which was in good shape, but not quite right for a law office," Steve says, "and I worked on it whenever I could find the time."

"And I managed to scrounge up the people to do whatever things Steve didn't know how to do," Mandy says.

"We helped." Kevin waves from across the room.

Jeff brushes his hand against his chin, clearly a little embarrassed that his brother grabbed the attention. "It was our pleasure to help."

"Now it looks like this." Steve waves his arm and nothing happens. He glares at Mandy.

"Really, Holden? Are you asleep back there?"

The photo finally changes, and now there's an image with a new sign that reads, "Double or Nothing Legal: Abigail Archer, Esq."

"You kept the 'Double or Nothing'?" Abby looks a little perplexed.

"Hear me out," Steve says. "When that store was worked over by Amanda, it was because of an idea you had. It might have worked, but it wasn't what she really wanted to do. When you two arrived, double trouble, no one here thought you'd stick it out."

"I did," Mandy says.

Steve rolls his eyes. "Okay, I hoped you would, and apparently Mandy knows everything."

Mandy smiles in a self-satisfied way.

Steve continues. "But everyone else figured you'd come for a few weeks and then leave."

"I thought we'd head back home to Houston too," Abby says.

"And now it's been almost a year since you arrived, and I've managed to shackle you into staying forever. You're a local now, and if we're good at anything here, it's doing more than one thing at once. We have a hardware store that's a grocery store."

People hoot.

"We have a restaurant that's also a hotel."

More cheers.

"And now, we have a law office, that's also a bakery that takes only custom or catering orders."

Izzy, Maren, Emery, and Whitney all poke their heads out from behind the wall at the front one at a time. Then they step out, smiling.

Abby narrows her eyes. "So, what exactly—"

"Holden!" Mandy shouts.

The image changes again, and this time, it shows the front room. The glass case is gone, and now it's a waiting room with a small table and chairs, a sofa, and some large armchairs.

"Again, Holden."

The image this time shows the next room back, which I've only been to once. It was a large kitchen, and most of that is still there—same sink, counters, dishwasher, fridge/freezer, and ovens. But the empty wall now has lines of filing cabinets.

"One more time, Holden," Mandy shouts.

"And now the back room that was two storage rooms," Steve says, "is your office."

The desk and side table and chairs look new. There's even a shiny computer resting on it.

"And the deed is ready and waiting to be put in your name, once you get it changed over to Archer," Mandy says. "Steve said you meant to."

Abby's hand is covering her face, but judging by the way she throws her arms around Steve, she's pleased. "Thank you so much."

"Why does he get the hug?" Mandy grumbles. "I'm the one who paid for everything *and* donated the building."

Abby turns to Mandy next, hugging her so tightly I swear I hear things creak and pop.

Almost everyone is oohing and aahing when I feel someone tug on my sleeve. I turn around and realize it's Beth. I've been an absolutely horrible aunt to her lately, thanks to the bad blood between me and her dad. "What are you doing here?"

Her face is as pale as I've ever seen it. "Can we talk?"

"Of course," I say. "Maybe we should go outside."

I notice Eddy and Amanda slipping back inside through the side door as I suggest it. Neither of them looks especially pleased. Hopefully whatever Beth has to say is more pleasant than whatever conversation they just had.

Once we successfully escape, I immediately ask, "What's going on? Are you alright?"

She shakes her head.

"What's wrong?" In spite of my attempt to remain calm, my heart rate spikes.

"I know Dad hit you," she says. "I'm sorry I didn't say anything before, but Mom made me swear to keep it quiet."

My heart sinks at that—Mom was always begging us not to say anything about Dad, more worried he'd go to prison than she was about us, apparently. "Beth, the thing is—"

"I know what you're thinking," she says. "That he's an awful guy, and that he should go to jail. I mean, you might even be right."

Hearing this from my niece breaks my heart. The damage my dad did just keeps spiraling down. "Beth, I am right. People who hit—"

"Mom left him," Beth says.

That gets my attention. "But you're here."

Her mother's from Seattle, and I'm absolutely positive that if she left him, that's where she'd go. Her family has a lot of money and a really nice place in Redmond. "I am—I'm trying to help Dad. If this year on the ranch goes badly, he could lose it."

I don't mention that if our hearing in less than two weeks goes badly, he'll lose it, too. It hardly seems helpful. "Sometimes something feels like it will destroy your world, but really—"

"Mom's been addicted to narcotics for years," Beth says. "She's been in rehab for it at least five times. And she has a shopping addiction. She's maxed out her credit cards so many times I lost count, and I didn't even find out about it until a few years ago. She's not an angel either."

How am I just hearing about this? Could Beth be making it up?

She pulls papers out of her purse. "I thought you might not believe me."

I stare at her face for a moment before finally looking down. The lighting's not the best out here, but I can make out enough to see that they're statements from seemingly posh rehab facilities, judging by the names. *Rise in Malibu. Seaside Rehab. The Spirit of the Mountain. Scenic Changes. Oceanside Harbor Rehab.* They sound more like resorts than rehab facilities. The patient name listed on the statements is Amelia Ellingson, and the invoice amounts are staggering. "Your parents took out the mortgage on the ranch, not my dad."

She swallows.

"And now you're here, to what? Beg me to just give your dad my money?"

"I know he shouldn't have hit you. I swear, he really has never done anything like that before. Mom left that night, and she begged me to come with her. Apparently she told him that if he ever did that, to anyone, anytime, she'd leave him. Figures that would be the one thing she ever kept her word on. . ."

"Are you telling me that your *mom* is the villain here?"

Beth purses her lips. "I know it seems like Dad's the bad guy. I mean, I'm not going to sit here and tell you he's great. You know him. But you also know that with all his flaws, the one thing he's always done well is love my mom. Actually, I think he's kind of enabled her. You know ranch proceeds come in all at once when the cows are sold."

I didn't live here this long and miss how auction works.

"Mom and Dad never had much in the few months right before, and we'd always get really strapped for cash. So putting stuff on credit cards was normal to them. Kind of. But then when Mom would get mad, or when she'd be stressed, or when she and Dad would fight, she started buying things. Expensive things—stuff she couldn't even sell later for anywhere near what she'd paid."

I knew Amelia was spoiled, but. . .

"Dad and Mom kind of did what anyone would do. They moved the debt from one card to the next. They consolidated cards. They took out short-term loans."

"To be clear, *not everyone* just shifts debt from card to card. Some people come up with a plan to pay off their credit card debt." That's what I did when bills piled up after Charles went to jail.

"I know, but when Mom had to be hospitalized the first time, it got worse. Dad had to take out a loan from the bank, and he took the most they'd give. So when she had to go back and their cards were already maxed. . ." Beth shrugs. "He wasn't sure what to do, and he had the power of attorney for Grandpa. So."

"So he committed fraud, taking money from an estate he didn't yet own."

Beth's shoulders slump.

"I didn't press charges," I say. "Your dad lied to me about our parents' will, and if he'd had his way, I'd never have known they left me anything. Does that seem remotely fair?"

"Your husband had money," Beth says. "He thought you were fine. And when you came home after the whole embezzling thing, well, he'd already taken out that loan and he was stuck."

I can't believe what she's asking me to do. "You want me to. . .what? Give all the life insurance money to Patrick? The money he tried to *steal from me?*"

She looks down at her feet. "I don't know why I came. Dad was right. I'm sorry."

"Is that really what you're asking me to do?" I ask.

Beth looks up at my eyes. "He wouldn't do it for you. I know it's not fair, but he's going to jail soon. There's been a judgment against us, and we're behind on the ranch payment, and they're about to take that, too. I just thought maybe—but never mind."

In this moment, as I stand outside of Abby and Steve's wedding, I think about what Abby would do if she were me. She should have told me off when Dad needed help at that hospital. She should have told me to jump in a lake when I asked her to represent me in the custody battle for Aiden and my divorce. She should have kicked Amanda to the curb about a dozen different times.

But she never did.

She's always busy, and always helping other people, and she's one of the happiest people I know. Could it be *because* she does the *right* thing, and not the crappy thing she'd be justified in doing?

I open my mouth to tell Beth that I'll think about it, but I can't even bring myself to say the words. *Give Patrick my entire inheritance? The one he tried to steal from me? The one that would make it so much easier for me to raise Aiden well?* I just can't say it. I want to be like Abby, but I'm just not.

"I'm going to go," Beth says. "Can you at least not tell Dad I came? I don't think I can deal with him telling me he told me so."

In that moment, I think about the cycle of abuse.

Dad hit us. Patrick hit me. No one ever has any confidence in their safety. No one ever has the strength to face things without reverting back to the old ways.

People are only out for themselves. And now my niece is asking me to let go of something, and I can't do it.

Or can I?

"Wait."

Beth stops in her tracks, but she doesn't turn around.

"Tell your Dad I have an offer." I sigh. "If he'll sign off on it, we can just settle. I'll be the executor, because I don't trust him, and I'll assign all but two hundred thousand dollars of the proceeds from the life insurance policy to him. That'll be just enough for him to pay off the mortgage he took out and get you square, but not much more. And he has to take and receive flying colors in an anger management course of my choosing. If he doesn't satisfy me, he'll have to take another. I won't assign the funds until he has done it."

Beth's crying silently when she jogs over to where I am and hugs me. It would be a miracle if it could happen —I really want to break this cycle, and the only way that happens is if *someone* doesn't do what their parents did. If someone does something good, something selfless, and something just.

"Thank you." Beth wipes her cheeks and squeezes my upper arms one last time. "You have no idea what this means to me."

"I'm not doing it for your dad or your mom," I say. "I'm doing it for *you*." She smiles with watery eyes and nods as she's leaving.

But as she disappears, I realize that I didn't really do it for her either.

I did it for *me*.

Knowing that this whole thing will be over? The fight with my brother, the constant legal battles that have eaten away at me for the past year, the uncertainty of how things will turn out, the meetings and the calls and the research. All of it will finally be over.

It helps me to know that Patrick's not just being greedy—I mean, yes. He *is* greedy, but his wife has the problem. It's not all him. And he's had consequences. She left him. It shouldn't make me happy, but it kind of does. I suppose I still have a ways to go.

Even so, I breathe a huge sigh of relief. Beth has been gone for a few moments, and it still feels like I made the right decision. I can put that two hundred grand in a savings account for Aiden and his college should be covered, and then there should be some left over for my retirement too, hopefully.

"I'm proud of you," a deep voice says behind me.

I spin around, my eyes searching the near dark of the area in front of the building, blinded by the interspersed floodlights hanging off the roof. I blink, but it doesn't help me to see him.

I don't need to see to know it's Will. I've been hearing his voice in my dreams lately.

"Proud of me?" I think about the Will I know. "How much did you hear?"

"I wanted to make sure you were alright," he says. "I wasn't trying to eavesdrop, but when Beth said Amelia has been in rehab, I couldn't go back inside."

I should be mad at him. He basically heard all of it. But he also said he's proud of me, and I really need to hear that right now. Plus, I'd practically give my right arm to have him talking to me again. "I'm alright."

"You look happier," he says. "Does that sound crazy?"

"A few million would have made me pretty happy," I say. "But it wasn't worth the misery, and even though he hit me, I do love Patrick."

Will's fists clench. "I can't believe he did that. He should be in jail."

"Frankly, it's probably shocking he hasn't done it before. You have no idea how often our dad hit us."

He's moved closer, and now I can make out the muscles in his jaw working in the silhouette of his face. "I am proud of you, but I'm also not sure what I'll do to Patrick the next time I see him."

I put one hand on his forearm. "Hitting is wrong, Will. Didn't you hear?"

"Hitting a woman is wrong," Will says. "Hitting a child. But hitting a man who hits women or children?" He shrugs. "I'm okay with it."

I laugh. "All the same, please don't."

"I'm sorry, too." He's not joking around anymore.

All my peace, all my calm, dissipates like fog burned off by the rays of the midday sun. He shifts a little, and suddenly, instead of a silhouette, I can see his face.

It's raw.

His eyes are *fraught*.

The strong jaw muscles I like so much are clenched.

"Why did you ask me to be your date to the wedding?"

I want to tell him, but I can't seem to say a single word.

"I didn't have a date when you called. I wasn't even invited to the wedding." His laugh is angry—harsh. "I'm such an idiot that after turning you down, I had to call Steve and beg him to let me come. Do you know what he said?"

I shake my head.

"He asked why I needed the invite, and I said I had to prove I was over you." He shakes his head and exhales. "He said if I needed to prove it, then I wasn't, and by God, he was right."

My heart surges. My lungs practically stop working. My hands shake so hard I'm forced to clench my fluffy tulle skirt to keep them from making noise.

"Donna, you always have something to say. Your last words to me keep playing on repeat in my head. *My answer is the same.*" His lips twist. "Your answer was no. It was always no. And I'm so stupid, here I am, asking again, bracing to be shut down again."

I open my mouth, words tumbling through my brain, but he cuts me off before I can say them.

"Rebecca says it's just what you do—you keep men on the hook to amuse yourself. She said that's why you called me, to string me along."

"She said what?"

"That you missed the attention, so you threw me a line."

"I hate her," I say. "She's cute and she's talented and she's probably an excellent mother, and I wanted to claw her eyes out when you walked in with her."

The hope that steals across Will's rugged face is like the sunrise over Morro Bay. It's like the bounding clumsiness of a puppy running toward its mother. It's the last piece being placed in a puzzle to form a beautiful mountain image.

"She's a perfectly lovely woman," Will says. "And she said she'd been waiting for me to ask her out for years." He crosses his arms. "Why would you want to claw her lovely golden eyes out?"

"I made a mistake, Will Earl. Is that what you want to hear?"

"Oh, I think I deserve to hear a little more than that."

"I'm an idiot," I say.

His hand covers my mouth, probably smearing my lipstick. "Don't ever insult yourself, but say more about me." He lowers his head so our eyes are on level. "Got it?"

I nod.

He releases me.

"Old Donna would have licked your hand," I say.

"No, she'd have bitten me," he says. "But I'm okay with that, too."

I laugh. "I haven't been this happy since that night— the night you kissed me and I ran away scared."

"You felt it too," he says.

"Felt what?"

"The earthquake when we kissed." He breathes my name. "The seismic shift." His arms reach for my waist, tugging me closer as he straightens. "Aren't you curious?"

About almost everything. "About what?"

"Whether it will happen every time?" His mouth is just above mine now, his eyes studying my face.

"I might be." I bite my lip. "But aren't you upset with me at all?"

He searches my face for answers—but to what questions?

"You're not?"

He presses a kiss against my forehead. "Would you be upset if a priceless work of art took longer to acquire? If it got stuck in customs, for instance?"

I blink.

"Or would you run out of patience if the wood for the handmade, one-of-a-kind piece of furniture you ordered took longer to cure?"

"I—"

"It took me months to get a part on a Shelby Cobra once. It took me hours and hours of searching before I found exactly the original Halibrand wheels that I wanted, and they got delayed over and over. But it's not about the time I spent waiting. It's about the joy it brings you when you finally get things *right*."

His hands tighten and pull, and his lips drop down to cover mine.

And the earth moves beneath us again.

The walls of my heart shake. The feel of him all around me is perfection. It's nirvana.

The air is crisp and cool, my soul is both at peace and ready to go to war, and I realize that he's correct. It's not about the years we missed. It's about how *right* this is right now. It's about how safe I feel with Will, and how happy I am that he hasn't changed his mind.

When he finally releases me, I almost moan.

"It's going to be really hard to go back in there and dance with Rebecca."

I grab his collar without thinking and drag his face right down to mine. "Don't you even think about it."

His devilish smile has me going up on my tiptoes and kissing him again.

And again.

And again.

S teve's phone has been buzzing in his pocket for almost twenty minutes.

"Maybe you should get that."

"It's my wedding day," he says. "Everyone who might call me with something urgent that I would leave my wedding reception to answer is already here."

He glances sideways at where his daughter is dancing with her feet on his dad's boots, both of them smiling happily, albeit a bit awkwardly. Gabe's dancing with Steve's stepmom, which might be an even funnier sight. He appears to be pointing things out to her here and there, and I kind of wish I could hear their certain-to-be-uncomfortable conversation.

"But what if it's the hospital?"

"I'm a shift worker," he says. "I'm not on call."

"If they had someone get sick, though, or die, they could be calling you." I hate even thinking about it, but you never know. I'm living proof of that.

"They've got six other people to call," he says. "People who aren't *getting married right now*."

But five minutes later, when it's still buzzing, I snatch it out of his pocket.

"It's Javi," I say. "Which means—"

"It's a horse thing." He sighs. "Fine. I'll call him back."

He's quiet as he listens, but his face doesn't look calm or relaxed. "Is Eddy still here?"

I glance around, and sure enough, he's in the very back row. I point.

Steve makes his way over to where Eddy's sitting, and they talk for a moment. When Steve comes back, he still looks grim. "He said he'll go."

"What is it?"

"Javier thinks that mare I adopted—the kill lot one —is pregnant. She's lying down and heaving and heaving, and nothing is happening."

"Wait." I can hardly believe what he's saying. "The one with the ribs?"

"If she's even more emaciated than we thought, she could have been pregnant and it wouldn't even have occurred to us that she was."

"Could they really have starved her that badly?"

"Outlook for that baby isn't good if she is—which I think she must be. What else could it be? The foal's probably coming early, or she'd have been bigger."

"You want to go," I say.

"Of course not," he lies.

I can tell by the way he won't meet my eye.

"We still haven't cut the cake or thrown the bouquet. We have more than an hour left in our celebration."

But I know him, and it's his wedding, too. "You know what matters more than the perfect wedding?" I arch one eyebrow.

478

"This feels like a trick question."

"The wedding night," I say.

His jaw drops.

I slug his arm. "I'm kidding, idiot. The *marriage*."

He shakes his head. "Right. I mean, I knew you were kidding."

I'm smiling as I shove him toward the door. When they notice us leaving, the dumb band stops playing.

"Hey," Amanda shouts. "What's going on?"

"Emergency at home." I wave at Amanda and Donna and Rebecca and every other unmarried gal I see, including Mandy. "All you single ladies, get over here." When Izzy and Whitney start trotting over, I scowl at them.

They just laugh.

And then I turn around and toss the wedding bouquet as close to where I think Amanda is as I can possibly get. I spin back around and see that it hit her feet. Bullseye. That girl needs some luck. Or a swift kick in the pants.

Or maybe both.

Donna snatches the flowers and clutches them against her chest. "Wahoo. Did you see that?" Her eyes sparkle. "It just flew right over to me."

At least Amanda's laughing at her obvious theft. "Clearly it's fate."

My last view of the reception is all our family and friends laughing and chatting. Everything may have gone wrong today, but we hit the important things dead center, right on target.

"Are you upset?" Steve's looking at me when he should be looking at the parking lot.

"I'm blissfully happy," I say. "I just married my best friend."

"You said that wrong," he says. "You meant to say that you married the hot doctor. Or the sexy cowboy. I'd accept either one."

I laugh. "Nice try."

"What?"

"You don't get to be sexy when you're yanking me away from our party for yet another horse emergency."

"For creatures who have highly evolved to run at unbelievable speed on the edge of a toenail, they sure do get sick and do stupid things at an alarming pace, don't they?"

He can say that again.

But when we get to his place, and I watch as Eddy and Steve deliver a tiny brown filly, even I have to admit that he's pretty sexy. I mean, he's probably ruined not one, but *two* nice sport coats today, but it was worth it both times.

"I think you should name her," Eddy says, looking my way. "I mean, she did ruin your wedding. It's only fair."

"How about Home Wrecker?" Steve asks.

"Or Mistress." Eddy snickers.

"Tart," Steve says.

"Or, I know," Eddy says. "Strumpet."

"The Other Woman?" Steve's grinning.

I realize they will just keep doing this all night unless I stop them. "I'll take it under advisement." I don't believe in naming anything until I know *something* about it first. "Don't rush me."

"You're still clean," Eddy says, looking me up and

down. "You could ditch this loser and go back to that cool party."

Steve mock growls.

"That might be a bad idea," I say.

But as it is, it's probably the worst wedding night ever. Almost immediately, the starving mother tries to eliminate the poor filly. And when the poor sweet baby stands on her wobbly, underdeveloped, knobby legs, and works her way over to try and nurse?

The mare bites her.

It leaves a terrible, bloody mark.

Then the whole thing happens again, three more times. She's so covered with bites and scratches that I finally intervene on her behalf. "Enough, right? I mean, when do we give up?"

Steve and Eddy share a glance, and then Steve sighs. "I was hoping she'd calm down." The mother's happily eating hay, but she still won't let the filly close.

"That mare's in really bad shape," Eddy says. "There's probably no way to know if she'd be a good mother in ordinary circumstances, because she's basically starving."

"Can we give her formula?" I ask. "Maybe after she's a little less starved and stressed, the mother will step up."

"Maybe," Steve says. "Formula isn't as good, but they do have some great supplements for situations like this now."

"Though some moms just aren't great," Eddy says. "Not all mares make good mothers."

"You don't have to tell me that," Steve says. "I was married to one."

Stephanie didn't bite her child, as far as I know, but I won't argue that she's an excellent mother either.

"What do we do?" I ask.

"She'll have to be bottle fed," Eddy says. "And I'll order some antibodies for her since I doubt she'll get much from Mom."

"Bottle feeding her is going to be hard to do from Canada," I say. "Do you think Izzy could handle it?"

Steve swallows, and that's when I realize our honeymoon's off.

Once I start laughing, I can't seem to stop. I mean, it's *not* funny, but also, it kind of is.

"What?" Steve asks.

"I just think it's funny how we make all these plans."

"We can go," Steve says. "Maybe Ethan can help Izzy and—"

"Steve." I may only have known my husband for eleven and a half months, but I *know* him. "You won't enjoy a minute of it if we're worrying."

I look at that sweet little filly who's so small that she can fit on my lap. "And neither would I."

"Uh, guys?" Eddy looks like he just saw mommy kissing Santa Claus. "I'm gonna go ahead and go get all the feeding stuff. I'll be right back."

Steve barely acknowledges his departure. He's too focused on me. "I'm sorry today was such a mess."

I sit down on the shavings and pull the filly closer. I pet her still slightly damp little head. "Today was just perfect."

This time it's Steve who laughs. "Perfect? Hardly."

"You know," I say, "when I got married the first time, I didn't feel like I had a choice. I was pregnant with Ethan. I loved Nate, or I thought I did, so it just kind of happened."

"That was probably hard." He sits next to me and

482

pulls me against him. My head drops gratefully against his broad, strong chest.

I sigh. "At first, I felt like I'd been robbed, really. I resented that my dress wasn't what I would have picked if I hadn't been pregnant. I fretted that my reception and ceremony were rushed. I hated that my mom made so many decisions, and my mother-in-law made even more."

"I get that."

"But after Ethan was born, all of that anger just. . .went away."

"Why?"

I run my hand down the tiny filly's little head. "Life isn't guaranteed. Nothing about it is. And nothing is the same for me as it is for anyone else. I realized that I could be upset and feel cheated for the steps that took me to where I was, or I could appreciate the miracle my son was in my life."

Steve's arms wrap around me. "I don't deserve you."

I snuggle against him. "You do, though. I had a wonderful life with Nate, and I thought I was broken beyond repair when he died. But then you came along and accepted me for who and what I was. Even now, you never cringe when I bring him up, and you never shy away from the kids talking about him either. You take my broken bits, like this little girl's floppy, unsteady legs, and you just do everything you can to accept them and heal them and love them."

"I do try," he says. "But if I didn't have all these horses, if I—"

"But you do," I say. "And that's one of the things I love about you, too."

The little filly kicks and shifts, I can't stop looking at the tiny white star in the center of her forehead.

"I've picked a name," I say. "I want to call her Supernova."

"Why?"

"A supernova is a star that explodes, you know. It's at the very end of its life—and it's spectacular to watch. People think of it as total death. But it's also life. Energy. Beauty. As it clears out, other stars that are still burning go on. Life is a sequence of spectacular explosions and death and darkness. And it's also birth and renewal and healing."

My heart feels like it might burst.

"When Nate died, that was a supernova to us. It ended what we knew. My family, mostly Helen, but my parents too, and Robert, none of them understood what we were doing, retreating from our lives to live out here, in the middle of nowhere."

"I got it, of course," Steve says.

I run my fingers up his bristly jaw. "You did, yes. And I think a large part of the reason we love it here is that I met you. But also, we needed a fresh start. Sometimes you have to fall back in order to regain your strength. You can't be reborn until you've exploded. Being here, doing something so different from what we knew, it gave us a chance to heal and expand in ways we couldn't in the aftermath of that utter destruction."

"So you're saying that you wouldn't have loved me in Houston?" Steve frowns.

I turn around and press a kiss against his warm, kind, wise mouth. "I'm saying that when things go wrong, like the rain, like the fight between Eddy and David and Helen's boy toy, we can run away and hide, or we can do our best to deal with it and focus on the good. Today was so much more good than bad. Perfect weddings are fine too, but they're sure boring by comparison to our supernova. And our lives are like that too—messy, eventful, and the best thing I could possibly imagine."

"I hope you remember this when you get the wedding pictures," Steve says.

"You're sassy," I say. "And I love that, too."

"Thank you," he says. "For being the absolute opposite of Stephanie. For making things around you brighter. For not demolishing everything when you don't get your way. And mostly, thank you for loving me, in spite of my imperfections."

"What imperfections?" I ask.

Steve pulls out his phone and starts typing something.

"What are you doing?"

"Me?" He grins. "Just setting a reminder."

"For what?"

"To get you in to see an optometrist. You clearly need your eyes checked."

I laugh. "Your flaws aren't flaws to me. They're what make you Steve, and boy am I glad you're exactly who you are, even if it turns my name into a laughingstock."

"Abigail Archer," Steve says. "It's a little corny, sure, but I think you can pull it off."

I roll my eyes.

"Plus, you'll be the first name in the phone book."

"No one uses phone books anymore," I say, "old man."

When his laughter dies down this time, his eyes meet mine and my heart skips a beat. When he kisses me, I don't even mind that our honeymoon has been

485

wrecked, our wedding photos will likely be disastrously bad, and my sister's date practically punched my sister-in-law's date.

Because this man I married? He's as good as it gets. And now he's all mine.

EPILOGUE: AMANDA

Mandy tries to wiggle out of the procedure, but I hold her feet to the figurative fire, and then when the morning finally arrives, I drive her to the hospital myself.

"I have a bad feeling about this," she says.

"About getting your last blockage repaired?" I roll my eyes. "I feel like if you *don't* do it, you may not be around to plague me, and argue over resort names, and harangue me about forgiving Eddy." Which I still haven't been able to do.

"Steve and Abby should be on their honeymoon right now, but after a rainy wedding, a disastrous reception, and a shocking filly birth, they're still in town."

"What does that have to do with this?" I exit the car, walk around, and open her door. "Let's go."

"You aren't superstitious at all?"

"Yesterday, you told me you couldn't go today because you had a toothache. This morning you said we should reschedule because your horoscope said 'bad things lie await this month.'" I sigh. "Amanda Francis Saddler, get out of the car."

"I'm not a toddler." She scowls. "Saying my middle name isn't effective with me."

"If you don't get out, I'll go get Dr. Hoover, and—"

She practically leaps out.

I knew that would work. Dr. Hoover gives me nightmares, if I'm being honest. She's like a drill sergeant who was trained by a dragon. Not the cute kind that submit to saddles and eat a lot of fish. One of the angry, burn-the-world-down dragons whom people are always trying and failing to slay.

"Why does that woman—"

"She's a talented cardio-thoracic surgeon," I say. "And last time, you had to just have *anyone* do the procedure, but this time, we had choices. I chose the best." Even if she's ungodly horrifying.

"Fine," she says. "Fine."

"And while we're waiting, we may as well be productive."

Mandy's scowl could peel the paint off a car.

"I polled dozens of people when I went into town yesterday and they all agree. Strike Gold is better than Gold Strike."

"Oh, fabulous. I'm delighted that your committee of flunkies who grew up in this podunk town sided with you, the fashionable New York influencer. I wonder if you might have, I don't know, *influenced* their opinions?"

"What does Gold Strike even mean?" I ask. "Our retreat is about giving women hope that they can find happier futures. They can Strike Gold—fix themselves, and then find new purpose."

"Gold Strike refers to the mentality that we can live

life in the moment. We can go for what we want. We can *not* waste our entire life because of a misunderstanding." She huffs. "Plus there was that cute little pony named Gold Strike who won the Kentucky Derby. I love stories like that."

"Strike Gold also gives people the hope they can grab what they want," I say.

She throws her hands up in the air. "I'm the one putting the money up, and I'm the one who owns the house, so how about we do this?" She rounds on me. "If I die on that table today, you name it Gold Strike in my honor. And if I survive, you name it Gold Strike so we can stop fighting."

"So heads you win, tails I lose?" I quirk one eyebrow.

She repeats it in her head, then beams at me. "Exactly."

I start walking again, tugging her along with me. "Mandy, you're lucky I love you. You're a difficult woman to put up with."

"All geniuses are."

An hour later, she's prepped and ready to go in her lime green, zebra print hospital gown.

"Do they make these things so ugly so that no one will ever be tempted to steal them?" Her eyes are sparkling, but the poor nurse doesn't know her at all.

"I'm sorry you don't like it," she says. "I might be able to find a blue one—"

I roll my eyes. "She's just kidding."

"It's uglier than a cross-eyed pig with an overbite," Mandy mutters.

"A cross-eyed what?"

"She's talking about her own beloved pet. Don't

worry about it." I wave the nurse out. "You can just ignore it and go."

"But I have to take her," she says. "They're ready."

And in that moment, looking at Mandy in her lime green and white hospital gown, her tiny stick arms poking out of the oversized feed-sack-looking thing, fear grips me. I didn't have time to think about my panicking last time—it all happened so fast.

But now, I can't help worrying. What if her anxiety was actually a premonition? What if she's right? Maybe today's not a good day. "Wait," I say.

Mandy smiles knowingly at me. "Hush, girl. I'll be just fine."

"You don't know that." Stupidly, tears well up in my eyes.

"No one knows what will happen five minutes from now, much less tomorrow, next week, or next year." She reaches out and takes my hand. "But I know that you'll be fine, whatever comes. You've grown up so much in the past year. I've been very proud to see it."

I swallow.

"And I'm happy you've got enough self-esteem now to make that stupid vet wait." Her voice lowers. "But don't make him wait too long, you hear?"

"Why are you talking to me like you're giving me death-bed advice?"

"Every time I get in a bed, it could be my death bed. That's what it means to be in your eighties." She cackles. "Now you listen to my advice, whether I wake up from this or not."

"Stop saying that," I say.

She cackles again. "This is more fun than I realized."

"I love you," I say, gripped by a stupid wave of emotion. "You know that, right?"

She nods. "I do, girl. I know you love me. And I love those babies of yours, too. You're doing a fine job."

When the nurse finally wheels her off, leaving me to sit and wait, tears run down my face. I'm not alone for more than ten minutes before Abby rushes into the room.

"Did they already take her back?"

"You just missed her," I say, my anxiety mounting. "What are you doing here?" Please, please don't say you have a bad feeling about this. I'll be sick.

"I'm here for *you*." She sits down and hands me a tissue.

"Excuse me?" I ask. "I'm fine."

"Sure you are." Her smirk is infuriating.

"I am just fine," I say. "No, I'm great, actually. I'm in perfect health."

"You're still single—no boyfriend to lean on—and your surrogate mother is going under the knife for a heart blockage. What's to worry about?"

"Shut up," I say.

"Amanda?"

I don't turn to look at her. She'll just mock me for having watery eyes.

"Everything's going to be alright. I promise."

ACKNOWLEDGMENTS

To my ARC ALL STARS: thank you. You are epic and I love you.

To Carrie: THANK YOU. Words cannot express my gratitude for how you squeeze me in last minute to help save me all the time. I hope money helps. HA!

To my readers: I LOVE YOU, from the bottom of my heart. You make this crazy thing I do for a job something that I can keep doing!!! I love making up worlds for you. I hope you can continue to enjoy my words for a very long time.

To my kids: thanks for your patience. And for letting me copy you shamelessly so that I don't get these kids all jumbled together in my head.

To my husband: you are my *everything*. My Steve. My Eddy. My Will. My every single hero in every single book. It's a good thing you're bald, or someone much better than me would probably steal you away.

And again to Steve Archer: THANK YOU for letting me steal your name for my book. You're the best horse trainer ever, and when I decided to write a horse trainer, I knew I couldn't name him anything else.

B. E. Baker is the romance and women's fiction pen name of Bridget E. Baker.

She's a lawyer, but does as little legal work as possible. She has five kids and soooo many animals that she loses count.

Horses, dogs, cats, rabbits, and so many chickens. Animals are her great love, after the hubby, the kids, and the books.

She makes cookies waaaaay too often and believes they should be their own food group. In a (possibly misguided) attempt at balancing the scales, she kick-boxes daily. So if you don't like her books, maybe don't tell her in person.

Bridget's active on social media, and has a facebook group she comments in often. (Her husband even gets on there sometimes.) Please feel free to join her there: https://www.facebook.com/groups/750807222376182

ALSO BY B. E. BAKER

The Finding Home Series:

Finding Faith (1)

Finding Cupid (2)

Finding Spring (3)

Finding Liberty (4)

Finding Holly (5)

Finding Home (6)

Finding Balance (7)

Finding Peace (8)

The Finding Home Series Boxset Books 1-3

The Finding Home Series Boxset Books 4-6

The Birch Creek Ranch Series:

The Bequest

The Vow

The Ranch

The Retreat

Children's Picture Book

Yuck! What's for Dinner?

I also write contemporary fantasy and end of the world books under Bridget E. Baker.

The Magical Misfits Series:

Mates: Minerva (1)

Mates: Xander (2)

The Birthright Series:

Displaced (1)

unForgiven (2)

Disillusioned (3)

misUnderstood (4)

Disavowed (5)

unRepentant (6)

Destroyed (7)

The Birthright Series Collection, Books 1-3

The Anchored Series:

Anchored (1)

Adrift (2)

Awoken (3)

Capsized (4)

The Sins of Our Ancestors Series:

Marked (1)

Suppressed (2)

Redeemed (3)

Renounced (4)

Reclaimed (5) a novella!

A stand alone YA romantic suspense:

Already Gone

Made in United States
Orlando, FL
11 July 2023

34956384R00300